Joy on the Mountain

Guarded Secrets Revealed

Wilma Styles

GRATEFUL STEPS
ASHEVILLE, NORTH CAROLINA

Grateful Steps Foundation
Crest Mountain
30 Ben Lippen School Road #107
Asheville, North Carolina 28806

Copyright © 2018 by Wilma Styles
Library of Congress Control Number 2018964146

Styles, Wilma
Joy on the Mountain
Cover photograph by Donna Rhinehart
Photograph on dedication page is from
the author's personal collection

ISBN 978-1-945714-21-4 Paperback
ISBN 978-1-945714-35-1 Ebook

FIRST EDITION

www.gratefulsteps.org

Praise for Joy on the Mountain

This is absolutely the best book I have ever read about the Cherokee people. Styles did such a beautiful job. I could hardly put it down. At each turn of events I felt as though I was right there in the midst of it all. A must read. Beautifully written!

> – SewSister, Hendersonville, North Carolina

Oh my gosh! Just finished reading *Joy on the Mountain* with tears running down my face. Best book I have ever read and I read every night. Wilma, you are the Phoenix! This should be a movie!

> – Vicky Harris, Clay Center, Kansas

I had stopped reading for such a long time. I was talked into reading *Joy on the Mountain*. I was so glad I did! The best book I have ever read! Thank you, for writing *Joy on the Mountain*! It gave me the incentive to read again! Thank you!

> – Nancy Harper, Fletcher, North Carolina

It was one of the best stories I have ever read! I was so into the story, I read it in a day and half. I don't read like that! Would make a great movie!

> – Don Gregg, Greenville, Tennessee

Good story! Margaret's inspiration and drive to find out about her childhood was riveting! I love the way nothing was going to stop Margaret, not even a war. Reads like a good movie script!

> – Michael Styles, Little Rock, Arkansas

Joy on the Mountain should be on the New York, Best Sellers list! I have read lots of best sellers, but this writer is better than anyone I have ever read! All her books are amazing and extremely entertaining!

> – Teresa Metcalf, Weaverville, North Carolina

to my Cherokee grandmothers

Hardenia (Deny) Daniels Black, my paternal great-grandmother, was born in Spartanburg, South Carolina, in 1857. She was a full-blooded Cherokee and came to Asheville, North Carolina, when she was 10 years old. She married Christopher Black in 1873 and made her home in Weaverville, North Carolina. She was the mother of fifteen children. She passed away February 19, 1953, at the age of 96. One of her children was my grandmother, Mary Lucinda Black.

Mary Lucinda Black Harris (below with her daughter Martha), my paternal grandmother, was born in 1878. She married Yance Harris in 1900 and lived in Burnsville, North Carolina, until her death, January 10, 1940. She was only 62 years old. Mary gave birth to my daddy, James Roy Harris, April 7, 1923. Daddy married Willie Mae King, September 21, 1940. They had nine children. I was the middle child, born August 22, 1948.

Acknowledgments

A special thank you to Donna Rhinehart for the cover photograph. Thanks also to Jacob Whiteside and Cynthia Rhinehart.

Contents

Contents

Contents

Chapter One

The Beginning

$\mathcal{I}$t was late October 1863. The sun was beginning to set when a mysterious wind stirred the wet leaves that lay thick on the rain-soaked ground. The wind quickly moved across the mountain, weaving through the gravestones and wooden crosses at Pine Mountain Cemetery. Only a glimmer of light remained. The rain had stopped, but sporadic flashes of lightning continued to expose deep purple and gray clouds in the distance. A thick mist had covered the crest of the mountain. Enormous pine trees swayed back and forth, hurling chilling moans over the crowded graves. At one time, each corpse had been filled with exuberant life. They laughed, loved and had children, grandchildren, jobs and a desire to live forever. Not one of them knew the hour the Grim Reaper would whisper in his or her ear, "I'm here for you." The essence of the Reaper was sucking the life force from the flesh, regardless of age.

Phoebe Thawbush was fifty years old when the Reaper first came calling. However, she wasn't ready for the trip he had planned for her. She fought with a

1

vengeance and won. The victorious battle had awarded Phoebe thirty-two more years of life. It had been a little over a year since she had yielded to the Reaper and taken her place in Pine Mountain Cemetery.

Margaret and Carolyn pressed their way into the harsh wind. To reach the secluded domain of the dead, it was a mile up the dirt road that had been rutted out by the heavy rain. Margaret cherished every memory of her grandmother and had been to the cemetery many times after her death.

Through the years, Phoebe had shown an abundant amount of love to Margaret. Phoebe had fifteen grandchildren, but there was something exceptional about Margaret Phoebe Black. Was it because that grandchild shared her name, or did Phoebe see something deeper in Margaret's spirit that was so like her own? Before she died, Phoebe took a small wooden bowl that she had carved, filled it with sweet smelling oil and summoned her grandchildren to the front porch of her meager log cabin. After the grandchildren surrounded her, Phoebe fixed her eyes on each one. A smile of pride captured her countenance. She knew her quiver had been filled with offspring who would carry on her legacy. Phoebe raised her aged hand from her lap, put it inside her wool shawl and pulled out a large eagle feather with intent to pray a distinct blessing over each grandchild. Margaret was next to last in line to be prayed over. When her turn came, she knelt in front of her grandmother who was sitting in a cane chair that her husband, Winter Snow Thawbush, had made for her as a wedding present. Phoebe dipped the tip of the eagle feather into the oil and glided it across Margaret's forehead. Phoebe's eyes widened and her hand trembled as she breathlessly whispered, "The Phoenix." Phoebe slowly stood, her expression changing from pleasant to gripping as she took the bowl of oil in her hands and slowly poured it over Margaret's head until it ran down her face and clothes onto the ground. The other grandchildren watched and listened, stunned at the mysterious words Phoebe boldly spoke over Margaret who was left speechless. At the time, Margaret had no idea what her grandmother was talking about, but still, daily, Phoebe's words burned in her mind.

"Oh, Great God of heaven and earth, breathe your Spirit into this child. From the ashes of death, cause her to arise like the mighty Phoenix and display your power in her for all to see. Cause her to spread her enormous wings and soar to the peaks of heaven, bringing a refreshing breeze to the souls of all mankind."

At the end of the blessing over Margaret, Phoebe held to the arms of the chair, slowly sat down, closed her eyes and slumped over, relinquishing to the Reaper who had returned. Willow Fine, the last in line to be blessed was devastated that she alone would live her life unblessed. In her heart she felt her grandmother had spent too much time blessing Margaret, or she too would have shared in the blessings.

Chapter Two

Stranger at Pine Mountain

Tonight, especially, Margaret could hear the words of her grandmother's prayer vividly as she started the exhausting journey, in the mud, to Phoebe's gravesite. Carolyn had brought a lantern, knowing it would be pitch black before they could get back home. The mist was so thick the women had to wipe their faces to see. Eerie moans and whistles from the wind sent chills down their spines. The derisive sound of some unknown creature flying through the air scared Carolyn; she slipped and fell in the mud. Margaret quickly turned and offered her hand to pull her dear friend to her feet. Almost in tears, her dress wet and covered with red mud, Carolyn snapped, "Good grief, Margaret! Look at my dress!"

"I'm sorry, Carolyn," Margaret said as she tried to wipe off some of the mud.

Carolyn slapped her hand and ranted, "Don't touch me! I'm too irritated right now to accept your apology or your help. Please tell me why we couldn't have come in the morning when we could enjoy the advantage of daylight? But no, you had to come when it's almost dark, in the mud. In addition, I only have a little oil for the lantern to give us enough light to get back off this god-forsaken mountain. I can barely see you standing right in front of me, and you want to go to the top of a mountain filled with dead people? Must I go on with why my frustration is piqued?"

Margaret reached forward to put her hand on Carolyn's arm to console her, but quickly pulled it back feeling her friend's irritation. "I know you're frustrated and scared, the same as me," Margaret said, "but I had to come tonight." Margaret looked around and concluded, "We'll talk later. It's getting so dark we have to go now."

Carolyn shook her head and muttered, "Why am I doing this?"

Margaret grinned and quickly replied, "Because you're my best friend and kindred spirit."

When they came to the fence, constructed of oak posts and chicken wire, Carolyn grabbed Margaret's arm, stopping her. "I'm lighting the lantern before we go through the gate."

Margaret swiftly agreed. Carolyn reached into her pocket for the matches that she made sure were there when they had left home. Panicked, Carolyn moaned, "Oh no! What are we going to do?"

"Carolyn, what's wrong?"

Frantic, Carolyn shouted, "I don't have the matches! I must have lost them out of my pocket when I fell. Now what?"

Margaret seized Carolyn's arm. "Come on, I'll hold you. Nothing is going to happen to us." Margaret turned the wooden latch and slowly opened the gate.

Carolyn grumbled, "It's too dark. You can hardly see anything."

Margaret took her friend's hand and pulled her through the grave markers toward an enormous pine tree that sat in the middle of the cemetery. Looking anxiously around her feet, Carolyn whined, "Oh, Lord, forgive us for walking all over these precious people's resting places."

"Hush your whining, Carolyn! We're here."

A wooden cross that had been painted brilliant white gave off more light than anything on the mountain. Margaret stood there in silence. Curious, Carolyn asked, "What now?"

"Shhh," Margaret whispered.

After a moment, Carolyn exploded. "Margaret, are you praying? If not I want to get out of here."

"Carolyn, please! We've trudged up the mountain, and I want to stay long enough to understand why we had to come tonight. There must be an important reason or else I wouldn't have felt the crucial need to come this late in the evening."

They anxiously waited for something to happen, although they had no idea what to expect. The wind had picked up, and the dark clouds began to race across the sky. The women were so nervous, unable to move anything but their eyes. As the wind moaned, lightning flashed in front of them, revealing a man standing at the head of Phoebe's grave. A pale blue light surrounded him. Medium-length, brown, curly hair framed his face. A long, snow-white tunic draped his tall muscular frame. Gold sandals were laced across the top of his feet.

Scared half to death but not wanting it to show, Margaret shouted, "I'm not afraid of you. I don't know who or what you are, but we're not afraid of you." Margaret nudged Carolyn to agree, but she said nothing.

"I'm glad you're not afraid," the man said. "My intent is not to harm you."

Margaret leaned her head forward and asked, "Did George send you here to scare me?"

The man replied in a firm voice, "I was sent by a much higher power than George."

Margaret shouted, "Then I demand to know who that higher power is!"

The stranger's sharp eyes stared intently at Margaret, and he responded, "I serve the Living God! The Great Eagle of heaven, the same as you."

Margaret swallowed so hard it was uncomfortable. After clearing her throat, she demanded, "What-what is your name and what are you doing at my grandmother's grave?"

The man placed his hands on his hips and stated, "My name is not important. I'm here for the same reason you are. I was summoned to the eagle's court and ordered to meet you here."

Carolyn whispered, "Eagle's court? Margaret, what does he mean by that?"

Margaret paused. "I don't know. Maybe it's a trick."

The man grinned and informed her, "Believe me, Margaret, this is no trick."

Margaret's mouth was dry. She licked her lips, rubbed her finger across her chin and said, "As crazy as it sounds, I believe what you're saying?"

He swiftly responded, "Because our spirits are one."

Margaret paused when she felt Carolyn's fingers tighten around her arm. She glanced at Carolyn, then shifted her widened eyes back to the stranger standing before her. Margaret squinted and uttered, "So tell me your name and why I was summoned to my grandmother's grave in the night."

He tilted his head and replied, "My name is Eagle Claw. I'm a warrior in the army of God Almighty. I can only say what I have been given permission to say."

"And what is that?" Margaret asked suspiciously.

Eagle Claw took a step forward, causing the women to gasp, and declared,

> From the ashes, a child will rise
>   and be transformed before everyone's eyes.
> A divine purpose will be fulfilled,
>   for this is the Father's will.
> In the forest, you will find the clue
>   that will show you what to do.
> Many years ago, a baby was taken,
>   but that was only God's plan in the making.
> Now go from this place and don't come again,
>   until you've solved the mystery
>   and penned it with your hand.

Thunder exploded causing the mountaintop to shake. A blinding sheet of lightning flashed, and the messenger disappeared, leaving the women in the dark. Margaret grabbed Carolyn, who was frozen in her tracks.

"Let's get out of here!" Margaret shouted. When Margaret took hold of the gate, a lightning surge stung her hand. She couldn't hold the latch; she had to leave the gate open. The high wind howled and beat against Carolyn and Margaret as they moved forward at a snail pace due to the strong wind. The darkness had vacuumed any hope of light. They thought they were on the trail but weren't sure. Unexpectedly, the wind calmed, the sky cleared, and they were at the foot of the mountain where they had left the horses. Terrified, they mounted their horses and raced back to Margaret's house.

Chapter Three

Explaining to George

The horses were sweating and panting heavily as they neared the house. Margaret's husband, George, was standing on the porch when they arrived.

"Whoa!" they said, pulling back on the reins. Instead of dismounting immediately, Margaret stared into space. Carolyn lowered her head, pressing her chin against her chest, trying to take deep breaths.

George shook his head and stated, "I knew you two were up to no good when you took out of here this evening. Where did you go anyway?"

Margaret slid off her horse, wearily squinted at George and declared, "George, I think it's plain that Carolyn and I are distraught. While I appreciate your concern, honey, I don't want you to ask any questions for a while."

George laughed and called Margaret by her nickname. "Toot, you look like you've seen a ghost. I hope you didn't go around Raven's Hill. Major Wright's scout saw signs that Silent Wolf and his warriors are back in the territory. I don't think I need to tell you there's a war going on. Not just the Indians, but Union and Confederate soldiers are fighting all around us. The soldiers here at Fort Howard can only guard so much land. They've designated what they think are safe areas, and I emphasize think. Which means, it's really just something they say to try and keep the people calm. Nevertheless, we're expected to stay in the confines of those boundaries. Do you ladies hear me?"

Margaret tied her horse. "We hear you, George, and rest assured we didn't go to Raven's Hill. Did we, Carolyn?"

"No we didn't. We visited Pine Mountain Cemetery. The people there don't have to worry about Silent Wolf or soldiers. They've already met their demise."

George exploded! "Why in the world did you go to that mountain at dark?"

Margaret put her hands on her hips and scolded, "Thank you so much, Carolyn, for sharing that with George. Now I'll never hear the end of it."

George walked over to Margaret, pointed toward the mountain and said, "I know what I'm talking about, Toot. I've never been one to boss you, and I take a lot of teasing because of that. I've let you come and go as you please, but that's going to end if you don't stay away from the mountain. And don't go back to Pine Mountain Cemetery until things settle down! Do I make myself clear?"

"George, I respect you, love you and even cherish you, but if I feel in my spirit to go to Pine Mountain Cemetery or Raven's Hill, trust me I'll go."

Carolyn smiled and muttered, "Speaking of going, I think I had better be going."

Toot squinted at Carolyn and cried, "NO! You're not bailing out on me just because I'm telling George where I stand on this matter."

Carolyn frowned and declared, "No, I'm not leaving because of that. I just don't want to be here, if by chance things should escalate."

George raised his hands and assured the women that enough had been said. "Carolyn please stay. I have to ride to the fort and see Major Wright about something. Besides, Toot is a strong-willed woman who will do pretty much what she sets her mind to. It's that fiery spirit I fell in love with." George kissed Margaret's cheek and started to mount his horse.

"George!" Margaret called out, "It's late, why would Major Wright need to see you tonight?"

"No idea. He sent a message and said it was important."

"You be careful, and I'll see you in a while."

George stopped his horse and looked at Margaret. "You're telling me to be careful and I'm only going to Fort Howard. However, you don't want me to tell you anything. Try to figure that one out. See you two later."

Margaret watched George ride away. "Carolyn, I wonder what Major Wright knows that would warrant George's attention this late."

"I don't know," Carolyn replied. "The last time he wanted to see George this late a battle was in the making. I pray that's not the case this time."

Chapter Four
George, a Scout for the Army

Fort Howard was nestled in the foothills of what the Cherokees called "Mountain of Blue Smoke" (Smoky Mountains). Major Todd Wright had been assigned there after a group of renegades, led by a Cherokee warrior named Silent Wolf, refused to stay on the reservation. Captain Ron Roland was killed during a raid by Silent Wolf. Major Wright was delegated to take Captain Roland's place. With Silent Wolf and Union soldiers in the area, Fort Howard was on full alert.

George had been a scout for Captain Roland for several years. After Roland's death, George retired but still assisted the military leaders at the fort. George was fifty-seven years old, born and raised in the Smoky Mountains and knew everything there was to know about the region. He also knew about the Cherokee people. Being married to one only heightened his knowledge. His expertise was tracking.

He was a rugged individual, yet with Margaret he was as gentle as a lamb. His dark skin accented his salt and pepper hair and matching mustache. He stood five feet nine inches tall and topped the scales at 175 pounds. His constant companion was a black Stetson hat with the tail feather of a golden eagle tucked inside the gray silk band. He wore black leather, knee boots with his pant legs stowed inside. Although he was no longer a scout, he maintained the look. The long scar on his stomach and smaller one on his arm served as a reminder of the many uprisings he had fought in.

Chapter Five

Margaret and Siblings

*M*argaret was born at White Oak Pass, a few miles outside the reservation. She was five feet three inches tall and weighed one hundred pounds. Her long, chestnut brown hair glistened, and her flawless light bronze skin had a gentle radiance. Her perfectly white teeth, sable eyes and pink lips provided a beauty that was harmonious with the breath-taking splendor of the Smoky Mountains. Although she was fifty years old, she had the looks of a thirty-year-old. Beauty couldn't take the tomboy out of her. She wore pants most of the time but could be very feminine or skin a bear; it made no difference to her.

Margaret was the youngest of three children. Her brother, Cody, was mild mannered. However, when pushed, his Indian blood would come to a boil and all hell would break loose. He had never married. His only love, Donna Felton, had been murdered when Silent Wolf led a revolt against the people who lived beyond the boundaries of Fort Howard. Cody had hardened his emotions in order to deal with the constant threat of an upheaval by the Cherokee rebels and the Union soldiers, but thoughts of Donna held tight to his heart. It wasn't that Cody didn't sympathize with the Cherokees, he just wanted the killing to stop on both sides.

Margaret's sister, Julie, was obsessed with wanting to go to Washington, D.C. She felt there she would at least be able to see some of the grandeur of her dreams. The big houses, parties, silk dresses, fancy buggies and live-in maids. She was married to Sgt. Creed Williams, who was stationed at Fort Howard. Julie was stuck at a place she despised. She prayed daily that he would be transferred. Julie did have a nice log house that she had decorated to a tee.

It was late when George returned home from the fort. Carolyn had gone home. Margaret, being exhausted, had pulled her shawl tight around her shoulders, rested her head on the table and fallen asleep.

George smiled as he looked at his wife of thirty years and whispered, "There is never a dull moment living with a Cherokee beauty like you." He stroked her dark hair that shimmered in the glow of leaping flames from their rounded-top, rock fireplace.

Suddenly, Margaret's face muscles tightened. She began to moan and move her head side to side. George leaned down to kiss her cheek. Margaret jerked her head back, hitting George on the end of his nose, causing blood to stream down his face. He held his nose with one hand while retrieving his handkerchief from his back pocket with the other. By then, Margaret had turned on the bench, facing George, and was swinging wildly into the air. George jumped back, wanting to avoid another hit, but he didn't move fast enough. Margaret stood and landed a blow to George's back, causing him to trip and fall.

In pain, he shouted, "Margaret, wake up!"

Margaret trembled as her wild eyes searched the room. It was as though she couldn't see George sitting on the floor in front of her. She didn't acknowledge him until he spoke again. "What in the devil's gotten into you lately?" he shouted.

Only then did Margaret notice George holding a blood soaked handkerchief to his nose. She held her breath and moaned, "Honey, what's wrong? Did . . . did I do that to you?"

George tried to stand, but paused on his knees and leaned to one side. Margaret hurried to try and assist him, but George held his hand out to stop her. "If you're not fully awake, stay away from me."

Margaret put her fingers to her lips. "Is something wrong with your back?" she whined.

George pushed himself up and growled, "Yes, there's something wrong with my back. You kicked me in the back and may have broken my nose. What's wrong with you? For the past few weeks, I've been almost afraid to sleep with you. You toss, turn and moan, and if I touch you, you wake up swinging. What's going on? Is it bad dreams, are you hurting, not resting well or what?"

"I'm so sorry, honey, you know I wouldn't hurt you on purpose. Let me get you a wet cloth for your nose."

George made his way to a rocking chair near the fireplace and laid his head back. Margaret took the handkerchief and put a cold, wet cloth on his nose. When it stopped bleeding, she sat beside him and placed her hand on his knee. "Are you all right, honey?" she asked.

George raised his head, still holding the cloth to his nose. "Yeah, I'll be fine. I may have a splitting headache and not be able to walk straight for a couple of days, but I'm sure I'll live." He patted her hand. "Now, I want to know what's going on in that head of yours that's making you act like a wild woman."

Margaret tightened her brows and began, "For the past few weeks, I've had a terrible nightmare. It's always the same. I'm walking around the house to the woodshed; when I open the door to the shed an Indian is standing in front of the woodpile. He grabs me and pulls me through the forest to a place where a palomino horse is tied. He takes a piece of leather from his pouch and ties my hands and lifts me onto the back of the horse and jumps on. He holds me so tight I can hardly breath. He smells my hair, sending chills down my spine. I try to fight, but his hold is firm. Then a host of warriors appears. He raises his hand in the air and does a scream so loud my ears ache. We ride away with the host behind us."

George frowned. "Well . . . do you think the dream . . . has a meaning?"

"I don't know for sure. I do know the dream has occurred almost nightly, and it scares me to think maybe there is something to it."

George put down the wet cloth and pulled Margaret onto his lap. "Toot, there's nothing going to happen to you as long as I have anything to do with it. Frankly, I don't think any man alive could fight more furiously than you've just fought me."

Toot stroked his cheek. "I pray it never comes to that," she whispered.

George tenderly kissed her. "I don't like the thought of any man touching you but me."

She stroked his cheek and teased, "Are you jealous?"

"Now, Toot, that's nothing to kid about."

"I was trying to take your mind off your bloody nose."

George held Margaret's chin. "I'm serious. In your dream, could the Indian be Silent Wolf? I mean like some kind of warning?"

Margaret thought a moment. "I'm sure it wasn't Silent Wolf, yet I couldn't tell who it was. I also saw a man with the party that was wearing the garb of a chief, but not a Cherokee chief."

George tightened his brows. "Not Cherokee?"

Chapter Six

Out-of-Season Honeysuckle

Late October was a time when the men at Fort Howard began to prepare for the long, cold winters the Smoky Mountains were noted for. The brightly colored leaves of fall rustled in the breeze. Margaret sniffed, trying to figure out where the sweet fragrance was coming from. She smiled in recognition but paused to ponder when she saw the honeysuckle bush at the end of the porch in full bloom. Out of season honeysuckles had opened overnight and their perfume had filled the air.

Margaret fixed breakfast and called George. She went outside, breathed the glorious aroma of the honeysuckles and checked the sky to see how the weather was shaping up for the day. George poured his coffee and joined her on the porch. He kissed her forehead. "Good morning, Toot," he said. "I trust that you slept well."

She shook her head and mumbled, "I've never seen anything like this before."

"Like what?"

"Like honeysuckles blooming in late October. This time of the year, everything is dying. Not blooming." She took a deep breath and sighed. "I think their fragrance is heavenly. Maybe God is giving us a special blessing. He knows how much I love the honeysuckles."

George raised his brows. "Must be, because they're sure out of season."

She kissed George's cheek. "By the way, good morning. Your breakfast is ready."

"Good, I'm starved."

As they were eating, Toot asked George about his meeting with Major Wright. He put his fork down and replied as he raised his eyes to meet Margaret's. "His scouts found a family massacred on the road coming from Franklin. It had all the signs of Silent Wolf and his men. The family had three young children; however, there was no trace of them. Major Wright thinks they were taken."

"Who was the family?"

"The Wilsons"

Margaret squeezed George's hand. "How old were the children?"

"Five, seven and ten. May God have mercy on them."

Margaret demanded, "What's Major Wright doing about this?"

"Toot, he's doing all he can. That's even more reason for you and Carolyn to stay close and watch yourselves."

"I know, and we will. Speaking of Carolyn, she said she had a jar of locust honey for me."

Suddenly, George laughed aloud and scratched his head.

"What are you laughing about, George Black?"

George continued to chuckle. "I was thinking Phoebe may not have lived long enough to bless Willow Fine, but Cody and I are going by and bless her poor husband today."

"What do you mean?"

"We're going to take him with us to fell some trees for firewood. We'll be at Balsam Gap if you need us." George started toward the porch but turned back, smiling. "Toot?"

"Yeah."

"Why don't you and Carolyn ride over and visit Willow. She is your first cousin, and Tim said she had been feeling down the past few days."

Toot sighed. "George, you know Willow hates me. All because Grandma Phoebe died before she blessed her. She said Grandma spent too much time blessing me, talking about the mighty Phoenix and so on. All that's really wrong with her is she's jealous. I was Phoebe's favorite grandchild, and Willow knew it."

"Toot, I'm not sure about the attitude you're displaying. Phoebe Thawbush loved all of her grand-children. Why she said more over you before she died, I don't know; nevertheless, if Willow needs some encouragement, it wouldn't hurt you to do the godly thing and encourage her."

"You're right. I'll go visit her and Julie today."

"That's more like it. I love you, Toot."

Margaret quickly dressed, saddled her horse and headed to see Carolyn, who was sitting on the porch ready to go when Margaret arrived. "What in the world are you doing with your horse saddled? Are you going somewhere?" Margaret asked.

Carolyn met her in the yard. "I know you, Margaret. You don't visit like normal people. We usually visit on horseback. I knew you were coming, so I saddled Betsy and I'm ready to go. So where are we going?"

"First, I promised George we would visit Willow."

"She hates you. Why would you promise that?"

"I'm just a nice person. Let's go and get this over with before I back out."

Chapter Seven
Three Captured Indians

Carolyn mounted her horse, and she and Margaret headed toward the settlement. Just outside the Fort, six Confederate soldiers were all but dragging three Indians into the fort. The Indians stared at Margaret and Carolyn as they slowly passed. Their wild eyes were red with fatigue. Their bodies were covered in mud and in desperate need of a bath. Their long, black hair was filled with burrs and feathers. Underneath the mud, Margaret saw splotches of red paint on their faces.

"I wonder where they captured these Indians," Margaret said. Curious, she beckoned Carolyn to follow them into the fort.

"Margaret, why does it matter where they were captured?"

"I just want to know."

Carolyn seized Margaret's arm. "Did you have that dream again?"

Margaret's weary eyes all but answered the question. "I'm not too proud to say I'm getting

24

concerned. Last night, I busted poor George's nose and bruised his ribs. I thought most of the night about the man, spirit, angel or whatever we saw at the graveyard. I dare not tell George about that. The things Eagle Claw said to me made no sense. What could he have possibly meant when he said that many years ago a baby was taken and deep in the forest I would find the clue that would show me what to do? Everything for miles in every direction is deep forest."

Carolyn shook her head and muttered, "I lost some sleep last night trying to figure that out myself." Suddenly, Carolyn gasped.

"What it is?" Margaret asked.

"In the blessing Phoebe spoke over you, she said, 'From the ashes of death cause this child to rise like the mighty Phoenix.' I remember that well because I've never fully understood the legend of the Phoenix and why Phoebe would use it in your blessing."

They tied their horses; Margaret squinted, bit her lower lip and asked, "Carolyn, do you remember the first thing Eagle Claw said?"

"I was trying not to wet my pants, but I do remember what he said about the Eagle's court. Do you remember what he said?"

Margaret sighed. "Of course I remember. He was talking to me. He said, 'From the ashes a child will rise.' Get it? Grandma Phoebe talked about the Phoenix rising from the ashes of death."

"That's right! What in the world would that have to do with you?"

Margaret tightened her lips and confessed, "I don't have a clue, but there is someone that might be able to help me."

"Who?"

"The oldest living Cherokee Indian around."

Carolyn frowned and shook her head. "Don't you even think about it."

"Too late," Margaret said. "I want this to be our utmost secret. George can never know. Promise me, Carolyn."

"Forget George!" Carolyn said. "She's a witch, for heaven sake. She does spells, curses and who knows what else."

Margaret furrowed her brows. "Do you believe in the Great Eagle of heaven?" she asked.

"You know I do."

"Then you shouldn't be so scared! The devil himself is no match for an offspring of the Great Eagle. Desan is close to one hundred ten years old. Should the need arise, and our faith fails us, we're still able to run."

"Do you know what her name means?" Carolyn asked. "Rock Pile!   I'm sure if she couldn't get us with a spell or curse, she would get a rock from a pile and try to stone us to death."

"I can always find her myself, you know."

"Oh, shut-up, Margaret. You know when you go I'll be right by your side, shaking all the way. If I can stand in a graveyard and listen to something named Eagle Claw, then an old witch like Desan will be a piece of cake."

26

Margaret giggled, "Speaking of a piece of cake, here comes one."

Carolyn quickly straightened her blouse and ordered, "Don't you dare embarrass me in front of Scott Taylor."

Confederate Captain Scott Taylor had been stationed at Fort Howard for three years. He was from Alabama and had never been married. A well-mannered man, Scott had the look of George Armstrong Custer—blond hair, beard, tall and pretty good looking. Carolyn thought he was gorgeous.

Carolyn Morris was forty-three and had lost her husband, Dale, ten years earlier in a logging accident. She was a lovely woman. Her long, sandy blond hair was beginning to show signs of gray. Her round eyes were emerald green and her skin, like fine porcelain. She stood a slim five foot eight inches tall. Not a tomboy like Margaret. She had taught school in Topeka, Kansas, where she was born. Carolyn's move to the Smoky Mountains to live with her aunt had proved to be a wise choice. Her aunt had passed away, but Carolyn chose to stay in Cherokee. She taught school three days a week and had been working with the Cherokee children who were becoming very familiar with the English language.

As Scott neared, Margaret smiled and greeted him. "Good morning, Captain Taylor."

He removed his hat and nodded. "Mrs. Black, it's a beautiful morning, made more beautiful by the two women standing before me." He nodded and smiled at Carolyn. "It's a pleasure to see you again, Miss Morris."

Carolyn blushed and apologized for her rugged appearance. Captain Taylor assured her that she looked radiant. With that said, Margaret excused herself.

"Where are you going?" Carolyn quickly asked.

"I wanted to find out about the three Indians that were just brought in."

Scott put his hat on and enquired, "What is it you want to know? Maybe I can help."

"Who are they? They're not Cherokee."

"You're right," Miss Margaret. "They're renegades from the Seminole nation."

Margaret frowned. "Seminole? Have they joined with someone here?"

"We've had reports of a group calling themselves Fiery Serpents. It's possible they're a part of that group. I'm sure George told you about the family that was slaughtered near Franklin."

"Yes, he told me this morning. He said, the slaughter had all the signs of Silent Wolf."

Scott looked down and moaned. "I'm not sure. Silent Wolf has always been consistent with everything he does. This scene was different. The woman was brutalized, left nude and only half of her scalp was taken. Silent Wolf is notorious for brutalizing women; however, I've never heard of him taking a woman's scalp, strange but true. What he does to men . . . the man bore no marks of Silent Wolf's mutilations. He may be trying to throw us off."

"I don't understand," Carolyn said. "If the evidence is so different, why would Major Wright settle that it was Silent Wolf and not someone else?"

"That was my question," Scott said. "I was told he didn't appreciate me questioning his findings."

Margaret snapped, "I don't care how long he's been here. It doesn't mean he can't possibly be wrong. I think I'll have a little talk with the good major."

"Please don't for a day or so," Scott said. "He would know for sure that I've talked with you. For some unknown reason, he doesn't like me and wants me away from Fort Howard." He smiled at Carolyn. "I would like to stay here as long as possible."

Carolyn grinned and rubbed the back of her neck.

He nodded and smiled. "Ladies, I had better be going. It was my pleasure to see you both again."

Carolyn swooned until Captain Taylor disappeared around the corner. Margaret put her hands on her hips and asked, "Are you coming or are you going to stand here all day?"

Carolyn closed her eyes and exhaled. "Did you see how he looked at me?"

Margaret shook her head and smiled. "You're acting like a young woman and I love it. Yes, I saw how he glared into your eyes. Do you want me to fix you up with him? I could always invite you two over to supper."

"Maybe."

Chapter Eight

Who Are the Prisoners?

*A*fter entering the fort, Margaret led the way straight to Major Wright's office. Deloris Hays, Major Wright's sister had volunteered to act as her brother's secretary, knowing how unorganized he was when it came to paper work. Union soldiers had killed Deloris's husband, Walter Hays, two years earlier. Being his only family, Major Wright liked having Deloris close by. He wanted to help her and make sure she was as safe as possible.

Deloris told the two ladies to be seated. "I'll let the Major know you are here." She was back in seconds. "He'll be right with you. Would you like a fresh cup of hot coffee?"

"No thanks," Margaret said. "But there is something you might be able to tell me."

Deloris stood. "If I can, what?"

Margaret stood, pulled her gloves off and worked into the question. "I know you hear almost everything that comes through Major Wright's office. I'm not asking you to break a confidence. Therefore, if you can't answer,

I'll understand."

Deloris raised her brows. "I must confess you have my attention, so ask away."

"The three Indians brought into the fort a few minutes ago . . . who were they and why were they arrested?"

Deloris appeared uncomfortable. "I think maybe you had better let my brother answer that question."

"Come on, Deloris. They're not Cherokee; that's plain to see by their features and the scarring on their chests. So what's the big secret?"

"Margaret," Carolyn interrupted.

Margaret waved her hand behind her for Carolyn to wait a moment. "Margaret," Carolyn said with a low tone.

Margaret stomped her foot, turned and growled, "Just a minute, Carolyn."

"Suit yourself," Carolyn muttered.

Deloris sat down, but Margaret was unyielding in her desire to know about the Indians. "Come on, Deloris. I won't tell a soul. I promise."

A stern voice questioned, "What's so important about three renegades that you are practically begging Deloris to tell you?"

Margaret jumped back and grabbed her chest. "Major Wright! You scared me half to death. You should clear your throat or something to let someone know you're around."

"Maybe if you weren't asking questions that don't concern you, you wouldn't be so jumpy."

Carolyn stood when she saw Margaret's face muscles tighten. "Margaret, we better go. It's getting late, and we have a lot to do."

"You're right, Carolyn; nevertheless, I would like to ask Major Wright a question before we go."

"What brought you here this morning, Margaret?" Major Wright asked.

Margaret propped her hand on her hip and responded, "I was curious about the prisoners. Just for the record, the question I asked Deloris does concern me. I heard about the family that was murdered and the three children that were taken. You say something like that doesn't concern me? It not only concerns me, but every person near Fort Howard. So, will you please answer my question?"

Major Wright raised his chin. "The Indians are a part of Silent Wolf's war party."

Margaret spoke up. "Silent Wolf is Cherokee, they're not Cherokee. The paint on their faces, the scarring on their chests, is not the way of the Cherokee people."

Major Wright smiled. "You're very observant.

"I have Cherokee blood in my veins, so don't try and tell me about the Cherokee. You've been here a short time, and you've done a great job, but those Indians are not part of Silent Wolf's group."

"I agree with Margaret," Carolyn said.

Major Wright was showing his agitation by his tight lips and clenched fist. "Mrs. Black, Miss Morris, I know my job and my surroundings. To be blunt, I don't need a couple of women telling me how to do my job. While it was good to see you, I'm sure you have many other things that need your attention, as Miss Morris stated a moment ago." He put his hat on, told Deloris that he would be back soon and went outside.

"I'm sorry I couldn't answer your question," Deloris said. "My brother is really strict about some things."

"That's fine, Deloris," Carolyn said. "We understand."

Margaret hastened to add, "We understand you couldn't say anything, but Major Wright is a different story. If there is a problem with renegades, or anything else, the people need to be aware of it."

Deloris raised her shoulders and sighed. "I agree, but what can I do?"

Chapter Nine
Sgt. Randy Mathis Says No

Carolyn and Margaret made their way to the lower side of the fort where prisoners were kept. "I don't think we need to be lurking around like animals," Carolyn muttered

"We're not lurking. We're going for a walk. There's a big difference."

"Sure there is. I don't understand why you don't knock on the jailhouse door and just ask to see the prisoners."

Margaret stopped and took a deep breath. "Carolyn, you're a genius." Margaret started to step onto the porch of the jail. Carolyn grabbed her arm. "Don't you dare, Margaret Black."

At that moment, Sergeant Randy Mathis opened the door. His eyes squinted. "What in the world are you two doing at this end of the fort?" he asked. He looked at Margaret and frowned. "I know George don't know you're here."

Margaret huffed, "Okay, Randy, I'll get right to the point. What do you know about the new prisoners?"

Randy was chewing tobacco. He spit. "What is it you want to know?"

"Who they are and why they were arrested."

Randy smiled at Carolyn and enquired, "Is there a question I can answer for you, Miss Morris?"

Carolyn shook her head. "No questions today."

Randy looked around. "I can't do this. If I get caught, I'll be the one in jail."

Margaret begged, "Come on, Randy. At least give me a hint."

Randy scratched his head. "I don't know."

Margaret squinted. "Don't make me bring up the fact that George has saved your life, loaned you money and—"

Randy interrupted. "You're sure not playing fair."

"That's because I'm not playing."

Randy observed the area again. "All right, I'll tell you this much, they're Seminole. About one hundred have been spotted making their way into the Smoky Mountains. Why, God only knows."

"Why were they arrested?" Margaret asked.

Randy spit and wiped his mouth. "They were found outside Franklin. With the Curtis family just being murdered, what else could the soldiers think?"

Carolyn commented, "The Major is being evasive about it."

"Major Wright's afraid of being replaced," Randy said. "As long as something big is going on, he can keep his job. Actually, he thinks that Captain Taylor was sent here to get familiar with the fort and take over in a few months."

Margaret patted Randy's shoulder and uttered, "Thanks, Randy, you're a true friend. I'll have to make you an apple cake and send it over by George." Margaret paused, tightened her brow and asked, "Randy, can I see the prisoners?"

Randy and Carolyn looked at each other and frowned. Through gritted teeth, Carolyn growled, "Have you lost your mind?"

Randy shook his head and declared, "There's no way in the world that you're going to see those heathens. No way. Besides, you saw them when you entered the fort."

"I didn't see them up close. Come on, Randy. I'll just step inside the door and no farther. They're locked up. I just want one look at their faces. Please, Randy, please."

Randy clenched his fists and thundered, "Margaret Phoebe Black, do you want me thrown out of the Army? You must or you wouldn't even consider asking me to do something that crazy. If someone found out, God only knows what they would do to me. That pitiful look is not going to work, so straighten your face."

Carolyn gasped. "I agree with Randy. What possible motive could you have?"

Margaret shrugged and whined, "I don't know. I just need to look at them for one second. Randy, just a quick peek and I'll leave."

Randy scratched his forearm and briefly closed his eyes. "You promise that you'll—"

"I promise."

Randy looked around the area once more.

Carolyn frowned and remarked, "You're not going to let her are you?"

"Umm, she did say there would be no more questions and she would leave. Okay, Margaret, you've got one minute. If you hear me cough, get your behind out here and fast."

Margaret gripped her hands together and whispered, "I will. Thank you, Randy."

He took hold of her arm. "Margaret, not so fast. You're not to touch anything. Go to the center of the floor and don't speak to them. Do you understand me? Do I make myself clear?"

"Completely!"

Carolyn crossed her arms, shook her head and sighed. "You've lost your mind."

Margaret patted her arm. "Trust me, Carolyn. I've not lost my mind. I'll be right back."

Margaret stepped onto the porch. Randy called out, "One minute."

Margaret nodded, swallowed hard, anxiously seized the doorknob, paused, stepped inside and closed the door. The prisoners instantly stood and vigorously grabbed the bars of the cell door. Their stares caused Margaret to tremble. Her eyes connected with the Indian in the middle. For a moment she couldn't move and her breathing was shallow. She questioned why she felt the need to see three possible murderers. They stared at her, talking among themselves. However, she couldn't understand their language. She started to leave, but suddenly turned and wildly gazed at the men in front of her.

The man in the middle pointed at her and grunted, "Phoenix, Phoenix."

Her mind raced. Without taking her eyes from him, she asked, "What . . . what did you say?"

The same man pounded his chest and announced, "Coosa, Coosa."

Margaret licked her incredibly dry lips and stated, "No, not Coosa, Phoenix. You said Phoenix."

Before she could say anything else, Randy began coughing profusely. Margaret hurried out the door. Major Wright was going back into his office.

Randy ordered, "You two get out of here."

Aggravated, Margaret uttered, "Randy—"

He held his hand up. "No! Now go before the Major sees you here."

Carolyn took Margaret's arm and pulled her. "He's right. Let's go."

They rode a short distance before Carolyn stopped her horse and questioned, "What's wrong with you? You were white as a ghost when you opened that door. Did they say something to you?"

Margaret frowned. "Yes. One of them did say something." She paused.

"Margaret, don't leave me hanging. What did he say that you could possibly understand?"

She fixed her eyes on Carolyn and whispered breathlessly, "Phoenix. He gazed at me with his cold eyes and blurted out, 'Phoenix.'"

Unsure what to say, Carolyn nudged her horse and rode toward the fort's gate.

Chapter Ten
A Visit to Willow

*T*hey didn't speak until they neared Willow's house. Carolyn cleared her throat and suggested, "Margaret, we need to leave this Phoenix thing behind us while we visit with Willow, don't you think?"

"Of course."

When they dismounted, Willow's dog began to bark furiously. Before they could knock, Willow opened the door and greeted them teasingly. "My heavens, if it isn't Margaret Black. Have you lost your way, dear cousin?"

Margaret grinned. "Willow, I must have lost my way. I thought this was the Trading Post."

Carolyn stated, "I for one haven't lost my way. It's good to see you again, Willow."

"Carolyn, it's a treat, to see you, too."

Margaret hugged Willow and assured her that she just wanted to drop by and say hello. Inside, Willow made them a hot cup of herbal tea.

"You have new curtains, don't you?" Carolyn asked.

"Yes, I do. They're not the ones I wanted, but until then they'll have to do."

"They're perfect for this room," Carolyn said. "You've done a wonderful job decorating."

Willow looked around the room, lifted her shoulders and replied, "It's all right, but nothing like a grand plantation in the South. That's the kind of house I yearn for and will have one day."

Margaret shook her head. "You sound exactly like Julie. I think you two are sisters."

Willow's tone changed drastically. "There's nothing wrong with wanting to better one's self. I'm not like you, Margaret, satisfied with . . . whatever."

Margaret quickly assured, "Don't take me wrong. I was only meaning that your dream . . . and Julie's, hasn't changed after all these years, that's all."

"Cousin dear, it really doesn't matter. I'll be here until the day I die. Then you can laugh and tell everyone what a dreamer I was."

Carolyn insisted, "There's nothing wrong with dreaming. I dream of finding a husband every day. Everybody should have dreams and goals for his or her life."

"She's right, Willow," Margaret said. "I have dreams. I'm fifty years old and realize if my dreams are ever going to become reality, they'll have to happen soon, or I'll be too old to enjoy them."

Willow tightened her lips and said, "Dreams! You have everything, Margaret. Maybe it was because Grandma Phoebe had time to give you her blessing. Maybe she took too much time on one and not everyone. I'm the only one that didn't receive a blessing."

Margaret threw her hands up. "Do you believe this, Carolyn? Willow is bringing up something that happened years ago. The nerve to blame Grandma Phoebe for dying before she could speak a few words over her." Margaret frowned and raised her tone.

"Willow Fine, you're self-centered and really don't care that Grandma died. It's all about the blessing to you. You're too blind with jealousy to be happy. I thought I would come by today to try and cheer you up. Evidently I'm not the one who can accomplish the impossible." Margaret put her hat on and headed toward the door. "Carolyn, are you ready?"

Carolyn nodded and patted Willow's shoulder. "Take care, Willow. Thanks for the tea."

Margaret and Carolyn mounted their horses and headed home. When out of sight of Willow's house, Margaret abruptly stopped her horse and dismounted. She pushed her hat back, sat on a rock, put her hands over her face and began to cry.

Carolyn put her arm around her friend, hoping to calm her. "Margaret, don't worry yourself sick over Willow's foolishness."

Margaret shook her head and continued to cry. She wiped her nose on her gloves and whimpered. "I don't know what's wrong with me. I wouldn't have let this bother me a few years ago, and now look at me. It's as though I just found out that Willow hates me. The graveyard experience last night . . . the Indians today . . . I don't think I can stand another thing today."

"Maybe you should go home and rest."

"That's just it, Carolyn, I'm afraid if I go to sleep. I'll have that dream again."

Carolyn insisted she cry and let it all out, assuring her she would go home with her and let her rest.

Margaret was sleeping and Carolyn was reading in a rocker nearby when something outside bumped against the house. Carolyn put the book down and listened to see if she could hear anything else. Her focus changed when Margaret moaned and kicked the blanket to the floor. Carolyn glanced back at the window, but Margaret's groans intensified.

"Margaret, wake up. Margaret!" Carolyn tried to stay clear, remembering how Margaret had battered George. Not responding, Carolyn tossed a pillow and hit Margaret's chest. Margaret seized the pillow and wildly tore at it. "Margaret Phoebe Black, wake up!" Carolyn shouted.

Trembling like a frightened child, Margaret fixed her eyes on Carolyn, held the pillow tight to her chest and breathlessly whispered, "Oh, God, I thought I heard . . ."

When Carolyn saw how frantically Margaret was trembling, she held her and asked, "Did you have that dream again?"

Margaret nodded yes.

Carolyn stuttered, "Wh-wh-why would you be having the same dream over and over?"

"I don't know."

"Should you see Doctor Whitt?"

"And tell him what? I've had the same nightmare for three months!"

Carolyn raised her hands and confessed, "I don't know what to do! If not Dr. Whitt, how about seeing Rev. Blare?"

Margaret pressed her fingers to her forehead. "I've asked God to help me understand the dream and why I'm having it. I can't explain it, but I need to see Desan. My insides scream it. Besides, anybody that old ought to be able to tell me something about everything."

"I've heard all kinds of weird stories about her," Carolyn said. "She's a recluse that lives in the backwoods where bears and rattlesnakes live in abundance."

"That's just it, Carolyn. You've heard from people who have never seen or talked to her, yet they have all these stories. So it's only hearsay. It's like being found guilty by hearsay with no evidence of any firsthand knowledge."

Carolyn smiled. "I suppose you're right. Let's put this behind us for now and do something fun."

Margaret grinned. "That sounds good. What do you have in mind?"

"Humm, do you have anything that belonged to your Grandma Phoebe?"

"No. There wasn't much to go around. My mother's brother Bill has a few things that belonged to Mom. The family has never had anything to do with him for some reason."

"What's your uncle like?"

"I've heard things about him, but I don't ever remember meeting him."

"Where does he live?"

"At Chestnut Cove, which is a two-day journey from here. Bill never wanted anything to do with his family after Mother died. I asked lots of questions about him, but no one seems to know why the separation. Or they weren't willing to tell. The last member of the family who went to visit with him was Uncle Tyler, but Bill wouldn't allow him on his land."

Carolyn sighed. "There has to be a reason he cut family ties."

"I asked and asked, then finally stopped asking. Now only Bill and Tyler are still alive. Bill is seventy-five and Tyler is seventy-eight.

The evening passed. Margaret walked out with Carolyn to say goodbye. Carolyn rubbed Margaret's forearm and asked, "Do you feel better now?"

Margaret hugged Carolyn. "Yes, I do. Thank you for being a dear friend."

Carolyn mounted her horse and fixed her eyes on Margaret.

"What's that look, Carolyn Morris?"

"I was just thinking."

"Thinking what?"

"Would . . . would you like to ride to Chestnut Cove and see if your uncle would be willing to see you? Who knows, he might."

"Carolyn, that's a great idea. Would you go too?"

Carolyn smiled and nodded. "What do you think? I'll see you tomorrow."

Chapter Eleven

Bad News

Expecting George and Cody home soon, Margaret made supper and hurried to the springhouse to get some milk. Margaret removed the wooden bar from the door and pushed it open. She stooped down to get a jar of milk. Instantly, she sensed someone staring at her. She swiftly stood and surveyed the area, but saw no one. She grabbed the milk, barred the door and hurried back to the house in time to see George and Cody tying their horses. George caught a glimpse of Margaret coming around the house.

"Hi, Toot," he said as he removed his hat and raked his fingers through his hair.

"Hi, Sis," Cody said.

Margaret hugged Cody and welcomed him to stay for supper. George and Cody pulled their boots off at the door, while Margaret set the table.

"It sure smells good in here," Cody said. "I'm glad you asked me to stay."

Margaret pushed Cody's shoulder and said, "You don't need an invitation. You're always welcome."

George asked grace, and the men ate as though they were starved.

George's eyes widened. "We saw one of the largest bucks today I've ever seen,"

"That's for sure," Cody agreed. "His rack was enormous."

George laughed. "Cody and I are going out Thursday, and we're bringing him home with us."

"How was Tim today?" Margaret asked.

"Actually, he was in a great mood," George said. "We worked hard, but had a good time."

Cody wiped his mouth and questioned, "Did you go visit Willow today?"

"Of course, why wouldn't I?"

George and Cody smiled at each other. "Let me see," Cody uttered. "Is it because Grandma Phoebe blessed you and died before she could bless Willow. I guarantee the visit didn't pass without Willow bringing that up. Am I right?"

Margaret finished her milk and answered, "You're right. It turned out pretty bad, but she'll get over it. I did apologize for saying exactly what I thought about her jealousy."

They had just finished supper when someone knocked at the door. George answered it. A soldier removed his hat and apologized for coming so late.

"Come in," George said.

The soldier stepped inside and announced, "Major Wright needs to see you right away."

George frowned. "Why tonight? Is it Silent Wolf or Union troops?"

46

"Unfortunately, Silent Wolf has struck again. There's been another attack on a family near Fontana Gorge."

Margaret stepped forward and asked, "Who was the family?"

The soldier lowered his head and answered, "The Curtis family."

George and Margaret gasped. "Are you talking about Ray and Sherri?"

"Yes. Did you know them?"

Margaret grabbed the soldier's arm. "What about the children?"

"I'm sorry, Mrs. Black."

Margaret closed her eyes and moaned. George put his arms around her.

"They were just small children. Amy was only six months old. They couldn't hurt anybody. Why?"

Through tear-filled eyes, George released Margaret and said, "Toot, I need to go check with Major Wright. Cody will stay with you until I get back."

Margaret hugged George. "You be very careful and hurry back."

George looked at Cody.

"Don't worry, George, I'll be here," Cody said.

George kissed Margaret's forehead. "I'll be back as soon as I can, Toot."

Cody fixed Margaret a cup of warm milk and put some wood on the fire.

"I saw Sherri last week," Margaret muttered. "She came to the Trading Post for supplies. Ray had been gathering wood for the winter. Those children were precious. How can someone's heart be so evil? How?"

"Silent Wolf doesn't have a heart. He killed Donna and countless others; still he continues to leave his evil on everything he touches. I hate him. I've asked God to take the hate out of my heart, but He hasn't yet."

Margaret patted Cody's knee. "There are some things God expects us to hate. Evil is to be hated. In time, God will help you to heal, and who, knows, He may have another woman in the picture for you."

Cody shook his head. "It's been five years since Donna died. I'll never know the joy of being her husband. You remember, we were to be married just a couple of weeks after her death."

"I know, honey. It must hurt so bad."

"At times, I get so lonely. Maybe there will be another woman. She had better hurry and make an appearance. I'm fifty-five and getting pretty set in my ways."

Margaret lowered her head. "I'll have to find out where the Curtises will be buried. I think their families live in Kentucky." She raised her head and stared intently at Cody.

Cody didn't understand her look. "What?" he asked.

Margaret put her hand on Cody's. "My mind is jumping all around. When I mentioned Kentucky . . . Cody, you're five years older than me, which means you had more time with Mama then I did. I know I've asked you a blue million times, but do you remember ever hearing anything about why Uncle Bill left the family after Mama died?"

Cody furrowed his brows. "What brought this up?"

Margaret shrugged. "I just wondered. There are only two left from Mama's family. Before they both die, I want to find out what was so terrible they couldn't reconcile. Why did Uncle Bill wait until Mama died to break all ties? Why wouldn't Grandma Phoebe ever speak of it? She would cut you off if you came close to the subject."

Cody shrugged. "I don't know why Grandma wouldn't talk about it. I think Tyler and Bill are too stubborn to make up. You may as well forget the reason. Besides, what difference does it make? That's been so many years ago."

Margaret began playing with her fingers. "I'm a curious kind of person. It's hard for me to let something die if it's important. This is important. Before one of them passes, I thought I might pay a visit to Uncle Bill. It's been a long time. Who knows, he may have softened."

"Margaret, Uncle Tyler made an attempt to visit Bill, and he stopped him on the edge of his property with a shotgun."

"And how long ago has that been?"

"I don't know. About twenty-five years."

"I rest my case." Margaret scratched her head. "I want to find out what happened, but there is another reason," she confessed.

"Which is?"

"Uncle Bill has a few of Mama's things. I want to at least see them and touch them because they were hers.

That's another thing I don't understand. Grandma gave those things to Uncle Bill right after mother died. Why would she do that and why all the secrets? Carolyn and I were talking today about maybe trying to visit Bill."

Cody's jaw and lips tightened as he pointed at Margaret. "You've just heard about the Curtis family being massacred, and you're thinking about going a two-day journey, unescorted, to try and visit someone who more than likely won't let you near him," he scolded. "Have no doubt, Margaret, Silent Wolf and his warriors are out there! They would love to find you and Carolyn riding down a trail alone, and who knows what they would do to you before they killed you? Get that crazy notion out of your head. Promise me you won't try to go until things settle and George and I can go with you?"

Before she could answer, they heard a horse coming. It was George. Stress gripped his face.

"Honey, what's wrong? What did Major Wright say to you?"

George pulled his hat off and put it on the rack behind the door. "He had several things to say. One of which made me furious."

Margaret knew George was told about her visit to the fort.

George shouted, "Why did you go to the fort enquiring about the Indians that were brought in today?"

Margaret started to speak, but George put his hand up and stated, "I don't care what your explanation is, it won't be acceptable. Those Indians have nothing to do with you. Stay away from them and don't go asking all kinds of questions and challenging the major's authority. Do you hear me?"

Irritated by the strong demands George had made, Margaret stated, "I was curious because of their war paint and wanted to know where they were from. As far as Major Wright, he doesn't know everything, even though he claims to."

George held Margaret's shoulders and ordered, "Stay away from those Indians and Major Wright."

Cody agreed with George. Margaret agreed, but knew she would do what she had to do when the time was right.

"What did the good major want to see you about?" Margaret asked.

"He wanted me to ride out with him and his troops tomorrow to the Curtis home."

"George," Margaret said, "what would bring Seminole braves to these parts?"

George's face muscles tightened. "Wait one minute! How do you know they're Seminole?"

Margaret realized she had said too much.

Cody moved closer, "I'd like to hear the answer to that question myself."

Margaret began playing with her fingers, not sure how to answer without incriminating Randy or Captain Taylor. She took a deep breath and looked at Cody's and George's impatient eyes.

George insisted, "Come on, Toot, I want an answer,"

In a low tone she muttered, "I heard someone say they were."

"Who did you talk to Margaret?" George asked.

Margaret raised her voice. "They dragged them through the street into the fort, so it's not like no one saw them."

"True enough," George said. "However, everyone didn't automatically know they were Seminole. Now, who told you they were?"

Margaret widened her eyes and declared, "If you think I'm going to give you a name, you're wrong."

George sighed and lowered his head. "You're right, Toot, I'm not thinking straight. When you think with your heart, sometimes your vision gets blurred. I love you, Toot, and God knows I couldn't stand for anything to happen to you. If the truth be known, you more than likely begged Randy Mathis to let you in to see them. What did you do, remind him of the time I saved his life?"

"I'm not confessing to anything." She quickly turned her attention to Cody and asked him to stay the night. Cody agreed.

Margaret breathed a sigh of relief, seeing George was willing to change the subject. She was thankful Cody didn't mention her wanting to visit Uncle Bill.

Margaret could see the concern on George's face. "George," she said, "I promise to be careful and watch my back at all times."

He smiled and gently stroked her cheek. "I love you, Toot. Let's put this behind us tonight and get some sleep." Later in bed, George pulled Margaret to him and pushed her hair behind her ear and whispered softly, "I love you, I love you, I love you, and I need you. I want you to stay safe."

Chapter Twelve
Sound of Horses

The wind blew hard all night. By morning the cool damp feeling in the air had the threat of several days of rain.

Margaret slept soundly all night but began to squirm at the distant sound of horse's hooves. She lay with her eyes closed listening for the sound again, but all she heard was the wind rustling the leaves on the big oak tree beside the bedroom window. There were a few seconds of silence, and then she heard the sound again. Instantly, the sound stopped. She listened for a few seconds, opened her eyes and stretched with all her might. George was up and maybe Cody; perhaps she heard them. Or maybe troops on their way back to the fort using the route past her house. Margaret tied her housecoat, twisted her long hair in a bun, grabbed a pair of George's wool socks, slid her feet into his slippers and stepped outside. On her way back to the house, she saw George and Cody bringing their horses around.

"Hey, you two," she called. "Where are you going this early without telling me?"

George tied his horse and hugged Margaret. "You know we wouldn't leave without telling you. I made coffee for you, but Cody and I will get some breakfast at the fort." George kissed her forehead and whispered, "You sure look beautiful this morning."

Cody cleared his throat, "Do you two need some time alone?"

Margaret grinned at George. "Yeah, that sounds like a good idea."

George teased, "That's just like a woman to say yes knowing I have to meet Major Wright. We need to be going."

"Are you going, Cody?" Margaret asked.

"Yeah, I thought I would."

"What are you doing today, Toot?" George asked.

"Hmm, I don't know, but I'm sure it involves Carolyn."

Cody said, "Speaking of Carolyn, I think I see her coming now."

Surprised, Margaret turned to look. "I wonder why she's out so early?"

George pulled his watch out of his vest. "Toot, it's not so early. It's 10:30, and we really need to be going."

Margaret put her hands on her hips and called out to Carolyn, "Is something wrong?"

"No, I just wanted to see if you heard about the Curtis family."

"Yes. We heard last night. George and Cody are going with Major Wright to the Curtis home to try to pinpoint who's responsible."

George helped Carolyn off her horse. "Thank you, George," she said.

Cody tipped his hat and smiled. "How are you this fine morning, Miss Morris?"

Carolyn pushed her hat back and pulled her gloves off. "I'm fine, just upset about the killings. They were a good family." Carolyn looked to the sky and commented, "The way things are going, I'm afraid of who will be next."

Margaret patted George's shoulder and turned to Carolyn, "These two have been preparing for the cold weather. Would you believe they've been chopping wood this morning? I think I would have asked the troops to grab an ax and help."

"Really?" Carolyn uttered. "I don't have that kind of energy until at least high noon."

Cody and George looked at each other. George offered, "We did chop some wood this morning, but there weren't any soldiers that come by. Cody and I got up, made coffee, chopped some wood and saddled the horses."

Margaret frowned and stated, "Well, who came by? It sounded like a group of horses."

Cody shook his head. "I don't have a clue."

Margaret looked toward the woodshed. "I know what I heard. I heard several horses ride past our house."

"The wind's been blowing pretty hard," Cody said. "Maybe the branches on that old oak were bumping the side of the house."

Margaret rubbed her cheek and took a deep breath. "Maybe so. You two be careful. Carolyn and I are going to have a cup of coffee." Margaret gave Cody and George a hug. "I love you guys."

The men mounted up and rode to Fort Howard.

Carolyn made pancakes while Margaret poured the coffee.

"Carolyn, I know what I heard this morning, and it wasn't tree branches. I've been around horses all my life. I know what they sound like."

Carolyn began to laugh hysterically.

Puzzled by her actions, Margaret asked, "And just what are you laughing about?"

Still laughing, Carolyn patted Margaret on top of her head and said, "I'm sorry, Margaret. It's just that you have more dilemmas in your life than I could have in two life times. In a day and a half alone, you've had event after event take place. God must have brought me here to spice up my life." Carolyn laughed so hard tears filled her eyes.

By that time, Margaret was laughing as well.

"That's why I stick so close to you, my friend," Carolyn said.

Chapter Thirteen
Margaret Visits Julie

*A*fter breakfast, the women rode to the settlement for supplies and to see Margaret's sister, Julie.

Julie was an attractive woman who dressed in the finest apparel. Her husband, Lieutenant Creed Williams, was a man whose family had made their mark raising rice on the Williams Plantation outside Charleston, South Carolina. The war had been devastating. Union soldiers had taken over the plantation, used it for their headquarters and burned it when they moved on. The Williams money had dwindled except for some that Creed's father had hidden a distance from the house. With some of that money, Creed built Julie a house that surpassed anything in Cherokee. Before the war, Creed spoiled Julie. He bought her anything she wanted. Though the war drastically changed everything, Julie tried to maintain her status as much as possible. She hired a white woman from the settlement and a Cherokee woman named Meco to help around her large log house. Julie loved to have dinner parties, mainly to show off her furniture from Charleston. She pulled back her long, auburn hair marked with gray and capped it in a crochet bun holder. Her pink cheeks and lips enhanced her medium-toned skin.

Julie greeted Margaret and Carolyn at the door, wearing a floor-length brown dress with tiny, white buttons up the front. A white lace collar draped around her shoulders was accented by a cameo necklace and earrings. Her petite waist was made to look even smaller by the hoop petticoats. Her round brown eyes danced as she held her head high.

All smiles, Julie expressed, "Margaret, Carolyn, what a surprise! I'm so glad to see you."

Julie quickly ordered Meco to serve hot tea in the living room. After a moment of chitchat, Margaret couldn't help herself. She had to mention Julie's magnified Southern drawl.

"What in the world are you talking about, Margaret? I'm talking no different today than any other day."

Margaret bit her lip to keep from laughing. "Sister dear, your Southern accent is straight from the heart of Georgia. I declare you and Cousin Willow are duplicates of each other. Don't you think, Carolyn?"

Stammering, Carolyn replied, "Th-they are family, and it's not that uncommon for them to have the same characteristics."

"Well, shoot! What kind of answer was that?" Margaret asked.

Carolyn, seeing the conversation needed to be changed, commented on Julie's beautiful home.

Margaret shifted her eyes to Carolyn and whispered, "Now you've done it."

It didn't take long for Carolyn to see what Margaret meant. Julie took Carolyn through every room, showing her everything visible. Margaret interrupted the grand tour by saying, "Julie, Carolyn and I really need to be going."

Julie sighed. "But why would you be leaving so soon? You hardly ever come around. Please stay for lunch."

"I'm sorry, sis, but I have a million things to get done today. Before I go, I wanted to ask you something."

Julie quickly responded, "Of course. What is it, dear? Do you need money?"

"No, Julie, I don't need money. What in the world made you ask that? At any rate, I know I've asked you about Uncle Bill too many times to count. I know your answer is always the same, but if you would answer my question one more time, I would so appreciate it."

"Okay, ask away."

"Do you remember anything about Uncle Bill? Think hard."

Julie placed her hand on her chest in surprise. "Well of course. I . . . I remember Uncle Bill. I've told you many times."

"I know, but please tell me again, even if it seems insignificant," Margaret said.

"Well, when I say I remember, I mean, vaguely remember. I'm not that much older than you. However, he is Mama's brother. I remember that."

Carolyn chuckled.

Julie peered at her and asked, "What's so funny?"

Carolyn shook her head. "What you're trying to say is you remember your uncle's name and that he's your mother's brother?"

Julie smiled and confessed, "You might say that."

Margaret suggested they sit down for a moment. "Julie, surely you remember more than I do. My memory is so vague for some reason."

Julie nodded. "I'm sure I do, but why are you going over this again?"

"Did you ever hear why Bill alienated himself from the family after Mama died."

Julie tapped her pointer finger against her lip. "Like I've said before, the only thing I remember was hearing Uncle Tyler say, 'Now that Mariah is dead, I won't have to pretend any longer.' I was young, and due to the tension that filled the room, I was afraid to ask what he meant. I've never said this to anyone before, but Tyler's statement about Mother being dead made me so angry. He sounded as if he were glad she had died. I questioned in my heart what he could have been pretending about. I did ask Aunt Lorrie about that day before she died. She said she didn't have a clue what Tyler meant by that statement. I didn't believe her for one minute."

"Why?" Margaret asked.

"Do you remember her best friend, Anna Rice?"

"Sure, Anna I remember."

"When I asked Aunt Lorrie that question, she breathed deep and held it in. Anna was standing at the table behind her pouring a cup of coffee.

She stared at me like someone had caught her stealing something. She run the cup over and burnt her hand. I knew then something wasn't right, yet Lorrie insisted she knew nothing. After that, I never mentioned it again. I felt maybe whatever the secret, it might be better on everyone if it remained a secret. Even after Mother's death, the way Grandma Phoebe acted, was so puzzling. Her lips were locked tighter than a vault."

Margaret tightened her brows and said, "There's a reason for Bill to take such drastic measures and Tyler to say he wouldn't have to pretend any longer." She sighed and continued, "Lorrie and Anna's response to a question they supposedly knew nothing about reveals something. What are they trying to hide and why? Do you think one of them murdered somebody?"

Julie put her hand to her chest and gasped, "Margaret! That's a bit drastic?"

Margaret shrugged. "Well, it's as possible as anything else. At least murder is something a person might try to cover up."

"Evidently, whatever it is, they have agreed not to talk about it," Carolyn said.

Julie squinted and asked, "What's going on, Margaret? Why are you so interested in something that happened thirty years ago?"

Margaret stood and pushed her hat down on her head. "For some reason, it's eating at me. I don't know why, but all of a sudden, I have to know what happened." She hugged Julie. "I love you, sis."

"I love you too. Whatever the reason you feel you have to know about these deep family secrets, I'm sure it will all come together in time."

Julie held Margaret's hands and spoke softly, "I'm so glad you came by today. Come back soon and you too, Carolyn."

Chapter Fourteen
J.D. Styles

The two women left and rode toward Fort Howard. "Margaret." Carolyn said, "You talk about every member of your family except your father. Why is that?"

"He wasn't around that much. His name was J.D. Styles. That, along with what Cody and Julie remember, doesn't amount to much. He was a trapper and gone most of the year. At the end of the year, he brought his furs home and sold them at the Trading Post. Daddy was tall and very thin, a heavy full beard and long, brown curly hair. He dressed the part of a trapper. He always brought us a big stick of peppermint candy. One thing I'll never forget is how happy Mama was when J.D. was there."

"Margaret, why are we going to the fort?"

"I need to get some bacon and flour."

"Is that all we're going to do?"

"I was going to check and see if anyone knows where the Curtis family will be buried."

Margaret passed the store and kept riding in the direction of the jail.

"Oh no," Carolyn moaned. "Are you going to the jail again?"

Looking straight ahead, Margaret answered, "I want to see if Randy knows anything about the arrangements."

"I'm not buying that!" Carolyn growled.

"Okay, Carolyn. If anyone comes while I'm visiting Randy, I'll quickly invite him to supper."

"George will have a fit Margaret."

"George isn't going to know. If you don't want to go in with me, that's fine."

"Of course I'll go in with you. I don't want to be seen hanging around in front of the jail."

They tied their horses and hurried to get to the door before Randy had a chance to keep them outside. Margaret opened the door and they rushed inside. Randy, who was sitting at his desk, jumped up and grabbed his heart. "God above, Margaret, you about scared me to death. What are you doing here?"

Margaret gazed at the three prisoners. Their black eyes stared vehemently at her and Carolyn. Today their faces and long black hair were clean.

Margaret squinted at them and stated, "I'm glad to see they had a bath."

Randy raked his hair back and put his hat on. "They smelled so bad we couldn't stand it. We tied them and scrubbed them down. Now what are you doing here?"

Margaret leaned toward Randy and remarked, "Do you see how they stare at me?"

"Yeah, I see. They would probably love to take your pretty scalp. I know you, Margaret Black, you've seen the prisoners, so get out of here before we all get in trouble."

"Well, Randy, I have *another* reason for dropping by," Margaret uttered.

Carolyn shook her head and mumbled, "I can't wait to hear this."

"Randy, you know everybody and everything about the Cherokee people. Right?"

Randy shrugged. "Pretty much. Why?"

"Umm . . . umm, where does the old Indian woman named Desan live?"

Randy looked stunned. "What in the world is your reason for asking that question?"

Margaret patted his arm. "I just want to know."

"You're up to no good, Margaret Black. And you, Carolyn, what part do you have in this?"

Carolyn shook her head. "I'm just with her that's all."

"Desan is an old witch and lives on a mountain over at White Oak Pass." He shook his finger at Margaret. "You don't want to go messing around with Silent Wolf out there. You know well about the Curtis family, and I don't want that to happen to you."

Margaret cleared her throat, "Randy, do you know if Desan speaks English at all?"

"How would I know that?" Randy snapped.

Margaret stared at Randy and boldly asked, "I'll get right to the point, Randy. Would you take us to see Desan?"

Randy exploded. "Are you crazy? No, I will not take you to see her."

"Calm down." Margaret laughed. "I'm only kidding to get you all stirred up. By the way, when would you like to come to supper?"

Randy frowned at Margaret and growled, "All stirred up thunder. You said you weren't going to ask for any more favors, and you ask me to take you to see Desan. George Black would have a fit."

"Okay, Randy. I told you I'm kidding. I know George would be furious."

Carolyn was stunned at the sudden change in Margaret's approach.

Randy rubbed his fingers across his forehead. "That's good to hear, and I'll let you know about supper."

One of the Indians pointed at Margaret and again muttered, "Phoenix."

Margaret swiftly looked to the cell. She frowned at him and stated, "Phoenix. You said, 'Phoenix.'"

Randy put his hand up and ordered, "Margaret, don't you be talking to them. You get on out of here."

Margaret tried to move closer to the cell, but Randy stepped in front of her. "Carolyn, get her out of here."

Carolyn took hold of her arm. "Margaret, Randy's right. Let's go."

"But did you hear him? He said, 'Phoenix.'"

Carolyn nodded. "I heard him. We'll talk about it later, Margaret."

Margaret blew her breath out and held her hands up. "You're right, Carolyn, we do need to be going."

Randy walked out with them. "I'm sorry, Randy," Margaret said. "I just heard him say something that I understood."

Randy sighed. "What is going on with you and the prisoner? What's the big deal about him saying Phoenix?"

"I was just surprised. Weren't you a little surprised?" Margaret asked.

"No, I wasn't. It's no concern to you either."

"You're right, Randy. I just got carried away. I don't know what the draw is, but the need to see them is overwhelming."

"You better shake the need off and stay away from here," Randy said gruffly.

Carolyn raised one eyebrow and agreed wholeheartedly.

Chapter Fifteen

Raven and Ortho

*A*s the women mounted their horses, sporadic drops of rain began to fall. They pulled their coat collars up around their necks to help block the muscle-tightening chill.

While they rode through the settlement, Carolyn was curious to know where Margaret was going when she turned in a direction away from her home.

"Where are we going?" Carolyn remarked.

"To visit Ortho and Raven."

Carolyn pulled back on her horse's bridle. "Whoa, Betsy," she ordered.

"What are you doing?"

Carolyn took a deep breath. "It's cold and drizzling rain out here, in case you hadn't noticed. For that reason alone, I want to know why you would be going on a day like this to visit someone you don't visit that often?"

"Carolyn, please trust me. I may sound like a repetitive fool asking about Uncle Bill, Mama and

Grandma Phoebe, but for some unknown reason, I have to do what I'm doing."

"I don't suppose Raven and Ortho are sick, and you want to check on their well-being."

Margaret tightened her lips and shook her head no.

"Are we going to be there very long?"

"No, I promise, twenty to thirty minutes."

Carolyn pushed her hat down on her head and mumbled, "Okay, lead the way."

Margaret grinned and, with a quick nod of her head, expressed, "Thank you, my best friend in the whole world."

Raven and Ortho were somewhat like historians of the Cherokee people. They were an older couple that still lived in a tepee. Ortho was blind in one eye and carried scars from past battles. His long, dingy, white hair was parted in the middle, and a leather headband fit around his forehead. Two, long, eagle feathers dangled on the right side of the headband. His face was lined with age, his nostrils flared and his narrow lips turned down. He was a small man, with a broad chest and short, stocky legs.

Raven didn't show her age like Ortho. Her hair was streaked with gray and pulled back with thin leather laces. Her dark skin and eyes had all the attributes of her people. She was about twenty pounds overweight, and one could tell in her youth she had been a striking woman.

When they arrived, Ortho was brushing his white horse down. Raven came out of the tepee right away when she heard horses approaching. Margaret smiled when she saw Raven was wearing a dress given to the Indians from the mission at Fort Howard.

Margaret greeted Ortho and Raven. She started by introducing Carolyn and commenting on Raven's dress. "My goodness, Raven, that dress looks wonderful on you. Don't you think, Ortho?"

Ortho smiled and spoke with broken English. "I told her to get dress. She didn't want at first, but then changed mind."

Raven ran her hand down the skirt of the dress. "I like the dress."

Ortho grunted, "It's not like our people, but looks so good on you."

Margaret teased Ortho, "Where are your new clothes. I'm sure you were offered clothing as well."

"They did, but I'll wear clothes made by my hands."

Ortho led the way into the tepee and spread animal pelts for Carolyn and Margaret to sit on. After a minute of small talk, Ortho asked if there was a reason for Margaret's unexpected visit.

Margaret cleared her throat and started, "I wanted to know if you can tell me anything about my Grandma Phoebe Thawbush and my mother Mariah Styles."

Ortho and Raven glanced at each other. "Why are you asking us about them?"

"Because you know the history of the Cherokee people. I'm seeking understanding about my ancestors. You should understand that better than anyone."

Ortho tightened his brows. "I know some about Phoebe Thawbush, but not much about Mariah Styles."

Margaret inched toward Ortho. "Please tell me anything you know. It would mean so much to me."

Ortho crossed his legs and rested his hands on them. He looked at Margaret and said, "Phoebe married a good man. Winter Snow Thawbush was a great hunter. He provided well for his wife."

Margaret shook her head. "No, no, I mean before Winter Snow and Phoebe were married."

Ortho looked at Raven. She nodded her head once and he uttered, "Phoebe's mother and father were killed by white men. They make their home at Fontana Gorge, by the river. Phoebe's mother and father were very young. One day while fishing, white men came. They killed Phoebe's mother and father and stole their furs that were to be used for winter coverings."

Margaret appeared puzzled. "What about Phoebe?"

"Phoebe was only a baby. The men left her by the river. A woman from settlement found her and took her to raise."

"Who was the woman?" Margaret asked.

"She was a preacher's wife. Her name was Helen. The preacher and his wife were killed shortly after taking Phoebe. They were at the same river, where Phoebe's mother and father were killed only a couple of months earlier. I know nothing else of Phoebe until years later. She came back to Cherokee with your mother, a young woman. Mariah had three children. Phoebe never spoke of her youth to anyone and neither did your mother."

Margaret's expression made clear her confusion. "Are you saying that Grandma Phoebe had Mama before she married Winter Snow Thawbush?"

Raven and Ortho looked at each other and then back at Margaret, yet said nothing.

"Please tell me," Margaret urged. "I need to know."

"You don't know about this?" Ortho asked.

Margaret played with her fingers and shook her head no. "We thought Mama was born here in Cherokee. Mama told us that Grandma and Grandpa Thawbush lived at White Oak Pass for years. That's where I was born. Mama was born at Fontana Gorge before they moved to White Oak Pass. We've been around one of Mama's brothers and sister all our life, but they never said anything to suggest anything other than what Mama had told us."

"Maybe I've said too much. Maybe my story is wrong," Ortho said.

Margaret widened her eyes. "Or maybe your story is right, and for some unknown reason, it was kept from us. I just want to know why."

Carolyn asked, "Your Grandma Phoebe died a little over a year ago. You had just turned fifty years old and your mother died when you were a little over twenty?"

"Yes, but I can't explain. It's like a big blur."

Carolyn frowned. "You were that old and don't recall that much about your mother?"

"I remember what we were told. Yet there're so many discrepancies, especially with what Ortho just told me."

Ortho pointed toward Margaret. "I know someone who can help you."

Raven squinted and muttered, "Ortho, I don't think that's a good idea."

Margaret straightened her back. "What's not a good idea? Please tell me."

Ortho looked at Raven. "A—"

Raven placed her hand on his forearm. "Please, don't do that."

Ortho patted her hand and then removed it from his arm. "Margaret has the right to know her heritage. We know ours. If we didn't know, we would do same as Margaret."

"But . . ."

"Woman, hold your tongue. My mind is made up."

Carolyn and Margaret listened with anticipation. Ortho and Raven stood. Carolyn and Margaret followed suit. Ortho dusted the seat of his pants and said, "Desan."

Margaret squeezed Carolyn's hand. "I told you I bet Desan could help."

"Be very careful around her," Raven warned. "I don't know if her magic is good or bad. I hear many stories about her. None is good."

"Can you tell me how to get to her home?" Margaret asked.

"She lives on the mountain at White Oak Pass. That's not a good place for woman. Silent Wolf's evil is out there. If you go to find her, be careful and watch."

Margaret held Ortho's hand and thanked him for his help.

Chapter Sixteen
Cherokee Woman Desan

On the way home, Margaret and Carolyn met Jack Sams, a scout at Fort Howard. He was standing on the porch in front of the hardware store.

He was a rugged man with rugged features. His hair, eyebrows and beard were bushy. His short, stocky frame was covered with buckskin from head to toe. Jack was married to a Cherokee woman named Rose.

He laughed and asked, "Ain't you two got sense? Don't you know it's rainin'?"

Margaret laughed. "Jack, only a good-looking man like you could come up with such a line."

"It's sure good to see you, Toot. How's that free-willed husband of yours?"

"He's just as mean as ever. He could wrestle a grizzly and win."

Jack nodded his head at Carolyn. "I suppose you're married to some lucky feller by now."

Carolyn grinned and lowered her head. Jack laughed and teased, "My lands, I don't believe I've ever witnessed a brighter shade of red. How about you, Margaret?"

"No, I haven't."

Jack rubbed his beard and said, "I've got a trapper friend about my size and age. Of course, he's not as pretty as me, but I might could fix you up. I think he's looking for a little lady like you to help with his traps."

Carolyn widened her eyes and gasped. "No . . . no, I already have a male friend."

Margaret swiftly cut her eyes to Carolyn, eager to hear who the lucky man might be.

"And who would that be?" Jack asked.

"Captain Scott Taylor. I've . . . I've liked him for some time now. We . . . we."

Margaret licked her lips to keep from laughing. She couldn't tell if it was beads of sweat on Carolyn's face or drops of rain that had intensified. "Jack, it's a match made in heaven." She slapped Carolyn on her shoulder and chuckled, "Right, Carolyn?"

With her countenance growing pale, Carolyn wiped the corner of her mouth and suggested that they get out of the rain.

"Jack," Margaret said, "why don't you join us for a moment. There's something I want to ask you."

Jack tied his horse and joined the women on the porch of the trading post. A couple of wagons piled high with furniture were heading out of the settlement. Jack quickly stepped off the porch and flagged the first wagon down.

"Where in the world are you going, Moses?" Jack asked.

"We're headed for Tennessee. We felt any place would be better than here with Silent Wolf on the rampage. We saw three Indians brought in a couple of days ago. God only knows where they're from. I can't stand by and let my family be butchered like the Curtis family."

His wife, Ellen, hastened to add, "My sister lives at Murfreesboro. She said there was no Indians in any of the surrounding areas."

Margaret frowned and shook her head. "Ellen, do you really think that Silent Wolf is confined to Cherokee? He's a renegade! Because you go over a state line doesn't mean they won't follow. At least here, at the settlement, you have the closeness of the fort and soldiers to help protect you."

"Margaret's right, Ellen., Carolyn added. "You have young children. Please think of them if not yourself."

Moses nodded at the men with him. "We have a couple of work hands going with us. Ellen will feel better being with her sister." Moses shook Jack's hand. Margaret and Carolyn hugged Ellen and the children.

Jack took his hat off and hit it against his leg. "Moses, won't you change your mind? You're going out of safety into an open field. As the good book says, 'like a lamb to slaughter.'"

"We've made up our mind," Moses stated. "Therefore we'd better be going before dark."

Margaret spoke up, "That's just it, Moses, you can't possibly make it to Murfreesboro before dark."

"Maybe not," Ellen said. "We'll go as far as we can and stop for the night."

"If you're ever over that way, stop in and see us," Moses said as he popped the reins. The team started moving. They watched as the wagons rolled out of the settlement.

"Lord have mercy!" Jack groaned through clinched teeth. "They must be crazy!"

Carolyn put her hand over her mouth and fought back tears. "The children. Didn't they consider the children at all? They're begging to be killed, putting themselves in harm's way like that."

Jack wrapped his big arms around Carolyn and held her tight, scaring her half to death. Her body jerked and her eyes all but popped out of her head. Again, Margaret bailed Carolyn out. "Jack," she said, causing him to release Carolyn from his grip. Carolyn put her hand on her chest and took a deep breath.

"Do you feel better now?" he asked.

"Oh, yes, oh, yes. Thank you," Carolyn replied breathlessly.

"I know when Rose is upset, she likes for me to hold her."

He looked at Margaret. "What was it that you were going to say?"

"Did you go out with the soldiers this morning?"

"Yes. You could smell Silent Wolf and his stinking savages. They're covering their tracks. We didn't see as much as a broken twig. Why do you ask?"

Margaret rubbed her face and replied, "I feel sick about Moses and Ellen leaving."

"We tried to stop them," Jack said, "but they wouldn't listen. Now the rest is up to the big man upstairs. Try to get your mind off it and tell me what you wanted to ask me."

"Carolyn and I stopped by Ortho and Raven's a few minutes ago. He told me that an old Cherokee woman named Desan lives on the mountain at White Oak Pass. Do you have a clue where on the mountain she lives?"

Jack put his thumb inside his belt and frowned. "Why do you want to know that?"

Margaret put her hand on his forearm and said. "Jack, you're the best trapper in Cherokee, outside of George, of course. You're smarter than any Indian alive, you speak several languages, and I could go on and on."

Jack put his hand up. "Please don't. Let's cut to it. What is it you want?"

Margaret bit her lower lip. "I need someone to take me to see Desan, and you're the man."

Jack turned and looked toward the end of town. Margaret glanced at Carolyn, anticipating his answer. He turned and stared soberly at Margaret. "Okay. When do you want to go?"

Stunned, Margaret's jaw dropped as she stared at Carolyn. "Did you say you would do it?"

"Yeah. I'm not afraid of her magic. Heck, Rose is rougher than any woman alive. Old Desan might try some magic on us, but she's nearly blind. Now I have a question."

"Sure, what is it?"

"Why ain't George taking you? I've worked with him, and he's as good a scout as I've ever seen." He tilted his head to one side and questioned, "He does know about this visit, doesn't he?"

Margaret slowly shook her head. "This isn't for George; it's for me."

Jack scratched his head and looked to the sky. "You know, Margaret, sometimes when I look to the sky I think I see the angels. Like right now, I see two looking down on us."

The women cut their eyes to each other, wondering what looking to the sky had to do with taking them to see Desan.

"Do you two believe in angels?" he asked.

They nodded.

He looked across the road to the general store. "Would you look there?"

"Look where?" Margaret asked.

"Over at the hitching post. There's an angel looking right at you."

Margaret and Carolyn found themselves squinting to see if they too could see something.

"I don't see anything," Margaret said.

Jack scratched his head and remarked, "It's a good thing we don't have to see them for them to be there. Don't you think?"

"I may not see them, but I surely believe the angels are here watching over us. Don't you, Margaret?" Carolyn asked.

Margaret looked at Jack and said, "Grandma Phoebe saw angels. She used to tell me that God allowed her to see the angels ever since she was a little girl. I may not see angels in front of me right now, but I see God all around me every morning I wake up. Like the special times when He allows me to smell the honeysuckles when they are not even in season."

"You smell honeysuckles out of season?" Jack asked.

"Yes, I do."

"I believe angels guided me to Cherokee," Carolyn said, "and I believe God will send His angels to watch after Moses, Ellen and the children."

"Amen," Margaret said.

Instantly, Jack turned his attention to Margaret. "When did you say you wanted to go see Desan?"

"I didn't say yet."

Jack stepped off the porch, untied his horse and mounted. He was talking to them, but his focus had shifted across the road to where he saw the angels. "Let me know when you decide to go. You know where to find me."

"Jack," Margaret called out.

He muttered, "Don't worry I won't tell George." He waved his hand over his head and said, "Good to see you, Carolyn."

She waved and whispered, "Yeah, you too."

"He got a little strange there, didn't he, Carolyn?" Margaret asked.

"Yes, and beyond. When he bear-hugged me, I thought he was going to squeeze the life out of me."

Margaret pushed a strand of hair behind her ear and remarked, "By the way, why did you resort to lying when talking about fixing you up with somebody?"

Exhausted, she replied, "It just came out of my mouth. I couldn't picture him fixing me up with one of his trapping buddies." She shivered and confessed she felt sick when he tried to squeeze the life out of her. "He smelled of wild onions or dead animals. I can't think about it right now."

"He does put some kind of oil on when he goes out scouting—to kill his human scent. When George uses it, I feel sick until he takes a long hot bath."

Carolyn's expression grew somber. "Margaret, I pray God will be with Moses and his family, but I have a sick feeling in my heart. They shouldn't have left."

"I have the same sick feeling. Let's go home and spend some time in prayer for them."

Chapter Seventeen

Strange Men Talking

Margaret looked out the window at the brightly colored leaves slowly falling to a rain-soaked ground. She jumped when she heard someone talking. She slowly turned and looked around the room. Carolyn had lain down on the bed in the loft; however, the voice she heard was not that of a woman. Quickly she glanced around the room, looked out the window, tilted her head and listened carefully for the voice she knew she had heard. Carolyn came from the loft.

"Margaret," Carolyn said after clearing her throat to get her friend's attention. She started to speak, but Margaret held her hand up to stop her.

"Carolyn, were you praying or something?"

Carolyn frowned. "No, we already prayed."

"I heard someone talking. It sounded like a man's voice to me."

Carolyn remarked, "What was the man saying?"

"I'm not sure," Margaret said. "It sounded like . . . like a war chant off in a distance. When the white people came and began their operation of removing the Cherokee from their land, from my Cherokee people's land, there was a howl in the voice of my people that was unmistakable—"

Carolyn interrupted. "Margaret, I don't know if you're aware of how you're talking. You're saying, 'my people and my land.' You're relating the Cherokee to yourself in a fashion that I've never heard you use before."

Puzzled by her statement, Margaret voiced, "They are my people. I'm half Cherokee! And this is my land, the only home I know. I love these mountains. I can't imagine being put in stocks or chains and being driven away to a strange place—the bad part being, most of my people had no choice."

Carolyn frowned. "Wait a minute. What's this all about? One minute, I'm talking to Margaret Phoebe Black and the next minute to a person I don't know. I'm trying to figure out what's going on."

"What you just said is true. I feel like two people. I feel as though I'm being forced from my home. Carolyn, there's something strange happening in my spirit."

Carolyn's eyes widened. "You don't have to convince me something strange is going on. I'm seeing it firsthand."

Before Margaret could respond, someone knocked at the door and called out, "Margaret. Margaret."

Margaret hurried to open the door. "Deloris. What is it? Is it George or Cody?"

Visibly shaken, Deloris put her hand over her mouth and slumped to the floor. "Carolyn, get her some water."

Margaret helped Deloris inside to a chair. Carolyn held the water, as Deloris took a sip. She took a deep slow breath and begin to sob. Margaret exploded.

She took Deloris by her shoulders and demanded, "Deloris! What is it? Is there something wrong with George or Cody?"

Trying to compose herself, Deloris groaned, "Moses, Ellen and the kids are dead."

Carolyn and Margaret gathered around Deloris. They held each other and wept until they could weep no more. Deloris stood and rubbed the back of her neck. "I just talked to them two hours ago. I told them not to go. I told them."

"So did we! What happened?" Margaret asked.

"Silent Wolf. They had only gone a few miles out of town. When they reached the tree line at Stone Creek, the renegades were waiting for them. They took the horses and burned everything else. Major Wright, George, Cody and the other soldiers are at Stone Creek now."

"George is there now?"

"Yes."

"How do you know?" Margaret asked.

"One of the soldiers who went to the Curtis home this morning rode to the fort to get back-up troops. Captain Taylor said for me to be sure and let you know that George and Cody were all right."

Margaret closed her eyes and lowered her head. "I'm going to Stone Creek."

Carolyn was crying. Hearing those words from her best friend made her furious. She grabbed Margaret's arm and shouted. "By God, you're not going anywhere! How could you think such a thing? Sometimes, I think you've lost your mind. You don't think about things;

you just go headlong into whatever. You're my best friend. I don't want to lose you too."

Margaret again lowered her head and embraced her. "I'm sorry. I just feel sick."

The three women consoled each other. Deloris went home, but Carolyn insisted on staying with Margaret until George and Cody arrived.

Chapter Eighteen
Union Soldiers

The dense clouds and drizzling rain had ensured that night would arrive early. Margaret and Carolyn hurried to get the chores done. As time passed, Margaret was frantic. She looked out the window every few minutes. Around 10:00 p.m., Carolyn put on one of Margaret's gowns and lay down. Margaret also prepared for bed, but sleep escaped her. She lay in the darkness, praying, crying and listening for George and Cody. Her mind was overwhelmed. A vivid picture of the three Indians she saw earlier whispering to each other and staring at her wouldn't go away. Also her mind was spinning with thoughts of the families that had been killed, secrets that had been kept from her, Cody and Julie, the man at the gravesite, how unbelievable it all was. She tossed and turned. Continually, the blessing that Phoebe had spoken over her about the Phoenix pounded like a drum as a constant reminder, but of what? Why now? And why all at once?

Margaret fell asleep, but was awakened when she thought she heard a horse snorting. She quickly put on her robe and anxiously looked out the window, but she saw nothing.

She lit a lamp and called Carolyn. Not waiting for her to respond, Margaret hurried to the porch, hoping that the horses she heard were George's and Cody's. She went to one side of the porch and then to the other, but still saw nothing. When she held the lamp high, her eyes widened and her mouth opened. In the dim light, she was now able to see three men on horses in dark blue uniforms. "Oh God," she whispered. Slowly she backed toward the door. The men began to dismount. Margaret raced inside shouting at Carolyn to bring the rifle, as she pushed the wood bar down, securing the door.

Frantic, not knowing what was going on, Carolyn raced into the room with a rifle. "What is it?"

Margaret grabbed the pistol that was beside the rocking chair. "It's Union soldiers."

"Oh God above." Carolyn gasped. "How many are there? Could you tell?"

"I could only see three, but it's so dark."

"What are we going to do?"

Margaret rubbed her lower lip. "We'll do what we have to, Carolyn. Prepare yourself for the worst. Can you do that?"

Carolyn's mouth was moving, but words were not coming out.

Margaret grabbed hold of her arm. "Carolyn, we don't know the intentions of these men. If we see they mean us harm, we'll have to kill them or they'll kill us. I, for one, don't intend to die without a fight."

They froze when they heard boots pounding against the plank porch. Suddenly, the pounding stopped at the door. Someone called out. "Why did you run inside? We mean you no harm. I'm Captain Albert Ross. My men and I only need some food, water and to rest for a while then we'll be going."

Margaret and Carolyn stared at each other. "What are we going to do?" Carolyn asked.

"I don't know, but we can't let them in the house."

The same voice called out, "Come on, Miss. Don't make us break the door down!"

"I'm not going to let you in. We have guns and will use them. The first one that tries to come in will meet his maker."

The man pounded his fist on the door. "Come on, lady. Give us what we want, and we'll be out of here. Now open the door! Or I'll kick it down!"

Margaret looked at Carolyn. Rapid beating on the door caused Margaret and Carolyn to raise their guns and prepare to shoot. The beating stopped. The women quickly surveyed the room.

"Oh God, Carolyn, I forgot to close the shutters over the window by the fireplace."

Before either could get to the window, it shattered into a thousand pieces. One of the soldiers jumped through. Margaret fired, hitting the man in the stomach. Blood went everywhere. Before he hit the floor, another soldier jumped through the window frame. Carolyn turned and shot, hitting the man in the neck. Margaret rushed to reload her gun. A harsh voice from the window demanded, "Put the guns down, or I'll kill you both.

Put them down!" The officer and another soldier came through the window. Captain Ross ordered his men to attend the soldiers who had been shot. Margaret and Carolyn slowly put their weapons down.

The soldier checked the men and called out, "Sir, Frank and Adam are dead."

Captain Ross tightened his face muscles and clinched his fists. He fixed his eyes on Margaret and moved close to her, glaring. Margaret stared back at a man three times her size. She was scared to death, yet she refused to let it show. He raised his hand and slapped her face, knocking her to the floor. Carolyn plunged toward the captain, only to be pushed to the floor. Carolyn helped Margaret sit up. Her mouth was bleeding and her head spinning. Carolyn tore a piece from her nightshirt and held it to Margaret's mouth.

They stared at Captain Ross, who was furious. "What the hell do you think you're doing? I told you all we wanted was some food and water. Now two of my men are dead."

"What was I supposed to do?" Margaret shouted. "Just take your word that all you wanted was food and water? Then, when they come crashing through my window, I didn't feel like putting out the welcome sign. Tell me, captain, what would you have done in the same position?"

Captain Ross looked at his dead soldiers. He slowly faced the women and pointed at Carolyn. "You, help Corporal Smith get these men into the bedroom and cover them up."

He frowned at Margaret and growled, "Clean this mess up."

Her head throbbing, Margaret pushed herself up and started to the kitchen area. Captain Ross grabbed her arm. "I'm watching every move you make. If you so much as cut your eyes in the wrong direction, I'll personally cut your throat." He shoved her, causing her to stagger.

Margaret took a rag from the table. "There's a bucket outside that's full of rain water. May I get it to clean with?" she asked.

He motioned for her to go and followed her outside. She got the bucket and mop and hurried back in. As she cleaned blood from the floor and walls, she prayed that George and Cody would come.

Carolyn and the soldier came into the room. "Hey you," Captain Ross shouted, "get something and put it over that window. I'm freezing."

Carolyn looked around the room for something large enough to cover the window. She started into the bedroom to get a quilt. The captain motioned for the other soldier to go with her. Margaret was finishing up mopping the floor.

"Hurry it up," the captain demanded. "I'm starving."

Carolyn and the soldier nailed the quilt over the window. Margaret picked the bucket up and looked at the captain for permission to take it outside. He opened the door and watched as she tossed the dirty water from the bucket and sat it off the porch to fill again with the rain that continued to fall.

"Now that you've cleaned up your mess, get me and Corporal Smith something to eat and a cup of coffee with it."

"There's some soup left from supper. Will that be all right?" Margaret asked.

Captain Ross nodded. "That's fine. Just hurry."

Carolyn looked at the captain and said, "I'll make the coffee while Margaret warms the soup."

He nodded for her to go ahead. Corporal Smith sat at the table to make sure they didn't try anything. Captain Ross sat in the rocking chair beside the fireplace, with his elbows propped on his knees. He cupped his hands and held his chin. Margaret cut her eyes toward Carolyn and then swiftly to Captain Ross. Carolyn knew from the look that Margaret had something in mind.

Margaret fixed two bowls of soup and placed them on the table. Carolyn put cornbread on saucers and placed them beside the bowls. Margaret asked Carolyn to pour the men a cup of coffee. She looked at Captain Ross and asked, "Captain, would you like a glass of milk with your soup?"

He sighed and rubbed his face, stood, placed his hands on his hips, rolled his shoulders and replied, "That would be good, thank you."

The women sat at the table while the men ate. Margaret was beginning to think that maybe she had been wrong about Captain Ross. Corporal Smith grabbed a bite of cornbread.

The captain stared at him and frowned. "Corporal, we don't eat until we say grace. You know that."

Corporal Smith slowly put the bread down and lowered his head. In a low tone, Captain Ross said, "Corporal, under the circumstances, you don't have to close your eyes."

The corporal acknowledged by nodding his head. Margaret and Carolyn glanced at each other.

With empty eyes and a broken voice, Captain Ross prayed, "God above. I want with everything in me to be thankful for this food and I am, yet at the cost of two lives . . ."

He paused and held his breath for a moment. "That's such a high price for a bowl of soup. Be with us, Lord, and take us home safely to our families. God bless this home and these women. Bring their husbands home soon, I pray. Amen."

Margaret stared at the captain. She began to tremble, realizing in her spirit that she had more than likely been wrong. How hungry they were became apparent as the two women watched the men eat. The first bowl of hot soup was consumed in seconds.

"There's plenty of soup. Would you like another bowl?" Margaret asked. Corporal Smith was quick to say yes. Captain Ross, on the other hand, stopped the corporal and asked Margaret, "When will your husband be home?"

Margaret swallowed hard and said, "I don't know. A family from the settlement was murdered today at Stone Creek. My husband does some scouting for the army, so he and my brother went with Major Wright to Stone Creek to check the area. They should have been home hours ago."

"Is there enough soup left for them?"

"Yes. I made a large pot."

"In that case, we would like another bowl."

"I'll get it," Carolyn said.

Margaret sighed. "I'm sorry about your soldiers. When they came through the window, I was scared and hell-bent on protecting me and my home."

"You're no more to blame than I. When you've been fighting away from home and family and you've watched the men under your command die one after the other until you're down to four, you don't always think clearly. They chose to break through the window. Maybe they wanted to die. Sometimes, you get tired of fighting. When you come to that place, death doesn't seem so bad. At any rate, I wish they were here eating soup with us."

Margaret shook her head. "You can rest assured that I would have never let you enter my home. Never."

Captain Ross tightened his brows and asked, "Do you mind if I ask your name?"

"I'm Margaret Black and this is my friend, Carolyn Morris. Please forgive me, but I forgot your name."

"I'll give you a hint. The chief of the Cherokee people has the same name."

Margaret frowned, then grinned. She knew the Cherokee history well. "You're John Ross?"

"Yes. This is Ned Smith."

"Where is your home?" Carolyn asked.

Captain Ross replied, "I'm from Albany, New York."

Carolyn looked at Corporal Smith. "And you, corporal?"

"I'm from Pittsburgh, Pennsylvania."

"Captain Ross," Margaret said, "can you tell me if there are many soldiers in this area?"

He pushed his empty bowl back and replied, "At the moment, you and I aren't shooting each other, but please don't take me for a fool, Mrs. Black. I'm not going to tell you about our soldiers, nor their location. I'm standing in Confederate territory, in a Confederate scout's home, talking to his wife, who is responsible for the deaths of two Union soldiers, and you ask a question like that."

Margaret shook her head. "No, no. You've misunderstood me. I'm not asking about Union soldiers as a spy tactic. I have a mission that I need to accomplish. That's my motive. Nothing more. Please believe me."

Carolyn looked on wide-eyed, wondering if this was the plan she had recognized in Margaret's eyes earlier.

Captain Ross stood and questioned, "And what would that mission be?"

Margaret began to play with her fingers as she addressed Captain Ross. "Sir, have you ever experienced something that's so much greater than you, to the point you feel driven to pursue the unknown? You make understanding the mystery a personal task. You gather bits and pieces of information until you find what you need to solve that unknown. Sir, I have been commissioned in my soul to find a lot of missing pieces and make the vision clear."

Carolyn stared intently as Margaret went on about her quest.

Margaret told about Phoebe's blessing and the man who appeared to them at Pine Mountain Cemetery. Of course she also told what was said about the Phoenix. Needless to say, the men stared at her, not having a clue as to what the point of the story meant to them.

Captain Ross put his hand up and said, "Mrs. Black, what could all of that possibly have to do with Corporal Smith and myself?"

"There's an old Indian woman named Desan who lives on a mountain near White Oak Pass. I need to go see her. I surely don't want to go if there is a planned battle or a lot of soldiers from both sides in that area. Believe me, that's the only reason that I asked about the soldiers."

Captain Ross tilted his head to the side and frowned, "Humm, for some unknown reason, I believe you Mrs. Black."

Captain Ross put his hat on and revealed, "There's not any soldiers, from either side, near White Oak Pass at the present, but things can change overnight. I pray you find the missing pieces to your puzzle. I do admire a person with enough grit to accept such a challenge. Corporal Smith and I will be going. We'll leave as soon as we attend our dead."

They took the men out and tied them on their horses. Captain Ross and Corporal Smith mounted. The captain looked at the women and tipped his hat. "I want to thank you for the soup. It was delicious. I'm sorry about the window. I must confess, the last part of our visit was quite pleasant." He tipped his hat again, and expressed, "Ladies. Mrs. Black, I pray your husband returns quickly and safely."

"Captain Ross," Margaret called out.

He turned his horse and asked, "Yes?"

"Take care. I pray the war ends soon and you and Corporal Smith can return home as well."

The men nodded and rode into the darkness.

Chapter Nineteen
Smell of Death

*I*nside, Carolyn and Margaret breathed a prayer of thanks for their safety. Carolyn began to tremble as tears flowed from her eyes. "Margaret, have you ever killed anyone before?"

Margaret closed her eyes and tilted her head back to rest on her shoulders, rubbed her neck and moaned. "Every muscle in my body aches."

Carolyn listened, hoping for an answer.

"To answer your question, yes I have, but only in self-defense."

The air in the house was deathly still, hanging like a heavy blanket all about them. Margaret looked around the rooms and stated, "Carolyn, I want you to help me scrub this house from top to bottom. One is to get the smell of death out of here. Second, I don't want any signs that anyone has been here when George and Coty return."

Carolyn frowned. "Are you saying you're not going to tell George about this?"

"Of course, I'll tell him. Or at least I think I will. I . . . I . . . I want to give Captain Ross and Corporal Smith time to get out of the region." Margaret paused, "Do you agree with that?"

"Yes," Carolyn said, "but, how will you come up with an explanation for the window?"

Margaret scratched her head, "I'll think of something while we're cleaning. I pray George and Cody are all right. Dawn's breaking. They should have been home hours ago. When we finish the house, we'll ride to the fort and see if anyone knows anything about the soldiers who went to Stone Creek yesterday. I'll stop by the trading post to see if Mr. Harper has any glass to fix the window."

By the time the women finished cleaning the house, dawn had turned into mid-morning. The rain had ceased, and a cool wind was pushing through the forest around Margaret's house. Margaret wrote George and Cody a note and left it on the table.

Outside, Margaret and Carolyn inhaled a deep breath of cool air, saddled their horses and headed to the fort. Margaret went to Major Wright's office right away. Deloris assured Margaret that she had heard nothing and was concerned about her brother as well.

As soon as Margaret and Carolyn left Deloris, Margaret instantly glanced toward the jail and then at Carolyn. "Go ahead," Carolyn uttered. "After what we went through last night, three Indians behind bars don't shake me."

Margaret hurried to the jail. She knocked on the door, but Randy didn't answer.

Carolyn was perplexed. "I wonder where he is."

Margaret shifted her eyes and said, "I couldn't tell you." She viewed the area and started to turn the doorknob. Carolyn pulled her hand away. "What are you doing? Don't you dare go in there without Randy here."

"I'm only going to take a quick look, and then we'll leave."

Carolyn sighed. "Go ahead. I don't care anymore. Go get your eyes full."

Margaret quickly opened the door and went inside. "Carolyn, come here," Margaret called.

Carolyn hurried inside. Margaret pointed at the jail cell.

"Where are they?" Carolyn asked.

"I don't know. Randy didn't say anything about moving them." She stomped her foot against the floor. "Shoot. I wanted to see them, at least one more time. Let's get out of here before Randy comes back."

Mr. Harper was opening the Trading Post when Margaret and Carolyn arrived.

"Good morning, ladies," he said as he put a box of nails behind the counter. "Margaret, have you heard anything from George?"

"Not a word. I'm worried sick about him. Do you know what's going on?"

He took a deep breath and offered, "I haven't heard anything, but there was a squad of about twenty-five soldiers went out early this morning."

"Who was leading them?" Carolyn asked.

"Captain Taylor. He came back to the fort for a while, rounded the men up and headed out. That's basically all I know."

"Will you let me know if you hear or see anything at all?" Margaret asked.

"I sure will. If I can't come personally, I'll send someone to let you know."

"Thank you!" Margaret viewed the store and asked, "Mr. Harper, do you have any glass left out of that shipment from Alabama?"

"Yeah. I think there's still a couple of pieces left. Do you need some?"

Margaret nodded. "Yes. One of our windows got broken, and it's pretty cool with just a quilt tacked over it."

Mr. Harper rubbed his chin. "Would you like for me to have Bert Williams bring a piece out and fix it for you?"

"That would be wonderful. Thank you so much."

The sound of several horses coming into the fort caused Margaret to race out the door, eager to see if George was with the riders.

"Captain Taylor," she shouted. "Where are George and Cody?"

He turned his horse aside, dismounted, pulled his hat off and ran his fingers through his hair. Frantic, Margaret asked, "Are they all right?"

Captain Taylor put his hand on Margaret's shoulder. "George is fine and Cody *will* be fine."

Margaret grabbed his shirtsleeve. "What do you mean, Cody *will* be fine? Is he hurt?"

"He took an arrow in his leg. Thank God, the arrow didn't hit a bone."

"Was It Silent Wolf?" Carolyn asked.

"I'm afraid so. There were more of them than we had estimated."

"Are you okay?" Carolyn asked.

"I'm so tired, I can hardly stand up. If you ladies will excuse me, I'm going to take a bath, have a cup of coffee and go to bed."

Margaret patted his arm. "You do that. Come on, Carolyn, I want to get home and see if George and Cody are there yet."

The women rode hard to Margaret's house, anxious to see the men. Margaret ran inside. George was checking the window. "George!" Margaret said breathlessly. They hurried to each other's arms.

Margaret gasped, "Shoot! I've been worried sick about you. Are you okay?"

He ran his hand down her cheek and held her tight. "Toot, I love you. I love you."

"I love you. Honey, Captain Taylor said Cody was wounded. Where is he?"

"He's in the bed. I'm sure he wants to see you."

Margaret hurried to the bedroom. Carolyn hugged George and expressed how worried they had been about their well-being.

Margaret rushed to the bedside where Cody was lying, knelt down and anxiously questioned, "Honey, are you okay? Are you in a lot of pain?"

Cody took her hand and assured her he wouldn't die from a flesh wound. George and Carolyn joined them. Carolyn put her hand on Cody's arm and asked if there was anything she could do. Much to her surprise, Cody boldly expressed, "I would certainly like to feel a woman's arm around me, other than my sister's."

Carolyn looked at Margaret, her face a bright shade of red.

"I didn't mean to embarrass you, Miss Morris," Cody said.

Margaret teased, "What do you mean you want someone's arms around you, other than your sister's?"

Cody voiced, "Every man, coming home from battle, needs a woman other than family to at least give him a hug."

Cody pushed up for Carolyn to accommodate his desire. She swallowed hard, slowly leaned forward and put her arms around him. George put his arm around Margaret and smiled, knowing Carolyn must be about to hyperventilate from the strange request. Carolyn rose up and shyly looked at Margaret.

George chuckled and suggested, "Carolyn, don't mind Cody. The doctor gave him some strong painkiller. Look at him."

Carolyn turned to see that Cody was already asleep—that fast.

George laughed aloud and said, "Cody will probably faint when he realizes he asked you to hug him."

Margaret pulled the covers up on his arms, and they left the room. In the living room, she put her open hand on George's chest and said, "Before you give me details about your trip, are you hungry?"

George closed his eyes, leaned his head back and moaned, "I'm too tired to eat. I just want to get some sleep." He kissed her forehead and whispered, "I love you, Toot."

Carolyn put wood on the fire while Margaret spread a quilt over George. She leaned down, kissed him and softly said, "Sleep tight, baby."

Margaret turned to go to the kitchen. George called out, "When I wake up, you can tell me what happened to the window."

Margaret tightened her lips and groaned, "Oh, no. Do you really want to know? I don't want to embarrass Carolyn. She didn't mean to do it."

"What did you say, Toot?" George asked.

"Mr. Harper is sending Bert Williams over to put new glass in the window. Do you want him to wait and let you sleep?"

"No. We need the window fixed, and besides it won't bother me. Enough said on the matter."

George had barely gone to sleep when Bert came up the dirt road and stopped in front of the house. "Whoa," Bert said as he pulled back on the reins, stopping the wagon.

"Good morning, Bert," Margaret called out.

He nodded. "Good morning, Mrs. Black, Miss Morris. Mr. Harper said you were in need of getting your window fixed."

Margaret chuckled. "Yeah, I told Carolyn to be careful, but she wouldn't listen."

Carolyn tilted her head and widened her eyes. "Is that right?" she said.

"No, Bert." Margaret laughed. "I was only kidding about Carolyn breaking the window."

Carolyn crossed her arms and teased, "I'm certainly glad that your conscience got the better of you."

"Bert," Margaret said, "if George were to wake up before you leave, would you tell him that Carolyn and I rode to the fort?"

Carolyn shook her head and stated, "Sorry, dear friend. I need to go home and groom myself. Ride over later, if you're not too busy getting into mischief."

"Mischief?" Margaret gasped. "That sounded as though you were talking to a child."

"Yeah, I guess it did." Carolyn said.

Chapter Twenty
Confederate General

*A*s Margaret rode toward the fort, she suddenly felt the ground shiver beneath her and heard a deafening sound as if a tornado was raging through the valley. She turned to see at least one hundred soldiers riding hard toward Fort Howard. In the center of the mass of soldiers was a black carriage drawn by four white horses. Margaret squinted, hoping to catch a glimpse of who was riding in the coach. She had never seen such a carriage. Black shades were drawn, preventing anyone from looking inside. Her curiosity got the better of her. She followed the soldiers into the fort.

Major Wright and Captain Taylor were standing outside, waiting for the fancy carriage to stop. A guard quickly opened the coach's door; a tall, lean man in a Confederate general's uniform emerged. He put his hat on, covering his dark hair. His long sideburns stopped on either side of his chin. The troops stood at full attention. The general returned the salute and extended his hand toward the carriage door. A heap of white lace petticoats covered with dark burgundy appeared. Margaret moved closer to catch a glimpse of the lady, who was obviously a woman of means. As the petite frame came into view, Margaret sighed. The woman's dark, burgundy, silk dress, had a high mandarin collar and long sleeves fastened with small ivory buttons. Ivory gloves fit tight on her small hands, an ivory lace collar outlined the rounded neckline and rested on top of her exposed full breasts, and a short fur cape dipped around the back of her tiny waist. Cultured pearls hugged her slender neck and small pearl earrings dangled from her ears. A dark burgundy hat with a small brim and mesh vale came over her eyes and relaxed across the middle of her straight nose showing the merest hint of irregularity, that only added to its perfection, if that were possible.

Her dark auburn hair hung in ringlets framing her radiant face. Her skin was porcelain white, and cheeks were a soft shade of pink. She smiled as she shook Captain Taylor's hand, revealing her perfect white teeth. She licked her full, yet delicate red lips. The woman's eyes shifted from left to right and then quickly back to the left where Margaret was standing. Briefly she fixed her stare on Margaret, then swiftly looked away.

When the party had cleared the gate, Major Wright ordered the gate closed. The Major and Captain Taylor led the general, and the woman accompanying him, into the major's office.

As soon as they were inside, Margaret caught a glimpse of Randy going toward the jail. "Randy. Randy," she called out.

Randy stopped and watched as Margaret ran toward him.

"Randy," she said breathlessly.

Randy chuckled. "What do you want from me today?"

She punched his shoulder and said, "Must you always be so suspicious?"

"Margaret, it has nothing to do with suspicion. It has all to do with your track record. You're very consistent. So just tell me what you want."

Margaret shrugged. "Well, there are a couple of things. First of all, what happened to the prisoners?"

Randy squinted his eyes and tightened his lips. "And just how do you know about the prisoners being gone?"

Margaret bit her lower lip and frowned. "I knocked, you didn't answer, so I looked inside the jail really fast and couldn't help but notice that—"

Randy held his hands up. "Please spare me. I received orders to have the prisoners moved to Fort Meade."

"That's in Chattanooga!"

"Yes. Now, what's your second question?"

"Who is in the carriage the general is escorting?"

"He's General Andrew Thomas, second in command under General Robert E. Lee. The fact that he's here ain't good."

"Who's the woman? And what's not good?"

"The woman is Suzie Chambers, one of the richest women in the South. Her daddy owns three active plantations on five thousand acres, two in Charleston and one in Georgia. There's no telling how many slaves he owns."

"What's she doing here in Cherokee?"

"She was on her way to Washington, D.C., to meet with none other than President Lincoln."

"Really?"

"Yeah. They met up with about three hundred unexpected visitors in blue uniforms at Red Ridge."

"Why would they be at Red Ridge? That's not the way to Washington, D.C., from Charleston or Georgia."

"Miss Chambers had left Charleston when the war started. She wanted to stay with her aunt on a plantation called Three Willows. She suddenly felt the need to visit a friend in Newport. Crazy woman. She wouldn't listen to General Thomas or the guards who were assigned to her. They warned her, but like most women, she wouldn't listen."

"Humm! There is one more thing, Randy, if you don't mind."

"What a surprise. Go ahead and ask."

"Why was the gate closed when they came inside? That's unusual, unless the special trumpet sounds."

Randy rubbed his chin and answered. "Margaret, honey, it's because they're rich and therefore considered precious cargo. It's all a big show."

Margaret smiled and patted Randy's arm. "Thanks. I can always count on you. I'm going to have you over to supper very soon."

"Speaking of supper, how are George and Cody? Captain Taylor told me that Cody took an arrow in his leg."

"They're both asleep. I'll make mention that you asked about them."

Margaret turned to walk away. "Margaret, the things I just told you are between us."

Margaret put her hands on her hips and whined. "Come on, Randy. The only one I'll tell is Carolyn. George will know anyway."

"Just understand the trouble I could get into if it gets back to Major Wright. I could be court marshaled or shot."

"Randy, I would never let anything happen to you. You're my buddy." Margaret patted Randy's arm and hurried to tell Carolyn what had taken place.

Carolyn taught a class at the fort at noon. Margaret asked her to have supper with them that night when she got off work.

When Carolyn arrived, supper was almost ready. Cody and George were still sleeping.

Margaret noticed Carolyn was acting differently from her usual carefree self. She also noticed her curled hair, tied back with a light blue ribbon.

Carolyn set the table, while Margaret took the potatoes from the fireplace. "Have you checked on Cody lately?" Carolyn asked.

"Yeah, when I first got home. He was sleeping soundly, so I didn't wake him. I did check to make sure that he wasn't running a fever. He wasn't."

George groaned, stretched and slowly sat up. "This is a wonderful way to wake up. I don't know what you're cooking, but it smells like heaven."

Cody called from the bedroom, "I agree with George. It smells like fried venison smothered with onions, which is perfect."

"Carolyn," Margaret said, "would you mind putting some hot water in the wash pan for Cody? I'll get him a towel and wash cloth."

George stood and grabbed Margaret's arm as she went by. He hugged her and then gently kissed her lips. "Toot, you drive me crazy, even after all our years together."

Margaret rubbed her finger down his cheek. "Likewise, my brave hunter, and even more so when you're clean shaven."

George rubbed his fingers over his chin. "Yeah, I need a shave and bathe."

"You're so right, my dear."

Carolyn cleared her throat. "Come on, you two, break it up. Supper is getting cold."

"And I'm starving," Cody called out from the bedroom.

Margaret fixed Cody's plate and asked Carolyn if she would mind taking it to him. Carolyn very eagerly agreed.

Cody took the plate from Carolyn and laughed. "Thank you for saving my life, fair maiden."

Margaret and George looked at each other and smiled. "That pain medicine has altered Cody's personality," George said.

Carolyn turned to leave the bedroom.

"Carolyn," Cody said.

She quickly turned. "Yes."

"Would you join a wounded soldier for dinner?"

She shyly smiled.

"Of course I will understand if you say no. This is not fancy, but it's the best that I can offer."

"I would love to. I'll be right back." She went into the kitchen where Margaret and George were waiting for her. Carolyn picked her plate up and asked, "Do you mind if I eat with Cody? He asked and I feel guilty to have him eat by himself."

Margaret grinned. "No, we don't mind. You go ahead."

They watched as Carolyn turned the corner into the bedroom. "Am I detecting a little something going on here?" George whispered.

Margaret squinted. "My thoughts exactly," she said. "Did you notice her hair curled and the ribbon? Humm! By the way, a General Andrew Thomas is at Fort Howard as we speak."

George frowned. "Are you talking about the second in command under General Lee?"

"Yes. He's the one."

George rubbed his finger across his lower lip and questioned, "Why would he be here at Fort Howard?"

Margaret told George about Suzie Chambers.

"I don't care about Suzie, but the general is a different story. The fact that he's here isn't a good sign, Toot. Lord," he groaned, "there must be something big coming."

Margaret frowned. "Could it be that he's here only to escort Miss Chambers?"

George slowly shook his head. "I wouldn't bet my life on it. The Union must be mounting an attack on or close to Fort Howard."

"But, honey, the fact that Miss Chambers is a very beautiful and rich woman, doesn't that mean anything?"

"Toot, a general like Andrew Thomas doesn't escort anybody anywhere unless it's troops into battle. After supper I'll ride to the fort and see what I can find out."

"Until then, George, tell me about Stone Creek," Margaret coaxed.

"Toot . . . I can't talk about it right now."

"Why not?"

George wiped his mouth, threw his napkin down and left the table. Margaret followed him to the fireplace. She tightened her lips and asked, "What's going on, George? I ask you a simple question and you huff away from the table like a child."

George seized her shoulders. "Didn't you hear what I said? General Thomas is here because of an attack that's sure to follow. That means every man that can walk will have to fight. God knows I don't want to have to leave you. After what we saw at Stone Creek, it's not easy to sit at the table and act as though nothing's happened." George's face muscles tightened as he faced Margaret. "And another thing, the scouts will be the first to leave home."

Margaret lowered her head. George took her in his arms and held her close without speaking. After a few minutes, Margaret raised her large dark eyes and stared into his. "Honey, it's getting dark. Why don't you wait until morning to go to the fort?"

"Maybe I will," he whispered as he pushed a strand of hair away from her face.

"I don't want Carolyn going home tonight," Margaret said. "She can sleep on the cot and we'll sleep in the loft."

George nodded and looked toward the bedroom door where Carolyn was standing. "Maybe you'd better ask Carolyn about that."

"Will you stay the night?" Margaret asked.

Carolyn smiled and answered, "Yes, I would love to." Carolyn warmed her hands by the fireplace. She turned and faced George and asked, "Do you really feel that there's going to be a battle here at Fort Howard?"

He tightened his lips and said, "If not here, then in East Tennessee."

Chapter Twenty-One
Cody Misspeaks

The sun shone intermittently the next morning, and the hard wind drove back the dark clouds that had hovered over Cherokee for two days. Indications of an early winter were clear. Margaret tried to move as she opened her eyes but was restrained by George's arm wrapped around her waist. She moved his arm and breathed in the awesome smell of fresh brewed coffee. Margaret sat on the edge of the bed and put her socks on. The chill in the room brought a shiver over her. She gently stroked George's disarrayed hair and went to check the fire.

Carolyn had left a note on the table:

I have an early class at the fort,
but I will be over later.

Margaret jumped when the door opened. "Cody," she said as she rushed to help him. "What are you doing out of bed? Why didn't you call me to help you get up?"

Cody insisted on sitting in the living room for a while. "How do you feel?"

Cody rubbed his head. "I have a splitting headache. I know the medicine helped me endure the pain, but it has destroyed my head."

"Can I get you anything?" Margaret put a pillow behind his back.

Cody groaned as he pushed himself up against the pillow. "A cup of coffee would be so good."

"How about something to eat?"

"No thanks, sis. Carolyn made me some oatmeal before she left."

Margaret brought his coffee. He took it and sighed. Margaret smiled and asked, "What?"

Cody cut his eyes to Margaret without raising his head. "I . . . I felt a little strange around Carolyn this morning. Is there is a reason for that?"

"Let me get some coffee and I'll tell you." Margaret grinned and pulled a chair close and said, "There could be a reason for feeling strange around Carolyn."

Cody frowned. "Tell me, Margaret!"

Margaret shrugged her shoulders. "You did ask her to give you a hug yesterday."

Cody's brows tightened and his mouth fell open. "Are you playing?"

Margaret had to bite her lip to keep from laughing aloud. "No, I'm serious."

Holding his breath, he asked, "What exactly did I say?"

Margaret rubbed the corners of her mouth and then said, "'. . . a wounded soldier needing someone to hug him other than his sister.' Or something like that. It's not important."

Panic filled Cody's eyes. "It is important. What else did I say?"

Margaret's lips quivered, trying to control her laughter. "You asked her to have supper with you last night."

Cody lowered his head. "Oh God! Did I make a complete fool of myself?"

Margaret stood and pulled the tie of her housecoat tight. "No, you didn't make a fool of yourself. If anything, you flattered my dear friend."

Cody shifted his eyes to Margaret. "What do you mean by that, Margaret Black?"

Margaret grinned and walked to the fireplace. "I mean Carolyn didn't mind hugging you and she didn't mind having supper with you. As a matter of fact, she curled her hair and tied it back with a ribbon."

"Really?"

"Oh, yes. I don't think you made a fool of yourself at all." By that time, Margaret could hold the laughter no longer.

Chapter Twenty-Two

The Kiss

*A*fter breakfast George brought his horse from the barn and tied him to the post in front of the house. "Toot," he called out.

Margaret hurried out. "Are you leaving now, George?" she asked.

George stood at the bottom of the steps and Margaret on the porch, which brought them eye-to-eye. He pulled her close to him and muttered, "If Cody weren't here, I'd take you inside and make love to you all day long."

Margaret smiled and whispered, "We could always go to the barn. Where there's a will, there is a way."

"If you keep talking like that, we'll make the way. Even if it's here on the front porch."

Margaret kissed the top of his earlobe. "You had better go. It's way too cold here on the front porch. By the way, I saw Julie yesterday. She wants Cody to come and recuperate at her house since she has a maid and everything she thinks I'm so deprived of. She's sending her carriage over later to pick him up. So we'll hold this thought, until tonight."

He twisted his mustache. "You light my fire, beautiful lady. I'll be back for you by night fall." He kissed her long and then quick. He mounted his horse, tilted his hat and rode away.

Margaret smiled.

Chapter Twenty-Three
General Thomas Meets George

*G*eorge greeted Deloris and asked if Major Wright was in. Softly Deloris said, "Yes, and I guess you know General Andrew Thomas is here."

"Yeah, Margaret told me that he was. Is he with Major Wright?"

"Yes, and so is Miss Chambers." Deloris tightened her lips and shook her head. "She is so hateful."

George patted her shoulder. "Everybody can't be as sweet as you."

Deloris smiled.

"Can I go in?" he asked.

"Just a moment." She knocked on the door. "George is here," she told Major Wright.

"Send him in," Major Wright said.

Major Wright met George at the door. General Thomas stood. "George, I want you to meet General Andrew Thomas. General this is George Black."

The general shook George's hand. "It's a pleasure to meet you. I've been told that you're one of, if not the best scout the Confederate Army has."

George raised his brows. "I don't know about that. I used to be a Confederate; however, now I only help out on occasion—"

Major Wright interrupted. "Before we go any further, let me introduce you to Miss Suzie Chambers."

The woman stood, lifted her chin and held her hand to George.

He gently shook her hand. "It's a pleasure to meet you, Miss Chambers. I've heard about your father. Actually, I met him in Charleston several years ago."

She tilted her head up slightly. "Was he there selling cotton?"

"No. He was there buying slaves."

"You would be surprised how many slaves it takes to operate a plantation properly," she said smugly.

"I'm sure."

"George," Major Wright said, "General Thomas has something to tell you. We were waiting for Jack Sams and some of the Cherokee scouts to arrive. He wants to fill you in on what his men have seen and what's about to take place close to home."

George took off his hat and scratched his head. "I must say, General Thomas, I was curious to find out what would bring you to Fort Howard. On occasion we receive important visitors, but not one that's second in command of the Confederate Army."

Before General Thomas could comment, Jack Sams opened the door. He smiled upon seeing General Thomas. Major Wright quickly said, "Jack, I want you to meet—"

Before he could say his name, Jack interrupted, "General Andrew Thomas."

General Thomas extended his hand. "Have we met before, Mr. Sams?"

Jack shook his hand and replied, "It's been awhile back. I wasn't properly introduced, but I did see you. I always remember a face. It's one of my . . . what shall I say . . . gifts." He set his eyes on Miss Chambers, removed his hat, nodded and said, "I know I haven't had the pleasure of seeing this beautiful face before, or your beauty would have definitely been burned into my mind."

Major Wright quickly said, "Jack, this is Miss Suzie Chambers."

Jack reached for her hand. She reluctantly held her hand toward him. Jack not only grasped her hand, he leaned down and kissed it. Miss Chambers swiftly pulled her hand back.

Major Wright appeared embarrassed by Jack's actions and abruptly said, "Jack, General Thomas has something to share with you and George. We'll go ahead and start, General. I'll inform the Indian scouts later."

The General placed one hand on top of his sword and soberly fixed his eyes on George and Jack. "There is an old cliché that says, "I have some good news and I have some bad news." Due to the severity of the bad news, I'll start with it. It appears that Red Eagle and his band of warriors have united with Silent Wolf and his braves."

George frowned. "General, I feel sure Major Wright told you about the three Indians that were captured near here yesterday."

"Yes, he did. That poses yet another problem. Word is they are from the Seminole nation. Why they would be here, I don't know. We'll have to deal with that matter as well."

Jack shook his head and grunted. "The Indians have a right to live anywhere in this land whether they be Cherokee or Seminole. All this fighting and killing just because white men feel they have to have black men to work their fields, and Indians on reservations. Men ought to be free except for murderers and men who rape women and children. It don't matter if they are from the North, South, black or red." Jack lowered his head and continued to mutter about freedom.

Miss Chambers stood, frowned at Jack and firmly stated. "What the devil is he talking about, General? Is this man on the side of the Confederate or not? There is no room for treason."

Jack wiped his mouth. "Look here, sweet cheeks, I'm here to protect my home, which happens to be in the South. However, I would do the same if it were in the North. I'll kill anyone or anything that threatens it or tries to take it from me."

Major Wright took Jack by the wrist and said, "I'm sure that Miss Chambers gets the picture, Jack."

George shifted his eyes from Jack to General Thomas. The general raised his chin and asked, "George, do you feel as adamant about your home as your friend Jack does?"

A quick nod of George's head gave the general the answer he wanted. Without taking his eyes from George, he said, "If I may continue, Major Wright told me the Seminole Indians were thought to have around a few hundred warriors. Which has proved to be false. My scouts have caught up with them and they number about one hundred. They are being followed at a distance to find out their intent." General Thomas took a map from a leather case and placed it on a table. "Gentlemen, we have a much larger problem than the Seminole." The men gathered around the table to view the map. The general drew a circle around Murfreesboro, Athens, and Clingmans Dome. "Gentlemen, there have been raids on Murfreesboro and Athens. Many were killed. Including women and children."

Surprised, George asked, "Why would you circle Clingmans Dome? It's rock cliffs and caves."

General Thomas put one hand behind his back and tapped the table with his pencil. "I circled it because those rock cliffs and caves are filled with Indians and Union soldiers. We could charge the cliffs; however, they would come down on us so fast we wouldn't know what hit us. I'm sending a message to General Lee that we need as many troops as possible to help take their stronghold out."

Jack scratched his head. "I can't figure out what the Seminole are doing here. They didn't come to war with only a hundred braves."

General Thomas put his hand on the back of his neck. "I agree. The troops we have would wipe them out in no time. Do you men have any ideas?"

Jack spoke up. "Sir, I think the Indians captured were scouting the area for something."

General Thomas cut his eyes to Major Wright. "Major, I'll let you answer that."

"Sir, I don't know about the Seminoles, but I know about Red Eagle and Silent Wolf. Right now they are the major threat."

The general snapped, "Of course they are a major threat."

A knock on the door caused Major Wright to jump.

Deloris opened the door. "I'm sorry to interrupt, Major Wright. One of the Indian scouts says that it is very important."

Major Wright moved away from General Thomas and walked toward the door. Tally, a Cherokee scout, hurried into the room. He saluted and said, "Major, there's been a raid on Townsend. Almost everything has been wiped out."

In haste, Major Wright asked George how far it was to Townsend.

"At least ten hours," he replied.

The general sighed. "Get as many men as you can spare, and we'll head out immediately."

"What about me?" Suzie Chambers asked.

General Thomas put his hat on and asked, "Is there someone Miss Chambers can stay with until I can arrange safe passage for her to Washington, D.C.?"

Major Wright immediately looked at George. George widened his eyes. "Are you thinking about Margaret?"

"Yes, I think she would get along just fine with Miss Chambers, and she won't be alone."

George ran his fingers across his lips. "Are you wanting me to go with you, now?"

General Thomas spoke up, "I'll answer that. Yes. When we go out, we need good scouts to go before us and fight with us. You being one of the best leave's you no choice."

Suzie stood and snapped, "Just one moment. You act as though I'm not here. Do I not have a say in where I stay?"

The general replied. "No! George will lead the carriage to his place. When we come back from Townsend, I'll try and get you out of here."

Chapter Twenty-Four

The Guest

Margaret came out on the porch when she saw George and the fancy carriage pull up to her house. Margaret's eyes connected with George's. She could tell by his expression that she might not like what was going on. Margaret cut her eyes to the carriage and quickly back to George. "What is it?" Margaret asked as George dismounted.

George tied his horse, started up the steps and then paused. Margaret frowned and asked, "Why is the carriage following behind you? That's the one I saw at the fort."

George held Margaret's shoulders and said, "Toot, there's been a raid on Townsend, and we have to go help now."

Margaret sighed. "Are you going back out so soon? You just got home."

"Honey, I have no choice."

"But George . . ."

George looked at the carriage and then at Margaret. Margaret watched as the driver opened the carriage door and helped a woman out. "That's the woman I saw at the fort with General Thomas. What's she doing here?"

"Toot, she needs to stay here until we get back from Townsend."

"George!"

"This is the best place for her to stay."

Suzie walked toward the porch. Margaret whispered, "What am I supposed to do with her?"

George extended his arm to Suzie and said, "Miss Chambers, this is my wife, Margaret."

Suzie nodded. "I'm sorry for the inconvenience. I seem to have no say in the matter."

"Forgive my manners. I was caught a little off guard." Margaret motioned for her to come in. "Welcome. I'll do my best to make you feel at home."

As Suzie started inside, she stopped and looked at Margaret. "I saw you at Fort Howard yesterday."

"Yes, we did get a glance at each other."

The driver brought her bags in and asked where he should put them. Margaret looked at George and then at their bedroom. She moved to the bedroom door and said, "In here will be fine."

"Has Julie come for Cody already?" George asked.

"Yes. She came right after you left. Miss Chambers if you would like to put your wrap and hand bag in here, feel free to do so."

Suzie walked past Margaret and put her things on the bed. Margaret stared at her beautiful pink silk dress. A large hoop petticoat made a perfect circle around her feet. The collar fit high on her neck. A narrow piece of white lace framed the top of the neck and around the bottom of the sleeves. Long, narrow pleats graced the bodice of the dress. A wide, pink belt with a gold hook hugged her small waist. White teardrop pearl earrings dangled from her ears. Suzie placed both hands on her medium size white hat with a small pink band. A pink, lacy veil rested across the top of her nose; she pulled a long hatpin from her hat and placed the hat on the bed. She looked around the room as she removed her white gloves.

Still glancing around, Suzie said, "You have a lovely home, Margaret. Small, but lovely."

Margaret didn't know what to expect. Nor did George.

"Toot, I've got to go."

Margaret and George embraced. "Honey, please be careful. I'll pray for you every minute you're away."

George and Margaret went to the porch. "I'll be praying for you, too. I think everything will be okay with her, Toot."

Margaret held George tightly. "Don't you worry about that. Carolyn will be here. That will help. I may have to take Suzie to visit Julie and Willow." Margaret looked at George and grinned. "They'll be so jealous. One of the richest women in the South staying here with me. They won't be able to stand it."

George gently stroked Margaret's cheek. "I love you, Toot. I guess our intimate evening will have to wait until I get back." He tenderly kissed her and mounted his horse. "I love you, Toot. If you need anything, go to the Fort and let Randy know."

Margaret awkwardly waved goodbye. "I love you, George," she whispered as he rode away.

"I'm sure that isn't an easy task," Suzie said. Margaret's eyes questioned her remark.

"I'm talking about saying goodbye to your husband. Not knowing if he'll be home again."

"Yes, it isn't easy." Margaret said as they went inside. "But I trust God will bring him safely home to me. It's getting pretty cold." She put a couple of sticks of wood on the fire. "Miss Chambers, would you like a cup of hot herbal tea?"

Suzie smiled. "I would love a cup. I'll never forget my first sip of herbal tea. When I was a little girl, my daddy bought a darkie in Virginia. Her name was Nellie. I was two when Daddy brought her to our Charleston Plantation. Her sole duty was to take care of me. I grew very close to her. There were times that I wanted to be with Mommy and Daddy, but they were always so busy. Mammy, that's what I called her, held me and sang to me. One day she came into my room with a big cup in her hand. I was curious, so I asked her what was in the cup. I had just turned six years old. Mammy motioned for me to come to her. She said, 'Princess, when I feel down or bad, or even a little sick, I drink hot tea. Not like your Mama and Daddy drink. This is a special tea. It's a magic potion.' She looked around to make sure no one was looking and said, 'I'll give you a sip, but you can't tell anyone.' Of course I promised not to tell because I wanted a sip of the magic tea. I took a sip. I remember it was so sweet. I loved it. I would pretend that it made me strong and gave me special powers. Mammy waited until I had three or four sips and then she told me how bright my eyes were or how my hair shone and how I looked like a princess after I finished the whole cup." Suzie paused. "I'm so sorry, Margaret. I didn't mean to go on and on."

Margaret smiled and asked, "So when did she tell you it was herbal tea?"

Suzie chuckled. "When I was twenty."

"Twenty?"

"Yes. She wouldn't have told me then, but Mama was feeling bad one day, and she asked Mammy to make her some hot herbal tea. To make a long story short, I took a sip of the herbal tea and it tasted just like my magic tea. Mammy told me that it was my magic tea. I acted as though it didn't matter that it wasn't magic, but actually, it broke my heart."

"I'm sure my tea won't taste as good as your Mammy's did," Margaret said as she went to the kitchen. "But it's pretty good."

Suzie and Margaret rocked in the rocking chairs that sat in front of the fireplace and drank their tea. Margaret had barely told Suzie about Carolyn when she heard her friend ride up. Before Margaret could get to the door, Carolyn tapped lightly and opened it. There was Margaret, standing ready to open the door. Carolyn screamed and grabbed her chest. "Heaven's, Margaret! You scared me. But no matter. Listen to this. Rumor has it that one of the richest women in the South is here at Fort Howard. Her name is Suzie Chambers."

Margaret grabbed Carolyn's arm and said, "Shhh!"

"Are you telling me that doesn't interest you? Her father owns too many slaves to count."

Unable to quiet Carolyn, Margaret said through gritted teeth, "Shut up, Carolyn. We have a guest." Margaret turned and pointed toward Suzie. "Suzie Chambers, I want you to meet my best friend, Carolyn Morris. Carolyn, this is Suzie Chambers."

Suzie smiled and commented, "One of the richest women in the South."

Carolyn quickly covered her red face with both hands. "Oh my goodness! I'm so sorry, Miss Chambers. I had no idea."

Suzie tilted her head. "So, I have already become a rumor. Should I be flattered, Carolyn?"

Carolyn shook her head. "I think that would be appropriate."

"Suzie is going to be staying with us until George gets back," Margaret offered.

Carolyn frowned and asked, "With us?"

"Yes. You always stay with me when George is away."

"How about Cody?"

"Cody is staying with Julie a few days." Margaret could see the disappointment in Carolyn's eyes.

"We'll be going over later to visit and let Suzie meet my sister."

Carolyn smiled and whispered as she went to the kitchen, "Julie will die."

"I know." Margaret chuckled.

Chapter Twenty-Five
Getting Acquainted

The women spent the afternoon getting acquainted. Margaret asked Suzie if she would like to change into something comfortable while she and Carolyn did the chores.

When outside, Margaret explained why Suzie was staying with her and how she was so different than she thought that she would be. Margaret insisted that Carolyn stay with them as well.

After supper, Margaret and Carolyn cleaned the kitchen and Suzie got a book from her room and settled into one of the rocking chairs by the fireplace to read. Margaret pulled the wooden shutters across the windows and latched them. "Suzie," Margaret said, "when you're ready for bed, feel free to say so."

She nodded. "I think I'm ready now."

"May I confess something to you, Suzie?" Margaret asked.

"Of course."

Margaret began to play with her fingers. "You're very different than I thought you would be. I felt sure you would be arrogant and hateful. Someone told me you were hateful and awful. Thus far, you haven't displayed those actions."

"Did you draw your information from a man? Men know nothing, except they can't stand for their judgment to be challenged," Suzie snapped. "My escort was angry with me because I wanted to go to Newport to visit a dear friend who's dying. It wasn't important to him; however, it was very important to me. I still may go to Newport, even if I have to go by myself."

"I know what you mean about wanting to go somewhere and the desire being so strong that you're willing to risk anything to get there. Your friend in Newport must be very special."

Suzie nodded as she headed to the bedroom. "Yes, very special," Margaret said.

"Is there anything that I can do?" Margaret said.

"You can take me to Newport."

Margaret looked at Carolyn and smiled. Suzie wasn't smiling. "Are you serious?" Margaret asked.

"Very serious. I want to see my Mammy one last time before she dies."

Suzie went into the bedroom. Carolyn and Margaret looked at each other. Carolyn shook her head and said. "What's that look in your eye, Margaret Black?"

"I was just thinking."

"About what?"

Margaret moved toward the fireplace. "I was thinking, Suzie wants to go to Newport and I want to go to Chestnut Grove."

"Humm. What's wrong with you? You can't go to Newport or Chestnut Grove. Think! Where is George? He's out trying to keep the Indians from killing all of us and you come up with a notion like that?"

"Carolyn, there's nothing wrong with me. Don't you remember Pine Mountain Cemetery?

"Do you remember Grandma Phoebe's blessing over me? And what Raven and Ortho told me about Grandma Phoebe and my mother and the three Indians looking at me and saying Phoenix? I haven't had the dream in two nights. I won't let anything take all this from me. I have to do what the Holy Spirit is pulling me to do. You have no idea how important this is to me."

"What about George? You're not sure how long he'll be gone, and besides, Jack said he would take you. Why can't you wait until George gets back?"

Margaret took a deep breath. "What if he doesn't come back for a long time? I know this territory as well as George or Jack."

Carolyn raised both hands and said softly, "And what about Suzie Chambers? She's not a mountain woman. She knows plantations, silk dresses and servants. Not only that, the weather is very unstable. It's so cold. With all the moisture and the cold combination, we could have an early snow."

Margaret took Carolyn by her shoulders. "I know all you've told me is true. I know the possible danger. I also know if Satan can stop you, he will. He's not going to stop me. God is directing me, and I know He'll take care of us."

Carolyn's eyes widened and her jaw dropped open. "Us? Are you talking about me and you?"

Margaret shrugged her shoulders. "Yeah, the thought did cross my mind. Didn't it cross yours?"

Carolyn shook her head. "You're hopeless."

"I sort of thought all that talk you were doing was your way of weeding the garden."

Carolyn frowned. "What are you talking about?"

"Cut it out, Carolyn. You're dying to go and you know it. As a matter of fact, you even suggested that we go after our visit to Pine Mountain Cemetery."

Carolyn and Margaret jumped when Suzie said, "Margaret's right, Carolyn. We could make an adventure out of this trip."

"Carolyn put her hand on her chest and sighed. "You scared the life out of me."

"I'm sorry, Carolyn. I couldn't help overhearing what you were saying."

Margaret looked toward the ceiling. "We'll need supplies and a time when George will be gone a few days. He can't know anything about this. He would have a fit."

"I have plenty of money for the supplies and whatever else we might need," Suzie said.

Carolyn put her hands up. "What about my job? Without it, I have no means of supporting myself."

Suzie asked, "Could you take some time off? Maybe have someone fill in for you until we get back?"

Carolyn massaged the back of her neck. She thought a moment and said, "I could ask Cool Breeze to teach for me a couple of weeks. Would that be enough time?"

Margaret quickly answered, "That would be more than enough time. It's only a couple of days to Chestnut Grove and another couple to Newport."

"How about horses?" Suzie asked. "The soldiers took mine back to the fort to be cared for until they return."

"We have an extra," Margaret said. "What about General Thomas—"

Carolyn interrupted, "Before you answer that question, what about clothing? A silk dress wouldn't be appropriate."

Suzie smiled and replied, "In the bottom of my trunk, I have the right kind of clothing. I even have a ladies' Stetson that looks almost like George's."

Margaret frowned. "Did you anticipate this kind of trip, Suzie?"

"I've learned a woman should pack for all occasions. Don't you agree?"

Margaret sat down in one of the rocking chairs. "I haven't really been any place that I needed to pack."

Suzie sat by Margaret. Carolyn got a chair and sat between them. "How will we explain being gone to Julie and Cody?"

Margaret stared into the leaping flames. "They won't miss me for a few days. I don't see them every day. I'll make sure I visit before we leave."

"One last question before retiring," Carolyn said.

Margaret cut her eyes to Carolyn. "And what would that one last question be?"

"What about Indians and soldiers? Union and Confederate?"

Margaret continued staring into the flames. "I guess we'll have to stretch our faith. I believe God has brought Suzie and us together for this trip; therefore, we'll trust Him to keep us safe as we endeavor to do His will. Whatever that is."

While Carolyn brushed her hair, Margaret and Suzie slowly rocked back and forth as the amber flames caused a slumber to overtake them. After a couple of minutes, Carolyn slapped her knee and announced, "Okay, I know I said I only had one more question, but I think I should have said two."

Margaret, who was almost asleep, jerked and said, "I felt certain you would ask one more question and I'll answer it without you asking. George isn't going to find out if we work this right. We'll get everything ready and when he has to go out again, we'll leave."

Carolyn glanced at Margaret and frowned, then quickly at Suzie.

"What's that look?" Margaret asked.

Carolyn tightened her lips and put her hand in front of her. "Are we going to do the hand thing or not?"

Suzie looked at Margaret and then put her hand on top of Carolyn's. Margaret quickly followed suit. Carolyn's timid voice transformed into a bold personification by declaring, "By the help and grace of God, we'll do what has been set before us."

Margaret grinned and commented, "This reminds me of a story in the Bible about the three Hebrew boys, who were not boys at all but men. They had to make a choice. They had come to a place where two roads joined together. They were servants of the living God, but were brought into captivity under another king's rule. They had to decide, will I bow to a pagan king and not have to face the fiery furnace or will I stay true to Jehovah and prove my allegiances to Him? God has brought the three of us down different roads to one place—Carolyn from Kansas, Suzie from Charleston and me from Cherokee—so we three could go down this new road together."

"Does that mean we'll be thrown into a furnace?" Suzie asked.

Margaret clicked her tongue and nodded. "Yeah, I think we can count on it."

Carolyn interjected, "The good news is the Hebrew boys came out of the furnace without even the smell of smoke on them and the guards that pushed them into the fire died from the heat."

The women stood. They agreed to make their plan and have everything ready when the time was right, to pursue their quest. As Suzie headed for her room, Carolyn asked, "Suzie, is it true that you were on your way to visit with President Lincoln?"

Suzie turned and faced Carolyn. "Yes."

"I was a little curious about that myself," Margaret said. "Was it a social visit or business?"

"It was business. I think he should leave slaves where they are and stop causing chaos over it. A war over slaves, it makes no sense to me."

Margaret frowned. "Maybe not to you, but how about the slaves? I'm sure if you asked their feelings they wouldn't agree with you."

"Yeah," Carolyn uttered. "How would you like for a colored man to own you?"

Margaret held her hands up and insisted, "Let's keep those feelings out of the picture. We have a mission before us, and there's no room for our personal opinions on slavery. And you don't want me to start about the plight of the Cherokee and all the other Indians in America. Therefore, let's get some sleep."

Chapter Twenty-Six

A Cry in the Night

Waves of light rippled through the starry sky. Falling stars appeared everywhere. The wind had stilled, yet the cold air forced the temperature into the low teens. Margaret's eyes sprang open. She held her breath as she listened keenly to what sounded like a woman wailing. She saw that Carolyn was sleeping soundly and chose not to wake her. Quietly she moved to the edge of the bed, tilted her head and again heard the eerie moans in the distance. Margaret pushed her feet into her slippers and took her robe from the chair beside the bed. She held it to her chest, paused briefly and then put it on. A gust of cold air swept through the room from underneath the door. The fire had died down and had only a few coals remaining; however, Margaret could see well enough and didn't have to light the lamp.

She paused halfway down the stairs and listened for the sound again, then proceeded down the steps and into the living room. The fireplace had plenty of wood and golden flames were leaping. So where was the cold air coming from?

Margaret saw that Suzie's bedroom door was open, but Suzie wasn't in the bed. The wailing had quieted, with only an occasional sob. Instantly, Margaret realized the sounds were coming from the porch. She moved slowly to the front door, put her hand on the knob and paused. She wondered what would be on the other side. Finally, Margaret opened the door to find Suzie on her knees with a quilt wrapped around her. She was slowly rocking back and forth.

"Suzie," Margaret said softly, "are you okay?"

Suzie lowered her head and then looked toward the sky, in silence.

"I heard you crying," Margaret said as she moved close to her. "I just wanted to make sure you were all right. It's freezing out here."

Suzie took a deep breath and blew it out. "I think we must be having a meteor shower. Have you ever seen anything so beautiful?"

Margaret stared toward the heavens and beheld the most extraordinary sight she had ever seen. The stars were falling in generous amounts, like streaks of lightning, rocketing through the clear sky.

Margaret didn't want to pry, yet was bursting to ask if that was why she was weeping. Shivering, Margaret put her hand on Suzie's shoulder and suggested, "Let's go inside and talk. You'll catch a death of cold out here. We have a quest to pursue, and you can't be sick when the time comes."

Trembling, Suzie looked up at Margaret who took her hand and helped her to her feet. When they opened the door, Carolyn was standing on the other side. Suzie pulled the quilt tight around her and said, "I'm sorry, I didn't mean to wake you up."

Carolyn pointed toward the kitchen. "There was some tea left. Shall I warm it up?"

"I don't care for any," Suzie said as she dropped the quilt and held her hands over the fire.

Carolyn asked, "What's wrong, that you two would be out on the porch in the freezing cold on a dark night, instead of being under the warm covers?"

Margaret shifted her eyes to Suzie, wondering if there would be an answer. Suzie pushed a strand of hair from her face and said, "I suppose I could say a lot at this moment to clear your curiosities; however, I don't feel I can. I don't want you to form opinions that aren't favorable. After all, we only met each other today."

"If you think that we'll judge you, you're wrong," Carolyn said.

Margaret watched as Suzie lowered her eyes and put her fingers to her forehead. Her eyes were swollen and bloodshot. "Carolyn's right. We won't judge you. We all have things that bother us and indeed haunt us, but we'll leave the judging to God."

Carolyn chuckled. Suzie and Margaret quickly turned their attention to her. "What's funny?" Margaret asked.

"Oh nothing." Carolyn said, trying clear the smile from her face.

"If there's something funny, now would be a good time to share it," Margaret said, as she began to smile.

Carolyn shrugged her shoulders. "I always thought if you were rich, you wouldn't have any problems."

Suzie hastened to say, "Nothing could be farther from the truth. Money doesn't exempt you from problems. Is that why you laughed?"

"Yeah. I thought when I married a rich man, it would be smooth sailing all the way," Carolyn said.

"Have you ever been married, Suzie?" Margaret asked. "Just wonderin'."

"No. There's not a man alive who would be suitable for me, according to my mother and father."

Margaret moaned, "I sure miss George. He used to be gone long periods of time when he was a full-time scout, but I never got used to him being away. I love him so much."

"Suzie," Carolyn said, "do you mind if I ask how old you are?"

"Not at all. I'm forty-five."

Carolyn shook her head and confessed, "I don't get it. Margaret's fifty, you're forty-five, I'm forty, and I look older than both of you."

Margaret threw a small pillow and hit her. "Stop your whining. You look beautiful and young. You're only fishing for compliments." Margaret stood and patted Suzie's shoulder. "Do you feel better?"

Suzie stood took hold of Margaret and Carolyn's hands and responded, "Yes, thank you so much."

Margaret yawned. "With that said, ladies, I will bid you a good night. I'm getting so sleepy."

Margaret put a couple sticks of wood in the fireplace and went back to bed. Carolyn followed behind and Suzie went to her room.

"I miss snuggling up to George," Margaret whispered.

Carolyn ordered, "You stay on your side of the bed."

Margaret giggled. "I'll do my best. Good night, Carolyn."

"Humm. It will be a good night if you remember that I'm Carolyn, not George."

Chapter Twenty-Seven
Sound of Heavy Boots

Carolyn's eyes sprang open, and she quickly sat up in the bed. She shook Margaret's arm. "Margaret, Margaret."

Margaret jerked and propped on her elbows. "What is it?"

Carolyn put her finger to her lips and advised, "Shhh. Listen."

Margaret asked softly, "What is it?"

Carolyn didn't have to answer. They heard the sound of heavy boots moving across the porch, promptly grabbed the pistols that were on either side of the bed and went down the steps to the living room. They paused when the boots stopped. Slowly, they faced each other as they remembered the horrid experience with the soldiers only a few days earlier. There was a stern knock on the door and someone called out, "Margaret!" Their breathless silence was broken when they recognized the low pitched voice of Sergeant Randy Mathis. Margaret breathed a sigh of relief as she opened the door.

"My word, Randy. You scared us to death. What are you doing here this early?"

Before he could answer, Margaret grabbed his arm and asked, "Is it George? Is something wrong with George?"

Randy put his hand on her shoulder. "No, there is nothing wrong with George, so calm down."

Margaret sighed, "Thank God! Come in, Randy. I'm sorry, it's just that to be awakened from hearing someone on the porch, gave us a bit of a scare with all that's been going on."

Suzie came from the bedroom. Randy removed his hat and raked his fingers through his hair. Suzie tightened the belt on her robe.

Margaret pointed toward Suzie. "Randy, have you met Suzie Chambers?"

"I haven't met her, but I did have the privilege of seeing her coming out of Major Wright's office the other day." Randy nodded at Suzie. "It's a pleasure to meet you, Miss Chambers."

Suzie tilted her head and smiled. "The pleasure is mine, Sergeant."

Carolyn chuckled and remarked, "Sergeant Mathis has spoiled Margaret beyond belief."

Margaret took Randy's arm, "He is my friend and a person whom I can turn to in time of need, right Randy Mathis?"

Randy blushed. "You . . . you know you can."

Carolyn frowned and fixed her stare on Margaret. She recognized Margaret's strategy from past experiences. "Carolyn," Margaret said, "why don't you put some coffee on so Randy can have a cup to warm him up before he leaves."

Randy patted Margaret's hand. "I almost forgot the reason for my visit. All this beauty in one room captivated my attention."

"And just to what do we owe this welcome visit?" Margaret asked.

"You asked earlier if George was all right; he's fine. However, Major Wright sent a rider back to let us know they had encountered Silent Wolf and Red Eagle."

Margaret's jaw dropped open and her eyes widened. "So, the Seminoles will be freed?"

Randy squinted. "I don't have a clue. You can bet Major Wright ain't going to release them. He'll find a reason to keep them locked away."

"But why?" Carolyn asked.

"Right now, every Indian is a threat to Major Wright. I'll not say any more than that. So don't ask."

"Why are they here?" Margaret whispered.

Randy scratched his temple. "Now there's a mystery. I got a little sidetracked there about why I'm here. There was quite a death toll at Morrisville near the railroad track. General Thomas and Major Wright, along with George and Jack, agreed they should pursue Silent Wolf and Red Eagle north toward Haden. The good news is, several hundred men from Fort Henry, Fort Powell and Fort Donelson are going to connect with them at the Tennessee River near Chattanooga."

Detecting a worried look on his face, Margaret asked, "That's the good news. Is the bad news worse than what you just told us?"

Randy tightened his lips and squirmed in his chair. "I'm afraid so. It's not just the renegade Indians they're going to be fighting."

Margaret lowered her head for a moment and questioned, "Are you talking about Union soldiers?"

Randy rubbed Margaret's forearm and replied, "Yes, General Grant has sent a large number of soldiers to the area."

Before Randy could finish his statement, Margaret grabbed his arm and frantically asked, "How many soldiers? A few, hundreds, what?"

Randy lowered his head without answering. Terror seized Margaret. "Does that look mean there's more than hundreds?"

Tears welled in Randy's eyes. "Yes," he said, "more than hundreds. A lot more."

Margaret put her hand over her mouth, slowly moved to the fireplace and stared into the glow of the flames.

Carolyn put her arm around Margaret's shoulders and whispered, "Margaret." Her friend didn't respond.

Suzie asked, "Sergeant, how many Confederate soldiers are being sent? Enough to make a stand against the Union soldiers?"

"Ma'am. There's a few thousand that's gathering. Margaret, there is one good thing to take note of."

Margaret swiftly turned. "What good thing?"

It won't be just Confederate soldiers who will fight Red Cloud and Silent Wolf. If the Union soldiers find them first, they'll fight them too."

"I don't understand all this madness," Suzie ranted. "Having to fight Indians, that for some unknown reason don't want to stay in their own territory, and white men fighting each other. I hate it all!"

Carolyn frowned and snapped, "Indians who don't want to stay on their territory. Their territory was taken away from them, and some would rather fight and die than be trapped in one place without freedom. It's obvious that you can't understand what that's like. You don't understand the black man wanting to be free from farming the white man's plantations. So how could you possibly sympathize with the Indians' dilemma?"

"Carolyn, Suzie, stop it!" Margaret ordered. "I can't think about anything right now but George."

"I'm sorry, Margaret. You're right," Carolyn said. "I'm sorry, Suzie. I must realize that you come from a different lifestyle than me. While I don't understand your reasoning, you are entitled to your thoughts. Our focus right now should be George and the other soldiers. I will agree with you, Suzie, about one thing, I hate it and want it all to end soon."

Suzie opened her arms. "I'm sorry too." They hugged and then opened their arms to Margaret. The three embraced as Randy watched. He put his hat on and cleared his throat.

"I guess I better be going."

Margaret, now composed, quickly pulled away, put her hands on Randy's broad shoulders and asked, "Is there anything else you can tell me?"

"Just pray for them, Miss Chambers. I don't have any idea how long it will be before General Thomas will be back."

Suzie took a deep breath. "He will be back when it's time and not until." She stared at Margaret and Carolyn. "Until then, I don't think I could ask for better company."

Randy cleared his throat. "If there is anything you ladies need, or I can help you with, I'll be at the fort."

Margaret bit her lower lip, took Randy's hand and pulled him toward the rocking chair. "Randy, please sit down for a minute."

Carolyn and Suzie looked at each other, realizing what Margaret had in mind. Randy sat down and Margaret pulled the other rocking chair close to Randy's. "Carolyn," she said, "would you please put that coffee on, and we'll have a cup together before Randy leaves." She looked at Suzie. "Suzie, would you mind cutting us a piece of cake to have with our coffee?"

Suzie smiled. "I would love to."

Margaret put some wood on the fire while Suzie and Carolyn prepared the coffee and cake. Carolyn and Suzie returned and pulled two chairs close around Randy.

Randy shook his head and whispered, "Oh God above, have mercy on me. I'm surrounded."

Margaret took a bite of cake and asked, "What would prompt you to say that, Randy? I thought you might enjoy a piece of cake and a cup of fresh coffee before you leave."

Carolyn took a sip of coffee and raised her eyebrows. "I do make a great cup of coffee, don't you think?"

Suzie joined the conversation by saying, "I can't take credit for making this delicious cake; however, I did cut it nicely. Don't you think, Randy?"

Randy's eyes widened. He groaned, "Lord, help me. Not you too, Miss Chambers."

"Why, Sergeant. Whatever do you mean? I only said that I cut the cake nicely."

"Eat your cake, Randy," Margaret said.

Randy took a sip of coffee and sat the cup on the floor beside the rocking chair. "I'm getting out of here."

Margaret swiftly stood and implored him to stay and hear her out. Randy held both hands out in front of him and boldly stated, "Margaret, I feel like I have been surrounded by Silent Wolf, Red Eagle and the Union Army. I'm not ashamed to admit that I feel like a trapped animal."

Margaret patted his knee. "Come on, Randy," she said. "You know that I tell you almost everything and I feel I need to tell you our plan."

"That's it!" Randy shouted. "I fear the plan. I know I won't agree with anything that you say. I can't tell you anything else about the Indians. I've told you all I know about George and the move toward the Tennessee River, so there is no more information I can give you. That's it."

"Calm down, Randy," Margaret said as she took his cup from the floor and handed it to him.

"I said that I wanted to tell you our plan. Someone needs to know, and you're the only one I trust."

Randy sighed and moaned, "My God, is this going to take trust from me? Why don't you just swear me to silence? That is what this is about, right?"

Margaret tightened her face muscles and clamped her teeth together. "Well, yeah, more or less. But, I can't sit here and worry myself sick about George. I love him more than my own life. I confess the thoughts that race through my mind can be brutal. Like, has Silent Wolf taken his scalp or has a Union cannonball blown him to shreds? No! I can't do that, and I'm not going to do that. This is something I have to do and frankly, I can't think of a better time to do it. At least it will help occupy my mind. I'll be doing something that needs to be done while George is away, and I'll be back home by the time he is. I can't just sit here, Randy. Please try and understand."

"Oh, all right. So go ahead and tell me. I'm not going to be able to leave until you do, whether I agree or not."

The women smiled and Margaret told Randy about going to Chestnut Grove and Newport.

Randy exploded. "You're wanting to drag Miss Chambers on a wild goose chase? I won't hear of it. General Thomas would have me skinned alive if something happened to her."

"No, no, no," Suzie hasted to say. "I'm the one who wants to go to Newport. I have a friend there who is dying, and I want to see her one more time, but I'm working against the clock. I don't have much time. As far as General Thomas is concerned, he's not my boss or my keeper. What he was doing wasn't out of the goodness of his heart. I was paying him handsomely for his escort. As I said before, his family had lost everything."

"But still, you have all this fighting going on. Three women can't be out there roaming around to God knows where." He looked at Carolyn and said, "Carolyn, you seem to always have a level head, tell them how foolish all this is."

Carolyn shrugged her shoulders, "Not this time, Randy."

Randy sat his coffee down and stood. "For the love of might, Carolyn. Where do you fit in this? Are you going to Richmond or somewhere?"

"No, Randy, I'm not. I don't have any destination in mind, but I do know I want to go with them and make sure they're all right. God forbid they should need any help, but if they do, I'm going to be there. We're going to do this with or without your approval. We would really prefer that you hear us out."

Randy hit his hat against his leg and snorted. "Dad blame! Go ahead and tell me so I can worry myself to death about you. It would be bad enough for three men to go off on some wild adventure, but three women. I can't even imagine what would happen if you were caught by the Indians or the soldiers. Yet, if you're going to do this outlandish thing, get to the point and tell me what you want from me."

Margaret put her hand on his arm. "You're a true friend to me, and I love you for that."

Randy shook his head. "I'm not a true friend. True friends wouldn't allow you to go. Somehow they would stop you. I just don't know how. So what do you want from me?"

"We need you to help get us supplies. No one will think anything about you buying the things we need, but they would notice us."

Suzie stood and said, "I have plenty of money for whatever supplies we need. Margaret can make a list, and what's left of the money is yours. I'll see you have more than enough to say thank you for your help."

"Miss Chambers, this is not about money. The concern you hear in my voice is genuine. I really care what happens to you."

Randy put his hat on, "When do you want to leave?"

Margaret replied, "In the morning, if we can get everything together."

"What about your family, Margaret? You know you'll be missed. You're all over the place. People are used to seeing you and Carolyn out. And you, Carolyn, what about your teaching classes? You'll be expected to be there."

"I'll ask Cool Breeze to fill in a few days. She'll cover me."

Margaret said, "I'll go by today and visit with Cody and Julie. I'll take Suzie with me."

Suzie interrupted, "I'll tell them I don't want to be bothered, and my staying with Margaret was Major Wright's idea. I'll be so rude no one will want to visit until I'm gone. That could also be the reason Margaret won't be so visible."

"What about your cows?" Randy asked.

"Would you milk them for me? You can have the milk or do whatever you like with it. Please."

"I can't promise you about milking the cows. What will somebody think if they see me out here every day while George is away?"

"You're right. Take the cows to the reservation and ask a family with children if they will milk the cows," Carolyn said. "They can have the milk for a couple weeks."

Randy headed toward the door.

"Randy." Margaret called out. He stopped but did not turn around. Margaret hurried over and took his hands. "Thank you," she whispered.

Randy tightened his lips and nodded.

"Randy," Suzie said as she hurried from the bedroom. She extended her hand to him. Randy hesitated and then took the money that was folded in her hand. He looked solemnly at the women. He opened the door and stepped onto the porch. "I'll try to have everything you need by nightfall." As he walked away he said loudly, "I'm not even going to mention the weather, but I'm sure you have already thought about the early snows that are likely."

The women watched until Randy rode out of sight and then hurried inside out of the cold.

Margaret smiled and slapped her hands together. "Ladies, we have much to do. Carolyn, go take care of your business, and Suzie and I will pay a visit to Cody, Julie and maybe Willow Fine."

"Margaret," Carolyn said, "do you mind if I go with you to Julie's?"

Margaret smiled. "You want to visit Julie?"

Carolyn shyly replied, "Well, yes, I like Julie."

Margaret chuckled. "No, I think it's Cody."

"Uh," Carolyn stammered, "I do like Cody, but I like Julie too."

"Of course you can go with us. We had better hurry. We have so much to do."

Chapter Twenty-Eight
Suzie Meets Julie

The cold wind was swirling the slate gray clouds across the morning sky, making the ride to the settlement not as pleasant as Margaret had hoped. She insisted they take Suzie's carriage for appearance sake. She knew Julie and Willow would be awed by its presence. Margaret drove and Carolyn sat alongside atop the coach. Margaret wanted Suzie, inside the coach, to get full attention.

Randy told Julie and Willow they would be bringing Suzie for a visit. As Margaret drove the carriage, her mind was filled with thoughts of George. She prayed in silence until they pulled into Julie's circle drive and stopped at the steps. As Margaret pulled back on the reins to stop the horses, she saw David Coats, a young Cherokee Indian, hurry down the steps to open the carriage door. He wore black pants, white shirt and a black bow tie. His long, black hair was oiled and pulled back. Margaret looked at Carolyn and frowned. The elaborate welcoming gesture was conspicuous. "Do you believe this?" Margaret asked.

Carolyn sniggered. "I'm afraid I do."

Julie emerged, arrayed in her finest attire. Somehow, she looked more like a Southern belle than Suzie. David opened the carriage door and extended his hand to Suzie. Her narrow hands were covered with black satin gloves, and a black, beaded drawstring purse with beaded fringe across the bottom dangled from her wrist. Suzie truly fit the role of a wealthy Southern belle in her flowing, dark brown dress with a high collar and narrow black belt. Her dark brown waist jacket, thin black collar and rounded black buttons were striking. However, the long, flowing dark brown cape—lined with black satin and outlined with black piping and a large black flower that hooked at the neck—was exquisite. The crowning touch was a small, brown hat with a slender, black satin narrow band and a large, black feather on the side.

Julie placed her hand on her chest and began to breathe as though she were going to hyperventilate. Margaret hugged Julie. "Sis, I want you to meet Miss Suzie Chambers. Suzie, my sister Julie Williams."

"Miss Chambers, I'm so honored to meet you. Please come in out of this horrid weather."

Inside, Julie clapped her hands and Meco appeared from around the corner and lowered her head in front of Julie. "Meco, take Miss Chamber's wrap."

Suzie unhooked the cape and handed it to Meco. Suzie surveyed the large room and commented, "You have a charming home, Mrs. Williams."

Julie quickly replied, "Please call me Julie. Meco has made hot tea and apple spice loaves for us. This way." She led the way to the dining room. "Miss Chambers, you sit here." David hurried to pull the chair out at the end of the table. Though they were only having tea and cake, the table was stunning. After they were seated, Margaret looked around the room. "Where is Cody?"

"He should be in to say hello in a moment. He is doing much better. He's up and moving around very well on his crutches."

Margaret watched as Julie, in her sheer elegance, displayed all the attributes of the upper echelon. This time, Margaret didn't want to tease, but admired her beautiful sister doing what she did best, being an elegant hostess for a state dinner or a small tea party. For the first time, Margaret prayed that Julie's longing would be fully realized. Why were her emotions being tapped concerning Julie's dream? Was it because she too had a dream that even she didn't understand? A vision that so far was totally confusing? A vision of finding her true roots that had been masterfully hidden for the fifty years of her life? As she observed, Margaret recalled what the Bible had to say about dreams and visions. When our vision fails, we die. Vision brings hope and hope breeds faith and faith moves God on our behalf.

Cody entered the room, hopping on his crutches. Carolyn's eyes sparkled. Margaret was about to stand to assist Cody, but Carolyn moved like lightning to accommodate the wounded soldier. Cody was soaking it in like a sponge. David brought a footstool for Cody to prop his foot on. Carolyn quickly took it from David and found the right spot to set it to make Cody comfortable. Margaret gave him a kiss on top of his head and introduced him to Suzie. Afterward, Margaret watched and listened, yet could not comprehend anything that was being said. The room was slowly spinning in circles. Everyone's voice had the sound of distant echoes. As the room spun, Margaret saw her Grandma Phoebe standing at the entrance of the room. With each spin of the room, Phoebe's appearance grew younger until Margaret saw a baby by a river in a basket.

"Margaret! Margaret!" Julie shouted.

Margaret looked around the table. Everyone was staring at her.

"Are you in some kind of trance?" Julie asked.

The room had stopped spinning and Phoebe had vanished. "I'm sorry, Julie. What did you say?"

"I said, are you okay? I've never seen you this quiet in your entire life."

Cody was quick to agree.

"I have a lot on my mind, with George away," Margaret said.

A solemn look covered Julie's face. "I know. I miss Creed. He was called to join them in Tennessee." Julie pointed at the table and confessed, "All of this show I am putting on is something to try to mask the fact that a serious battle is going to take place. Then of course there is the morbid thoughts that somehow seize your mind regardless. Creed told me the South had lost portions of West and Middle Tennessee and were hell bent to regain it."

"I wish I could be there to help," Cody said. "I feel worthless sitting here sipping tea with the women, while George and Creed are with the troops."

Suzie wiped the corners of her mouth and said, "Cody, we know you would be there to fight if possible."

"Margaret," Cody said, "did Randy tell you that thousands were gathering for this battle at Knoxville?"

Margaret lowered her head and replied, "Yes, he did. Sometimes truth is a hard thing." Margaret's brows tightened. "Julie," she snapped, "you said that Creed told you about this before he left?"

"Yes."

"I don't understand. George didn't know about having to go back out to Knoxville."

"He must have known," Cody said. "We were briefed about the troops gathering before George and I came back from Stone's Creek."

Bewildered, Margaret asked, "Cody, why didn't you tell me?"

"Because you would worry yourself sick. George didn't want that for you. Julie and I are only talking about it now because we know that Randy told you."

Suzie stood, put her hands on her hips and said sharply, "So that's why General Thomas agreed to escort me to Washington, D.C. It wasn't out of his way at all. He was coming this way for the battle. I paid him a bounty for that escort. He lied to me. He said he would escort me because of the respect he had for my daddy." Suzie looked sternly at Margaret, "It appears the truth has been withheld from both of us."

Margaret looked at Julie and Cody. They in turn were watching Margaret. "I can't do this," Margaret said.

Julie stood and asked, "Do what?"

Margaret took a deep breath and blew it out. She lifted her head, paused and announced, "Julie, Cody, I love you very much. I can't lie to you about what I'm going to do."

Julie and Cody looked at each other. "What do you mean, going to do?" Julie asked.

Cody furrowed his brows and muttered, "What is it, sis?"

Cody and Julie weren't the only ones who wanted to know. Margaret had captured Suzie and Carolyn's attention as well. "I know George didn't tell me about any of this to keep me from worrying, but I don't like it. I may have wanted to say one more I love you, or hold him one last time. I just don't like deception, whatever the reason. The sad thing is, we came here today not only to visit, but to try deceive you."

Julie shook her head. "You did what?"

Cody didn't give her time to answer. "What are you talking about? You came here to visit and deceive us? Are you saying that Miss Chambers and Carolyn were going to deceive us as well? If that's it, I want to know why. And deceive us about what?"

Carolyn and Suzie stood. Margaret asked them to please sit down.

"Let me explain," Margaret said. She exhaled, massaged her temples and then began.

"I've watched Julie since we've arrived, doing what I know she has been gifted by God to do, being the perfect hostess to rich and poor alike. Julie, I'm very proud of you because you don't hide that fact. You're open and extremely honest about your gifts. Your excellence in performing your duty astounds me. Cody, you have always been forthright with your desires, fears and dreams. You've worked hard to fulfill, overcome and conquer your pain and loss."

Margaret lowered her head, closed her eyes briefly and continued, "Suzie Chambers, I admire you. A complete stranger, and you also were open and honest about your pursuit. You didn't care whom it made mad. You felt the pull in your soul to go to Newport to see your mammy before she dies. Your pursuit withstood a general second in command under General Robert E Lee. You had the nerve to set out for Washington, D.C. to protest our president's decision about the war over slavery. Whether I agree or not isn't the question. You knew what you had to do, and you're doing it. And you're being very honest about it."

Margaret looked at Carolyn and said, "Carolyn, you're my best friend, and you have stuck beside me in everything, whether you agreed with me or not. As my friend, you have always been open and honest with me. Today, I apologize to you for pulling you into my deception."

"For God's sake, Margaret, what are you talking about?" Cody asked.

Margaret sat down and told them everything. She started with the event at Pine Mountain Cemetery. It was Monday. All morning I had Grandma Phoebe on my mind. It was like hearing a voice calling to me. It kept saying, "Come to the mountain." Margaret ended with her plan to visit them and sneak off and pursue her destiny. When she had finished, everyone continued to stare at her. When no one said anything, Margaret said, "We're going no matter what you say and that's that."

Julie cleared her throat and agreed, "I think you should do whatever you feel you should. The years are slipping away, along with my dreams. I may never go to Washington, D.C., and yet I do continue to prepare in case. I don't want that for you, Margaret. I'm not sure where the search will lead you, but our roots are the same and I will do anything I can to help. Will I worry about you? Of course I will, but I'll trust God to bring you home safely. If there is anything I can do to help, please tell me."

Margaret couldn't believe Julie's response. She turned her eyes to Cody. His eyes displayed his reservations. Margaret softly said, "Cody, I need to know your true feelings."

"As your big brother, my emotions are mixed. My first instinct is to protect you and not wish you well on a quest that could be very dangerous. However, my heart is crying out, 'Go and find what it is you're looking for. Follow your heart and come home safe.'"

Tears rolled down Margaret's face as she felt the overwhelming support from the two she thought would throw a fit. They embraced and cried together. Suzie and Carolyn gathered behind them. Julie and Suzie embraced, as did Carolyn and Margaret. Margaret noticed Cody looking at Carolyn as she hugged Julie. Carolyn turned and faced Cody. He smiled at Carolyn and said softly, "It would sure be nice to have a hug from someone other than your sister." Carolyn looked at Margaret and then slowly moved toward Cody to embrace him. Cody put his arms around her and whispered in her ear. Carolyn's face turned a soft shade of red. She looked at the others and then Cody. Cody pulled himself up with his crutches and tenderly looked into Carolyn's eyes. He reached his hands out to her. Carolyn swallowed hard, took his hands and moved close to him. Margaret, Julie and Suzie watched, not sure what would happen next. Carolyn put her face close to Cody's, and for a second, they stared into each other's eyes. Cody tilted his head and gently kissed Carolyn lips. Margaret took Julie's hand and the tears started again. Carolyn and Cody had not taken their eyes off each other. Everyone was a captivated as Carolyn gently ran her fingertips down Cody's cheek. As she did, he closed his eyes. Carolyn pressed her lips to his and this time Cody kissed her passionately. Margaret and Julie were ecstatic. Cody hadn't kissed a woman since Donna's brutal murder. Carolyn looked at Margaret but said nothing; her eyes said it all.

Julie said David could milk Margaret's cows while they were away, and she would keep a close watch on the house. Margaret told Cody the route they would be taking, while Julie, Carolyn and Suzie discussed other aspects of the trip. Julie thought it would be a bad idea for Margaret to visit Willow and so did Cody. Carolyn headed for the settlement to talk to Gentle Breeze about her classes, to pack lightly and to meet back at Margaret's before dark.

Chapter Twenty-Nine
Finding a Guide

*R*andy pulled down his hat on his head to prevent the blustery wind from blowing it off. The thoughts of Margaret and the others heading out in such threatening weather gave him a sick feeling. Randy insisted on knowing their itinerary. He also insisted that they promise not to change it. Randy put Suzie's carriage in the barn and helped bring the firewood in before he left. He held Margaret's shoulders and said, "If you're not back in two weeks, I'm coming after you."

Margaret hugged Randy and thanked him for all his help. He hugged Carolyn, paused and then hugged Suzie as well. As he stepped into the yard, he mumbled, "Did they even think about the possibility of snow?" He went a couple of steps and stopped. Margaret watched, thinking he was going to turn around and try once again to convince them not to go. Randy held his finger out, shook it, swiftly turned and hurried to the porch. "Margaret, I don't know why I didn't think about this earlier."

"Think about what?" she asked.

Randy pressed his pointer finger to his lips. "You know the old Indian Lighted Path?"

"Yes, of course. Why?"

"I trust him completely. I want you to take him with you."

Margaret frowned. "I don't know, Randy."

"And why not? He got the name Lighted Path when he was a young boy and there was a reason for that. He knows every crook and cranny in this part of the country, and he can speak just about every language spoken in the Smoky Mountains and beyond. You said you were going to see Desan. How do you know that you can communicate with her?"

Margaret crossed her arms and held her chin in her fingers. She raised her eyes to Randy's and asked, "Will he go?"

Randy's eyes widened and excitement filled his voice. "Yes. Yes, he will. What do you say, Margaret?"

Margaret's smile made Randy a happy man. "Okay, he can go with us."

Randy grabbed Margaret's shoulders and ecstatically agreed to ask Lighted Path about going. "I'll have him here by daylight, I promise." Randy wasn't the only one who felt more at ease; so did Margaret.

As Randy rode away, Carolyn opened the door. "Randy just leaving? I thought he left already."

Margaret muttered, "I'm glad he didn't."

Chapter Thirty
Lighted Path

*I*nside the house, Margaret shared Randy's idea about Lighted Path taking them. Suzie and Carolyn were pleased as well. After supper, Margaret told Carolyn and Suzie they would go to Uncle Bill's first since his place was on the way to Newport.

"Margaret," Suzie said, "I know that Indian names all have special meanings that are somehow attached to the person. However, aren't those names usually given at birth?"

"Not always. There are cases when other names can be given when a person is older. Why do you ask?"

"The man that's going with us, Lighted Path . . . did Randy say he was given that name when he was a boy?"

"Yes, he did."

"Well, what warranted the name Lighted Path?"

"His original birth name was Morning Light. The reason for that name was obvious. He was born at daybreak after a hard night of labor. His mother was so thrilled to see the morning light again that she named her son Morning Light. When he was a young boy, I think around nine years old, some white men killed his mother and sister, but Morning Light and his father were able to get away; however, his father was wounded in the process. I think they ended up lost somewhere in Kentucky. They had never been even half that distance from Cherokee, so the problem was being able to return home without knowing the way. Morning Light said one night his father stood in the midst of a vast forest with only shafts of light from a full moon. He took a long cape covered with eagle feathers from a bag he was carrying. Morning Light said his father stared at the sky for a long time and then placed the cape around his shoulders and began to moan and make strange sounds. Then he began to dance and cry out to the Great Eagle of the Universe, asking him to light the way home for him and his son. He danced all night and then collapsed. Morning Light thought he had fainted from exhaustion, but he died. Morning Light buried his father with leaves and brush. He put the eagle cape back in the bag and started his journey home. He said at night, the path in front of him lit up with every step he took, enabling him to find his way."

Suzie frowned. "Do you believe that?"

"Of course I believe it. Why wouldn't I?"

"It sounds made up."

Margaret furrowed her brows, "Don't you believe in God?"

"Well, yes, but to dance all night thinking that would bring God to make the ground light up so a boy can see in the night is a little extreme."

"If that's what you choose to believe, that's up to you. I will tell you this, I don't limit the Mighty Eagle, the God I serve. If he is God to me, I know I can trust Him in whatever situation arises. Otherwise, why would I call Him God?"

Suzie sighed. "I suppose you're right."

Carolyn came from the bedroom. "I think we had better get some sleep. Suzie, do you have your things ready to go?"

Suzie stood and stretched. "Yes. I might add I'm eager to get started. Therefore, I bid you a good night."

"Sleep well," Margaret said.

Carolyn and Margaret put wood on the fire and went to bed. Margaret was lying on her back with her hands under her head. "Carolyn?"

"Yeah," Carolyn groaned.

"Does Cody kiss good?"

Carolyn gasped and pushed Margaret. "That's none of your business."

Margaret chuckled. "It sort of is. He's my brother, and I have to look out for him. Exactly, what are your intentions?"

"My heavens," Carolyn groaned.

Margaret laughed. "Only kidding. I think it's great."

"You think what's great? That your brother and I kissed?"

"No. I think it's great that we're leaving in the morning. Good night, Carolyn."

"Good night."

After a brief moment of silence, Carolyn whispered, "He's a wonderful kisser."

Chapter Thirty-One
Cold Morning

*R*andy and Lighted Path were at Margaret's before dawn. To Randy's surprise, the women were ready. Lighted Path was riding his brown and white pinto. He was dressed in buckskin and wore a dark brown coat made of beaver skin. His gray hair hung loosely under his beaver hat. His dark skin was lined with age, yet his dark eyes danced with excitement, like a young man going out on the first hunt of winter. Margaret quickly went over her plans, gave Randy a hug and assured him that they would be back soon. Right on schedule, they left the clearing and rode through the forested gates before dawn.

The first gray light of morning crept through the multitude of trees. The morning was cold, and the sky was white with high snow clouds.

Though Margaret knew the way to Chestnut Grove, she allowed Lighted Path to take the lead. The cold weather made the trip slow and very tiring. Margaret and Lighted Path knew they couldn't make the trip in one day, but they would go until nightfall, make camp and continue on at daybreak. With any luck at all, they would arrive at their destination in two or three days.

They took only short breaks to eat, feed, water and rest the horses. With winter fast approaching, daylight rapidly withdrew her light and forced the group to find shelter for the night.

Lighted Path knew of a cave in that area. He found it and went inside to make sure it was clear. They tied their horses, and Lighted Path gathered wood for a fire he feared might attract attention. He gave in to build one long enough for them to warm up. They ate beef jerky and fried bread. No matter how badly Suzie and Carolyn wanted coffee, Lighted Path said no, the smell might attract unwanted visitors. After they had warmed themselves and eaten, they wrapped up in their blankets. Margaret made a pillow of her clothes bag. Lighted Path said he would watch so the women could rest. Of course Margaret wouldn't agree to that unless she could take half of the watch. Carolyn and Suzie joined rank; however, Margaret and Lighted Path said no.

Lighted Path put the fire out, wrapped up in his blanket and sat in the mouth of the cave. He propped his long-barreled rifle across his lap, drew his knees to his chest and wrapped his arms around them.

Carolyn and Suzie were fast asleep, but not Margaret. Thoughts of George prevented that. She missed his strong arms around her. She prayed in silence, yet still was unable to sleep. She sat up and whispered, "Lighted Path."

"Yes."

"Do you mind if I join you a few minutes?"

"Come," he grunted.

She took her blanket and sat down beside him. "It sure is cold tonight, don't you think?"

"Not as cold as I expected. The snow didn't fall. The Great Eagle has smiled down on us."

"Lighted Path, tell me about the old woman Desan."

"What's to tell? She's old like me. Many moons have passed since her birth."

"Is she . . .," Margaret paused and said, "crazy?"

"Not crazy. Desan carries the wisdom of the Mighty Eagle. She chooses to be alone. No one understands the kind of power she possesses."

"What kind of power?"

"The power of the Creator of all things. He gave that power to her when she was a young girl. With that power, she was able to see things others could not see. People were afraid of that kind of power. Yet they were afraid to kill her or have her put to death."

"How do you know so much about her?"

"I used to go and visit her on occasions. She taught me many things. I haven't seen her for many seasons."

"Why haven't you visited her?"

"I moved to the settlement, and she moved to the top of White Oak Pass."

Margaret pulled the blanket over her head and moaned. "It's so cold and damp."

"The rings around the moon tell from the sky the weather is going to get worse."

"Yeah, I know. I pray that George is safe and warm." Margaret sighed. "Lighted Path, did you find it strange that we didn't see or hear anything relating to soldiers or Indians today?"

"You'd better get some sleep. Your watch will be here soon."

"I don't think I can sleep right now. I'm just too wound up."

Lighted Path took the rifle from his lap and handed it to Margaret. "You take your watch now. I'm very tired." He stood and said firmly, "Don't go to sleep on your watch. If you get too sleepy to stay awake, call me."

Margaret placed the rifle beside her and pulled her scarf tightly around her neck and over her mouth to stop the cold air from hurting her lungs. In silence she prayed that Uncle Bill would agree to see her. Thoughts raced through her head. What will I find at my uncle's home if he does agree to see me? Will he be glad to see me? Most importantly, will he share the mysterious cover-up about my mother and Phoebe? What caused the division of Bill from his brother and sister after Mariah's death? Was it all in vain? Will he close me out as well?

The forest was draped with silence, except for the screech of the wind and an occasional hoot from an owl close by. After what seemed forever, Margaret was getting so sleepy she couldn't hold her eyes open. She tried to stand. Her leg muscles began to cramp. Instantly, Lighted Path leapt up with his knife drawn.

Groaning and trying to rub her leg, Margaret moaned. "It's me, Lighted Path. My leg is cramping."

"Open your mouth," he ordered. When Margaret opened her mouth, Lighted Path put something that tasted like birch bark on her tongue. "Chew it. It will relax the muscle."

In seconds her muscle calmed and the pain diminished. By then Carolyn and Suzie were beginning to stir. "What is it?" Carolyn asked.

Margaret limped around and moaned. "I had a leg cramp, but it's better now. What did you put in my mouth? It tasted like birch."

"I'll tell you later. Get some sleep. We'll leave at first light."

"Margaret, Margaret."

Margaret sprang up breathlessly. "Oh, my! You scared me."

Carolyn and Suzie laughed. "You had better get up," Carolyn said. "Lighted Path has made a fire long enough for us to warm our bodies and bread."

Suzie extended her hand to Margaret. "Let me give you a hand. I know your body is going to be stiff."

"Oh," Margaret groaned as she grabbed her back and tried to bend her aching knees. "I need to pee-pee."

Carolyn chuckled, "Good luck, my friend. It's freezing out there."

"That's an understatement," Suzie added.

Margaret stretched her back. She patted Lighted Path's shoulder as she went by. "Good morning, buddy."

Lighted Path pointed beside the cave. "You go right here and no farther."

"I'll watch," Margaret said, "but I want to go just a couple steps higher. Okay?"

Lighted Path nodded. "But no farther."

Chapter Thirty-Two
Chestnut Grove

As soon as they ate, they mounted their horses and headed on to Chestnut Grove. Late evening they rode out of the mountains into the peaceful surroundings and log homes of the small community. A trading post sat in the middle of the valley with a small white church down from it on the other side of the road. A meager plank schoolhouse and a blacksmith shop sat beside the trading post. Margaret looked around trying to imagine which house was her uncle's. They rode slowly into town and halted at the blacksmith's shop.

A big man was shoeing a horse but paused when the group stopped their horses in front of him.

"Howdy," the blacksmith said as he put his hammer down and wiped his hands.

The group dismounted. "Hello," Margaret said.

The blacksmith scratched his eyebrow. "Is there something I can help you with?" he asked.

"I'm Margaret Black. This is Carolyn Morris, Suzie Chambers and my guide Lighted Path. I'm looking for Bill Thawbush. Could you tell me where he lives?"

"I'm Conley Day, the local blacksmith as you can tell. Bill Thawbush lives in the only white house in town." Conley stepped out in the road. He pointed toward the end of town to a white house that sat on the hill near the tree line. "That's his house, but he's not there. I saw him go into the Trading Post right before you rode in."

Margaret thanked Conley. She took a deep breath and asked, "Conley, can you tell me what kind of man he is?"

A quick jerk of his head and Conley replied, "He's one of the nicest men that I have ever known. How is it that you know him?"

"He's my uncle."

Carolyn asked, "Do you want us to go with you to the Trading Post?"

Margaret bit the side of her lip. "I think I should go first and introduce myself. He doesn't know me, and I don't know him."

Margaret gave Lighted Path her horse's reins.

"You're welcome to bring your horses inside and water them. I have some fresh hay as well," Conley said.

Lighted Path led the horses inside the barn.

Margaret took a deep breath, looked at Suzie and Carolyn and said, "Pray for me. I'm scared."

"Be brave," Suzie commented. "You'll be fine."

Carolyn tilted her head. "You know, Margaret, you just said something my mother used to scold me for believing."

"What's that?"

"The villainous 'they.'"

Margaret tightened her coat. "What in the world are you talking about?"

"You said, 'I'm what they call a nervous wreck.' Actually, there is no 'they.' A person uses the word they, only to cover what's coming from within themselves. In other words, you're nervous because you say that you're nervous, not because someone else says so. I want you to ask God to calm you and go in that Trading Post believing your Uncle Bill will see you."

Margaret cut her eyes to Suzie. Suzie nodded in agreement.

Margaret itched her nose and nodded back. Accepting the challenge before her, she walked toward the Trading Post. Her heart pounded as she went up the steps. She paused at the door before entering. Her fist tightened then relaxed as she took hold of the knob and went inside. The combination of the smell of tobacco, wood burning and vanilla flavoring was almost overwhelming. One side of the room was filled with furs. Some were hanging and others were lying on a pallet on the plank floor. The other side of the room had everything from cloth to hard candy. Margaret frowned and glanced around the room. A couple of men, a woman and a big man behind the counter appeared to be the only ones in the Trading Post.

"What can I get for you, Miss?" a friendly voice from behind the counter asked.

Margaret took a couple of steps toward the man and stopped. "Actually I'm looking for someone. I thought he was in here; however, I don't see him so I must have been mistaken."

"Who are you looking for, and I'll let you know if you're mistaken or not?"

"I'm looking for Bill Thawbush. I saw the blacksmith outside, and he said he thought he came in here a few minutes ago."

"That I did," a voice said from behind her.

Margaret quickly turned, widened her eyes and whispered, "Uncle Bill?"

Bill had the looks of someone much younger than seventy-five. Although he was an older man, he carried himself with grace and poise. His hair was as white as cotton and hung loosely around his neck. He sported a full, white mustache and stood around six feet tall. His tan skin showed very few wrinkles. He wore a brown hat and a medium-length brown, checked wool coat. He squinted, gasped, slowly removed his hat and said breathlessly, "My God. You're the spitting image of Mariah."

Margaret trembled and tried to manage a smile without crying.

"Are you Margaret?" he asked.

"Yes," she said barely above a whisper.

A tear rolled down his cheek as he opened his arms to Margaret. She slowly made her way into his strong embrace. Margaret could not contain her tears. Exhilaration sprang forth as Bill introduced Margaret to the people inside the store. Margaret was so overwhelmed at his acceptance of not only seeing her, but embracing her.

Suzie and Carolyn waited outside, desperate to know what was going on. Carolyn rubbed her forearms and said, "I wonder what's taking so long? She's been in there ten minutes."

"Maybe that's a good sign," Suzie said. "Otherwise she would have been out by now."

Those words were barely out of her mouth when Margaret came out of the store, holding her uncle's hand. Carolyn slapped her hands together and muttered, "Thank you, God."

"Amen," Suzie whispered.

Margaret introduced Carolyn, Suzie and Lighted Path to her uncle. Bill went to the blacksmith's shop and asked him to board their horses. "Let's get in out of the cold," Bill said.

Chapter Thirty-Three
Uncle Bill

*B*ill's house was masculine, yet elegant. Margaret was surprised. A large group of window panes graced the living room and peered out over the lofty snow-covered mountains and down on the valley. She looked out at the small, white streams of smoke that crept upward into the freezing atmosphere from the chimneys of the houses below. The living room was vast, and to her surprise, several oil paintings were displayed, one of which left her breathless. Hanging above the stone fireplace, encased in a gold frame, was a painting of her Grandma Phoebe Thawbush. The likeness was astounding. She was adorned in a ceremonial Cherokee dress, white with colorful beaded fringe down the long sleeves and around the V-neck. Her brown moccasins were also fringed down the side with vibrant beads. Phoebe's long ebony hair lay loose down her back, with a braid on either side of her face. The braids were interwoven with the mutli-colored beads. The braid on the right side had a long eagle feather attached to it. She was holding a dark-colored wooden box overlaid with turquoise. Phoebe's large brown eyes, white teeth and dark skin epitomized the beauty of the Cherokee people. Not only her beauty caught Margaret's attention, but also the extraordinary turquoise necklace that lay against her tanned skin. In the center of the turquoise was a large, black eagle claw.

Margaret stared at Bill and asked, "Where did you get this painting?"

Bill looked down and then raised his head. "I painted it, several years ago."

Margaret's mouth opened and her brows furrowed. "You painted this?"

"Yes. It's one of my favorites."

Margaret sighed. "Did you do all of these?"

Bill's smile showed the pride of the work in the paintings. "Yes, I love to paint." Bill called out, "Sara!" In seconds a middle-aged Indian woman entered the room. She was heavyset and very attractive. Her face beamed as Bill introduced her to Margaret. Sara is my best friend, cook and housekeeper, Bill said. He asked Sara to prepare supper for his guests. She assured him that she would fix something very special.

Bill took their coats, and everyone but Margaret was seated. She continued to look at the portrait of Phoebe.

"Margaret," Bill called out, "Come sit with us. I have many questions for you."

Margaret reluctantly left the painting and sat down directly in front of Bill.

Bill shook his head. "My, Margaret, you're so beautiful. So like Mariah. I have waited for this day for so long. I'm elated that you've come."

"You sound as though you were expecting me."

"I have been expecting you for a long while."

Margaret sighed. "If you wanted to see me, you know where I live and have lived most of my life. Why didn't you come?"

Bill clicked his tongue and said, "For the same reason you haven't come until now. It wasn't time."

"What do you mean, it wasn't time?"

Bill put his hands together and responded, "It's like the good book says, 'there is a time and a season for every purpose under heaven.' Many seasons had to pass before the time and the purpose would manifest. The fact that you're here proves that your season has arrived. We'll talk about the season later. Now, I want to know how Cody and Julie are doing."

"They're doing fine. Cody hasn't married yet. However, Julie is married to Sergeant Creed Williams."

"Do they have children?" Bill asked.

"None living. She lost two and then stopped trying. The thought of maybe losing another one was too great."

"And your husband. What's his name?"

"George Black. He's the most wonderful man in the world and was a scout for the Army for many years. He semi-retired to do some farming, but scouting was so in his blood, he couldn't stop. As a matter of fact, he's gone to Knoxville with Major Wright and General Andrew Thomas. There's a significant battle there.

"Yes, I heard about that." Bill frowned and remarked, "Andrew Thomas? The commander under General Lee?"

"Yes."

"What's a man like General Thomas doing in Cherokee?"

"I'll let Suzie answer that."

Suzie smiled, and with her Southern drawl proceeded to tell the story about her escort to Washington, D.C. and the reason that she was with Margaret.

Carolyn chuckled and uttered, "I'm along only for the ride."

Bill turned his attention to Lighted Path. "Lighted Path sounds very familiar. Is that your birth name?"

"No. My birth name was Morning Light."

Bill moved to the edge of his chair, squinted and said, "I remember you. You're the young boy who was lost, and you prayed to the All Mighty and He lighted your path home. Did I get the story right?"

Soberly, Lighted Path said, "Yes. I thank the light of this world every day for His guiding light."

Before Bill could respond, Sara entered the room and announced that supper was ready.

A banquet of fried chicken, boiled potatoes, corn on the cob, cabbage and cornbread filled the table. There was milk, coffee and tea to drink. After a hefty meal, Sara brought dessert bowls filled with blackberry cobbler.

Chapter Thirty-Four

The Paintings

*A*fter supper, Sara prepared the guest bedrooms. She filled hot-water bottles and placed them on the sheets to warm the beds. When the others had gone to bed, Margaret and Bill stayed up to talk. There were so many questions Margaret wanted to ask, the first being if it were possible to see her mother's things.

Margaret looked at a painting that hung over a small table. Other than the painting of Phoebe, it was the most extraordinary portrait that she had ever seen. As she stared at the face of the Indian chief decked in full headdress, she asked without taking her eyes from it, "Uncle Bill, who is this remarkable-looking chief? He's not Cherokee."

Without answering her question, Bill took Margaret's hand. "Come sit with me."

When they sat down, Bill asked, "How is Tyler?"

Margaret leaned back in her chair. "He's old and not doing very well. While we're on the subject of Uncle Tyler, there's something I need to ask of you. Would you please tell me what happened after Mother died that separated you from your family?"

Bill rubbed his lips. "Many things happen in a person's life. Some things are hard to explain. Complicated things. Tyler, Lorrie and I didn't agree on many things. Things that I can't, or chose not to discuss."

"Uncle Tyler said when he last came to visit you, that you wouldn't let him on your property. Why? He's your brother."

Bill turned his head to the side, looked down and said nothing for a moment, then slowly raised his head. "I loved your mother more than anything. When she died, it tore my heart out. I have something of hers that I want you to have." Bill stood and asked Margaret to follow him. Her heart raced as she followed him into a room filled with unfinished paintings, empty canvases, books, a large walnut desk and an easel. On the wall behind the desk, hung a portrait with the images of three children—a boy and two girls.

"Uncle Bill, who are these children?"

"It's Cody, Julie and you."

"How could you possibly know what we looked like? We've never seen you before. I was twenty years old when Mama died. I didn't see you at her funeral. Where were you? If you loved my mother so much, why didn't you come to visit her? While we're on the subject, I didn't see you at Grandma Phoebe's funeral either. Your own mother! Is there any wonder I'm so confused?"

"You're wrong, Margaret, I did see you. I used to visit Mariah once a month, until she died. We met outside the settlement. There were times I came close enough to see you, Cody and Julie. Years ago, your Grandma Phoebe brought Mariah, Tyler, Lorrie and me back to Cherokee." Bill gently touched the painting and said, "Mariah, brought her three children with her."

"How could that be? We were born in Cherokee and our father was a trapper named J.D. Styles. We only saw him two or three weeks out of the year, but we loved him."

Bill smiled. "J.D. Styles was a wonderful man. He sure loved your mother."

"Why didn't he stay home more? There are lots of trappers who stay near home and still get plenty of furs."

"What did your mother say about that?"

"Nothing. She talked so little about everything. Now I'm hearing what we've been told isn't necessarily the truth. I don't know what to believe. That's one reason I wanted to see you. Your reception of me has also been a shock. I was expecting some awful man that growled instead of talking. You've been anything but what I expected. I need to know the truth, Uncle Bill. Only you and Tyler know the truth. Because of your age alone, I need to know. For the past few weeks, the need to know the truth has burned in my soul like a fire. It's not that I just want to know, I must know. If that makes any sense to you."

Bill took Margaret's hand and said, "It makes all the sense in the world. I would've been shocked had you not come." Bill pointed to a chair and asked Margaret to sit down. When she did, he opened a desk drawer and took out a hand-carved wooden box that was overlaid with turquoise. He looked at Margaret, slowly opened the box and told her to look inside. Margaret held her breath as she touched the side of the box. "This is the box that Grandma Phoebe is holding in the painting."

Bill nodded yes.

In awe Margaret gently stroked the shiny, brown eagle feather that lay on top. She gradually picked it up and raised it to her face. Still holding her breath, she shifted her eyes to Bill. "What . . . what is this?"

"What do you think it is?"

Margaret stared at the feather, released her breath and said, "It's an eagle feather."

Bill nodded. "That's right."

"This was my mother's?"

"Yes. She treasured it."

"Is this like the one Grandma Phoebe was wearing in her hair?"

"No. It's not like the one she was wearing. It is the one she's wearing."

Margaret's mouth was getting dry from sheer exhilaration. She swallowed hard as she put the feather on the desk. Anticipation was high as Margaret took a turquoise necklace from the box. It was exceptional. Unlike anything that Margaret had ever seen. She held it before her face and marveled at the unique piece of jewelry. The one thing that made it unique, was the large black eagle claw that hinged in the center of the large pieces of turquoise. Margaret looked at Bill in unbelief and asked, "Is this the necklace that Grandma is wearing?"

"Yes, it is."

"Did Grandma Phoebe give it to my mother?"

Bill nodded yes. She carefully placed the necklace beside the feather. Margaret squinted at the third remaining item—a small piece of tanned leather with tiny slits cut around the top. It was pulled together by a narrow piece of rawhide. Margaret gently touched the pouch, paused, looked at Bill and picked it up. She squeezed the pouch. Whatever was inside felt soft. She gazed at Bill and questioned him with her eyes.

Bill grinned. "Go ahead and open it."

Carefully, she untied the bow and pulled the pouch open. Margaret frowned and quickly looked at Bill. "What is this?"

"What does it look like to you?"

Margaret rubbed her fingers through it and uttered, "It feels like some kind of powder or maybe ashes. I'll say ashes, due to the grayish hue."

"You're right. It is ashes. And yes, that too was your mother's. As were the other two items. They were priceless to her. Not just in a monetary value, but highly spiritual."

"What are the ashes from?"

"A fire that was kindled many years ago is all I can tell you."

Margaret held each item again and then placed them in the box. She closed it and pushed it to Bill. "I don't know how to express my appreciation for allowing me to see my mother's things. Not only my mother's, but Grandma Phoebe's as well. I'm so thankful."

Bill picked the box up and handed it to Margaret. "I want you to have it. You're the rightful owner, not me.

Mother gave the chest to me after Mariah died. I was to keep it until the rightful owner came for it. The owner is you."

In disbelief, Margaret took the box and held it to her chest. In silence, she embraced Bill.

"That's enough for tonight," Bill said. "You need to get some rest. If you don't, you'll never be able to keep up with your friends who have been in bed for the last hour and a half. Besides, you want to go before the hot-water bottle turns cold. You can trust me on that."

Margaret placed her open hand on Bill's chest and thanked him again for making her dream of having something of her mother's come true. Margaret looked at the painting of the three children and then at Bill. "Why would I be the rightful owner and not Julie or Cody? And how could you so vividly remember what we looked like as children?"

"You never forget someone you love. Good night, Margaret." Bill turned and left the room.

Margaret fixed her eyes on the three children in the painting. She gently placed her fingertips on each child and tried to remember that time, but everything seemed out of place. She moved to the living room and again marveled at the brilliant likeness of her Grandma Phoebe standing like a tower above the leaping flames of the oversized fireplace. Margaret held the box tightly as she focused on the feather in Phoebe's hair and the beautiful box that she was holding. Just knowing that she was holding the same box sent a chill through her.

Margaret's mind was whirling like a tornado with a question she prayed her uncle would answer.

As she looked around the room, she couldn't help but think of Julie and Willow. The excellence of the house and the decoration were definitely a gifting that had been passed from Bill to them. As Margaret turned to leave the room, her eyes connected with the painting of the Indian chief. A shiver shot through her body. She sighed and whispered, "How could a painting that excellent not send a chill?" She smiled and gently touched the chief. "Goodnight. Whoever you are."

Chapter Thirty-Five
Much Needed Sleep

$\mathcal{A}$ light tapping on her bedroom door made Margaret moan and try to open her eyes. She sat up, but only a grunt came from her exhausted body. With her eyes still closed, she slowly lay back down and snuggled tightly to her pillow.

Carolyn opened the door and smiled as she looked at Margaret. For Margaret not to get up early was totally out of the ordinary. Carolyn quietly closed the door.

"Is she awake?" Suzie asked.

"I think she's in a coma," Carolyn muttered.

The morning passed and the noon hour had arrived. Sara entered the living room where Bill and his guests were getting acquainted. Sara looked around and asked, "Where's Margaret?"

"She's still sleeping," Bill said.

Sara frowned, "It's one o'clock."

"I know," Bill said. "No matter about the time. She evidently needs the sleep."

"You're right, Uncle Bill. I desperately needed the rest," Margaret remarked as she came down the stairs. "How long have you all been up? I'm so embarrassed"

Carolyn laughed. "The smell of breakfast woke *us* up, not dinner."

"Honestly," Suzie commented, "Sara made the best sweet rolls and coffee I have ever tasted."

Margaret stood behind Bill's chair, leaned down and kissed the top of his head. "I trust you rested well, Uncle Bill."

Bill put his hand on top of Margaret's. "I could hardly sleep at all. I'm so excited that you and your friends are here."

Margaret glanced around the room and asked, "Where's Lighted Path?"

Bill stood. "I sent him to check on the horses."

"He's been gone almost an hour," Suzie said. "Conley must be a big talker. Lighted Path hardly speaks at all."

"Good morning, I mean good afternoon, Mrs. Black," Sara said. "I wanted to let you know that dinner is ready, when you are."

Margaret put her hand on her stomach and moaned, "I'm ready right now."

"Should I go get Lighted Path?" Carolyn asked.

Bill looked out the window, "Here he comes now." Bill opened the door for Lighted Path and asked. "Is everything okay?"

Lighted Path rubbed his hands together. "Everything is fine." He looked past Bill and said, "Good morning, Margaret."

"Good morning. I sure proved to be a lazybones today, didn't I?"

Bill asked Margaret to say grace. Afterward, they talked about their plans to go with Suzie to Newport.

"Newport is only a day from here," Bill said. "Margaret, will you come back by Chestnut Grove when you return to Cherokee?"

"I think I speak for all of us when I say we would love to."

Everyone wholeheartedly agreed.

Bill quickly asked, "You will stay tonight and leave in the morning, won't you?"

Margaret looked at the others. Carolyn and Suzie spoke up, "It sounds good to us."

Margaret looked at Lighted Path. "What do you think?" she asked.

"It's too late to leave today; we'll leave at daybreak

Bill put his arm around Margaret's shoulders. "I'm so glad that you're staying. There's still much to catch up on." Bill stopped and then added, "I have an idea. Carolyn, Suzie, I want Lighted Path to escort you to the Trading Post. I want you and Suzie to pick out something nice to take with you from me."

"You don't have to do that," Suzie commented. "Allowing us to stay in your home is more than sufficient."

"I insist," Bill said. "By the way, tell Martin, the man that works behind the counter, to just put what you get on my account. Lighted Path, tell him to put some of the best cured tobacco on my account for you."

"Uncle Bill," Margaret said, "Lighted Path doesn't smoke, do you?"

Lighted Path grinned. "I smoke only on special occasions. I love the smell of tobacco though."

Chapter Thirty-Six

My Two Sons

𝕸argaret watched as her friends made their way down the road to the Trading Post.

She looked upward, when a sudden surge of light burst through the dreary gray clouds that had occupied the sky for the last five days. "The sun would surely be a Godsend for a few days. After several days of continuous dark clouds, I yearn for bright warm rays to lift my spirit." She turned to face Bill and quickly stated, "Although I can't imagine my spirit being lifted more than it has in the last twenty-four hours. The only thing that could possibly make it any greater would be if George were here to share this time with me."

"I agree, Margaret." Bill stared out the window. "Do you see the church at the end of the road?"

Margaret smiled. "Yes I do. It and your house are the only two white buildings in town. Therefore, it would be hard to miss either one of them."

"That's true. I go to that church often and pray. After Ellie and my two sons were killed . . . I . . ."

Margaret interjected, "Uncle Bill, you had two sons?"

Bill took a deep breath and looked toward the church. "Yes. Jim and Marty. Jim was twenty and Marty was twenty-five."

"I didn't have a clue. I knew you were married, but I didn't know about children. Did Tyler or Lorrie know?"

"No, we had cut all ties before they were born."

"How did they die?"

Bill rubbed his lips and revealed, "A group of white men came through Chestnut Grove and decided to rob the Trading Post. I had gone to Pole Creek to buy furs, to make sure I would have plenty in stock with winter coming on."

"You own the Trading Post?"

"Yes. I built it too many years ago to count. I didn't go away that often, maybe three times a year to buy supplies in bulk. The boys and Ellie stayed behind and ran things for me. When I came home from my last trip out, for the winter, they had already been buried for three weeks. I was gone five weeks. I lost all will to live. I felt that God had let me down. I trusted Him to watch after my family when I was away. The people here at Chestnut Grove rallied around me. It took a year, but with their help and the help of God, I was able to start putting my life back together. One of the first things I did was build the church. It was my way of thanking God for my friends and for His healing touch. When I bought the paint for the church, I got enough to paint my house as well. Ellie always wanted a white house. She didn't get to enjoy it, but I sure do."

Margaret looked around the room. "Do you have any paintings of Ellie and your boys?"

Bill lowered his head and responded, "Yes, but I put them away after their deaths. I tried to look at them, but it proved to be too difficult. I couldn't stand the constant reminder that they were gone."

Margaret took a deep breath and asked. "Can I see them?"

Bill turned and took hold of the back of the chair. "I . . . I don't know."

Margaret put her hand on his arm and implored, "Please, Uncle Bill. It would mean so much to me."

Bill thought a moment and whispered, "Okay."

Margaret followed Bill up the stairs. He went to the bedroom Margaret had slept in, opened the door and motioned for her to come inside.

He stopped in front of an oak wardrobe and gently ran his fingers across the detailed carving of birds and vines. He breathed in and quickly blew it out. With his fingers close to the bronze knobs, he paused then rubbed the tips of his fingers together. Margaret could tell how difficult it was for him. She was about to tell him it was okay, but before she could, Bill swiftly took hold of the knobs and pulled the double doors open. He took another deep breath and quickly blew it out. On one side of the wardrobe, were a couple of men's shirts and a pale blue dress with a white collar and long sleeves with white cuffs. Under the clothing were two pairs of black, men's shoes and a pair of women's black, button-up high heels. Bill took hold of the sleeve of the dress, held it to his nose and took a deep breath, smelling the faded perfume. Gradually, he looked at the other side of the wardrobe where a sheet was draped over several paintings. A sweat broke out on his upper lip as he removed the sheet and placed it across a chest at the foot of the bed. Bill touched the back of the painting, paused and then pulled it from the wardrobe. He turned to face Margaret. Margaret gasped as she stared at two of the most handsome men she had ever seen. A beautiful woman was standing between them. They all had dark skin, dark brown eyes and black hair. To Margaret's surprise, the clothing in the wardrobe was exactly what they were wearing in the painting. The antique frame was incredible, but there was something else that caught her eye. They were all smiling. In any pictures that Margaret had ever seen, no one smiled. But Ellie, Jim and Marty wore big ones.

"Uncle Bill," Margaret whispered, "your sons are so good looking, and Ellie is radiant."

Bill was slightly turning his head from left to right and taking short breaths. Margaret put her hand on his arm. "Uncle Bill, I know how hard this must be for you. I wish I could do something to take all your pain away."

"You have no idea how you have helped take the pain away. I could have never taken the paintings out if you hadn't been here to encourage it. As I look at my wife and sons, I realize how much I've missed by hiding the images of the ones I loved so much. I think I'm going to hang them up again and enjoy their presence."

Bill set the portrait aside, smiled at Margaret and said, "There is another painting that I have hidden away for much too long. I think this one may surprise you."

"Really?"

"Oh yes." Bill pulled another painting from the wardrobe. Margaret held her breath, awaiting the surprise. Bill turned the large painting around. Margaret's breath escaped her. She put both hands over her mouth, looked at Bill and then the painting. Tears welled up in her eyes and rolled down her cheeks. She whispered through her fingers, "Mama."

Bill had to wipe a tear from his cheek. "Margaret, you're the image of Mariah. When I saw you in the store my spirit leapt. It was as though I was seeing and talking to Mariah."

Margaret knelt down and stared at her mother's picture. "This likeness is astounding."

"Yes, it is."

Margaret felt dizzy when she saw the eagle feather in her mother's hair and the wooden box overlaid with turquoise in her mother's hands and the turquoise necklace with the eagle claw her mother was wearing around her neck.

Margaret trembled as she asked, "Is there a reason for Mama having on the same attire in this picture as Grandma Phoebe?"

"Yes," Bill said softly.

Margaret looked at Bill and whispered, "What about the feather, the box and the necklace? Is there something I should know about them?"

Bill propped the picture of Mariah against his desk beside the picture Ellie and his sons. He gently patted Margaret's shoulder. "For everything, there is a season."

"Uncle Bill, I have so many questions and so much to share with you, I don't know where to start."

"Why don't you start by sharing, and we'll do more questions later. Let's go back to the living room where we can be more comfortable."

Margaret told Bill about the dream she had been having and about her trip to Pine Mountain Cemetery. And she told him what Eagle Claw had said about the clues she would find deep in the forest. "He also told me not to come back until I had found those clues and penned them. I don't understand any of that."

"Tell me more about this Desan you mentioned."

Margaret proceeded to report all that she knew about Desan. She told of her Grandma Phoebe's blessing over her before she died. Before she could tell, or ask, anything else, Suzie, Carolyn and Lighted Path came through the door with the gifts they had chosen. Carolyn couldn't wait to show Margaret and Bill the beaded, black drawstring purse she treasured. "Suzie has one something like this one. I loved it." Carolyn kissed Bill's cheek, "Thank you, Uncle Bill."

Bill was taken by surprise. It was evident from the light shade of red that had settled on his cheeks.

Suzie took a book from her sack and said, "I love to read and every time I read the beautiful poetry from this book, I'll think of you, Uncle Bill." Suzie kissed Bill's glowing cheeks.

Lighted Path held up a pouch of tobacco. "When the special occasion is here, I'll smoke this fine tobacco and think of you."

Bill held his hands up. "Lighted Path, please spare the kiss."

Lighted Path and Bill went to the church to spend some time together. Margaret, Carolyn and Suzie went to Margaret's bedroom. Margaret was eager to show the paintings of Bill's wife and sons, but more importantly, the painting of her mother. Carolyn and Suzie were stunned at the painting of Mariah.

"Margaret, the painting looks just like you," Carolyn said.

Suzie sighed. "What is the box that she's holding? It's beautiful."

Before Margaret could answer, Carolyn said, "Your mother is dressed exactly like your Grandma Phoebe."

"That she is," Margaret said. "Suzie, you asked about the box. Let me show you something."

Margaret opened a dresser drawer and took out the box. Carolyn whispered, "Oh my goodness, Margaret. That's the box in the picture."

Margaret showed the contents of the box and carefully put them away. "What does all of this mean?" Carolyn asked.

"I don't know," Margaret answered. "I do know this visit has been unbelievable. God has opened so many things to me. Yet there is still so much that I want to know, but morning will come fast."

Margaret put her hand on Suzie's and uttered, "I pray that your visit with your Mammy is just as wonderful as this trip has been. Cody and Julie won't believe all that has taken place."

Margaret breathed heavily and shook her head. "George would have a fit if he knew we were here."

"I would have a fit too," Bill said, "but I knew in my spirit you were supposed to come."

Margaret smiled then returned her thoughts to George. "I miss him. My mind is filled with questions. Is he all right? When will they come home?"

Carolyn chuckled. "You had better pray that he has a day or so before he makes it home. Otherwise things could prove to be very bad."

Chapter Thirty-Seven
Thanks for the Surprise Gift

*D*ark clouds were beginning to form again as they returned from the Trading Post.

There was a light tapping on the door. Sara called out, "Supper will be served in ten minutes."

After supper, Lighted Path, Carolyn and Suzie said goodnight and went to bed. Margaret lingered with Bill in the living room. "Uncle Bill."

"Shhh." He put his hands on her shoulders and said, "Tomorrow will be a long day. I want you to go to bed. I am." He kissed her forehead and said goodnight. Again Margaret stared at the painting of Phoebe. In her mind she prayed for God to give her even more understanding. After several yawns, Margaret agreed that it was time for bed.

Margaret was up before daylight, and so was everyone else. The smell of bacon, coffee and hot biscuits was overwhelming. Margaret hurried to pack her things, anticipating the trip to Newport. She buckled her bag and draped her coat across the bed. Her eyes went immediately to her mother's painting. She stooped down in front of it and gently touched Mariah's face. "Mama," she whispered, "I love you. I sure don't understand why you kept so many things from us, but I'm sure there was a reason."

A soft knock on the door caused Margaret to stand. "Mrs. Black, breakfast is ready."

"I'll be right there." Margaret took her bag and coat and headed for the door. She put her hand on the doorknob and turned for one last look at her mother's portrait. She took a deep breath and opened the door. As Margaret entered the dining room, her eyes widened when she saw everyone was at the table. Bill stood and pulled her chair out. Margaret tightened her lips and said, "What is going on? I am usually the first one up. I must be getting old or something. Carolyn has been up two mornings in a row before me."

Bill laughed. "It's not age. Both Lighted Path and I were up before you. We'll place all the blame on exhaustion."

Suzie pushed a strand of hair behind her ear and announced, "I'm up early because I want to make it to Newport by dark. My Mammy will be so surprised."

"By dark? That would be perfect," Margaret said."

Bill blessed the food and asked a special prayer for safety and a prosperous journey over his guests.

After breakfast, Sara brought a bag filled with bacon and eggs, biscuits and fresh fried apple pies for the trip. Conley brought their horses and tied them in front of Bill's house. Carolyn, Suzie and Lighted Path said goodbye and mounted their horses. Margaret slowly filled her saddlebags. She thanked Sara for her wonderful care, and then, with tear filled eyes, she put her arms around Bill and whispered, "Thank you for everything. Words escape me when I try to come up with some appropriate way to say thank you for all you've done."

"I love you, Margaret. This has been a special time that only God could have given to me. I'll see you on your way back home."

"That you will. Thank you for giving me the box and the contents, and thank you for sharing some of your insight."

"The box was destined to be passed to you."

"I'll treasure it forever. I love you, Uncle Bill."

"I love you. I pray the weather will hold out for you."

Margaret mounted her horse, and the foursome turned and rode toward the end of town. Margaret stopped in front of the church, turned and waved once more to her uncle and Sara who were still standing on the porch.

Chapter Thirty-Eight
Ned Alexander

The sky teemed with slate gray clouds as the morning sprang forth. It was twenty-nine degrees with no wind. Shadowy silhouettes were all around as Lighted Path led the way off the trail into the massive woods. They traveled at a rapid, steady pace for an hour and a half, stopping only to allow their horses a breather. During these brief stops, they munched on the tasty biscuits and pies and discussed what Newport would hold.

Their travel pace remained brisk and true to Lighted Path's estimations. Shortly before nightfall, they spotted a modest log house in an open field, just outside Newport.

"That's it. That's it," Suzie shouted. "That's Mammy's house." Suzie put her hand on her chest and breathlessly exclaimed, "I can hardly breathe I'm so excited."

They rode through the field toward the house. White smoke spiraled from the rock chimneys on either side. A split rail fence surrounded the house. A small woodshed and a barn sat on the right side. As they approached, a big brown and white mixed-breed dog barked nonstop. In front of the woodshed, a tall Negro with a brown and white checked coat, dark pants and brown hat was chopping wood. His tightly kinked black and white hair showed that he was older. But his face had no wrinkles. He was wearing a pair of dark-colored gloves. He swung the double-bladed axe with a slow, even rhythm, spraying chips each time it came down. You could tell from the blows there was no shortage of strength from the six-foot-three woodsman.

As they drew near, he put the blade of the axe on the ground and rested his hand on top of the handle. He spit and said, "Howdy. Can I help you?"

Suzie slid off her horse and stepped toward him. She took her hat and scarf off and said, "Ned Alexander, I'm Suzie Chambers."

He squinted, took his hat off and muttered, "My Lord above. Miss Chambers, it good to see you. It's been a long time."

"It's good to see you. Are you staying with Mammy?"

"Yes, me and my son, Willie, stay here and help Aunt Nellie."

Suzie hesitated. "Willie?" she said. "I haven't seen him for some time now."

Ned shook his head, "He sure has made a good-looking man. I guess he took after his daddy."

Everyone laughed. Ned wiped the corner of his mouth. "I'll take care of your horses. Tie them there at the post. Miss Chambers, would you like for me to let Aunt Nellie know you're here?"

Suzie quickly responded, "No, thank you, Ned. I want to surprise her."

Everyone dismounted. Ned and Lighted Path took the horses to the watering barrel. Suzie looked at Margaret and Carolyn, put her hand on her stomach and took a deep breath. "I am so excited and nervous at the same time."

"I know exactly how you feel," Margaret muttered.

Chapter Thirty-Nine
Suzie and Mammy

Suzie led the way to the front porch, paused and looked around. A wooden, upright chair and a large stack of firewood were on the dark planked floor. Suzie held her breath and knocked. When the door opened, Suzie's eyes widened. She slowly took a step back. "Willie," she whispered.

He ran his tongue across his pearly white teeth and said softly, "As I live and breathe, if it isn't Suzie Chambers."

Margaret and Carolyn focused on the beautiful, light brown man standing before them. His skin was flawless, along with the rest of his being. A light blue shirt with a white pocket enhanced his handsome smile and body. His black pants lay on top of his dusty, black leather boots.

"Who is it?" someone called out from behind him.

His sexy, round, dark eyes examined the three women standing in front of him. "It's three of the most beautiful women that my eyes have ever had the pleasure of beholding."

Suzie started past Willie, who had not moved. She paused when her body brushed against his, stared into his eyes and said, "Will you please excuse us, Willie?"

He stepped aside. "Forgive me. I'm not used to such exquisiteness."

"I want to see my Mammy now."

Willie moved from the door and uttered, "By all means, Miss Chambers."

Suzie stepped in front of the bedroom door and stopped. "Mammy," she said softly.

A heavyset, elderly, black woman with white hair was lying in a small bed that sat beside the window. Upon hearing Suzie's voice, her eyes sprang open and she sat up. "Baby Suzie. Is it really you?"

Tears welled up in Suzie's eyes as she took a step forward and stopped. "Yes, Mammy, it's Suzie."

The old lady opened her arms, and she too began to cry tears of joy. As they embraced, Suzie said "Mammy" repeatedly.

Mammy held Suzie's face in her hands and kissed her cheeks. "Lord be praised. My Baby Suzie has come before I go home. I've been praying for this moment for ten years." She took Suzie's hands and said, "Just let me look at you a minute."

Suzie ran her hand across her hair, "I must look a mess. We've ridden hard all day to get here by dark."

Mammy smiled. "My eyes have never seen a more beautiful sight."

She looked around Suzie at Margaret and Carolyn standing at the foot of the bed. Suzie stood and motioned for them to come closer. "Mammy, I want you to meet my dear friends, Carolyn Morris and Margaret Black."

Margaret put her hand out to shake Mammy's. "Lord, child, give me a hug. Any friend of Suzie's is a friend of mine."

Margaret smiled and embraced the old woman.

Suzie sat on the edge of the bed. Mammy called for Willie. "Willie, why don't you get our guests a chair?"

Willie looked at Margaret and Carolyn, nodded and said, "I'd be delighted to do so."

In only a moment, he brought two rough-finished wooden chairs. "Could I get you ladies something to drink? We have some fresh ground coffee, tea or some Kentucky whiskey Daddy bought at the store in Newport."

Mammy frowned and scolded, "Willie, that's enough of that. You don't offer proper ladies Kentucky whiskey. Carolyn, Margaret, forgive Willie for his foolishness. He's a joker. He meant no disrespect."

Willie grinned. "Mammy's right. I was only teasing. Would you like coffee or tea?"

"I would love a cup of hot tea," Margaret said.

"I want coffee," Carolyn said quickly.

"And you, Miss Chambers?" he asked.

"I think I'll have a cup of hot tea. How about you, Mammy?" Suzie asked.

Mammy leaned back against the pillows. "I don't care for anything, thank you."

Suzie stroked Mammy's hair. "How long have you been sick?"

Mammy coughed and uttered through a strained voice, "How did you know I was sick?"

"Abe Turner, who owns Twin Gates Plantation, said he saw Ned when he passed through Newport a while back. Ned told him that you were pretty sick."

"Well, I have been feeling pretty bad."

Suzie kissed her forehead. "I love you. More than you know."

"I love you, Baby Suzie."

"Is there anything I can do for you or get you?"

"No, thank you though." She paused and muttered, "How's your daddy?"

"He's fine. He didn't want me to come on this trip because of all the fighting."

Willie brought the drinks and served the women. "Tell me, ladies, did you see any Union or Confederate soldiers on your way here?"

Margaret sipped her tea and replied. "No we didn't. Maybe there're all in Townsend. Union and Confederate troops are assembling along the Tennessee River. And renegade Indians are everywhere."

Willie shook his head. "It's not safe for three women and an old Indian man to be out with those kinds of goings on."

"Willie," Mammy said, "go bring my guests' things in and show them where they can sleep."

Willie nodded and left the room.

"I'm sorry we don't have a bigger house," Mammy said. "Suzie, you can sleep in here with me. Willie will bring a cot in for you. Carolyn, you and Margaret can sleep in the other bedroom. Ned and Willie can make a bed in the living room. I'll have Willie heat you some water for a bath, while Ned fixes supper."

"A bath sounds heavenly." Suzie sighed.

"It's just a tin washtub," Mammy said, "but you'll be able to sponge off."

After bringing their things in, Willie fetched the washtub and began filling it with water.

"Willie," Margaret said, "Carolyn and I will help with the water."

"No, thanks, Miss Black. It won't take me but a few minutes."

Margaret shook her head. "But it's so cold outside, and besides, three working is better than one. The faster the water is brought in and heated, the faster I can get a bath."

Chapter Forty
Ned Confronts Willie

*N*ed made fried potatoes, scrambled eggs and fried cornbread cakes for supper. After their baths, Ned called them to come and eat. The women sat down in rough-finished chairs and slid them under a table made from two wide planks that were set on two sawhorses. Ned quickly poured cold milk that he brought in from the springhouse. The blessing was asked and the conversation swiftly turned to how delicious the meal was. "These potatoes are wonderful!" Carolyn said.

Suzie ate in the room with Mammy. "Suzie has anticipated this trip for some time now," Margaret remarked, wanting to make small talk to feel more at ease.

"Miss Chambers' daddy sure has been good to us," Ned uttered. "He gave us our free papers and helped us get this place. He's a good man."

Margaret tilted her head and asked, "Why did you buy here in Newport and not closer to Charleston?"

Ned took a bite of cornbread and replied, "I think Mr. Chambers knew the person who owned this place. I never fully understood. That was mainly between Aunt Nellie and Mr. Chambers. I call her Aunt Nellie, but she was a mama to me. She raised me. My wife, Kayla, was sent to work at the Albert Smith plantation. That was fifteen years ago. I don't know if she is alive or dead. The Smith plantation was somewhere in Louisiana."

Margaret frowned. "Was it Mr. Chambers who sent her to Louisiana?"

"It was Mrs. Chambers who sent her away."

Willie put his fork down and growled, "Why don't you tell Mrs. Black why she sent her away, Daddy?"

Margaret quickly stated, "That's all right. I was just curious."

Willie's jaw tightened. "I'll tell you why. Mr. Chambers was sending for mama almost every night to warm his bed. My mama is a beautiful woman, like you, but beauty was a curse to her. Not only did Mr. Chambers send for her, but so did the overseers."

Ned stood and boldly stated, "That's enough, Willie. I'm sorry, Mrs. Black. My son has a way of shooting his mouth off when he needs to keep it shut."

Carolyn and Margaret glanced at each other and then at Ned. "That's okay, Ned. There are times we all have to vent. I understand the anguish of being put in a position that binds your hands. So there is no need to apologize."

"He just needs to control his venting in front of our guests."

Willie tightened his lips and pushed his chair under the table. "I'm sorry, Miss Black, Miss Morris."

Margaret wasn't sure what to say. Willie grabbed his coat and hat from a hook on the wall, put it on and headed toward the front door. Suzie was standing in the doorway of Mammy's bedroom as Willie passed. He stopped, and with eyes of stone, he stared at her, tightened his fist and then went out the front door.

The look in Ned's eyes showed that Suzie must have heard what Willie had said. Suzie quietly closed the bedroom door and moved slowly toward the table. She took hold of the back of a chair and sighed. "Mammy went to sleep." She rubbed her thumb against the wood and said, "Ned, I don't want you to worry about what Willie said. He has always had a different nature than you. I'm not proud of what my father did to Kayla. It tore my mother's heart out. He wasn't discreet with his adultery. After Mother sent Kayla away, another slave took her place. I don't approve or excuse that kind of action from anyone." Suzie straightened her posture. "I just wanted you to know that. I also wanted you to know I understand the pain that Willie feels. It wasn't easy to see it happening."

"Why . . . why thank you, Miss. Chambers."

Suzie nodded and sat down. "Margaret, Carolyn, did you enjoy Ned's fried pies?"

Breathing a sigh of relief, Carolyn responded, "They were the best that I have ever tasted."

Margaret was quick to agree. Margaret and Carolyn cleared the table while Suzie asked Ned about Mammy's condition.

"She's been sick for some time now. It started with a cough, back last winter. The doctor gave her some medicine, but it hasn't seemed to help. I'm really concerned."

Suddenly Ned jumped up and said, "Miss Margaret, Miss Carolyn, you don't be doing no dishes. You're our guests. You come on over here and make yourselves comfortable."

Margaret held her hand up. "Thank you just the same, Ned; however, I have been sitting my horse all day. I prefer to stand."

"I sure do appreciate that."

"Ned," Margaret said, "You mentioned a bit ago that Lighted Path went into Newport. Did he say when he would be back? I'm beginning to worry."

"Yeah. I was thinking the same thing," Carolyn said.

Ned got a corn-shuck broom from the corner and began to sweep the floor. Suzie quickly took it from him and stated, "We're not on the plantation any longer, so I'll sweep the floor."

Ned stepped back. "Oh Lord, have mercy if Aunt Nellie were to see you sweeping the floor."

Suzie stopped and looked at Ned. "Why don't you go check on Willie?"

"Yeah, I guess I had better," Ned muttered.

Margaret dried her hands and asked, "Ned, did Lighted Path say why he was going into Newport?"

Ned rubbed his head. "No, he didn't." Ned put his coat, hat and gloves on and went outside.

Carolyn and Margaret fixed their eyes on Suzie. Realizing they were staring at her, Suzie put the broom down, put her hands on her hips and asked, "What's the matter, haven't you ever seen anyone sweep a floor before?"

They moved close to Suzie. Margaret squinted and remarked. "You don't have that mental sickness where a person has six or seven personalities do you?"

Suzie frowned. "Why, Margaret Black, what kind of a question is that?"

"What kind of question? You have gone from one extreme to another—from a Southern aristocrat to sweeping a plank floor. I don't get it."

"When I need to be an aristocrat, I will. If I need to sweep the floor, I can do that as well. I don't know why that would be so shocking to you."

Margaret eyes widened. "Because the way I am today is the way I'll be tomorrow."

Carolyn shook her head. "I have to agree with Margaret on this one, Suzie."

"What you see is what you get with me as well," Suzie informed. "You just might see a different role today than tomorrow."

Carolyn looked out the window. "I'm beginning to worry about Lighted Path."

Margaret was quick to say if he wasn't back in thirty minutes, she was going to look for him.

"You can't be out in the dark and freezing cold," Suzie said. "Besides, I'm sure he can find his way back by himself."

"I wonder why he didn't tell us that he was going." Margaret muttered.

Suzie said she was going to read for a while.

Margaret suddenly said, "Carolyn, get your coat. You and I are going out for a ride—"

Before Carolyn could make her case about the cold, Suzie interrupted, "Margaret Black, if you're going out, you take Ned with you. I mean it."

"What if he doesn't want to go?"

"He will," Suzie insisted.

"What about me?" Carolyn asked. "What if I don't want to go?"

Margaret put her coat on and said, "Then stay here. I'm going."

"I was only kidding," Carolyn mumbled as she put her coat on.

"Come on, Margaret!" Suzie said. "At least wait until Ned or Willie comes back." Suzie grabbed her coat, lit a lantern and said, "If you're not going to listen, let's at least look and see if Ned is at the barn."

When they opened the door, a gust of cold air shot through Margaret's bones. There wasn't a cloud in the sky. A large, full moon was surrounded by a million twinkling stars. "Lord above, it's so cold," Margaret exclaimed.

Carolyn wrapped her wool scarf around her head and face. Nearing the barn, the women heard a rustle coming from the trees. Margaret put her hand on her pistol and called out, "Who's there?"

"It's Ned, don't shoot."

The women breathed a sigh of relief when Ned approached. "What in the name of goodness are you doing, Ned?" Suzie asked. "You almost scared the life out of me."

"What in the world are you women doing out here? It's freezing."

Margaret responded, "I've decided I'm going to look for Lighted Path."

"There's no need of that," Ned said. "Miss Margaret, if you'll come with me, I'll show you where he's at."

Suzie urged, "You all go on, I'll stay here with Mammy. She and I will love the alone time." She paused and then asked, "By the way, Ned, did you find Willie?"

"Yeah. He went to visit Sally. She's a woman he courts from time to time. We'll be back in a few minutes," Ned assured Suzie.

Chapter Forty-One
Dance in the Dark

$\mathcal{N}$ed led them through the bare oak trees as quietly as possible. Margaret pulled her scarf over her nose and mouth to prevent the cold air from hurting her lungs. They had only gone a short distance; however, it seemed a long way in the frigid weather. Ned put his hand up and whispered, "We're almost there so follow my lead."

Margaret could hear moans and chanting in the distance. As they continued forward, the chanting grew louder. Suddenly, Ned stopped and squatted behind some bushes. Margaret and Carolyn did the same. A shadowy blue haze infiltrated the forest. The women were immobilized as their eyes fixed on the sight before them. Margaret's head began to spin as she watched Lighted Path arrayed in his long eagle cape, bearskin boots and a dark fur hat with eagle feathers dangling from his long white hair, dancing in a small clearing surrounded with an audience of tall straight oaks and the radiance of the lights of heaven. After a few minutes, Lighted Path lifted his spear over his head and cried out in the Cherokee tongue, "Great Eagle of Heaven and Earth, I accept your wisdom. Thy will be done." With the strength of a young warrior, Lighted Path knelt on one knee, and with his other one bent, he brought the spear down and broke it in the middle. Margaret gasped and clamped her hand on Carolyn's forearm. Lighted Path stood slowly, lifted his eyes and hands toward heaven and stood in silence for a few moments. He then began to move his arms and body from side to side and the chanting resumed.

Ned looked at Margaret and motioned for them to move back. In silence they moved away. When they were out of hearing, Ned stopped and said, "Margaret, I understand you have Indian blood in your veins, so when we get back to the house, maybe you can explain all that to me."

Chapter Forty-Two
Unwelcome Guests

*B*ack at the cabin, Suzie was reading to Mammy. Ned immediately stoked the fire and spoke to Mammy. Mammy pushed up on her pillows and asked, "Ned, do we have any more of the apple cider that Mrs. Branch gave us?"

Ned pulled his hat off. "Yes, Aunt Nellie, we have plenty left. Could I heat you a cup?"

"If you would. I love the smell of it in my house. So sweet, and the smell lingers for a couple of days. Why don't you fix our guests a cup?"

Ned smiled, tilted his head and asked, "Ladies, do you like your cider warm or hot?"

After serving the cider, Ned asked Margaret about the dance that Lighted Path was doing.

"I'm not sure," she said. "It could mean many things. It depends on what the individual need for the ceremony is. I do know what he said in Cherokee and that was, 'God, Great Eagle of Heaven and Earth, I accept your wisdom. Thy will be done.'"

Carolyn stood, put her hands on her hips and groaned as she stretched from side to side. "I think I'm going to retire for the night." She went in to say goodnight to Mammy. "Mammy, or should I call you Nellie or Mrs. Alexander?"

Mammy took Carolyn's hand. "Please call me Mammy," she insisted.

Carolyn patted the top of her hand. Mammy smiled and said, "God bless you, child. I can feel through the warmth of your hand that you're such a caring person. Are you married?"

Carolyn blushed. "I was married, but my husband was killed."

"You will marry again in the near future. You can count on that."

Carolyn gave a tight-lipped grin. "I accept that insight. Thank you."

"Do you mind if I say a prayer over you since I'm holding your hand?"

"Mind? I welcome your prayer."

Suzie stood at the foot of the bed as Mammy prayed. Margaret smiled, hearing that Mammy shared her thoughts about Carolyn finding a mate soon.

Carolyn went to bed. Suzie sat by the fireplace reading the book of poems that Bill had given her. Ned set the cot up for Suzie. By that time, Margaret was ready for bed also. Suzie pushed the cot beside Mammy's bed and lay down. Margaret went to the other side of the bed to say goodnight. Mammy stretched her hand to Margaret. When Margaret took her hand, Mammy's eyes widened and she gasped. Suzie quickly asked if something was wrong. Mammy's response puzzled both Margaret and Suzie.

"No, Baby Suzie, nothing's wrong. To the contrary, something is exceptionally right." Mammy patted the bed for Margaret to sit. Mammy gently laid her hand on Margaret's. She looked at Margaret's hand and then stared into her eyes. Margaret tightened her brows and questioned, "What is it, Mammy?"

Mammy slowly shook her head. "Something very unique will soon take place in your life. I don't know what, but it will be soon. Your husband will be home soon. Goodnight, child," Mammy muttered.

Margaret glanced at Suzie and left the room. She lay on her back with her hands on her stomach. She wanted to wake Carolyn and release the emotions that were overwhelming, but didn't. She knew they would have to leave soon in order to accomplish the task before her. Lighted Path had also added to her wonderment. She may not have known the reason for the chant and dance in the moonlight, but she did know it was significant.

Margaret had barely dozed off when she gasped and sat upright, cocking her head, listening for something. She heard horses' hoofs stomping. Instantly, she tensed. Quietly she slipped out of bed and reached for her pistol.

Carolyn moaned, "Margaret, what are you doing?"

"Shhh, I heard horses outside the window."

Suddenly the sound of unshod horses pounded against the earth. Margaret quietly opened the door to find Ned and Willie with their rifles in hand. Suzie hurried through the bedroom door.

"Ned," she whispered.

Willie was standing by the door when she came out of the room. He whispered, "Miss Chambers, can you shoot this?"

He handed her a rifle. By that time, Carolyn had joined them in the living room. She too had her pistol. "Margaret, can you tell how many are out there?" Carolyn asked.

"There's at least a dozen. It's too hard to tell, but they are Indians."

"How do you know?"

"Their horses are unshod."

They all gasped when they heard a horse come up on the porch. The horse stopped at the front door. The snorting was loud. After a long minute, the horse whinnied and stomped its hooves on the planks. Then suddenly the horse turned and went off the porch. They could hear the Indians talking, but no one understood the language. A sigh of relief was breathed when they heard the beating hooves going away from the house. Ned put his head to the door and waited to make sure that no one was outside. After a few minutes of silence, Ned took the bar from the door and slowly pushed it open. He grabbed a torch at the end of the porch, and lit it. Margaret, Ned, Willie and Carolyn looked around the house, but saw nothing.

Margaret gasped and breathlessly shouted, "Lighted Path! We've got to find him."

"Miss Margaret," Ned said, "we're not going out in them woods tonight. I'm surprised the Indians didn't try to come in. What was the point of circling the house and one bringing his horse on the porch? It sounded like the horse's nose was pushed against the door the way it was snorting."

"I didn't understand their language. It wasn't Cherokee," Margaret said.

"Do you think they'll be back?" Suzie asked.

Willie rubbed his temple. "I don't know," he said. "What do you think, Dad?"

"I think we need to get in out of this cold."

Inside, Ned told Willie that they would take turns watching and listening for anything that might move. Willie offered to take the first watch. Ned insisted that he get some sleep.

"Dad, you get some rest."

"Willie," Ned snapped, "I said I'd do the watch. You go to bed and sleep the whisky off. If Indians or soldiers were to come around, I need you with a clear head."

Chapter Forty-Three
The Smell of Coffee

*E*arly morning sunlight streamed in through the kitchen window. Ned and Willie were having a quiet cup of coffee, waiting for the women to awaken.

"Good morning, Miss Margaret," Ned said. He moved to pull her chair out and hurried to get her a cup of coffee.

"You didn't have to pour me coffee Ned, but thank you anyway."

Carolyn came through the bedroom door and sniffed the air. "My heavens, the coffee is breathtaking."

Ned started to get up, but Willie beat him to it. "Let me do the honors. Did you ladies rest well after our excitement last night?"

Margaret replied, "I think I speak for me and Carolyn, we hardly slept at all."

Carolyn glanced toward Mammy's door and chuckled. "I take it that Suzie and Mammy are resting just fine."

"After I finish my coffee, I'm going out to look for Lighted Path. He's another reason I didn't sleep."

Those words barely left Margaret's mouth, when they heard someone on the porch. Ned reached for his pistol and stood. A light knock on the door caused Margaret to tense. Ned peeked through the window. "Well, Miss Margaret, we don't have to go looking after all. Lighted Path has arrived."

Margaret put her coffee cup down and stood. Ned removed the bar and opened the door. Lighted Path nodded and said good morning.

"Lighted Path," Margaret said, "I've been worried sick about you. Where have you been?"

"I needed some time alone. So I went into the forest."

"There were some Indians here last night. Did you see anything at all?"

"I saw about ten or fifteen men, but I couldn't see their clothing or paint."

"You saw them? Where were you?" Carolyn questioned.

"I slept in the barn under the hay."

Ned pulled a chair out and told him to sit down. Willie got him a cup of coffee. As they sat and talked, suddenly a scream from Mammy's bedroom drew them all. Margaret swiftly opened the door to find Suzie lying on Mammy's chest screaming. "No, no, no. Mammy! Mammy!"

Ned hurried into the room. "Aunt Nellie. Oh, Lord." He groaned. Willie hurried to comfort his daddy.

Margaret and Carolyn helped raise Suzie up.

"She must have passed while I was asleep," Suzie cried. "I didn't hear her. I should have stayed awake."

Suzie's body trembled as she sobbed. Ned and Willie were visibly shaken as well.

Ned sent Willie to tell their neighbors about Mammy's passing. Suzie and Margaret rode into town to find a coffin and someone to dig a grave. Some friends came that night to sit with Ned and Willie. Suzie didn't sleep at all that night. The next day, at noon, they buried Mammy on a hill near the house.

Chapter Forty-Four
Willie's Kiss

The sun had been darkened and snow clouds filled the sky, casting shadows over the forested foothills. A slight breeze had picked up and the temperature was dropping.

Suzie had gone to thank neighbors for the food they had brought. Carolyn was resting and so was Ned. Margaret felt restless, so she bundled up and went to the barn to think, check on the horses and have some privacy. She climbed the ladder to the loft, lay back on the hay and went to sleep. Her eyes sprang open when she heard the barn door open. She tried not to move, not sure who had entered the barn. It was Willie bringing his horse inside to feed him. In a few minutes she heard another horse nearing the barn. The door opened, and she heard Suzie talking to her horse as she entered. She released the reins and closed the door. Margaret started to call out to Suzie, but stopped when Willie came out from the stall next to where Suzie was standing.

"You always had a way with horses," Willie said.

Suzie jerked and took a deep breath. "Willie, you startled me."

He took the reins from Suzie and insisted that he put her horse in the stall. When he took the reins, Suzie swiftly turned to leave the barn. To Margaret's surprise, Willie dropped the reins and seized Suzie's arm. She struggled to break free from his hold. Margaret was going to call out for him to release her, but stopped when Willie pulled Suzie tight to his body and kissed her lips. At first Suzie struggled, but then she kissed Willie back and passionately. Margaret sank back into the hay and said nothing.

Willie was trying to kiss her again, but Suzie tried to push away. "I can't do this, Willie. Not again. I only let you kiss me because my heart is broken over Mammy."

"I've tasted your lips for ten years. I've felt your body pressing against mine. I hated your daddy for sending us away. He could lay with my mama, but I was forbid to love you. I didn't want to use you. I loved you."

Suzie gasped. "You know that we could have never married. I was young and you were younger."

Willie grabbed her shoulders and uttered, "I was old enough for you to have my baby. I hated your daddy for sending you away to have our baby, and then sending our baby away. I didn't even get to see our little girl. I gave her a name. I call her Freedom. My mama always told me there is nothing more precious than being free. I can't tell you how she knew anything about freedom. She was anything but free. Because of our baby, your daddy sent us here with our free papers. He could have cared less about our freedom. He wanted me away from you. Everything was taken away from me. You and our baby. She would have been ten years old in the spring. Tell me that you didn't want our baby and me. Tell me."

Suzie closed her eyes and lowered her head. "Of course, I wanted you and our baby. But it never could have worked."

"Love never fails, Suzie. I still love you the same as I did back then. Can you tell me that you don't love me?"

"I can't love you, Willie. I can't."

"Why? Because I don't have a big plantation and fine things to offer you? Is that it?"

"I don't need your money. I have plenty of money." Suzie pulled from his hold. "Willie, you were so beautiful and even more beautiful now. I've thought of you and grieved for you and cried over our sin. I wept a million tears over my beautiful baby girl who was pulled from my arms as soon as she was born and sent off to someone else to raise."

Willie took her shoulders and said, "Not just your baby, our baby. What sin are you talking about? I loved you and still do. Is that a sin? Stay here with me, Suzie. I'll build us a house or I'll be content to slip into your bedroom, or anywhere I can spend time with you."

"Day after tomorrow I'm leaving for Washington, D.C.," Suzie said with her head lowered. "There's a stage leaving Thursday morning. My plans were to go back to Fort Howard with Carolyn and Margaret. However, I heard about the stage that's going to Washington and decided that I want to get on with my life. I only came to Newport because of Mammy."

Willie released her shoulders and shifted his eyes from left to right. "I don't believe you."

"Well, it's true."

"You really don't care for me?" Willie asked with tears in his eyes.

Suzie gently wiped a tear from his cheek and said, "It's over. I'm sorry, Willie. I know you'll find someone else. How about that Sally you went to visit? Maybe you can get with her."

Willie tightened his fist and growled through clenched teeth, "You're the only woman I'll ever truly love. You were the first woman I made love to and the only woman I've made love to. My love for you is that strong. How can you act so cold toward me?"

Suzie put her hand on Willie's chest. "Society will never let your beautiful, brown skin and my white skin go together. I'm sorry." Suzie took a couple of steps, stopped and looked at Willie. "Goodbye, Willie," she whispered and turned to go, but Willie grabbed her and pressed his lips hard against hers. Suzie struggled to break free, but Willie was too strong. He picked her up and went into one of the stalls. She was fighting him and telling him to stop. He stumbled and fell with her into the hay.

"Stop, Willie! Stop it!" Suzie groaned.

Willie held her arms down and sat on top of her. "You stop it, Suzie. If you're so willing to act as though I'm nothing to you, then I don't mind taking you one last time."

He forced his lips on hers. She struggled for a moment and then relaxed in the hay. Margaret didn't know what to do but keep quiet. Suzie wasn't fighting, but she wasn't participating either. After a while, Willie groaned in ecstasy and his body relaxed. Suzie quickly pushed him off her.

"You were wonderful," he moaned.

Suzie sat up, slapped his face and through tears shouted, "I hate you for this! I hate you!"

"Suzie, I thought that you really wanted me when you stopped struggling."

Suzie stood and straightened her clothes. "I stopped struggling because I knew I couldn't stop you." She rushed out of the barn, leaving the door open. Willie lay in the hay and cried like a baby.

Margaret was stunned by what she had heard. Her emotions were torn. Should she have done or said something? At that point, all she wanted to do was get out of the loft and back to the house. For now, all she could do was lie in silence. After a few minutes, Willie saddled his horse, led him through the barn door, slammed it shut and rode away. Margaret gradually stood and looked around. In haste, she went down the steps and out the back door so as not to be seen.

As Margaret hurried through the yard to the porch, Carolyn opened the door and said. "I was just coming to look for you. Where have you been?"

"You were asleep, so I went out for some time alone." Margaret glanced around and asked, "Where's Suzie?"

"She came in a few minutes ago and said that she needed to lie down for a while."

"What about Lighted Path?"

"He and Ned are sleeping like babies. I'm not sure about Willie."

Chapter Forty-Five
Don't Go

That night at supper, Margaret and Carolyn warmed leftovers that were brought by friends after the funeral. Margaret knocked on Suzie's door. "Suzie, supper's ready."

She didn't respond. Margaret knocked lightly. Still there was no response. She opened the door to check on her. Suzie was lying in the center of the bed—on her back staring at the ceiling. Her arms were lying straight by her side and her legs were hanging off the side of the bed.

"Suzie, you need to come and eat. I know you didn't eat breakfast, and you were gone during lunch."

Suzie didn't respond, only stared at the ceiling without as much as a blink of her eyes. Margaret closed the door and sat on the bed beside her. "How are you doing?" she asked. "I know that you've had a hard blow, and if I were put in the same position I would probably be lying here doing the same thing."

Margaret put her hand on her arm; still Suzie didn't respond. Margaret patted her arm. "I'll save you a plate for later . . . when you're ready." Margaret stood to leave the room.

Suzie whispered, "I loved Mammy more than my own life. She was good and so loving to everyone."

Margaret turned and waited for Suzie to continue. She watched as Suzie lay lifeless across the bed.

"Please don't go. I need a friend," Suzie said.

Margaret sat beside Suzie.

"I would sit up," Suzie groaned, "but I don't have the energy."

"That's fine. Why don't you talk and rest at the same time?"

"Margaret, have you ever been so torn in your emotions you feel like you're losing your mind?"

"Yes, many times."

Suzie groaned as she sat upright. "Mammy was the only true mother I've ever known. When I needed anything, she was the one who was always there for me. She could see right through me. I could hide nothing from her."

A light tap caused Suzie to take a deep breath. Carolyn slightly opened the door and peeked inside. "Come on in," Suzie said.

"I thought I would remind you two that supper is getting cold." From their somber looks, Carolyn knew something was wrong.

"Come sit down," Suzie said. "There's something I want to tell you both."

Carolyn pulled a straight-backed chair close to the bed. Suzie looked at Carolyn and Margaret and sighed,

"I've thought it over and decided I'm not going back to Fort Howard."

Carolyn frowned and asked, "Why? All your things are there. What will you do?"

"There's a stage leaving Newport Thursday morning for Washington, D.C. I wanted to ask if you and Margaret would send my things when you get back to Cherokee. I have plenty of money with me. I'll do some shopping for essentials until my trunks arrive. I have a friend who lives there; I'll give you her address."

"What about your carriage?" Margaret asked.

"Do you mind if I leave it at your place? You may have it if you like."

"I'll just leave it in the barn until you can come and get it."

"Thank you, Margaret."

"We'll sure miss you," Carolyn said.

Suzie took their hands. "I'll miss you. However, I promise to come back and visit."

Margaret sighed. "We'll miss you. I'll send your things when we get back home." Margaret smiled. "I had hoped you would go visit Desan with us."

That brought a much-needed smile. "I think I'll go with Suzie," Carolyn joked.

"When will you be leaving?" Suzie asked.

"Thursday morning. We'll all leave at the same time, even if it's in different directions.

That night Ned asked Suzie if she wanted to go through Mammy's belongings and find something of hers to take with her. She found a brooch made of porcelain and ivory. Before bedtime, Suzie sat by the fire and read. Carolyn borrowed a book from Suzie and joined her. Margaret cleaned her pistol as she and Lighted Path discussed the trip ahead. Ned sat snoozing with his chin propped against his chest. Suddenly, the sound of heavy boots pounded on the porch. "Ned!" someone called out. Ned jerked his head, grabbed his pistol and called out, "Who is it?"

"Matt Fox."

Ned hurried to open the door. Matt Fox stood there holding Willie upright. "Willie had way too much to drink, so I brought him home."

Ned put his arm around Willie's waist and helped him inside. "Thanks for getting him home, Matt. I'll take it from here."

"Okay. I do have to get back. Nellie is sure going to be missed. I've never known Willie to have more than a casual drink. I figure Nellie's death drove him a little further into the bottle tonight."

"Yeah, he loved Aunt Nellie."

"If there's anything you need, let me know."

"I will and thanks again."

Ned brought Willie inside. As they came through the door, Willie began to cry and reach his hand toward Suzie. "Suzie, I need you, Suzie."

Ned squeezed Willie's waist and growled, "Shut up, boy. Your mouth is always bigger than it needs to be." Ned took Willie into Mammy's bedroom and closed the door. Lighted Path put his coat on and went outside. Carolyn looked at Suzie and asked, "What's going on with Willie? Why would he say those things to you?"

Suzie looked nervously from left to right, clearly shaken by Willie's actions. She grabbed her coat and ran out the door. Carolyn started after her, but Margaret caught her arm as she went by.

"Let her go," Margaret said.

Carolyn frowned and asked. "What? Can't you see she needs us?"

"I can see she needs some time alone."

Carolyn raised her hands and asked, "What is going on here? Am I the only one who doesn't have a clue?"

"She's upset. Maybe she needs a good cry."

Carolyn groaned. "I'm totally confused. Losing Mammy, which in itself is devastating enough . . . but their actions are not those of someone who has lost a loved one. Willie is acting like a discarded lover and Suzie is responding accordingly. And your actions, Margaret Black, are not normal either. If you know something, you better tell me."

Margaret told Carolyn all that she had heard in the barn.

"My heavens, Margaret, remember the night Suzie was out on the porch in the freezing cold crying her eyes out?"

"Of course I remember."

"Do you suppose that had to do with Willie and the baby?"

Margaret sighed. "More than likely."

"I wonder if Ned knows about the baby."

"Of course he does. Ned is Willie's father. Suzie's father moved them here to keep Willie and Suzie apart; therefore, he must know."

"Should you tell Suzie you know what happened?"

Margaret eyes widened. "No!"

Carolyn chuckled and shook her head.

"What's so funny?" Margaret asked.

"This trip! We were going to visit Uncle Bill, find out what we could, another day with Suzie to Newport and head home."

"I know." Margaret grinned. "Carolyn, would you like to look again at the things Uncle Bill gave me?"

"I would."

Margaret sat the box between her and Carolyn on the bed. She gently touched then opened it. "It sends a chill down my spine to touch it."

Carolyn reached for the necklace. "Let me fasten it for you. I want to see what it looks like on the third generation of Thawbush women."

Margaret stood in front of the mirror and Carolyn put it around her neck. "Well, what do you think?"

Margaret gently touched the eagle claw. "None of this seems real. It's like a dream." She took the feather and the leather pouch out and looked inside the bag. "What do you suppose these ashes are from?"

Carolyn scratched her head. "I'm almost afraid to know. A mystery may be a blessing."

Margaret shrugged. "I don't know either; however, I do thank God for giving them to me."

Margaret placed them back inside the box. "Maybe one day we'll know the meaning. Until then, I'll put them away."

Chapter Forty-Six
Ned Shares a Secret

𝒩ed was sitting at the table when Margaret and Carolyn came into the living room. Suzie still hadn't returned. "Come sit with me," Ned said. He put his hands together. "I know you're wondering about Willie's actions toward Miss Suzie. You know that we used to live on one of the Chambers' plantations. Miss Chambers is ten years older than Willie. When he was born, he was the most beautiful baby that my eyes have ever seen. Miss Suzie took care of him. Aunt Nellie let her hold him, change him, bathe him and play with him.

"As he grew, they played together all the time. When Willie was sixteen, he and Miss Suzie were playing in the barn. Willie kissed her. Then she kissed him. One of the hands came and told me. I went in and broke them up. I told Miss Suzie they would sell Willie if Mr. Chambers found out about them kissing. I thought that everything had stopped. When Willie had just turned twenty, Miss Suzie and he were in the barn one day and I walked in on them. They were, well you know, like man and wife. I didn't know what to do. Miss Suzie got pregnant. Even though Suzie was thirty years old, her daddy controlled her every move. When Mr. Chambers found out, he was going to sell us, but Miss Suzie begged him not to. She promised to stop seeing him. That pleased her daddy. He sent her to England to have the baby. He came to Newport and bought this place for us. Willie had to promise to never try and see Miss Suzie again. When he promised that he wouldn't, Mr. Chambers gave us our free papers and moved us here. That was ten years ago. They haven't seen or heard from each other until the other day when you all arrived here. We found out that the baby was a girl. Mr. Chambers gave the baby to someone in England to raise. At least there she's free. We swore never to talk about it here and we haven't. Willie grieved over that woman like someone had died. He loved Aunt Nellie, but she wasn't the reason for his drunkenness. It's another kind of love that makes a person hurt like he's hurting. I felt I owed you some kind of explanation. Please don't judge them. They were so in love."

"Thank you for telling us," Margaret said. "And we don't judge them. There is only one judge, Ned, and it's not me or Carolyn."

"I know she wanted to see her Mammy before she died, but I wish she hadn't come here. Her daddy would have never let her come, had he known. She told him she was going to Washington but didn't mention dropping by here first."

About that time Suzie came through the door. She stared at them and they stared at her. She looked at Ned and asked, "You told them?"

He rubbed his chin and nodded. "I felt they deserved an explanation."

Suzie took her coat off and put it on the hook beside the back door. "I was going to tell you, but I was afraid you would think I was some awful person and I'm not."

Margaret put her hand on Suzie's arm and assured her they didn't feel that way.

"Suzie," Carolyn said, "is that what you were crying about that night on Margaret's porch?"

Suzie nodded yes.

At that moment, someone knocked on the door. Ned opened it. Matt Fox smiled and said, "I bet you didn't expect to see me again so soon."

Ned shook his head. "No, I didn't. Is there something wrong?"

"No. Mack at the stage office said that Miss Chambers was wanting to take the stage to Washington D.C."

Suzie called out, "Yes, I do."

"Well, Mack wanted me to let you know the stage came in today, and it will be leaving in the morning at seven thirty."

Suzie glanced to Margaret and Carolyn and said, "That's great. I'll be there."

Ned closed the door and looked at Suzie. "I think in the morning, before Willie wakes up will be perfect."

Margaret asked, "Where is Lighted Path?'

No one knew. Margaret, Carolyn and Susie gathered at the table while Ned went to find Lighted Path.

"It's been rewarding to meet you two," Suzie said. "What will you do next, Margaret?"

"I need to find the old woman Desan. I pray finding her will give me more answers to my quest. I want to make sense out of the dreams and the man, Eagle Claw, we saw at the cemetery. I would really like to make some sense out of Grandma Phoebe's blessing over my life . . . about the phoenix rising out of the ashes. I guess as much as anything, I want to know why Mama and Grandma Phoebe weren't open about our past."

"How about you, Carolyn?"

"I don't know. I hope your Mammy's words over me will swiftly come to pass. Sometimes I get so tired of being alone. Of course, Margaret will suffice as my friend, but not as a husband."

"And what about you, Suzie?" Margaret asked.

"I'm really not sure. I have all this built up inside about meeting with President Lincoln and protesting freeing the slaves, but now I don't know. I may travel abroad for a while. I love Paris and Rome. I have your address, Margaret. I'll be sure to keep in touch with you and Carolyn."

Lighted Path and Ned were standing by the fireplace. The women joined them.

"Where have you been all this time, Lighted Path?" Margaret asked.

"In the forest. Ned said that we are leaving first thing in the morning."

Margaret nodded yes. "We had better rest. Tomorrow will be a long day."

Ned brought Suzie's things and the cot from Mammy's bedroom. She would sleep in the room with Margaret and Carolyn.

Chapter Forty-Seven
Departing in Different Directions

*I*t was still dark when everyone but Willie arose. Ned and Lighted Path brought the horses from the barn. Suzie moved past Mammy's bedroom door where Willie was still sleeping. She stopped and put her hand flat against the door. She took a deep breath and moved on.

Margaret and Carolyn tensed as they stared at the sky. Morning's first light was approaching. The clouds were pregnant with the threat of snow. The air was cold, and the stillness in the atmosphere was eerie. Margaret, Carolyn and Lighted Path mounted their horses. Suzie was going to ride with them to where the trail parted. One last goodbye to Ned, and they were on their way.

At the parting of the roads, Suzie pulled the hood of her coat tight around her face. "I'll keep in touch." They all waved goodbye and rode off in different directions.

By noon lazy wet snowflakes began to fall. Lighted Path wanted to stop and give the horses a break.

When they dismounted, Carolyn started to say something. Margaret put her hand over Carolyn's mouth. Lighted Path knelt down and put his ear to the ground. He quickly rose and informed them that many people and horses were coming in their direction.

"Do you think it's soldiers?" Margaret asked.

Lighted Path groaned. "Yes, and many of them. I need to go scout the area. You stay here."

Margaret grabbed his arm and said a resounding no. "We'll come with you. I don't want to be left standing here like open prey."

"You know to keep quiet and low," Lighted Path cautioned. "We'll tie the horses here and go to the top of that knoll."

They tied their horses and started up the knoll through the trees. At the top, Margaret gasped and Carolyn whispered, "Oh, God."

Lighted Path furrowed his brows. "Shhh," he said.

In the distance, walls of men in gray uniforms covered the rolling hill. On the other side of the valley, the hill was barricaded with dark blue Union uniforms. Margaret's eyes widened when they heard what sounded like men and horses, all around them. Lighted Path motioned for them to lie still and be quiet. Margaret and Carolyn joined hands and prayed in silence for God to get them out of that place safely. The deafening thuds of horses' hooves sounded as though they were headed straight toward them. On the slope below, a Union officer stood at attention as he looked out over his troops. He was dressed in dark blue with two rows of gold buttons down his chest and gold bars on his shoulders with tassels dangling down his sleeve. White, wide-topped gloves covered the end of his coat sleeves. A wide gold stripe stretched the length of the outer seam of his pants. A dark blue hat with a wide band crowned his long brown hair. His face revealed that the horrid task before him was one he wished did not have to take place.

Two lower-ranked soldiers came alongside him, pulled back on their horses' reins and stopped directly below them. Margaret's eyes quickly shifted when several men on foot gathered beside the three men on horses. Their chests were crossed with ammunition. The Union officer shouted, "The enemy must never be granted too much time." He leaned over, seized the hilt of the saber protruding from his saddle scabbard, and drew it out. "See that the bugler and flag boy stay close to me," he shouted. A young boy approached with a bugle in his hand. He looked thirteen or fourteen. The Union officer raised his sword over his head. The bugle boy placed the bugle to his lips and the flag boy held the flag high. In seconds, the officer yelled, "Charge," and headed down the slopes. The young boy played his bugle so loud the women's ears rang. The boys followed their leader down the slopes.

The gray uniforms on the other side followed suit. The attacking brigades made a rippling wall of men and horses, all advancing with not a gap anywhere along the lines.

As the two armies drew near the valley, a cannonball hit in the midst of the gray lines. Screams from young boys and older men exploded through the valley.

Instantly the battle was full blown. "Spread out, spread out!" The Union soldier shouted as the enemy's artillery flashed.

"Lighted Path," Margaret shouted, "we have to get out of here. Now!"

They started to pull back but stopped when they felt the ground rumble from pounding boots nearing behind them.

"Margaret," Lighted Path shouted. "I'll get the horses. Meet me by the big oak east of the hill."

Lighted Path headed toward the horses. Margaret and Carolyn pulled off toward the east side. "Carolyn, keep your head down!" Margaret shouted.

They had gone a short distance when they heard the steady hammering of men, horses and wagons coming toward them. Margaret and Carolyn saw a small ditch just inside the treeline. They grabbed a batch of tree limbs, leapt into the ditch that was so small they had to lie on their sides and pulled the branches over themselves. It was so tight the women could hardly breathe. Their hearts pounded. Exploding muskets shook the earth. Screams from dying and wounded soldiers caused the women to tremble.

A yell stuck in Carolyn's throat when a body landed on top of the brush, forcing a limb into her arm. The soldier's blood streamed through the limbs covering Margaret's pants. Carolyn managed to break the limb and pull it from her arm. The pain was excruciating. She pressed her hand over her mouth to quiet her moans. Another body fell on the branches at Margaret's head. She gasped as she looked into a pair of pale eyes that stared down at her. Fear gripped her, not knowing if he was dead or not. She watched to see if he would blink. After a few seconds, blood dripped from his mouth onto her neck. She wiped her neck with one hand and held her pistol in the other.

"Carolyn," Margaret whispered, "can you hear me?"

"Yes." She groaned. "My arm hurts so . . . so bad I can hardly stand it."

Margaret's body jerked as she cried silently. The thought of life being lost, whether blue or gray, was overpowering. She had to fight the horrid thoughts of George being only one of thousands of casualties. She could only ask that God would bring him home safely, not only George, but also Carolyn and Lighted Path and herself as well. She prayed for God to touch Carolyn's arm and take the pain away as she continued to wipe the blood from her neck. It was freezing cold. Snowflakes were covering and penetrating the branches. The women had lost all perception of time. The screams had stopped and the sound of horses' hooves had diminished. Not sure what to do, Margaret whispered, "Carolyn?"

Carolyn groaned. "Yes."

"Are you okay?"

Carolyn began to cry.

"Honey, hold on a few more minutes. Hey, Carolyn, do you remember how it felt when Cody kissed you?"

"Yes . . . yes, I do."

"I want you to think about how it felt when he held you in his arms. You need to keep your mind off the pain until we can get out of here. If we don't hear anything in a few minutes, I'll try to push the bodies off and see if the way is clear. Can you do that for me?"

"I'll try. I wish Cody were here to hold me now."

"I know. I feel the same about George." After a few minutes, Margaret began trying to push the bodies off. The awkward position she was in made it almost impossible. The limbs were white with snow. As Margaret pushed, the snow sprinkled through on them. She managed to put her foot against the branches and heave with all her might. One of the bodies rolled off. "Thank you, God," she whispered. She proceeded to push until the body at her head rolled away. "I did it, Carolyn."

"Thank God."

"I'm going to try and see if I can see anything. Just hold on." Margaret took a deep breath and slowly pushed the limbs up just enough to raise her head. She didn't see or hear anything. "I think it's clear, Carolyn. I'll get out first and make sure."

Margaret cautiously moved the branches and tried to stand. She felt her muscles cramping, and just breathing the cold air made her throat hurt. After a moment, she grew dizzy. She squatted, leaned forward and threw up. Her body trembled from shock. The massive battleground lay full of bodies, men and horses. Margaret felt disoriented. Her hands and feet were freezing. She knew she had to help Carolyn out of the ditch. Trembling, she called out, "Carolyn, cover your face. I'm going to move the limbs."

Margaret threw the branches from the ditch. She gasped. Carolyn was covered in blood. "Carolyn," she cried, "I'm so sorry. I never should have brought you on this . . . this hell quest." Margaret helped Carolyn from the ditch and embraced her.

Carolyn felt faint and sick to her stomach. Through the snow, the women were aghast at what they saw. The snow wasn't white on the battlefield, but red.

"Carolyn, we've got to move from here. I can only pray that Lighted Path is safe." She put her arm around Carolyn's waist and moved across the field. It was the most horrible sight that the women could have ever imagined—bodies with limbs twisted or missing were everywhere; some were decapitated. Margaret's head began to spin again. She came to a standstill near the edge of the field. Though dark was setting in, she could still make out the body of the young bugle boy, lying in a mass of blood. His bugle had been trampled. Only a few feet away lay the dashing Union officer who led the charge. The women stood speechless. The breathless silence was broken when they saw, through the shadows, a rider coming toward them leading two horses.

Ecstatic Margaret and Carolyn waved and tried to hurry through the snow that now covered the ground. Lighted Path raced to the women, slid off his horse and embraced them.

"Are you all right?" he asked breathlessly.

"A tree branch stuck in Carolyn's arm."

"Let me see," he said. Margaret helped take Carolyn's coat off. Lighted Path took a salve from his pouch and put it on top on the wound. He then took snow from the ground and placed it on top of the salve. After helping Carolyn put her coat on, and get on her horse, Margaret gave Carolyn a piece beef jerky and a quick swallow of water.

The sound of muskets firing echoed in the distance, indicating there was no time to wait.

"We have to get out of here now. I'm sorry to say that it can't be toward your Uncle Bill's. We have to go east. There are soldiers all over Chestnut Grove. If we ride tonight, I know a safe place where we can stop and rest in the morning."

Lighted Path took their blankets from the back of their saddles and unrolled them. "Margaret, you ride with Carolyn for warmth and to make sure she doesn't fall off her horse. Besides you're light, so the weight won't hurt your horse."

They wrapped their blankets around them and rode into the forest. The snow had ended, and a full moon graced the heavens and shined through the trees on the perfectly white snow, lighting the way. Margaret wasn't sure of the direction that Lighted Path was going. He appeared sure, so she didn't question his guidance.

After a couple of hours, Lighted Path stopped at a small clearing of gray-barked beech trees on the side of a gentle knoll. Through the trees, they had a clear field of vision across the opening and could detect any advancing troops in time to retreat farther into the forest.

"In this cold we need to stretch our legs and keep the circulation moving," Lighted Path said. "We need to feed the horses and give Carolyn some jerky or biscuit. She needs to keep her strength up."

When they were settled, Margaret asked, "Where are we, Lighted Path? I don't recognize the area."

"This is called Coosa."

"I've never heard of Coosa before."

"It's named after a very brave warrior."

"Really?"

"Yes. He is not known by many, but I know him."

Carolyn groaned.

"What is it?" Margaret asked.

"I feel so dizzy."

Lighted Path stood. "We had better be going."

They mounted and continued east. Margaret's mind was filled with the images on the battlefield. The smell of blood that dried on her clothing and in her hair kept a fresh reminder of the young bugle boy, his life cut short without seeing all the things a young teenage boy should experience. And a reminder of the officer who sat with such poise only to be brought down by the enemy's saber. Holding Carolyn was a benefit. The warmth of their bodies helped ward off the cold. They rode and rode. Morning seemed an eternity away. Carolyn leaned her head back against Margaret's shoulder. Margaret hoped that she would sleep until they reached the safe place that Lighted Path talked about.

The trail through the trees was one of rugged, twisted, contours with abnormal paths that continued to take them higher into the mountains. Margaret was so sleepy that her eyes warred to stay open. Her body was no longer tensed from fear, but limp from the cold. Suddenly, Margaret's body jerked in response to a noise that sounded like a twig breaking off to the right.

"Lighted Path."

"I know," he said. "Just stay calm."

Carolyn rose up and quickly looked around. "Margaret is it soldiers?"

"No, I don't think it's soldiers at all. What about you, Lighted Path?"

"It's not soldiers. Just stay calm and make no quick movements." He rode cautiously in front of them, scanning the area with his eyes.

"Oh God above," Margaret whispered. "My heart is about to explode." Margaret looked through the trees, and through the shadowy light of daybreak, she sensed that the trees camouflaged a mass of Indians. She sighed and then said breathlessly, "Carolyn, look at the paint on their faces."

Carolyn sat upright and stared into the trees. She took a quick breath and said, "Oh my goodness. They look like the three Indians that were at Fort Howard."

"Exactly. Lighted Path, do you think they're Seminole?"

"Yes, I do."

As the three moved up the mountain so did the Indians. Carolyn and Margaret prayed in silence with the fervor of Elijah. The women held their pistols under the blanket.

"Lighted Path, I think we should stop," Margaret said.

"No. We need to go forward."

Margaret tightened her brows. "That doesn't make sense to me. We don't know what we're riding into. If we get to the top of this mountain, we may not be able to turn back."

"We can't turn back now. We're totally surrounded."

As they neared the summit, Margaret gasped at the sight before her. A band of warriors lined the rugged trail, and the ones that had been following beside and behind them closed in. Margaret's horse moved restlessly. She pulled on the reins to control him. A lone rider made his way to the front of the other warriors. He was riding a dark brown mare with a strip of white between her eyes to the end of her nose. The rider sat on a colorful blanket. The bridle was adorned with feathers. His boots were made of leather and fur. His pants were leather with fringe down the outer seam. His shirt was bright colored with long, full sleeves. A hooded, light gray and black wolf-fur cape draped around him like a robe of royalty.

The riders were well armed with rifles and long spears. The feathered ends of sharp, flint-tipped arrows protruded from the quivers that they wore around their shoulders. He didn't have face paint on as some of the others did. Long feathers hung on both sides of his long ebony hair. The warriors glanced at each other but said nothing. Their dark eyes danced with excitement. The rider carried a long spear with feathers dangling from the top. He said something to Lighted Path. Lighted Path responded, but Margaret and Carolyn couldn't understand their language.

"Lighted Path, what did he say?"

"He said they want us to follow them; they mean us no harm."

Margaret questioned, "Do you believe them?"

"They could have taken us a long way back if they had wanted to hurt us. Besides, what choice do we have? Just stay calm."

"Why would they want us to follow them?" Carolyn asked. "What could they possibly want?"

Margaret sighed. "I don't know."

Chapter Forty-Eight
Taken Hostage

They traveled along the summit for quite a distance, surrounded by about fifty Indians. The proud warrior who spoke with Lighted Path led the way. The wind had picked up, sending a chill through their bones, but they were thankful that the snow had not started again. Suddenly, Margaret cocked her head. Before she could say anything, Carolyn asked, "What's that?

Margaret listened a moment then answered, "It's drums, but not war drums."

"How do you know?"

"By the intensity of the sound. If they were war drums they would be much stronger."

Margaret looked ahead, and to her surprise she saw two, long, narrow rocks that towered at the height of the evergreens surrounding the area. A narrow passage was carved at the bottom of the rocks. Only one at a time could enter the passage. Margaret filed in behind Lighted Path. The drums grew louder, like a heart beat in their ears.

As they exited the opening, Margaret saw several tents and a least fifty more warriors standing near the dwellings, staring at the procession as it entered the camp.

"Carolyn, are you all right?"

"Margaret, I have no words in my vocabulary to describe how I feel at this moment."

"We'll be all right. God will take care of us."

One of the first things Margaret noticed was there appeared to be no women and children in the camp. There wasn't the sound of a dog barking. She felt dazed as her eyes surveyed the surroundings. "Where are we?" she muttered. She still had no clue, even though she had paid close attention to anything that could possibly be a landmark. If the opportunity presented itself, she wanted to know how to get back to the valley.

The Indian leading the way stopped in front of the warriors. Everyone followed. When he stopped, the drums stopped. The leader and Lighted Path dismounted and stood in front of their horses. The other warriors dismounted, leaving Margaret and Carolyn the only ones on their horses.

"Should we get off?" Carolyn asked.

"No," Margaret whispered. "Not until they tell us to and keep your gun close."

The men in front of the nearest tent parted. Margaret's eyes widened in expectation of what would happen next. In a few seconds, the flap of the first tent opened. Two women, wrapped in the most beautiful beaver fur capes that Margaret had ever seen, exited the tent. Their long, ebony hair glistened even in the grayish hue of dusk. Each had two, long braids, interwoven with brightly colored beads, hanging across her shoulders and resting on her chest. Their long, tan buckskin dresses lay on top of their fur boots. One stood on either side of the tent opening. The one on the right held the flap open. Margaret and Carolyn fixed their eyes on the opening and could only wonder who would appear next. Without warning, Margaret began to tremble, but she didn't know why. It was freezing cold, but it was not the kind of shiver that results in chill bumps covering the body but the kind of tremble when running a high fever.

Carolyn quickly turned her head and frantically asked, "Margaret, what's wrong with you?"

Through chattering teeth, Margaret said breathlessly, "I don't know. Oh, God, what's wrong with me?"

Carolyn took her hand, trying to calm her. Margaret's other hand went limp and her pistol fell to the ground. Lighted Path swiftly turned to check on the women. Margaret's head was spinning. Her breathing was shallow. The last thing she remembered seeing was an Indian chief in full headdress coming from the opening. Lighted Path caught her as she fell from the side of her horse. The chief motioned for Lighted Path to bring her into the tent. Carolyn slid off the horse. When her feet hit the ground, the jar caused agonizing pain in her arm. Her blanket dropped to the ground, exposing the pistol she clutched in her hand. The Indian who had led them to the camp grabbed the gun as she groaned. Holding her arm, Carolyn started toward the tent only to be stopped by the Indian who had taken her gun. She shouted, "I want to see Margaret!"

Lighted Path quickly left the tent to aid Carolyn. He took her hand and assured her that everything was all right. He slowly removed her coat to look at her wound. The chief came to the opening and motioned for Lighted Path to bring Carolyn inside. After they had entered, Carolyn hurried to check Margaret. She was lying on a large, brown bear fur and covered with the same. Pelts were scattered around the large tent. A fire in the center of the tent was a welcome sight. She put the back of her hand on Margaret's cheek, checking for an elevated temperature.

"Thank God she's not running a fever," Carolyn said as she looked up at Lighted Path. She leaned close to Margaret and said softly, "Margaret! Margaret. Can you hear me?" Fear gripped her face as she looked to Lighted Path. He stooped down and put his arm around Carolyn's shoulder. "She's all right. She only fainted. More than likely from the cold . . . and your wound shows that you two have been through some traumatic times."

Tears began to stream down Carolyn's face. "My arm hurts so bad, and if that's not enough, these Indians scare the life out of me. I'm still covered with a young soldier's blood who lay on top of me forever, and now Margaret has the nerve to faint on me."

She lowered her head and began to sob. The two women, the chief and the Indian who had led them to the camp stood around the room looking at Carolyn. The chief said something to the two Indian women, and they left the tent. In seconds they were back with a bowl of warm water and a salve that smelled horrid. They knelt beside Carolyn and started to touch her arm. Carolyn looked at them and swiftly pulled away. Lighted Path assured her that the women meant her no harm but wanted to help her. Carolyn reluctantly allowed the women to clean the wound and apply the dreadful-smelling salve. They wrapped her arm in a clean white bandage. Carolyn wondered where the white cotton cloth came from. Almost on contact, the salve numbed her arm. She was so grateful just to have the pain stop for a moment. Carolyn looked at the women and managed a grin and a nod of her head to say thank you.

Carolyn noticed the chief had removed his headdress and knelt beside Margaret. He looked as though he was in a trance as he stared down at Margaret's face. Carolyn asked softly, "Why is he staring at her like that?"

"I think we need to answer that later," Lighted Path said.

The women brought Carolyn and Lighted Path hot herbal tea and a piece of roasted rabbit. After they had eaten, Carolyn asked Lighted Path a question. "How do you know these people? And what are we doing here?"

Lighted Path nodded for her to look at the chief who was still in a daze as he continued to look intently at Margaret's face. Lighted Path shifted around and extended his hands toward the fire. He rubbed his hands together without answering the question.

Carolyn insisted, "Lighted Path, answer me. How do you know these people?"

Lighted Path sighed and replied, "The chief's name is Coosa. He is one of the bravest men I have ever known. Margaret told you the story about my father and I running for our lives after soldiers killed my mother and sister. My father was wounded and died as a result. I was left alone in a place that I knew nothing about. All I had ever known was the beautiful land of the Cherokee people. I prayed and asked the Great Eagle to show me the way home. There came a time on my journey that I didn't know what to do. My will to even live had diminished. All the things that I had been taught as a young brave evaded me. I was cold, tired and hungry. My emotions were in chaos. Seeing my mother, father and sister die was taking a toll. One evening at dusk, I sat down in the edge of a clearing and leaned my back against a tree. I drew my knees to my chest and rested my head on them. I had made up my mind that night I wasn't going any farther.

"I actually prayed that a bear or snake would inflict a deadly blow to my thin frame and get me out of the degradation that had befallen me. As I sat there with my eyes swollen from crying, I sensed that someone was staring at me. I slowly looked up and there stood a young Seminole brave. His eyes were set on me. I glanced into his eyes and lowered my head. He stooped down and offered me a piece of roasted mountain trout. At first I couldn't eat. He continued to offer me the fish and water. I realized that he wasn't there to end my life as I had prayed for, but there to preserve my life. He wrapped his blanket around me and told me, 'Rest, I will watch for you.' I was taken by the fact that he could speak the Cherokee language very well. He was Seminole; how could he possibly know my language? I was amazed that he knew the area. So I asked the obvious questions. 'How do you know my people's language and what are you doing so far from your home?'

"He didn't answer my questions; however, he did stay with me until I came back to the borders of Cherokee—I might add at great risk to himself. He called me his brother. I said, 'How can you call me your brother? I'm Cherokee, not Seminole.' He put his hand on my shoulder and said that we are all the children of one, the Great Eagle of heaven. I never saw him again . . . until he was a warrior. I know the Great Eagle sent him to light my path and lead me home. He didn't want any credit for helping me. He told me to say the God of heaven and earth lighted the path for me. That's what I did. Everyone began calling me Lighted Path. The Mighty Eagle had sent a trusted eagle of His to guide me, and his name is Coosa. That's how I know him."

Carolyn turned her head, expecting to see Coosa, but he wasn't in the tent. "I don't know what to say. Your story is the most touching one I have ever heard. Nonetheless, I want to know what that has to do with us being here now?"

Lighted Path stood and said, "Get some sleep. You're safe."

Carolyn stood. "Are you not going to answer me?"

"Not tonight. I need some rest and so do you. You'll know the answer to your question soon enough."

"What about Margaret?"

"She needs the rest too. She'll be fine by morning."

Lighted Path lay down on one of the pelts and covered himself with a woven blanket. Carolyn lay down beside Margaret and pulled one of the furs over her. She was afraid to close her eyes, although the fear had calmed somewhat. The battle to keep her eyes open ended, and she drifted off to sleep.

Chapter Forty-Nine
Meeting at Sundown

*T*he night swiftly passed and welcomed rays of sunlight illuminated the land. Carolyn wasn't sure what had awakened her, the drums or Margaret's groans. Carolyn sprang up with exhilaration and breathlessly called, "Margaret!" She embraced her. Margaret squinted, rubbed her head and questioned, "Where are we?"

Before Carolyn could answer, Lighted Path stretched and yawned. He quickly asked, "Margaret, do you feel better?"

She tried to stand, but sat back down and held her head. "Lord above, my head is spinning." She suddenly looked around. "What are the drums? Where are we?"

"We're in a safe place," Lighted Path replied.

"Where's my pistol?" she asked frantically as she looked around the tent.

"You don't need a gun here," Lighted Path stated. "We're among friends."

Margaret looked at Carolyn and frowned when two Indian women entered the tent with meat and water. They bowed their heads and set the food on the ground beside Margaret and exited. Her knees felt weak but Margaret managed to stand. Carolyn held her arm until she was stable.

"How's your arm, Carolyn? You're holding me, when I should be helping you."

Carolyn lightly touched her arm and said, "I don't know what the smelly salve was they put on my arm, but whatever it was, I love it. My arm hasn't hurt since. I'm very cautious of it, but it isn't hurting."

"Lighted Path," Margaret stated, "I need to be excused, really bad."

Carolyn hurriedly agreed.

"Wait here," he said. He went out and returned almost as fast. "The women will take you."

Margaret looked at Carolyn and frowned. "At this point, I don't care. I just need to go."

The north wind sent a chill through them as they stepped outside the tent. Margaret observed the warriors standing around the campfire, covered in all kinds of animal skins. A lone warrior who sat on a log kept the constant beat of his drum pounding. Carolyn looked around for the chief, but didn't see him. The Indian women, one in front and the other in the rear, led them into the trees away from camp. "Carolyn, have they tried in any way to touch you?"

"No, they haven't. It's weird, Margaret. Lighted Path knows Chief Coosa."

Stunned, Margaret asked, "How?"

"Margaret, look," Carolyn whispered, "the women have their backs turned. Do you think that we could get away?"

"Not without the things Uncle Bill gave me. I won't leave them behind. I won't."

One of the Indian women motioned for them to come on. "So we do . . . nothing?" Carolyn asked.

"For now we do nothing, but wait and see what they have in mind. Listen, the drumbeat is different. It's more like a celebration sound. I will ask Lighted Path about it."

As they came back into the camp, the Indian who had led them into the camp was standing by the tent. His chest swelled and his dark eyes were set on Margaret in a way that made her feel apprehensive. Carolyn noticed the stare and commented, "I don't have a good feeling about that one. Did you notice the thorough examination he was giving you? His mouth was all but watering."

"Of course I noticed. How could I not? He was about as subtle as a skunk releasing his odor."

The two women who were watching after Margaret and Carolyn brought a large bucket of water and a big wooden bowl into the tent and sat them beside the fire. One stoked the fire, causing sparks to leap into the air. Margaret and Carolyn glanced at each other, not sure what the women were doing.

Lighted Path entered the tent. "I don't think this is the time for a talk." He turned to leave, but Margaret called out, "Lighted Path."

He turned back. "What is it?"

"Where are you going?" Margaret asked.

"I'm going out now to allow you to take your bath in private."

The women left the tent. Margaret was eager to know why there were no children or more women, other than the two waiting on them. She asked the women's names.

Lighted Path smiled and replied. "The shortest one is called Sky. The other one is Windy."

Margaret asked, "Who is the man who led us into the camp?"

"His name is John."

Margaret glanced at Carolyn and frowned. "John? What kind of a name is John for a Seminole warrior?"

Lighted Path chuckled. "You'll have to ask him about that."

"All right, enough about the names," Margaret said. "I want to know what we're doing here. Are they going to let us go, or hold us hostage, or worse yet, kill us?"

"They would never kill you. You'll have to ask Chief Coosa why you're here."

"About that chief," Margaret uttered, "Carolyn said he was staring at me in an unusual way while I was unconscious. Do you know if there's a reason for that?"

At that time, Sky and Windy entered the tent with two changes of men's clothes. They laid them on the pelts and pointed to Margaret and Carolyn.

"Are these for us?" Margaret asked.

Lighted Path repeated Margaret's words for the women. Sky pointed to Margaret and ordered her to take a bath and change her clothes. Margaret tapped Sky on the shoulder and said, "Thank you."

The women nodded and left the tent. Margaret looked at the clothes that she was wearing, covered with dried blood. Lighted Path smiled and left the tent. The women bathed and washed their hair. The clothes Sky had brought were a little big, but clean. Margaret lowered her head toward the fire and shook her hair dry with her hands.

When dry, Margaret sat on one of the pelts and Carolyn brushed her long shiny hair. She brushed the front back and braided it.

"Carolyn, how is it that a simple trip to visit Uncle Bill could turn into all of this?"

"Only God knows. What I do know is, if that drum doesn't stop soon, I may scream.

"You're right, it's getting very annoying."

Carolyn put the brush down and sat beside Margaret. "I think about Cody. I still taste his lips. His touch staggered me. I wonder how he felt?"

Margaret laughed. "Oh, I'm sure he has thought about that kiss constantly. He hasn't courted a woman since Donna Felton. You know the story, they were going to be married, until Silent Wolf changed his plans and brutally murdered her."

"Can I tell you something and you promise not to say a word to anybody?"

"Of course. What?"

Carolyn bit her lower lip. "I . . . I . . . I just can't say it."

Margaret frowned and asked, "And why not? I'm your best friend and friends share things that everyone doesn't know, so tell me."

Carolyn raised her brows and uttered, "You promise, right?"

"I promise."

"I hope things work out with Cody and me, even though he has only kissed me once. Sometimes one kiss is all it takes to know for sure, and I feel that way with Cody. I hope he feels the same way."

Before she could respond, Lighted Path asked if he could come inside. Carolyn told him to come in.

The women looked at him with anticipation, hoping he came with word about when they could leave.

"The weather is good today," he said.

Margaret stood. "Forget the weather!" Margaret snapped. "I didn't come this far to be stuck on a mountain as a hostage. If they're not going to hurt us, why are they holding us here?"

"Holding us? They've made no attempt to hurt us. They gave you water for a bath and clean clothes. They've given us food and treated you as a guest."

Margaret took a deep breath, put one hand on her hip and said, "I'm thankful for the bath, food and clothes, but I'm ready to go. If we're not prisoners, does that mean we can walk out of here right now and not be stopped?"

Lighted Path lowered his head and didn't respond.

Margaret shook her head. "Then we are prisoners?"

Lighted Path turned to leave. Margaret was furious. She grabbed his arm. "Just what is your part in all of this? I agreed with Randy for you to go with us only because I thought we could trust you. Boy, was I wrong. You led us to these people. I want to know why. Where is the chief that gazed at me while I was unconscious? Like he had never seen a human before."

Lighted Path shifted his eyes to Margaret's hand that was holding his arm and then cut his eyes to hers. "Chief Coosa will meet with you at sundown."

Margaret released his arm.

Carolyn asked, "Lighted Path, can you tell us why the one drum has been pounding for hours now?"

"The drum is a symbol of a great chief who is rejoicing, yet grieving at the same time. It symbolizes a great man's soul and flesh in a battle that one can't understand until they reach that place."

"What place is that?" Carolyn asked.

"The place of the great water. His soul wants to cross that water, but the warrior in him wants to stay on this side and fight, never relinquishing his place."

"What does that have to do with me and Carolyn, or with you?" Margaret snapped.

Lighted Path stared into Margaret's eyes and solemnly replied, "Chief Coosa will be in to see you at sundown."

Carolyn and Margaret looked at each other and could only wonder what that statement could possibly mean. Margaret managed a smile. "We could talk about Suzie. That would help take our minds off our dilemma for a while."

Carolyn readily agreed. "Where do you think she is about now?"

Margaret lay down and replied. "I don't know. She sure was a mystery. You know, I never would have guessed that she would have had a child, and by Willie.

Love is a strange thing. I know I've said it at least a million times; nevertheless, I'll say it again, I miss my love terribly." Tears welled up in Margaret's eyes. "I pray he's all right." She turned on her stomach and began to sob aloud.

Carolyn sat beside her and rubbed her back, trying to console her. Instantly, Sky and Windy entered to see what was wrong. Carolyn shook her head and motioned for them to leave. Carolyn and Margaret slept for a while and were awakened when John entered the tent. The women quickly stood. He stared at Margaret. She gritted her teeth and boldly said, "Get out of here! Now!"

"Do you think he can understand one word you said?" Carolyn asked.

"I don't know, but I don't like the way he stares at me."

Margaret pointed to the flap and shouted, "Go!"

He seized her wrist and said in a low voice, "If I go, I take you with me. I would like to make sons with you."

Margaret's eyes widened. She was stunned that he could speak English. She tried to pull free, but he only tightened his grip. "I have a husband, and I'm too old to make sons."

He released his grip and she jerked her wrist free. He squinted and ordered, "You come with me, while the women prepare the tent."

"Prepare the tent for what?" Margaret questioned.

He put his face close to hers and whispered, "For you, lovely one."

Margaret stepped back and said nothing.

"You had better wrap up. It's cold outside," he said softly.

"Where's Lighted Path?" Margaret said.

"He'll be here for the ceremony. Until then, you'll stay in my tent." John held the flap open for the women to exit. To their surprise, the warriors were still in a circle around the fire and someone continued to play the drum. All eyes turned to them as they went past the campfire to a tent near the back of the camp. It was a relief to see Sky and Windy standing at the tent door they were to enter. This time, the women didn't go in with them. Margaret frantically surveyed the tent. Carolyn watched as she moved around the room. At the back of the tent, Margaret stopped and moved her hand up and down a section of the cowhide wall.

"What are you doing?" Carolyn asked.

Margaret faced Carolyn. "We've got to get out of here now!"

Carolyn frowned. "How are we going to do that?"

"I looked at our surroundings as we were coming to this tent. There's only one other tent behind this one and the woods are right beside us." Margaret pulled a small knife from her boot and said, "We need to go relieve ourselves. While we're out, I'll check the area even more and see where the braves are stationed. Of course there will be some in the front of the tent, but hopefully not in the back where we go to pee-pee. They don't know I have a knife. They won't expect us to go out the back. When we come back, we'll wait a few minutes and then make our move."

"Oh, Margaret, I don't know."

Margaret put her hand on Carolyn's shoulder. "Do you want to stay here and have who knows what happen to you? I don't. For all we know this ceremony is some kind of wedding for John. I don't want him to touch me. He's all but raped me with his eyes. I'm not going to wait for that, are you?"

Carolyn shook her head. "No. I'm not. What about Lighted Path?"

Margaret put the knife back in her boot. "He brought us here. I'm sure he can find his way back. I'll motion for Sky. When we get out, be sure and check the area with me. Of course we have to be careful so Sky and Windy won't notice."

Margaret opened the flap. John was standing beside the opening. "Do you need something?" he asked.

"I need to see Sky. We need to go relieve ourselves."

He stared at her and then told her to wait. Sky and Windy came immediately and led Margaret and Carolyn to the back of the tents. Margaret and Carolyn observed everything. They saw right away there were no guards to be seen at the back of the tent. After coming back from the woods, they waited for almost an hour and then Margaret pulled the knife from her boot and whispered, "It's time."

They joined hands and prayed for safety. Margaret put her ear to the back wall of the tent to make sure she heard nothing. She slowly made a small slit in the wall and peeked out to make sure no one was around. As the drum continued to pound, Margaret glided her knife through the rawhide. She grabbed the chest that was rolled in her blanket, and they quietly went through the slit. They stood still for a moment, listening. After a few seconds, Margaret whispered, "Carolyn, once we're in the woods, we'll move quickly down the mountain." She took a deep breath, glanced around and rushed to the tree line. For a short distance, they wove through the maze of trees and snow as fast and quietly as possible. The cold air made it hard to breathe, and the bright sun on the snow was blinding. They ran until their lungs ached. Margaret stopped, leaned her head forward and tried to catch her breath. Carolyn stooped down and placed her hand on her chest, gasping.

When Margaret could speak, she said breathlessly, "We need to go." She glanced at Carolyn and asked, "Is your arm all right?"

Carolyn's face was gripped with pain, yet she nodded that she was fine. After a couple of deep breaths, the women proceeded down the mountain. They didn't look back, afraid of what they might see.

Suddenly, Margaret stopped and motioned for Carolyn to get down. "What is it?" Carolyn groaned in breathless anticipation.

Margaret pointed toward a mound of snow that was near a clearing. "I think it's a cabin. It is a cabin! And there's a shed to the left of it. The only bad thing is I don't see any smoke coming from the chimney."

"What should we do? Check it out or keep going?"

"We'll check it out. There could be someone there, but they would have a fire going. Be careful and stay low until we get closer."

They made their way to the edge of the clearing, and still there was no sign of life. "Do you want to stay here while I go and check it out?" Margaret asked Carolyn.

Carolyn snapped. "No, I don't want to stay here. I ran down the mountain the same as you, and we're not going to separate now. If you go, I go."

As they neared the side of the house, Margaret's heavily booted feet sank into a snowdrift that came above the top of her boot. "Shoot!" she growled. The snow was mounded around the cabin. "The wind must have been blowing directly toward this place." Margaret groaned. "Snow is in my boots. For heaven's sake." She pulled her feet from the snow mounds and managed to get to a window; however, it was boarded up.

"What now?" Carolyn asked.

"We'll check the door, and if we need to, we'll pull the planks off to get inside. I need to empty my boots soon, before the inside of my boot soaks the water up."

To their surprise, the door wasn't barred. Their eyes met briefly looked at each other and Margaret slowly opened the door. "Is anyone here?" she called out. There was no response. The room was empty except for a small table and a bench. The fireplace was cold. There hadn't been a fire in it for some time. Margaret dropped on the bench and swiftly unlaced her boots. "As soon as I empty my boots, we'll have to go. It won't be long until they realize we're gone."

"If they don't know already." Carolyn groaned.

"How's your arm holding up?"

"It only hurts bad when we're running. I wish I had some more of that stinking salve. That stuff worked like magic."

"When we get home, I'll take you to see Dr. Whitt," Margaret said as she tied her boots.

Carolyn rubbed her forehead. "How many days have we been gone? I've lost all track of time."

Margaret sighed. "Me, too. I'm not sure even what day it is. I'm going out and check the shed to see if there is anything we can use for a weapon. You stay here and rest. I'll be right back."

"Margaret."

Margaret turned to face Carolyn. "Yeah."

Before Carolyn could say anything, a savage gust of wind rattled the windows and whistled through the crack of the door. Margaret frantically glanced around the room. "The wind must be really picking up."

"Yeah, considering it wasn't blowing at all when we arrived five minutes ago."

"What were you going to say?" Margaret asked.

Carolyn's eyes showed the hopelessness she was experiencing. "Do . . . do you think we'll get home?"

Margaret took Carolyn's hands. "Of course we're going to get home. I know we've been through quite a bit, in a short time, but we can't give up hope. God will keep us and take us home. You repeat that until you feel it in your heart. George needs me and I need George. Remember what you said about Cody? He needs you and you need him. With God's help, the four of us will be together soon. Don't you dare think anything else, promise?"

Carolyn nodded and whispered, "I promise."

Margaret stood and ran her hand down Carolyn's cheek. "I'll be back in a moment."

"Okay."

Margaret slowly opened the door, stepped outside and looked around, surveying everything as she trotted to the shed. Before opening the door, she took the knife from her boot, gradually lifted the latch and pulled the door open. When she did, a scream stuck in her throat.

John stood on the other side of the door.

Margaret's hand rose high to stab him, but he seized her arm. Struggling to free herself, she found he was too strong. His hand squeezed her wrist until she dropped the knife, but not before putting a small cut on his chest. After kicking him, she tried to crawl away, but he grabbed her by her braid and pulled her back. The excruciating pain caused her to raise her hands to her head. "No!" she screamed. Catching his wrists, she dug her fingernails into his flesh. His hand came forward and slapped her to the ground.

As Margaret tried to get up, Carolyn screamed, and in seconds two Indians pulled her from the cabin.

Margaret tried to move but was dazed from the blow. John picked her up by her coat like she was a rag doll. Three or four warriors came around the shed with their horses.

Carolyn shouted, "Margaret are you okay?"

"Yes," she groaned.

John tied her hands and sat her on his horse. After she felt him mount behind her and push his body so tightly to hers, she could hardly breathe. His fingers began to massage her stomach as he pressed his face to the back of her head, smelling her hair. Margaret tried to ward off his advances as John's strong fingers moved upward to her breast and then pushed into her shirt as he pressed his body even closer. Margaret rammed her elbow into his ribs. John quickly moved his hand from her breast to his ribs. With one hand, he grabbed her hair and pulled her head back, leaned forward and kissed her lips so hard it hurt.

Carolyn was screaming for him to stop, which caused things to grow worse.

Sliding from his horse, he pulled Margaret off and pushed her to the ground. His hand seized her skirt, pushing it to her waist. Tightening his face muscles, he sat on top of Margaret. Her struggle proved to be hopeless, and the smell of his breath was appalling.

Just as he started to violate her, Margaret heard something whiz past her head and go deep into the ground. John instantly turned to see who had shot the arrow. Lighted Path ordered, "Get off her now, or the next one will go through your head."

John slowly stood and straightened his clothes. Margaret looked at Lighted Path, relaxed her head and closed her eyes.

"Untie her, now!"

John stooped down and took the ropes from Margaret's hands. Margaret pushed her body up and adjusted her clothing. Lighted Path ordered the others to untie Carolyn. Margaret mounted behind Carolyn.

Lighted Path frowned and stared at John. "I think Chief Coosa will have a few words for you. If I see you as much as look at her again, I'll kill you."

John mounted his horse and they started back up the mountain.

"Did he hurt you, honey?" Carolyn asked.

"Not as bad as I did him. The thought of his hands touching me made me sick. Did they hurt you?"

"No, thank God, they didn't."

Margaret put her arms around Carolyn and took the reins, turned the horse and followed Lighted Path up the mountain. As they neared the camp, pounding of the drum echoed down the valley; this time, there were several drums beating.

Chapter Fifty
Phoebe's Story

Sky and Windy were waiting for Margaret and Carolyn's return. They immediately helped them from the horse and took them into another tent. Lighted Path followed them.

He gritted his teeth and questioned, "Why did you leave? I told you they wouldn't hurt you. You put yourselves in danger by taking off."

Every muscle in Margaret's face tightened. "Don't you dare scold us for trying to get away. We didn't put ourselves in danger. You did by bringing us here. I wasn't going to stay around and have who knows what happen to me and Carolyn."

Lighted Path tightened his lips. "Sky will be in shortly. I'll have Windy bring you some food and water." He turned and left the tent.

In moments, Windy brought food for Margaret and Carolyn; she looked at them and set the food beside the fire. Margaret could tell she wanted to say something. She gently placed her hand on Windy's shoulder. "What is it? Can you understand?"

Windy nodded and said in broken English, "Stay. Don't go way. Don't go way." She was pleading with Margaret through her eyes.

Margaret nodded and replied, "Okay. We won't go away."

Windy lowered her head and left the room. The drumbeats had intensified, bringing Margaret and Carolyn to the conclusion that something would take place soon, but what? Windy had barely left the tent before she came back. Margaret and Carolyn were sitting on the furs eating but quickly gave their attention to Windy when she entered. She extended her hand to Carolyn to give her some of the smelly salve. When she left, Margaret put some of the ointment on Carolyn's arm.

"I wonder if it would help a sore head," Margaret said. "Where that beast pulled my braid is so sore."

Carolyn moved her arm up and down. "I've never witnessed anything like this stinky stuff; my arm has already stopped hurting. I don't smell really good, but there is no one here to impress."

Margaret wasn't sure what time it was, but knew that soon the sun would be going down.

The flap of the tent came open, and Sky entered with her arms outstretched holding the most extraordinary white dress Margaret had ever seen. Lighted Path followed her inside. Margaret and Carolyn swiftly stood. Lighted Path said. "Margaret, it's time."

"Time for what?" Margaret snapped.

Sky held the dress out to Margaret.

"She wants you to put it on," Lighted Path said.

Carolyn gasped. "Margaret, this dress is like the one your Grandma Phoebe was wearing in the portrait that was over Uncle Bill's fireplace."

Margaret put her trembling fingertips on the dress and drew a breath in and held it. "Oh, my. You're right. It's just like it." She cut her eyes to Lighted Path and asked, "What's going on? Don't tell me 'nothing'! This dress . . . why do they want me to put it on and why is it exactly like Grandma Phoebe's?"

A voice from behind Margaret said, "Let me answer that question."

Margaret's body jerked at the familiar voice. She swiftly turned and breathlessly said, "Uncle Bill!"

She stood, stunned. Carolyn put her arm around Margaret. "Uncle Bill, what are you doing here and how did you know we were here?"

He stepped forward and extended his hand toward Margaret. The room was spinning as Margaret shifted her eyes to Lighted Path, then to Sky and Windy. Again she touched the dress with her fingertips and slowly looked back at Bill. Bill took the dress from Sky and asked everyone to leave but Carolyn and Margaret to give him a few minutes alone with them.

The drums outside were pounding faster. The warriors were dancing around the campfire and whoops of joy were echoing across the mountain. The sun was setting and the gray hue of dusk was sending a chill across the lofty peak of the mountain that appeared to reach into the heavens.

Uncle Bill sat on the furs that were spread around the fire. He motioned for the women to sit with him.

Margaret looked at Carolyn, who took her hand and led her to the pelts. Tears welled up in Bill's eyes as he straightened the dress across his lap. He wiped his tears and put his hand on Margaret's.

In a broken voice he said, "I know you don't understand what's happening. But I want you to know, I have waited for this day for many years. When you were at my house, you asked me what had happened to separate our family after your mother's death." He took a handkerchief from his pocket and wiped his face. Margaret's blank stare made it hard for him to speak without crying.

"I'll try and explain it to you. Years ago, some Seminole Indians who were on their way back to Florida, found Phoebe Thawbush beside the White Oak River. The man and woman who had been raising her were dead. They had been shot and robbed. The man was on the edge of the river and the woman was lying beside a big boulder. When the Indians rode up and saw the man and woman, they dismounted and checked them for any sign of life. That is when they heard a baby crying. The chief followed the sound into the bushes, and there on a blanket was a baby around six months old. The chief didn't want to leave the child, so he took her to his village and raised her as his own. There was a white woman in the village. She hadn't been kidnapped, but rather was there because she had fallen in love with one of the chief's sons. Her family had been killed, and she willingly came to the village and married the brave. She had a small baby and the chief gave the baby he had just found to his son's wife to breast-feed and help care for her also.

"The woman taught Phoebe to speak English and the Seminole tongue. Phoebe wasn't like the other women. She excelled in everything from hunting to shooting a bow and arrow accurately with every pull of the bowstring. She made her father very proud. The chief prized her over his own children. She was so beautiful. Another of the chief's sons, Winter Snow Thawbush, married Phoebe when she was thirteen. They had four children—Tyler, Lorrie, Mariah and me. We grew up with the Seminole because we were part Seminole, however, we were part Cherokee and a part of Phoebe yearned to come back to the place of her birth.

"Tyler, Lorrie and I were content not to marry, anticipating the move back to Cherokee. For some reason, we felt as though we had been kidnapped, but not Mariah. She was so like her mother. She too excelled in everything. She beat the young braves in every event. Mariah fell in love with a brave named Coosa. By the way, I failed to mention that Winter Snow Thawbush was part white. His mother was white. She too was a victim that the Seminole took in and raised.

"She was nineteen when they found her, therefore her tongue was English, and so we were taught to speak the English language well. As fate would have it, we took our genes from our father, thus our light skin. Winter Snow was so light-skinned that he could have passed for all white. Coosa's father was white. He was a trapper named Alvin Wells, and he also lived with the Seminole. Many blacks lived with our tribe as well. They too took wives from the Seminole women. That's why some of their people have such a dark color. Anyway, Mariah married Coosa. He, in later years, became Chief Coosa."

Carolyn put her hand up and said, "Wait a minute. Did you say that Mariah married a man that is now Chief Coosa?"

"Yes."

Carolyn tightened her brow and whispered, "Margaret, that's the Chief's name who I said stared at you when you fainted."

Margaret had not spoken up to that point. Now she frowned at Bill. "Raven and Ortho told me that I wasn't born at White Oak Creek . . . as I had been told by my mother and grandmother. Ortho said that Phoebe came back to Cherokee when her children were grown. He also told me that Cody, Julie and I were already born when they came back." Margaret shook her head and asked, "If not our father, who was J. D. Styles?"

Bill licked his lips and answered. "J. D. was a trapper who loved your mother with a passion. She loved him too and lived with him a long time, against Phoebe's wishes. J.D. was away so much and worse than that, to Mariah, was the fact he didn't believe in marriage. He saw no use for it. Mariah, on the other hand, felt that he should marry her if he loved her as he said he did. They fought many battles over that. He went away and didn't come back for almost three years. Mariah had fallen in love with Coosa, thinking that J.D. wasn't coming back. Coosa married her and shortly afterward, J.D. did come back, but it was too late. In the time period that J.D. was away, Mariah truly fell in love with Coosa. J.D. always made a point to come by and visit Mariah even if she was married.

"Winter Snow died a young man. I think it was his heart. After that, Phoebe was adamant about coming back to Cherokee. I don't know why, but she was set on coming back to a place she didn't remember. When Phoebe set a time for the move, Mariah had to decide if she wanted to stay with Coosa or come back with Phoebe. Coosa could tell that Mariah's heart was to follow her mother. Because of his love for her, and you, he backed away, told Mariah to go and she did."

Margaret asked, "Why did J.D. come around and call himself Daddy to us. He really wasn't there enough to be a daddy, but we always looked to him as our father."

Bill lowered his head and explained, "He identified himself as father to Julie and Cody because he was their father. You alone are Coosa's child."

The expression on Margaret's face was one of total confusion. She tried to form a word two or three times before the question came out. "Are telling me that I have a different father than Cody and Julie?"

Bill nodded. "Yes."

Margaret put her finger to her temples and frowned. "So my real father is here, now?"

"Yes. Chief Coosa is your father. He's old and knows his time is short, so he sent spies to Cherokee to find you. A while back, Coosa sent word to me and to Lighted Path that he wanted to see his daughter before he died."

Bill looked at the dress Margaret was holding. "Phoebe and Mariah were two exceptional women. They had the spirit of the Mighty Eagle burned in their souls. The necklace and the feather I gave you, they wore for the ceremony that was only befitting women of great strength and character. Two women with a strong belief in the Mighty Eagle of heaven displayed it for all to see. They both had those qualities and you have the same spirit. Phoebe passed the blessing to Mariah, but she didn't accept the blessing as Phoebe did. Phoebe embraced the blessing and yearned to pass it to one of her grandchildren. She would not be sure which grandchild until the Mighty Eagle revealed to her you were the one. That's the reason your blessing was different from the others. She saw the mighty Phoenix arise in you. Phoebe died in peace after she gave your blessing. More than anything, Phoebe wanted to see the Eagle mantel passed, and she did. There's a ceremony that is considered most holy when the Eagle mantle is passed. Chief Coosa wants to perform that ceremony for his only daughter before he dies. I believe that was the reason you came to visit me when you did. I call it divine intervention."

Margaret pressed her fingers to her brow. "I really don't understand what you're talking about. I know each tribe of people celebrate events in their own way nevertheless, I don't understand the ritual that Chief Coosa wants to have me participate in. I'm really no one special. I know about having the same spirit, but to me, that's not uncommon. Of course I would have some of their same spirit in me; they were my mother and grandmother."

Bill patted Margaret's hand. "You may not comprehend everything now, but you will in time."

Margaret rubbed the back of her neck and remarked, "I'm . . . I'm very nervous about meeting Chief Coosa. You say he's my father, but I don't know him as my father." Margaret squinted and said, "I didn't say this earlier, but the instant before I fainted, I saw a chief coming from the tent. I didn't see his face, but he had to stoop to leave the tent opening. When I saw him bend over, I . . . I recalled an event, or at least I thought I did. It was like the same thing had happened before, but I didn't know when. That was when everything began to spin and I blacked out."

Bill ran his hand up and down Margaret's forearm and said, "I'm not surprised you recall that kind of event."

"What do you mean?"

"When Phoebe had gathered her family to head back to Cherokee, you cried and cried, not wanting to leave your father. Coosa was sending a guard of Seminole warriors with us to make sure we found our way and would be safe. Coosa knelt down to hug you goodbye. When he did, you threw your arms around his neck. Mariah had to pry your hands loose from him. Coosa pounded the ground with his fist and wept bitterly as we rode away. He feared he would never see you again."

"Why can't I remember? I was nine years old. I should remember something!" Margaret muttered, "Do Cody and Julie remember this and just didn't tell me?"

"You must remember, Margaret, you all were young, and time has a way of protecting one's emotions. Besides, J.D. came often, right after the move back to Cherokee. He wanted to help you kids adjust as soon as possible. He called himself father to you and more than likely, Cody and Julie didn't think anything about it. Mariah told you J.D. was your father and everyone accepted that."

"Okay, I can understand some of that; however, I want to know what happened between you, Tyler and Lorrie and why you left after mother's death? Why?"

"Oh, Lord! Just thinking about it makes me feel sick. Tyler and Lorrie were ashamed of Mariah for marrying a Seminole and not marrying, or at least staying, with J.D. They wanted to pretend they were white and could do so due to their fair skin, but Mariah didn't care who knew, until she saw how hard it would be for her and you kids.

The government had begun the relocation of the Cherokee people. So Mariah agreed to go along with J.D. and pretended he was her husband and the father of you children. It broke Phoebe's heart. To be ashamed of your heritage, she felt was like Esau selling his birthright. I wouldn't be a part of it. I was Indian no matter how fair my skin. We argued over those feelings time and time again.

They were in constant fear I would tell their dreaded secret. I loved Mariah so much. While I was around, she at least had someone with whom to share her emotions. After she died, I didn't want to be a part of anyone who caused her such hurt. She felt as though her life was a lie. Because of her love for Tyler and Lorrie, she suppressed her own feelings to accommodate theirs. I believe it took her to an early grave.

She didn't want Phoebe to know how she felt, so she put on a daily show, displaying how happy she was. Mariah was never happy. She grieved over Coosa until the day she died. I really believe that Phoebe knew down deep but didn't know what to do about it, so she did nothing. The day I decided to move to Chestnut Grove, Tyler, Lorrie and I got into an awful fight. I tried to kill Tyler. I told them what hypocrites they were and I couldn't stay and be a part of their lies. I left and settled at Chestnut Grove. There I didn't care who knew about my descendants or the color of my skin.

"Tyler did try to visit me a few years later. When I met him, his first words were, 'Have you come to your senses yet?' I asked what he meant. He said, 'Are you ready to admit that you're white, like Lorrie and me?'"

"I was furious. I told him to get off my land and not to come back. He was a disgrace to the white man and the Indian. I didn't see him or Lorrie ever again."

"I want—"

Before Margaret could finish her sentence, Sky and Lighted Path entered the tent. Margaret and Carolyn's attention quickly shifted to them. "It's time. The sun has set," Lighted Path said.

Margaret looked at Bill without blinking. She swallowed hard and asked, "What do I do now?"

"Let Sky and Windy dress you for the ceremony."

"I want to dress myself. Carolyn can help with my hair. I remember vividly the way Grandma Phoebe looked in the painting. I can get ready myself. If that's okay?"

Bill looked at Lighted Path. Lighted Path nodded yes. "But you must hurry," he said. "The drums will stop soon and you must go out before then."

Everyone stood. Bill gave the dress to Margaret and asked, "You do have the necklace, feather and the pouch, don't you?"

"Yes, of course I do."

"Bring the box with the contents inside when you come out."

"I don't get to wear them?"

Bill smiled. "You most certainly will, but not until the ceremony starts."

"We must hurry," Lighted Path said.

Chapter Fifty-One
Seminole Chief

hen left alone, Margaret and Carolyn both took deep breaths and shook their heads. "Do you believe any of this Margaret?" Carolyn said.

"Yes, for some unknown reason, I do. That's why I want you to help me get the dress on."

Margaret was unlacing the front of her shirt when Sky entered the tent with a pair of brown moccasins that went up to Margaret's knees and a bowl holding brightly colored strung beads for Margaret's hair. Sky smiled, handed the bowl to Margaret and hurried out.

"Carolyn, do you remember how the beads were in Grandma Phoebe's and Mother's hair?"

Carolyn could see the excitement in Margaret's eyes as she pulled the dress over her friend's head and shoulders and down past the calves of her legs. Margaret glided her hands down the front of the dress and lifted her eyes to Carolyn.

"You look wonderful," Carolyn said. The dress looks tailor-made for you. By the way, I do remember the last beads were placed in Phoebe's and Mariah's hair."

Margaret hurried and put the moccasins on; they fit perfectly. She then sat for Carolyn to do her hair. Carolyn braided the strands of beads into Margaret's long shiny hair. When finished, Margaret and Carolyn stood. My Lord, Margaret you are the spitting image of your mother and Phoebe. You're stunning."

Margaret blew out and looked down at her dress. She slowly ran her fingers over the beads in her hair. "My heart is beating louder than the drums. The thought of meeting my real father is mind-boggling. Just pray I don't stumble and fall or faint again."

"You'll be fine. Are you ready?"

Margaret picked up the box, took two deep breaths and said, "I'm ready. It's so cold outside. Do I wear a blanket or coat?"

Carolyn tightened her face muscles and shook her head. "No! Besides, you'll be by the fire."

Carolyn went out and held the flap of the tent open for Margaret. Margaret drew in a sharp breath and released it slowly. The beat of her heart was loud in her ears as she lowered her head to go out of the tent. When she raised her head, the first sight she saw was a striking Seminole chief decked in brown leather from head to toe. Long fringe dangled down the outside of his sleeves and the outer seam of his pants. A breastplate of long beads strung together covered his chest. His long eagle-feathered headdress was the most exquisite Margaret had ever witnessed. He was tall with squared shoulders, and his nostrils flared. His face was filled with strong features, and his dark eyes leapt brightly with shock and disbelief as he beheld the daughter whom he hadn't seen in forty-one years.

Margaret's entire body trembled, and yet suddenly, she felt in total control. With her head held high, her posture straight, she took a step forward as she gripped the box with both hands.

Chapter Fifty-Two
Margaret Meets Her Father

*T*he drum stopped instantly, and a hush fell over the camp. All eyes were on Margaret. Bill gasped and covered his mouth with his large hand. He felt as though time had been turned back and he was looking at his mother or sister.

There was a significant pause. Chief Coosa wiped the tears from his face and moved toward Margaret. He swallowed hard and softly said, "I'm afraid to close my eyes. I fear that when I open them, this day will be only a dream, and you won't be standing before me. Your beauty is greater than the mountain peaks covered with virgin snow and more lovely than the delicate petal of a red rose. I see Mariah when I look at you, my daughter. It would please an old man's heart if you would allow me to embrace you."

Margaret's breathing had relaxed until she stepped forward to her father's outreached arms. With her first step, she experienced the same kind of feeling when she had fainted earlier. The images were so strong she could hardly breathe as the father and daughter placed their arms around each other. At their touch, the images became clear. For the first time, Margaret remembered the nine-year-old girl who had embraced her daddy forty-one years earlier. Her body trembled at Coosa's touch. With her recall, came a mass of tears. Coosa hit his chest and groaned loudly. The drums began to beat, and a joyous celebration filled the mountaintop. Carolyn, Bill and Lighted Path joined the celebration with tears and shouts of joy.

Windy and Sky went into one of the tents and came out with a burlap sack. They set it beside the campfire. One of the warriors spread a pelt on the ground and then emptied the contents of the sack on top of the fur. Chief Coosa lifted his arms over his head. When he did, the drums stopped and the mountaintop fell silent. In a loud voice, Coosa cried, "I lift my voice in praise to the Great Eagle of heaven and earth for bringing my daughter to this special place for my eyes to see and my arms to hold . . . one last time before I make my journey across the vast river."

Sky gently took Margaret's arm and led her to the pelt where the contents had been emptied. Margaret looked at the powdery substance on the skin and frowned. "It's ashes," she muttered.

Sky pointed to the ashes, wanting Margaret to sit in them. Margaret quickly glanced to Bill and Carolyn. Bill nodded for her to do as they asked. Margaret held to the box and sat down with her legs crossed. Not knowing what to expect, she fixed your eyes on Coosa. He stood in front of her and pointed to the box and said, "My daughter, will you please open the box?"

Margaret glanced at the box, then Coosa. When she reached toward the opening of the special box, Margaret pulled back slightly, wanting to protect what she now cherished.

"It's okay," Coosa whispered. Margaret relaxed and Coosa took the necklace from the chest, held it to the sky and said, "Great Creator who sees all things, this treasure has been passed to my daughter. It represents royalty and the signet of my people." Coosa placed the necklace around Margaret's neck. He took the feather from the box and held it to the sky and said, "Mighty Eagle of heaven and earth, thank you for releasing your Eagle spirit into my daughter." He placed the feather inside a strand of beads at the top of the braid, allowing the feather to hang at the side of her face. Coosa took the small pouch from the box, opened it, poured the ashes into the palm of his hand, held it to the sky and then held it over Margaret's head. Slowly he opened his hand, and the ashes covered her ebony crown. In a loud voice, Coosa shouted, "The fire has burned and only the ash remains. Hell has tried to destroy us with a large gulf that separated us. We will not be denied the destiny the Great Eagle has called us to. Holy Spirit, let your fire consume us and raise us from the ashes that remain."

After those words, one drum began to play at a slow pace. Chief Coosa removed his headdress and gave it to one of the warriors. At first he moved his feet in the snow to the rhythm of the lone drum. After a moment, the drum tempo picked up and so did Coosa's feet. He danced and chanted in a tone that was unlike anything

Margaret had ever heard. He took a spear from one of the nearby braves. Holding it over his head, he danced and chanted around the fire with the stamina of a young warrior. The dance went on for at least ten minutes. Without warning, Coosa stopped and hurled the spear into the ground beside Margaret. When the spear hit the ground, the drum stopped instantly. He stood before Margaret, fixed his eyes on hers and shouted, "Oh great God of heaven and earth, blow the spark that this mighty woman possesses in her heart and bring new life to her and her people! Cause the spark to ignite within her and illuminate her path that she may light the way for others. From the ashes of death, cause her to arise like the Mighty Phoenix and display your power for all to see. Cause her to spread her wings and soar to the peaks of the highest mountain. Allow the wind from her wings to bring a refreshing breeze to the souls of all mankind. Always fill her with peace and may she forever find joy on the mountain."

He extended his hand to Margaret. When she placed her hand in his slowly, he helped her from the ground. Windy emerged from a tent with a large piece of bleached leather lying across her arms. Coosa took the skin and opened it. Margaret gasped. Coosa held a long cape up, opened the front and placed it around Margaret's narrow shoulders, the bottom of the cape resting on top of her moccasins. The cape was constructed from fine leather and lined with the same. The outside of the cape was layered from head to toe with overlaid rows of large eagle feathers. Margaret trembled as she stared into to Coosa's eyes, dumbfounded and unable to find words to express what her heart felt. He leaned forward and kissed her cheek, took one step back and started to say something when a loud bang caused everyone to scurry around the camp. Coosa fell into Margaret's arms and they both went down. A shrill scream shot forth when she saw the blood that swiftly covered his back. "Father!" she shouted. Gunfire rang out across the mountain. Warriors dropped lifelessly all around her. She frantically called out to Carolyn who was checking Lighted Path and Bill for any signs of life, but there were none. They both lay in a pool of blood on the snow-covered ground. Gunfire continued to ring out and the warriors continued to fall. Margaret grabbed the drawstring pouch, the small chest and the skin that the cape had been wrapped in. She started away, then turned back and grabbed a handful of ashes. Hurrying to Carolyn, she seized her arm and pulled her into the trees.

They had only gone a short distance when Margaret stopped suddenly. "Carolyn, take the cape off me while I put the ashes in the pouch." She pulled the string to close the pouch and hurriedly broke a piece of fringe from her boot and gave it to Carolyn to hold. Swiftly, taking the necklace from her neck and the feather from her hair, she put them in the chest. Even though the weather was freezing, sweat was beading on Margaret's forehead. Spreading the hide, she wrapped the cape and chest inside, then hid it under a mass of bushes. "Give me the fringe," she said breathlessly. Finding a limb toward the bottom of the bushes she tied the strand to it.

"What are you doing?" Carolyn asked.

"So I can find it when I come back."

"Why don't you take it now?"

Margaret grabbed Carolyn's arm. "Oh God, Carolyn, the shooting stopped. We've got to get out of here."

Chapter Fifty-Three
Captured

The women ran as fast as they could, using caution in the dark so as not to go off a cliff. Margaret stopped abruptly and stooped down.

"What is it?" Carolyn whispered.

"Listen. I hear men's voices. It sounds like they're coming up the mountain."

Their eyes had adjusted to the night, although the snow-covered ground helped tremendously. They looked around for a place to hide. Margaret led the way to a couple of gigantic trees. As the voices grew louder and closer, there was no doubt that there were several men. But who were they and why did they ambush Chief Coosa and the others?

The sound of tree limbs breaking and the crushing sound of boots pressing into the snow sent a chill down Margaret's spine. She propped her forehead against the tree and prayed. Amid great jubilation in having seen her Uncle Bill and receiving the treasures that belonged to her mother and grandma and ultimately meeting her real father, she had also experienced the most devastating time of her life. She wanted to thank God for all He had revealed to her, yet she couldn't understand why she had been exposed to all the death that had woven its way into her joy. Her emotions were so torn that everything that had happened had to be put on hold until they were out of the dangerous situation now presenting itself.

Suddenly, Margaret gasped and froze when she felt the barrel of a gun push hard against her back. A deep voice growled, "Move and I'll kill you." The same happened to Carolyn. Someone behind them lit a lantern and held it up. The man pressing his gun into Margaret's back whispered, "Well, well. What do we have here?"

The one holding Carolyn called out, "Lieutenant Coats! Come take a look at what we've found."

Several pairs of boots scurried through the snow and stopped behind the women. A stern voice ordered, "Turn them around." The man grabbed Margaret's arm, forcing her around, then pushed her back against the tree. Margaret eyes quickly shifted to Carolyn to make sure she was okay.

The soldiers were wearing Union uniforms. One man laughed. "Hey, we've got ourselves a couple of lookers," he cried.

The Lieutenant took the lantern from the soldier and held it close to Margaret's face and then to Carolyn's. "This one's a squaw! The other one is a white woman!" He took a step back and frowned.

The man holding Margaret's arm put his face close to her, sniffed her hair and said, "Hey, Lieutenant, what do you think of this one?"

"Or this one?" the man holding Carolyn chuckled. The lieutenant's solemn stare gave Margaret the creeps. The man holding Margaret pushed the end of his nose to her cheek. She swiftly turned her head. His breath was so disgusting, Margaret felt sick. He grabbed her face and turned it back. "What's the matter pretty thing? Don't you like me or something?"

"That's enough, Corporal! Bring them to camp. Untouched! Understood?"

The man pulled away from Margaret and stuttered, "Yes . . . yes, sir. I didn't mean anything. I was only having some fun."

The lieutenant snapped, "You're not here to have fun; you're here to win a war. Nothing more."

"Yes, sir. I'm sorry, sir." The man grabbed Margaret's arm and pulled her through the snow.

The man with Carolyn seized her arm and she screamed out in pain. "What's the matter with you?" he scolded.

"Her arm is wounded," Margaret shouted.

The man jerked Margaret's arm and told her to shut up. Every muscle in Margaret's body had tensed from fear and the cold. They had walked only a few minutes but it seemed forever. The terrain had leveled; the base of the mountain was a welcome sight. By then Margaret was visibly shaking from the freezing cold. The wind had picked up, dropping the wind chill, but there were no signs of snow clouds in the perfectly clear sky. Margaret had never seen the moon so full. It's rays of light shown through the massive trees. Margaret glanced at the heavyset man who continued to pull her down the trail and into the clearing. There were a number of lit lanterns and torches hanging around several tents. Two campfires were burning brightly at either end of the camp. Every eye turned to Margaret and Carolyn as they were ushered into the base camp. The stern looks on the men's faces was chilling. Their eyes were aloof, like those of someone who had lived with danger a long time.

Lieutenant Coats got off his horse and gave the reins to a soldier nearby. "Corporal Brigs, get that woman a blanket and bring them to my tent."

"Yes, sir. Right away."

Margaret noticed the way everyone jumped when the lieutenant spoke. He wasn't a big man; in fact, he was thin and about five feet eight. His face didn't show one wrinkle. His sandy-colored locks were full around his neck but cut neatly around his face. He had the saddest hazel eyes that Margaret had ever seen, full lips, a thin mustache and slightly pointy nose. The blue uniform gave him a very distinguished look. However, his disposition thus far had been earnest with no sign of pleasantries. A soldier handed Margaret a blanket. She hurriedly wrapped it tight around her shoulders to ward off the bitter cold. The man pulled her forearm, causing one side of the blanket to fall from her shoulder. She scurried to pull it back into place. He was rough and crude with a full, bushy beard and long, brown, curly hair that was in need of being brushed. His eyebrows were a perfect match to his hair. He was chewing tobacco and wasn't careful about keeping it cleaned from his lips and beard. His accent was straight from the backwoods. The men pushed Margaret and Carolyn into the tent. The fire inside was welcome.

The lieutenant motioned to them and said, "Warm yourselves. Corporal, get these women some hot coffee." He looked over his glasses and asked, "You do drink coffee, don't you?"

They both were quick to say yes. The lieutenant sat in a wooden chair at a medium-size crate. A small cot was visible just past the crate. The lieutenant looked at a map and didn't speak until the soldier brought the coffee in and gave it to the women. The corporal continued to stand beside the fire. "Corporal Stills, you can go now." He nervously nodded his head and went out.

Without looking around, Lieutenant Coats said, "You may sit on the cot." He didn't look up until they were seated. Then he glanced over his glasses, pulled them off and put them on the crate. His sad eyes focused on them with no sign of a smile or a frown. His face was thought-provoking. Margaret could only wonder what had brought him to such an intense place. Is it the war? Has a lover, wife or friend jilted him? Or is he serious about his work and the demands placed on him by rank? Or could it be that his will to live is at an end?

Lieutenant Coats pointed to Margaret and asked, "Are you a squaw?"

"I am part Cherokee, but the truth is we were taken hostage two days ago by the Seminole Indians, who took us to the mountaintop where your soldiers just now killed them."

"Why did they dress *you alone* like this and not the other woman?"

"They were having some kind of ceremony and wanted me to put the dress on. I had no choice."

The lieutenant pointed to Carolyn. "Tell me, where is *your* dress?"

"They didn't give me one."

"What's your name?"

"I'm Carolyn Davis."

"Where do you live that you would be taken hostage?"

Carolyn cut her eyes toward Margaret, then quickly back to Lieutenant Coats. "I live in the settlement at Fort Howard. I'm a teacher. How did I get to this place? I went with Margaret to Chestnut Grove to visit her uncle."

"Where's your husband?"

"He died a few years back."

The lieutenant shifted his eyes toward Margaret. "What's your name?"

Margaret tightened the blanket around her shoulder and replied, "My name is Margaret Black. My husband is George Black. He's a semi-retired scout for the military."

"For which side?"

"I can truthfully say he has scouted for both sides."

"What was so important that you had to visit Chestnut Grove when there's a war going on? Before you answer that question, let me ask, did your husband agree to such an endeavor?"

Margaret lowered her head and said softly, "No. He doesn't know that I'm not safe at our home in Cherokee. If he knew my whereabouts, he would surely explode."

"I'm still curious about the dress. Were they going to marry you off to one of the braves?"

"I really don't know what all they were going to do."

The lieutenant stood and put his hands behind his back. After a moment, he looked at Margaret and asked, "Exactly where is your husband that he doesn't know where you are?"

Margaret knew that her answer had to be carefully thought out. She didn't want to tell a Union officer that he was fighting with Confederate troops. She took the last sip of her coffee, trying to buy enough time to get her explanation together. After putting the cup on the ground by the cot, she wiped her mouth and said, "I don't know if you're familiar with a brutal savage called Silent Wolf or another group called . . . called . . ."

Lieutenant Coats furrowed his brows and said, "Fiery Serpents?"

Margaret didn't want to tell what Randy had told her about there being no Fiery Serpents so she nodded yes to the Lieutenant's question.

"I believe we put an end to the so called Fiery Serpents. I'm only thankful that we were able to spare you two."

Margaret fought back tears as she listened to a man who understood nothing about the Indians on the mountain. She wanted to scream from the pain that gripped her heart. In her mind she could see the look on her father's face as he fell into her arms. All of them murdered, because an old Seminole Chief wanted to see his daughter one last time—badly enough, that he made the long journey from his home to the Smoky Mountains, never to return. Margaret knew it was imperative to keep her focus and do what she had to do to be freed from the Union camp and get home. Therefore, she continued her explanation about her husband.

"My husband, George, went out to investigate the first two barbaric murders by Silent Wolf in our area. They were ordinary country folk with small children, including infants. My husband has seen many things in his years of being a scout, but seeing small children murdered and a couple of little girls taken for who knows what purpose . . . well, I'm sure you get my meaning."

"Yes, I do, Mrs. Black; however, that doesn't explain to me where your husband is at this present time. So if you will oblige me with that information, I would appreciate it."

"I would be glad to do so, but I can't."

"And why is that?"

Margaret licked her upper lip and replied, "A few days ago, there was an attack on Townsend. Major Wright at Fort Howard asked George to guide them to Townsend to investigate the attack. It was believed to be Silent Wolf, but they weren't sure."

Lieutenant Coats folded his arms and sighed. Margaret hoped the sigh would be a link to his emotions.

She took advantage by asking, "Do you know anything about Townsend or maybe someone there?"

His sad eyes looked down to meet hers. She could tell that she had struck a nerve, so she swiftly interjected, "I hope I didn't say something that maybe I shouldn't have about an attack on Townsend. I was only answering your question."

"When exactly did you say the attack took place?"

Margaret shrugged her shoulders and glanced at Carolyn. "It was a couple of weeks ago, wasn't it, Carolyn?"

Carolyn nodded slightly. "Yes, at least that." Carolyn looked at the lieutenant and asked, "Have you ever lost all perception of time? I think I speak for Margaret and myself when I say since we left Cherokee, going to Chestnut Grove, time has become a blur."

Margaret quickly added, "That's for sure."

Lieutenant Coats sat down on the crate and crossed his legs. He said nothing for a moment and then he turned his focus to Margaret. "Did he go only to scout for Major Wright, or did he go to fight with him?"

Margaret frowned. "He went as a scout, but I'm sure if the need should present itself, he would fight. There's no way that he would be put into danger and not defend himself."

"What was the importance of going to visit an uncle with all the uprising and attacks going on?"

Margaret tightened her lips. "Can I be honest with you about the visit?"

"I would expect nothing less."

"My mother passed away when I was a young girl. She had two brothers and one sister. The sister passed away a couple of years back. After mother's death, my Uncle Bill moved away, cutting all ties with his brother and sister. They're all up in age and would never talk about the reason for the split. Are you a family person, Lieutenant Coats?"

"Yes, I am."

"I am too. I think family is the most important thing we have, outside of God. To see the family torn apart and not many years left for any of them was more than I could stand. When George left, I felt that should be the time I made the trip Chestnut Grove. Otherwise I would perhaps never be able to make the trip. George would fuss about it, and I wouldn't want to add to the problem, so I left the morning after he did. I can't explain it, but I had to try and find out what the problem was and see if there was any way possible to fix it before another one of them died."

Lieutenant Coats tilted his head and asked, "Did you accomplish your mission, Mrs. Black?"

"Well, not exactly. The Indians took us hostage before I could complete it. Lieutenant Coats, I want you to know we're not here by choice, and we weren't at the mountain by choice. All we want to do is go home. To say I'm not anxious about being here would be a lie. I'm somewhat terrified; yet I feel you are a fair and decent man."

Lieutenant Coats leaned back in his chair and crossed his hands across his stomach. "What am I to assume from your words? Would you be asking me to let you go?"

Margaret leaned forward and replied, "Yes. That's exactly what I'm doing. We're no threat to you or your men."

"You have pleasant words and a cunning way with your words; however, I'm not sure what your fate will be. I know what my men would like for your fate to be, but I don't hurt people for the sake of what some might call fun. I'm in this war to free the slaves that the South holds in bondage. I'm not out to kill women and children, nor to rape women to satisfy my desires. I don't know what I'm going to do as of yet. I'll have to think about it. For tonight, I'll put a guard around you and get back to you in the morning. We have other troops who haven't come in from their mission. I'll have . . ."

Before he could finish his sentence, one of the soldiers shouted, "Riders approaching!"

Lieutenant Coats quickly stood as the horses drew near and stopped outside the tent.

Carolyn and Margaret looked at each other. Margaret whispered, "I've been praying God will get us out of here. How's your arm?"

"It hurts, but the ointment really helped."

Lieutenant Coats showed his first sign of emotions by telling Carolyn and Margaret, "No talking."

At that moment, an officer entered the tent and greeted Lieutenant Coats. Lieutenant Coats was standing in front of the women, blocking the view of the officer. "How was your mission, Captain?"

"Very successful. I heard you have a couple of female prisoners."

"Yes sir, I do."

Lieutenant Coats stepped aside, opening the view for the Captain. Carolyn and Margaret gasped and their eyes widened. The Captain chuckled and in disbelief, muttered, "My heavenly days."

Lieutenant Coats swiftly asked the captain, "Sir, what's so funny?"

"Mrs. Black and Miss Morris?" The captain continued to laugh.

Lieutenant Coats was shocked by his actions. "Captain Ross, what is it?"

"I'm just a little shocked at your prisoners."

Carolyn and Margaret smiled as they looked at their first ray of hope out of the predicament they were in.

"Lieutenant, I know these women. I'm not sure how they became your prisoners, but they're no threat to us."

"But, sir, how do you know?"

"These women came to my rescue not long ago. I might add they also served Corporal Smith and I a tasty meal and didn't turn us in." Captain Ross took his hat off and put it on the crate. "Lieutenant, have Corporal Smith come here please."

The lieutenant left the tent. Captain Ross extended his hand to Margaret. "I can only imagine how you two were captured," he said.

Margaret took his hand and breathlessly replied, "It's quite a story." Margaret started to stand, then quickly asked, "Is it all right for us to stand?"

"Of course you may."

Carolyn stood and nodded. "I can't believe this," she said.

Captain Ross shook her hand. When he did, she flinched and groaned. "What's wrong?" he asked.

Margaret answered, "A tree limb hit her arm."

"Let me take a look," he said as he helped her take her coat off. He sniffed and asked, "What is that smell? Is your arm infected?"

"No," Carolyn moaned as he took the cloth from the wound. "The Indians put some kind of salve on it. It helped so much. On contact, it numbed the wound and the area around the wound."

He raised his brows. "It smells awful, but looks clean. We don't have a doctor here, but we do have some whiskey if you would like some."

"No, thank you. I want to stay alert as long as possible."

"If you change your mind, let me know."

"Thank you."

He looked at the dress Margaret was wearing. "Why are you in a squaw's dress? And where did you get it?"

Before Margaret could answer, Corporal Smith entered the tent. "You wanted to see me, sir?" His mouth opened in surprise. "Captain, we know these women. They're the ones at Cherokee. Mrs. Black and Miss Morris."

Captain Ross grinned. "I thought you would remember them."

"Are they the prisoners?" Corporal Smith asked.

"One and the same."

Corporal Smith took his cap off and nodded to the women. "It's good to see you again. Of course I'm surprised at the circumstances."

"Are you ladies hungry?" Captain Ross asked.

Margaret moaned, "Yes. We're starved."

"We can fix that for you. Corporal Smith, go see what you can round up for our guests."

Corporal Smith saluted. "It will be my pleasure, sir."

Lieutenant Coats returned with a question. "Captain, what should we do with these women?"

"First of all, we'll feed them and then I'll find out what they're doing here. Then, they can get some sleep. That's what I suggest you do, lieutenant. We have a long day ahead of us tomorrow."

Lieutenant Coats nodded his head, said goodnight and left the tent.

Captain Ross sat down in the chair and crossed his arms. "Ladies, I want you to sit and share your story with me. I don't care who talks first."

They sat down and Margaret began. "I don't know if you remember our conversation about a quest that was burning in my soul. I asked you if there were any other soldiers in the area. You thought I was asking for military reasons, but I wasn't."

"I remember well. You asked if I had ever experienced something that's so much greater than one's self. You mentioned something about a mystery, and that you needed to find the missing pieces in order to solve the mystery. . . if my memory serves me right."

"My goodness," Margaret said, "your memory serves you very accurately. I was endeavoring to find those missing pieces when all of this took place."

Corporal Smith brought in food and gave it to the women. "Corporal, bring another cot and some blankets for the ladies."

"Yes, sir."

"Margaret, why don't you fill me in on your adventure as you eat."

Margaret started at the first and told Captain Ross everything that had taken place. He listened without comment, until she told about the soldiers killing Chief Coosa, Lighted Path and her Uncle Bill. "That part I don't understand," Margaret said. "They didn't even fire a warning shot, yell out or anything."

"In defense of my men, I must say there was a reason for the ambush. They actually thought they were freeing you and Miss Morris. A couple of our men had watched the group for three days. When they saw the two squaws that watched you everywhere you went, that was a definite sign to my men that you were being held against your will. Please try and understand there is a war going on. Nevertheless, I'm sorry about Lighted Path, Chief Coosa and your uncle. In the morning, we'll go to the mountaintop and see that they are buried."

"I would be so grateful," Margaret said.

"Are you going to let us go home after that?" Carolyn asked.

"Yes, I am."

"With horses, I hope?" Margaret groaned.

Captain Ross stood. "That request, I can't fill even if I wanted to. The United States Army says no."

Margaret spoke up, "But one of those horses was mine to start with."

"Even so, I can't give one to you. We need every one of them for our men."

"But . . . but how can we make it home in the snow without horses?"

"Oh, you'll be all right. You two must be as tough as nails with all you've been through. You'll find your way home, I'm sure of that. Get some sleep. I'll see you in the morning." He tipped his hat and said goodnight.

Corporal Smith passed the captain as he left the tent. The women could hear them talking but couldn't make out what they were saying. Corporal Smith came into their tent, smiled and said, "Here's the cot and some blankets. I'm sorry we didn't have any pillows."

"Trust me, corporal, this is more than we ever expected," Margaret said.

"Captain Ross said that Private Carver and I will stand guard over you tonight."

"That's a comfort to know," Carolyn said.

"This isn't the best place for two nice looking women, if you know what I mean."

"We know exactly what you mean," Carolyn replied. "Thanks for your concern."

He gave a tight-lipped grin and said, "I'll bring some wood in for the fire. I'll be right back."

When he left, Carolyn and Margaret embraced. "I knew that God would help us," Margaret whispered.

"I just want to get home," Carolyn uttered.

After the corporal put wood on the fire, Margaret blew the lamp out and lay down. She pulled the covers up tight around her neck. Carolyn went to sleep as soon as her eyes closed. Margaret, however, couldn't clear her mind enough to sleep. She hadn't had a chance to grieve over her Uncle Bill, Lighted Path or her newly found father, Coosa. The images were indelible of Sky and Windy lying face down in the snow; and her heart felt as though it could explode wanting to feel George's arms. She smiled, remembering his tender kiss on the steps before he left and the promise of a romantic rendezvous. Still, her quest wasn't over. With hopes of finding more information about Phoebe, the need to see Desan was stronger than ever. *I used to have such a normal life,* she thought. Margaret hugged her arms recalling the nine-year-old girl having to be pried loose from her father's neck. Even more vivid now was the recall of Coosa wailing as they rode out of his sight, his land and his life. She could hardly wait to get back to the mountain to bury Coosa and the others before wild animals got hold of them. More than anything, she wanted to make sure the rare treasures that had been passed to her were safe. Even with her mind so full, Margaret's tired body finally gave way to slumber.

Chapter Fifty-Four
Captain Ross's Plan

The sound of boots scurrying outside the tent caused Margaret to spring up breathlessly. Her eyes frantically assessed the tent. "Carolyn," she called out softly.

Carolyn yawned and rubbed her eyes. "I can't open my eyes. I'm too tired."

Margaret swiftly got up and folded the covers and the cot. "Carolyn, get up. Captain Ross said he would take us to the mountain today. Then we can get you home and to a doctor."

Carolyn sat on the side of the cot but said nothing. Margaret noticed the somber look on Carolyn's face. She quickly squatted in front of her and took her hand. "Are you okay?"

Tears welled up in Carolyn's eyes, and her chin began to quiver. "I've tried to be brave and keep up with you and I was doing all right, until the tree limb." Carolyn began to cry. She tried to be as quiet as possible so not to be heard outside the tent. Margaret wiped Carolyn's tears. "I really need to see a doctor," Carolyn said

319

between sobs. "Through the night, I realized that all the smell wasn't just from the salve. I think my arm is as risk of getting infected. I don't want to die from an infection if I can get to a doctor and get something to prevent it."

"Oh honey, I'm so sorry." Margaret couldn't hold her feelings down. She wept aloud. Through her tears, she tried to speak. She didn't know that Captain Ross was standing outside the tent, hearing all that was said.

Margaret laid her head on Carolyn's knees. "I've been so wrapped up in my own selfish plans, I really haven't been considerate of you at all. You're my best friend, and I'd rather have you than any foolish dream that I could ever pursue. Please forgive me. We'll forget about the going back to the mountain. I'll ask Captain Ross to point us in the right direction and we'll go home."

Margaret jerked when she heard a soft voice say, "I'll see that you get to a doctor, Miss Morris. I can't give you a horse, but you can ride with Corporal Smith. He can take you to the area that borders Cherokee."

Margaret stood and seized Captain Ross's hands as he entered. "Thank you, thank you. I don't know what else to say."

Captain Ross grinned, "I think you just said all you need to say."

"Do you think Corporal Smith will mind taking us?" Carolyn asked.

Captain Ross stepped aside and allowed Corporal Smith to enter. "It would be my pleasure, Miss Morris."

"There is one catch," Captain Ross said.

Margaret dried her eyes. "What's the catch?"

He and Corporal Smith drew closer to the cot where Carolyn was sitting. "The catch is, no one must know that Corporal Smith is doing this . . . including Lieutenant Coats. It's against regulations. Not to mention the fact that Lieutenant Coats would love to find anything out of order so he could see me hanged."

"If that's the case, how will you manage to keep it quiet?" Margaret asked.

"When we leave for the mountain this morning, the moment we're out of sight Corporal Smith and Miss Morris will head for Cherokee. You and I, on the other hand, will go bury your dead and then you too will be free to go home, but without a horse."

"No," Carolyn said. "Why can't Margaret come with me and Corporal Smith?"

"Miss Morris, three people can't ride on one horse for this kind of trip. I'll need some help in order to get back on time. I could tell last night, from the looks of your arm that you were in desperate need of a doctor and soon. I'm not trying to scare you, but I don't want to see you die, as many of my men have. Margaret is healthy and I'll point her in the right direction. She'll make it home in a couple of days. I'll see she has some food and a warm coat and a pair of wool socks. She'll be fine."

Carolyn looked anxiously at Margaret who was quick to say, "He's right, Carolyn. You need a doctor, and I know how to survive. I'll leave as soon as we attend our dead."

Carolyn looked down and asked, "What about Windy and Sky?"

Margaret looked at Captain Ross. "We can take care of them as well," he said.

At that time, Lieutenant Coats entered the tent and the conversation quickly changed.

"Good morning, ladies," Lieutenant Coats said with a nod.

"Good morning," Margaret said.

Lieutenant Coats put his gloves on and asked, "What's the agenda for this morning, Captain Ross?"

"This morning I want you to take some men and scout the northern section that leads around the caves we saw day before yesterday. I want the caves searched and make sure they're clear. I'm going to take the women back to the mountain to retrieve their things, take the tents down and cover the bodies. We should be back by nightfall."

"What about the women after that, sir?" the lieutenant asked.

"Then as far as I'm concerned, they can go home."

"How many men are you taking with you?"

"I'll take Corporal Smith."

"That's all?"

"Yes, lieutenant."

"Sir, won't that be a lot to accomplish with just two people?"

Captain Ross frowned. "The women can help."

Lieutenant Coats looked at Carolyn and Margaret. "Yes, sir, I never thought of that."

The lieutenant turned to leave, stopped and asked, "What time will you be leaving, sir?"

"After the women eat."

The lieutenant tipped his hat to Carolyn and Margaret. "I hope you find what you're looking for, ladies."

Margaret smiled and thanked him. Captain Ross told Corporal Smith to get the women something to eat and get some extra for Margaret to take with her. The corporal quickly left and Captain Ross assured the women that everything would be all right. He checked Carolyn's arm. "You should be back at Cherokee by nightfall. Corporal will take my horse. He's faster than the wind."

"In a few hours!" Excitement filled Margaret's voice. "Are we that close to home?" she asked.

Captain Ross smiled and said, "By horse, yes. Didn't you know?"

"No, I didn't. Actually I didn't know where we were. Lighted Path broke from the trail, and I didn't have a clue where he was leading us. He said he knew a closer way, so I didn't question him. I did observe our surroundings; however, I didn't recognize anything about the area."

Margaret hugged Carolyn. "That relieves my mind, knowing we're that close to home. I must confess you're not the only one I'm relieved for. A few hours' journey is not bad. Without a horse, I should still make it in two good days."

Corporal Smith entered with coffee and bacon wrapped in fried bread. Margaret took a slow easy breath to absorb the aroma. "Oh, Corporal, that smells so good."

Captain Ross smiled. "We'll leave as soon as you get through eating. I'll make sure we have everything we need to take with us in the meanwhile." The captain and corporal left the tent. Carolyn and Margaret gobbled down the food in a couple of minutes. When they came from the tent, every eye focused on them. Lieutenant Coats had already left on his mission, which was a relief for Captain Ross. As Margaret started to mount the horse behind Captain Ross, one of the soldiers called out to the captain. "Sir, would you like to use my horse for the women to ride? I'm assigned camp duty today. I won't be needing it. It would sure make it a lot easier on you and the horses."

"Actually, that's a splendid idea, private."

Chapter Fifty-Five
Carolyn's Wound Worsens

When out of sight of the camp, they stopped. Captain Ross told Margaret to dismount and ride with him. Margaret slid off and patted Carolyn's hand. "Home in a few hours. Keep that thought and pray for me. Listen, when you get home, take the horse from the barn and go straight to Randy at the fort. Tell him what's happened, and I'll be home in two days. If I'm not, tell him to please come looking for me. I want you to stay with Julie. Randy will send the doctor there immediately." Margaret sighed. "If by chance George is home, tell him what's happened, and he'll be on his way to meet me. Promise me you'll do as I ask. Promise."

Carolyn nodded. "I promise. I feel so bad to leave you, like I'm a deserter."

"Don't start that again. You get to a doctor and . . . I love you."

"I love you," Carolyn said as tears filled her eyes.

"We've got to be going, Captain Ross said. "Corporal Smith, take care, ride like the wind, and I'll meet you back here as soon as you can possibly get back."

"Yes, sir. I'll need a miracle to be back by morning. We'll ride as hard as possible."

Captain Ross looked to the sky and responded, "You'll be back before morning. God will see to that."

The corporal grinned. "Yes, sir."

"Miss Morris, I pray for God's speed and healing to your arm."

Carolyn wiped her tears and replied, "I pray for you, Captain. Thank you for everything."

"It's my pleasure to repay the favor bestowed on Corporal Smith and myself. Maybe we'll meet again . . . under different circumstances."

Margaret waved as they rode away. Captain Ross took Margaret's hand and pulled her up behind him and started up the mountain.

Chapter Fifty-Six
The Burial

$\mathcal{I}$t was cold, but the sun shone intermittently through the trees. Margaret held tight around Captain Ross's waist as they made their way up the trails winding through the forest. Her emotions were evident as they neared the top of the mountain. Margaret hoped the captain didn't hear her crying or feel the subtle movement of her body. It was evident that he did, when he gently pressed his hand against hers. For an instant, the touch of a strong hand felt so comforting.

Out of exhaustion, Margaret rested her head on his back. This wasn't her character. She was always strong and very independent, but not this time. She felt like a little child who desperately needed someone to hold her, if only for a minute. With her eyes closed for a brief moment, she pretended it was George holding her hand. In her mind, she could feel the stroke of George's fingertips pushing her hair from her face and the gentle way that he would rub his cheek to hers. Soothing thoughts of the man she loved caused her body to stop trembling and a calm to cover her like a warm blanket. Captain Ross had stopped the horse, but Margaret continued to hold tight to his waist. After a couple of minutes, Captain Ross patted her hand and said, "Margaret, Margaret."

She quickly released her hands and cut her eyes around the area. The first thing she saw was tents and then dead bodies lying in the snow. Pain gripped her soul as she remembered the last few minutes before the guns sounded, changing her life forever. Captain Ross dismounted and extended his hand to help Margaret, who continued to stare at the lifeless bodies scattered throughout the camp.

"Margaret."

She slowly turned her head and fixed her uncomprehending eyes on his and muttered, "Why? Please tell me why? They weren't doing anything except having some kind of ceremony that honored me. I didn't understand all that was going on, but it was something good, not bad."

Captain Ross didn't answer. He knew at that time, no matter what he said, it wouldn't ease her pain. "I have to get to work," he said. "I'll never make it back by dark if I don't. I really need you to help me, if you will."

Margaret responded, "Of course. I need to be busy."

"I understand. Just do the best you can. We need to start by burying bodies first." Captain Ross took a shovel from his horse and looked at Margaret. "Is there anyone in particular that you want to bury first?" he asked.

Margaret looked at Bill, then Coosa. "I want to bury Chief Coosa first, then Uncle Bill."

Captain Ross looked around the area and asked, "Is there any place you have in mind?"

"I want to bury him here by the fire, where he fell."

"Okay. The holes are going to be pretty shallow because of the frozen ground. I'll dig a hole for Coosa, Bill and Lighted Path. The others will have to be covered with whatever we can find."

"Not Windy and Sky. I'll dig their place."

"I'll do it. While I dig, you can take the tents down. I have a hatchet in my saddlebag you can use to cut the straps from the stakes."

Margaret got the hatchet and started to the first tent. As she passed Coosa, she paused and looked for any likeness in his face that she could relate to as her own, but saw none. She passed Bill and paused. She thought of the portraits of Phoebe, her mother and Coosa he had painted. What would happen to them now that he was dead?

Margaret began to work frantically taking the tents down. She didn't know where the energy came from; nevertheless, she would accept it whatever the source.

After the graves were dug, Margaret helped Captain Ross put the bodies in the holes. They shared a prayer over each one and then covered them up. Margaret picked a special place under an oak tree for Sky and Windy. They rolled the others into a large ditch and spread the leather from the tents over them and piled brush and tree limbs over the leather. Margaret put aside the beautiful headdress of Chief Coosa. She wanted something to remember him by. So she rolled it in a pelt and put it by the horse.

Daylight was quickly fading. Captain Ross sat on a piece of rawhide and leaned back against a tree to rest a few minutes. Margaret started to go into the trees from the clearing. Captain Ross called out, "Where are you going?"

"I left something down the hill just a short distance from the clearing. I need to find it before we go."

Captain Ross rose quickly and followed after her. Margaret checked every large mass of bushes for the piece of leather she had tied to mark the spot. After a few minutes, she called out. "Here it is! Thank you Lord for letting me to find it."

Captain Ross watched as Margaret pulled a long piece of hide from the bushes. She held something to her chest. "What is it?" he asked.

"Treasures. This small cedar chest holds my inheritance. It may mean nothing to anyone else, but it's everything to me."

Back at the clearing, Captain Ross informed Margaret that they should be going.

"Could I have a moment?" she asked.

"Yes, but only a few minutes." He led the horse down the trail and waited for her.

Margaret stood by the campfire that had burned brightly a few hours earlier and remembered. There, she thanked the Mighty Eagle for bringing her to the mountaintop and her father. She absorbed the moment, then headed toward Captain Ross. The ride to the foot of the mountain went fast. The twilight deepened and the gloom of the forest melted into an indistinct mass darkness.

When they arrived at the base of the mountain, Corporal Smith had just arrived.

Captain Ross chuckled. "Corporal, that is what you call timing."

"Tell me about Carolyn," Margaret hurriedly asked.

"I took her to the boundary of trees behind your place. We rode hard, but she did okay. It was as though angels picked up the horse and we glided. I'm astounded how fast our horses went. It's unbelievable."

Captain Ross raised his brows, "You said you needed a miracle; it would appear you got one."

"Yes, sir!"

Captain Ross took Margaret's things from his horse and put his hand on her shoulder. "I wish I could give you a horse, but you know I can't. I could be shot for that, and if I die, I don't want it to be over a horse."

"I understand," Margaret said.

"Are your feet warm?" Corporal Smith asked.

Margaret smiled. "Yes, thanks to Captain Ross's generous donation of a pair of his wool socks. Thank you, Corporal, for a pair of your pants and you, Captain Ross, for one of your shirts and coats."

Captain Ross saluted Margaret, "Keep south, soldier, and you'll make it home without any problem."

Margaret smiled and quickly hugged Captain Ross and Corporal Smith. "God bless you two. I can't imagine what would have happened to Carolyn and me without you. Again, thank you for everything."

Margaret turned to walk away alone. Captain Ross called out. "God keep you, Margaret, and may your path be lighted."

She nodded. "And your steps, Captain. I'll never forget your kindness."

The men mounted their horses and rode back to the camp. Margaret walked into the night with the treasures of heaven and earth in her heart and hands.

Chapter Fifty-Seven

The Barn

The sky was clear and millions of stars twinkled, enhancing the radiance of the half-moon. The air was freezing, but the wind was calm. For that, Margaret was most grateful. Her eyes were big, and her adrenalin pumped. She went as fast as possible while she made her way through a valley that was all but devoid of trees. Her lips were dry and the cold air hurt her lungs, forcing her to wrap her scarf around her mouth. At times her brisk walk turned into a trot. Margaret was thankful the snow wasn't frozen but a powdery mix that made it much easier for walking. She trekked for several hours, only stopping for water, to relieve herself and to take a few bites of beef jerky.

The night passed quickly, and the first gray light of morning crept across the wooded area. Her muscles ached from the cold and overexertion. She scanned the area for a place to rest; her eyes burned like fire from the cold.

After walking for almost a mile through the trees, she stopped abruptly, immobilized by total exhaustion.

Flinging her things to the ground, she grabbed and quickly removed the scarf that felt as though it was smothering her. She leaned her body forward and held her knees with her hands. A deep breath of cold air actually felt good as she stretched her tired body. Then she straightened and turned her head to the right and to the left. She whispered, "Oh, my God!" What she saw to the left caused her to lose her breath for a moment.

Smoke from a chimney spiraled upward. Promptly surveying the grounds around her, she moved slowly to the top of the hill. From behind a large tree, she saw a log cabin and a barn nearby. Margaret knew going to the house could be risky, but if she could make it to the barn, perhaps she could hide and get a few minutes of sleep. It was the barn or the snow. It didn't take her long to decide her chances in the barn were better than the lying against a tree out in the open.

Margaret picked up her things and moved cautiously toward the barn. It was plain there were no windows in the back or on the left side of the house; that was a blessing in itself. Knowing this, she ran as fast as possible to the back of the building. Leaning against the barn, she tried to catch her breath and to listen for sounds from inside. Hoping to hear the sweet sound of a horse, mule, pony or anything she might borrow, she was disappointed to hear nothing except the low moan of a cow. Margaret peeked around the side of the barn to make sure the way to the front was clear. She noted the door was secured by a latch. Swiftly running from the side, she lifted the latch, opened the door and hurriedly closed it. "Shoot," she whispered. "How am

I going to resecure the door on the outside?" Looking around, she found a long, slender piece of wood with a curved blade attached to the end. Putting the blade to the bottom of the door, she pulled the door to, which dropped the latch, securing the door. Margaret saw a rugged, makeshift ladder at the end of the barn. Four large nails held it to the floor of the loft, which was filled with hay. Margaret cautiously went up the ladder and to the other end of the loft. In the corner, she placed her things to one side and spread the hay out. After taking a small blanket from her roll, she put it around her shoulders and sat down. She licked her dry lips as she opened the canteen and took a drink of water; she ate beef jerky and then lay down and pulled the hay over her. It felt so good just to have the opportunity to rest. After praying that Carolyn's arm would be okay and George was somewhere safe and warm, she also prayed that God would protect her and help her find her way home.

Margaret groaned and turned from her back to her side. She halfway opened her eyes only to see two sets of shoes beside her. With caution she turned her head and gradually moved her eyes up the legs to the faces of a middle-aged woman and a boy who looked about twelve or thirteen. The woman had a pitchfork in her hands pointing at Margaret's stomach.

"What are you doing in our barn?" she snapped.

Without moving anything but her eyes, Margaret answered, "I don't mean you any harm. I just needed some sleep. I'll be on my way. I . . . I don't want any trouble. I just want to get home, that's all."

The boy frowned and asked, "Why didn't you knock on our door if you needed some help?"

"I . . . I was afraid. I didn't know if I would find a welcome smile or an unwelcome frown. I didn't want to take a chance on the latter, so I chose the barn."

The boy tightened his lips and turned to his mother. "Do you believe her, Mama?"

"I don't know, son." She pulled the pitchfork back a little and said, "Stand up and let's take a look at you."

Margaret pulled the blanket aside, and like lightning, the woman pushed the pitchfork back at Margaret. "What are you doing with Union britches on?"

"And the shirt, Mama," the boy added.

Margaret leaned away from the pitchfork. "Please, allow me to explain."

The woman furrowed her brows. "You had better do something. I don't care for any stinking Union soldier or anybody that's on their side."

"I assure you I'm not Union anything. My name is Margaret Black, and I live in Cherokee. As we speak, my husband, George Black, is out scouting for Major Wright who's over Fort Howard."

"If that's true, where did you get them clothes?"

"I was taken hostage by some Indians and the Union soldiers rescued me a couple of days ago. The Indians made me put on some of their clothes. Two of the soldiers were nice enough to give me something to wear instead. They didn't fit, but I took them. At least they will keep me warm until I can get home."

"Do you believe her, Mama? Or should we put an end to her right now?"

The woman pulled the pitchfork back and hesitated. "I think her story could be true. You say you live in Cherokee?"

"Yes, I do."

The woman nodded toward Margaret's things, "What's in that cloth?"

Margaret's eyes saddened as she laid her hand on the cloth. "These are very precious to me. It's some things that were given to me for safekeeping."

"Open it up and let's see," the woman said.

Margaret unrolled the skin. The first things they saw were the headdress and the eagle cape.

"What are you doing with that stuff?"

"They're souvenirs taken from those who took me."

The boy sneered. "What's in that box?"

"May I show you?" Margaret asked.

The boy nodded.

"Do you mind if I sit up?" Margaret asked.

The woman paused and then said, "Okay, but if you try anything, this fork goes through you."

Margaret held to the box and slowly sat up.

"That sure is a pretty box. Is that turquoise on the top?" the woman asked.

Margaret hesitated, not sure what the woman's curiosity would produce. "Yes, it is turquoise.

Before Margaret could open the box a squeaky little voice called out, "Mama, are you in here?"

The woman quickly cried out. "Diana, didn't I tell you to stay in the house?"

"Yes, but Dan's crying and he won't stop."

The woman furrowed her brows and, in a voice of

sheer frustration, shouted, "Where's your coat, Diana? You know better than to come out in this god-forsaken cold without a coat. Now get to the house."

The boy lowered his head and said, "Mama, I'll go see about Dan if you'll be okay without me."

"Yeah, you go on. I'll be fine," she said. "I'll be there in a few minutes."

The boy pointed his finger at Margaret and frowned. "If you hurt my mama, I'll kill you."

"Franklin! They ain't nobody going to hurt me. Now go on and see about the baby."

Franklin snarled his nose at Margaret as he passed by. Before Franklin could get down the steps Diana shouted, "Mama, Dan won't shut up!"

"Blame it!" The woman shouted. She jabbed the pitchfork at Margaret and growled, "Get up, dad-blame it. Don't you try anything with me, or I'll run you through. I'm just in the right frame of mind to do it, too. I love my children better than anything, but they get on my last nerve sometimes."

Margaret held tight to the box but left the cape and headdress rolled in the cloth. The woman went down the ladder first and stood at the bottom, holding the pitchfork at Margaret as she came down. As they drew near the house, the women saw that the front door was open. The woman with the pitchfork ordered Margaret inside. Franklin was walking around the only room, bouncing a screaming baby.

"Franklin," the woman said, "put Dan in the crib and while I feed him, get some rope and tie up our trespasser."

The little, blond-haired girl stared as Franklin tied Margaret's hands behind her. The woman propped the pitchfork against the wall and picked the baby up. "Franklin, put some wood in the heater please. Diana, I've told you, 'Don't leave the door open.' Try to remember to shut it next time, okay?"

"Okay, Mama." The child hugged her mother, who was breastfeeding a now contented baby. The woman continued to hug the little girl with one arm and hold the baby with the other. Silence filled the meager home. Franklin sat at a table that was covered with an off-white cloth. There were benches on either side. A potbelly heater sat near the wall in the living area. There was an upstairs that looked similar to the loft in the barn. Two kerosene lamps hung from the ceiling, one over the table and one in the living area. A small, hand-carved settee with a brightly colored quilt draped across it sat near the heater on one side and two, high-backed cane chairs on the other. A low bed with a feather tick, sat close to a hand-carved crib.

Chapter Fifty-Eight

Making Friends

*L*ike his mother and sister, Franklin had blond hair and fair skin. His pale blue eyes were striking. He stood about five feet six inches tall with a slim frame. His blue pants were a little short, revealing his hand-knitted wool socks. He sat at the table reading a book.

Diana looked to be about six or seven with long blond hair and large blue eyes. She wasn't shy, but neither was she outgoing. It was plain that she loved her mama. Dan couldn't have been more than six months old. Margaret looked at the mother and wondered where her husband could be. Or did she have a husband? She was medium height with a slim frame and wore her long, blond hair twisted in a bun on the back of her head. Strands of hair hung around her face. Her skin was flawless, and her lips were full. Up to this point, it was as though Margaret wasn't in the room. How long would they go without speaking to her? Finally, after the woman had put the baby down, Margaret asked, "How old is your baby?"

The woman cut her eyes to Margaret and said, "He's six months."

"You have beautiful children," Margaret said.

"Yeah," the woman muttered.

"Do you mind if I ask your name?"

The woman frowned at Margaret. "This is not a social gathering."

"I . . . I know. I . . . I was just trying to make conversation. That's all."

The woman pushed a strand of hair behind her ear. "My name is Holly."

"That's a pretty name."

Holly glanced at the floor and softly said, "Thank you so much."

Franklin's face hardened. "Mama, what are we going to do with her?"

Holly sighed and said, "I don't know. I don't really think she's here to harm us, so I'll probably need to let her go."

"Shoot," Franklin grunted.

His mama put her hands on her hips and asked, "What do you suggest we do with her? Do you want us to string her up for trespassing?"

Franklin didn't respond. He looked down and continued to read. Diana sat near the heater and played with her doll. It was made of straw and covered with cloth from a flour sack.

"Holly," Margaret said, "would you mind if I call you Holly?"

Holly frowned at Margaret. "That's my name. What else would you call me?"

Margaret wanted to make conversation to ease any tension she may have caused. "Franklin, do you like to read?"

He lifted his eyes but not his head. "If I didn't like to read I wouldn't be sitting here reading, would I?"

Holly snapped, "Franklin, you mind your manners."

"But, Mama, it was a stupid question."

"Stupid or not, you respect your elders."

"She's not that old."

Holly tightened her lips. "You hush."

Diana had made her way to her mother and asked, "Are you going to keep her hands tied?"

Holly patted her shoulder and said, "For now."

"But, Mama, if you're going to let her go home, why keep her hands tied? Is she going to hurt us?"

"No, baby, she's not going to hurt us."

Franklin closed his book. "Diana's right Mama. If you really think she's not going to try anything, why keep her tied?"

"You two stop bugging me." Holly paused a moment then took a knife from a small table in the kitchen area and looked at Margaret. Franklin's eyes widened, he jumped up from the table and shouted, "Are you going to kill her, Mama?"

Holly frowned at him. "My God in heaven. Have you lost your mind? You just got through asking me why I didn't untie her, and now you ask if I'm going to kill her?" Holly shook her head and cut the rope, freeing Margaret's hands. Holly squinted at Franklin and stuttered, "D-d-did you really think I would kill somebody?"

Franklin sat back down and muttered, "No I didn't. That's why it surprised me when you got the knife, Mom."

Margaret rubbed her wrist. "Thanks for cutting me loose. I was telling the truth when I said that I meant you no harm. All I really want is to get back to Cherokee."

Holly motioned for Margaret to come sit at the table. "Do you want something to eat?"

"I would love some coffee."

Franklin put his book down. "I'll get it, Mama."

Diana snuggled up to Holly, and Franklin brought the coffee and sat it in front of Margaret. "Thank you so much for the coffee."

"You're welcome," Holly said.

Margaret watched as Holly stroked Diana's hair. Holly stared at Margaret with sad eyes and asked, "Did you say that your husband was a scout for the troops at Fort Howard?"

"Yes. He's semi-retired, but so many things were going on with the Indians and Union soldiers he felt had to do what he could."

"You said your husband was out on a mission now. Do you know where he is?"

"The last I heard, he was going to Townsend."

Holly put her hand over her mouth and breathed hard through her fingers. Franklin looked up and asked, "What is it, Mama?"

"I'm pretty sure Townsend was where your daddy was going."

"Your husband is in the Army?" Margaret asked.

"Yes. He left three weeks ago. I haven't heard anything since. You say that there was a mass of soldiers?"

"Yes. I know how you feel. I haven't heard from my husband since he left either."

"You say you know how I feel. Do you have children?"

Margaret shook her head.

"Then how can you possibly say you know how I feel?"

"I know how you feel about your husband. I miss George beyond any words."

Diana looked at Margaret and said, "What's your name, lady?"

Margaret grinned. "My name is Margaret."

The little girl quickly responded, "My whole name is Diana Kay Meadows."

Margaret smiled. "That's is a beautiful name for a beautiful girl. My whole name is Margaret Phoebe Black."

"That's pretty, but not as pretty as mine."

"Diana, that's not very nice," Holly said.

Holly looked at Margaret and said, "It will be night soon. You're welcome to stay with us if you like and get a fresh start in the morning."

"Thank you so much for the invitation. I walked all last night. That was the reason I took refuge in your barn. I couldn't go any further."

"Franklin, you need to bring in a couple of loads of firewood. I milked the cow early today; that's when we found you. Franklin and I were going to throw some fresh hay down for the cow. He went up to the loft and there you lay. I'm sure you covered yourself with the hay—although the hay was all at your feet."

Chapter Fifty-Nine
Saying Goodbye

That night after the kids were in bed, Holly and Margaret sat and talked about missing their husbands and the children.

"Tell me," Holly said, "What brought you to these parts? Cherokee is a good journey from here."

Margaret shared her story. Holly frowned and asked, "You want to find the old woman Desan. She's a strange one."

Margaret leaned forward, her eyes widened. "You know Desan?"

"Yes. Well, we're not good friends or anything, but I have talked with her a couple of times."

Eager to hear, Margaret asked, "What's she like?"

Holly raised her brows. "She can be scary, but I think that's all show to keep people away from her cave. She lives at the top . . . and I do mean the top . . . of White Oak Mountain. Do you mean you're familiar with the area?"

"I do know about the surrounding area, but I've never been to the top of White Oak."

"There's one word that describes it—awful. If I were going to go, it would be in the winter while the rattlesnakes and bears are hibernating. I don't know how the old woman has lasted as long as she has. Some say that she put a curse against anyone who tries to come around the cave."

"Was she in the cave when you visited her?" Margaret asked.

"Yes, she was. Franklin and I were picking blackberries. He fell and cut his leg. It was a terrible gash. I didn't know she was anywhere around. I was so close to her cave, I could have spit on it. I would have probably had a heart attack, had I known. She heard him crying and came out to see what was wrong. When I saw her, I froze for a second. I was scared to death due to all the tales I had heard; yet I knew I had to do something for Franklin or he would bleed to death." Holly held her hands up.

Margaret gasped. "Oh, my."

"It was so strange," Holly continued. "She put something on Franklin's leg she said would keep the infection out. After that, she put some kind of bandage on it to pull the cut together. and then she prayed. All I remember her saying was, 'Great Eagle of heaven and earth.' After that she took the bandage off and . . . and it was healed. The cut had knit together, leaving only a hairline scar. I know this sounds like something I made up, but I'm telling you the truth when I say I don't remember getting home." Holly pointed toward the door. "The next thing I knew, I was standing in my front yard with Franklin in my arms. Don't ask me how."

Margaret's eyes widened. "Can you remember anything she said other than Great Eagle of heaven and earth?"

"No I don't. I know Franklin would have bled to death if she hadn't done whatever she did. Some said it was witchcraft. I don't really think that, but I don't know what to think. At that point I didn't care. I was so thankful, magic or not."

"I sure hope my friend Carolyn is okay. Her arm looked pretty bad when she left for home."

Holly put her hand on Margaret's, "I wish I had a horse I could lend you. I have a runty mule, but he's all we have to pull our wagon."

Margaret's eyes widened. "Are you saying you have a wagon?"

"It's an old buckboard, but it's all we have. I could take you, but with three children in this cold and the threat of soldiers . . . or worse yet, Silent Wolf . . ."

Margaret lowered her head. "I couldn't expect you to take the children out in this weather. I'm so thankful for the warm place to sleep tonight. I'm sorry I scared you and Franklin. I must confess our meeting has turned out to be very pleasant. When the weather breaks, you and the children will have to come visit me at Cherokee."

"I would love to. There aren't many people around here. Only a couple of families that live not too far from here, but we don't get to visit much in the wintertime."

"Holly, do you mind if I go to bed? I'm so sleepy, I can hardly hold my head up."

Holly stood. "For heaven sake, I didn't mean to go on and on. Would you like a gown to sleep in?"

"Yes, that would be wonderful."

Chapter Sixty
Goodbye to New Friends

Margaret slept soundly through the night but was awakened by low grunting sounds from the baby's crib. Margaret saw that Holly was still sleeping, so she picked Dan up and tried to quiet him by rocking him. To no avail. Dan was frantically searching for his mother's breast. Margaret bounced and bounced. Finally, she realized only his mother would be able to calm him. She called gently, "Holly!"

"I'll be right back," Holly said as she headed for the door. "Necessity calls."

Franklin called from the loft, "Did Mama go out?"

"Yes." Margaret called as she continued to walk and bounce the baby.

"Let him bite your knuckle," Franklin said. "His gums are swollen. Mama said he's cutting teeth."

Margaret bent her knuckle, and Dan took the bait until his mother returned. Margaret watched as Holly wrapped a blanket around Dan, rocked him and give him his much needed breakfast. She wondered what it would have been like if she and George could have had a baby. They had tried for many years; however, she had been unable to conceive. They had questioned God as to why He hadn't blessed them with a child but accepted that God knows best.

Margaret made fried bread and eggs for breakfast. Franklin bundled up and went to milk the cow and feed the mule. Margaret helped clean the dishes and put wood in the heater.

Franklin came through the door. "Man alive, it's cold outside. I don't envy you, Mrs. Black, having to be out in this."

"Neither do I," Holly said. "You're welcome to stay as long as you like. We don't have anything fancy, but you're welcome to share what we have—a warm fire and a place to sleep."

Margaret was touched by their kindness. "I don't know how to thank you for all that you've already done. Under different circumstances, I would be delighted, but I better be going. Besides, I have warm boots and a heavy coat and gloves. I'll be fine."

"I'll fix you some food and water to take with you," Holly said.

"Thank you. I think I have a few pieces of beef jerky left, but my canteen is almost empty."

Holly put Dan in the crib and told Franklin to go get Margaret's things from the barn loft. Holly hurried to the kitchen area. "I have some leftovers from breakfast."

After Franklin brought her things and Holly wrapped her food, Margaret was ready to leave.

"You take care and stay warm," Holly said. "It's looking pretty cloudy. I sure hope that don't mean snow clouds."

"Me too," Margaret said. She patted the top of Diana's head and kissed Dan's cheek. Franklin extended his hand to her. "You keep safe. We'll say a prayer for you. Won't we, Mama?"

"We most certainly will." Holly quickly hugged Margaret. "I enjoyed our visit last night. I hope your husband comes home soon."

"And yours, Holly. Goodbye and thanks again for everything. Franklin, you're quite the young man. I'm sure your dad is very proud of you. If I had a son, I would want him to be just like you."

Franklin blushed and grinned. Margaret looked at the sky and started down the road.

Chapter Sixty-One

Home

The overcast was a combination of light and slate gray clouds that were steadily moving across the sky. There were only two inches of snow on the ground at the moment, and Margaret prayed that it would stay that way. She moved close to the tree line, so as not to be noticed. After about thirty minutes, she heard what sounded like a wagon coming in the distance. She hid behind the trees. As the wagon drew nearer, Margaret realized it was a mule pulling the wagon and a young boy driving it. She squinted, trying to make out who the driver was. After the wagon drew closer, Margaret stepped from the trees and shouted, "Franklin! Franklin!" Margaret cautiously ran toward the road.

Franklin pulled back on the reins, bringing the mule to a stop. "Mama, it's Mrs. Black."

Holly quickly turned to see Margaret moving hurriedly across the snow.

"Is something wrong?" Margaret shouted as she drew near the wagon.

Holly, who was sitting in the back of the wagon under the quilts with Diana and Dan, stood and answered, "No nothing's wrong, except we let you go out in this cold when we had a means of helping you get home."

"Holly," Margaret said breathlessly, "I can't expect you to bring your children out in this snow. I appreciate the wonderful thought, but you need to go home. I'll be fine."

Franklin shook his head. "No, Mrs. Black, we're not going back. We're taking you to Cherokee. The vote was unanimous, so you may as well climb aboard."

Margaret looked at Holly who gave an assuring nod of her head. Margaret climbed into the wagon and looked back at Diana who quickly said, "I voted yes, too."

"What a surprise! I don't know what to say. Are you and the baby warm?"

Holly chuckled. "We're more than warm. I have about twenty quilts back here. We're sitting on half and covered with the rest. I brought some food and water and plenty of cloths for Dan's diapers. I'll be honest with you, Margaret, we wanted to get out of the house. The fear of staying there was greater than taking you to Cherokee."

"But what if your husband comes home and you're not there?"

Holly lowered her head. "I'll tell you about it later. For now, we need to take advantage of the daylight."

Franklin looked around. "Is everybody ready?"

Holly sat down and pulled the quilts over her and the kids. "Now we're ready," she said. That was all it took for Franklin to pop the reins and start down the rough road to Cherokee.

They stopped occasionally, to rest the mule and eat. Everyone was thankful that by noon the dark clouds had evaporated and the sun beamed down, softening the frozen snow. Margaret took turns sitting in the back with Diana and Dan, allowing Holly to sit up front with Franklin. What Holly had said about the quilts, turned out to be true. Margaret, Diana and the baby snuggled under the covers and took a long nap. They were awakened when Franklin stopped to relieve himself. That occasion also proved to be a perfect time to feed the baby. Everyone was in such a good mood, including Dan. Margaret watched as Franklin, Diana and Holly laughed as though they were taking a vacation, not a bumpy buckboard ride through the cold and snow. At one point, Holly said what a wonderful time she was having. Margaret gave Franklin a break and drove the wagon. He held Dan in his arms and Diana snuggled to his back. They went to sleep immediately. Holly sat up front with Margaret.

Margaret popped the reins and said, "Holly, you said you would explain later about your husband. I was curious to know what you were talking about."

Holly pulled her coat tight and adjusted her fur hat. "There's so much that I haven't told you. First of all, I've only known you a few hours, but I feel very free around you. You're so easy to talk to. I . . . . I told the kids their father had to join the Army because of fighting to keep what freedom we have. I said that he had no choice; therefore, he left to meet up with the soldiers at Murphy." She paused and sniffed.

Margaret glanced at her. Tears were rolling down her face. "I understand your feelings. I miss George so much right now I could cry with you, but I fear the tears would turn into icicles."

Holly covered her face with her scarf, yet continued to talk. "I said I told the kids their father joined the Army. The truth is, he left us. I didn't know how to tell them. I thought it would be better for them to believe that he was killed in the war than to know he deserted us."

"Holly, I'm so sorry."

"I'm only telling you now while the children are sleeping. That's why I didn't care if I left or not. You're the first adult I've spoken to in a while and it feels good to talk to a grown up. Franklin is very mature for his age, but I can't drop all of this on him. I have to remind myself not to expect adult actions from a boy. He wouldn't understand his dad leaving us. Diana would forget with time, and Dan is too young to know anything. I just couldn't let Franklin know . . . not yet."

"What are you going to do?"

"I have enough money to get supplies and when they run out, I'll take it day by day. If I can make it until spring, I would like to move up North near a big city. I hate living in a deserted place where you constantly worry about Indians taking your scalp. Enough sadness! Tell me about your friend Carolyn."

"Her husband was killed a few years back. She decided to move to Cherokee to live with her aunt.

She took a teaching position at Fort Howard, where she teaches white children and Indian children who live in the settlement. She has a crush on my brother, Cody, and she's the best friend a person could have. I've prayed for her in my mind almost every minute. I wish I knew if she was okay. I want her to be happy and fulfilled. I . . . I want you to be fulfilled as well, Holly. You're a pretty woman. You're still young and strong, and you have three beautiful children. I think any man would be blessed to have you for his wife."

Chapter Sixty-Two

A Ride to Cherokee

The night sky was clear, and the moon shone brightly on the snow-covered ground, allowing ample light for traveling. When Dan had to be fed again, everyone took advantage of the time. They ate and walked around to stretch their legs. It also gave the mule time to eat and get a few minutes of much needed rest. The wagon had four short posts on the sides. Holly and Franklin draped a couple of quilts over the posts to create a tent and secured the quilts down to keep the cold air out. They used their pillows for back rests. Holly and Diana pretended they were camping.

Franklin was wide awake after a lengthy nap and wanted to drive. Holly said if they traveled all night, they should arrive in Cherokee by nightfall.

As the cold night passed and the dawn slowly emerged, Margaret and Franklin talked and shared their thoughts on many things. With the light of day, Margaret saw familiar landmarks. She put her arm around Franklin's, squeezed and announced. "We're almost there." Margaret was so excited she could hardly contain her emotions. "Holly! We should be there in about thirty minutes."

Holly pulled the quilt back and looked around. She grasped Margaret's arm and said, "Thank God! Diana, we're almost there."

As her house came into view, Margaret saw smoke coming from the chimney.

"Margaret, maybe George is home," Holly said.

They pulled into the yard. The front door abruptly came open. Carolyn, Julie and Cody rushed out to greet them. Carolyn shouted, "Margaret!"

Margaret jumped down almost before the wagon stopped and ran to greet them.

Julie hugged Margaret. "We've been worried sick about you. We came here last night to build a fire in case you made it home sooner than we thought. I made some breakfast, and it's a good thing that I made plenty." Julie hurried to take the baby while Holly pulled her and Diana's coats and gloves off. Cody poured coffee for Margaret and Holly and hot chocolate milk for the kids.

"Holly, I have some warm applesauce for the baby if you like," Carolyn said.

"Thank you. I'm sure Dan will enjoy that."

Carolyn started to the stove, but Cody stopped her. "I'll get it. You take it easy."

Margaret put her hand on Carolyn's cheek. "How is your arm?"

"The doctor said the stinky stuff the Indians put on my arm did a miracle. It wasn't infected."

Margaret frowned. "It wasn't infected?"

"No. It was irritated, but not infected."

Cody and Franklin brought the many quilts inside. Franklin went out and came back in with the roll of skin and gave it to Margaret. "What's that?" Julie asked.

Margaret grinned. "After we eat and I get into some of my own clothes, we'll talk about it."

At breakfast, Margaret shared the story about her meeting with Holly and Franklin and the trip home. She also explained about their Uncle Bill and how he had played a big part in her meeting her real father, Chief Coosa.

Margaret fixed a place for Holly and the kids. Cody put a cot in the room for Franklin. Holly chuckled and said, "I know it's hard to believe, but I'm so tired and sleepy. We napped quite a bit on the road, but I'm still exhausted."

"Me too," Diana muttered.

When they were in bed, Margaret was ready to show Julie and Cody what Coosa and Bill had given her. She rolled the skin out on the table to reveal the eagle cape and the chief's magnificent headdress. Cody held the cape up and put it around his shoulders. "Wow! This is unbelievable, and so is this headdress."

Julie exclaimed, "Margaret, you said that this Chief Coosa was your real father. I don't understand that. J.D. Styles was our father."

"Part of that statement is true. J.D. was your and Cody's real father, but he wasn't mine. Of course, J.D. was the only father whom I remembered; therefore, he'll still be a father to me forever. I don't know how much Carolyn has told you about our trip."

Carolyn interrupted and said, "I told them some, but not about Coosa. I felt you should be the one to share that story."

Margaret's hand trembled and tears filled her eyes as she looked at Cody, Julie and Carolyn. "I can't explain how I felt when I looked into Chief Coosa's eyes. I was having flashbacks to a time that I didn't remember existed. I could see the nine-year-old girl who cried hysterically as she was pulled from her father's arms. I remembered hearing the wailing of my father as we rode out of the village. Now the eyes that danced with jubilation at seeing his daughter after forty years have been burned into my soul. The blessing he spoke over me was unbelievable. When he placed the eagle cape on my shoulders, my knees grew weak and my spirit melted within me. He held me with his last breath." Margaret began to weep aloud. Julie, Cody and Carolyn wept with her. After everyone's tears had dried, Margaret took the chest from the cloth, opened it, took every piece out and explained the significance of each. About how their Grandma Phoebe and their mother had treasured the things before her. And the painting their Uncle Bill had done and how he had them in places of honor in his home. Margaret then unveiled the mystery of the separation of Bill from Tyler and Lorrie after their mother's death. Julie and Cody listened intently to every word. When Margaret had finished, Julie asked, "Didn't you say you felt that you needed to talk to the old Indian woman Desan?"

"Yes, I do and as soon as possible. Cody have you heard anything about George and Major Wright?"

Cody didn't want to upset Margaret after all that she had been through, so he didn't tell her that ten thousand had died outside of Townsend. "The battle had spread out toward Stone River, Tennessee," Cody said. "But there is some good news out of all of this."

"What's that?" Margaret asked.

"Silent Wolf is dead. He was killed at Townsend."

"And his warriors?"

"Wiped out."

"Thank God," Margaret whispered.

Julie furrowed her brows. "What is the story with Holly and the children? How is it that she would take her children out in this weather to bring you home?"

Margaret explained Holly's situation with her husband and how the children didn't know. She then stood. "While they're sleeping, I need to go into town and see if Randy can have someone escort them home. I'd like for them to stay in Cherokee, if they will. They have a cow and some chickens, and of course the mule that pulled the wagon, but not much else. I hope Holly will agree to bring her things back and stay here at the Fort or in the village at least." Margaret put her coat on and said, "I need to see what Randy can do about getting somebody to make sure she gets home safely, and to help bring her things back if she will move here."

Carolyn quickly said, "Let me get my coat and I'll go with you."

"No," Cody said. "You stay here with Julie and I'll go with Margaret."

Carolyn looked at Margaret who agreed with Coty.

Chapter Sixty-Three
Margaret's Request

*A*s they rode into Fort Howard, there appeared to be something going on. People were out for some reason other than the joy of being in the freezing cold. As they neared the center of the fort, Margaret saw the three Seminole Indians who had been sent to find her. They were being held by some of the townsmen. The townspeople were demanding that they be hanged. Margaret's breath froze within her. She grabbed Cody's arm and frantically said, "Cody, we can't let them be strung up in the street. Chief Coosa sent them to find me. They didn't come to hurt anyone. Please help me do something."

"Sis, that's a pretty tall request right now."

She pleaded, "Please, Cody. Please!"

"Let's see what's going on first before we do anything rash."

Margaret's body jerked when someone fired a gun over their heads. Randy and several soldiers hurried to take charge of the Indians. "What the devil is going on here?" Randy shouted.

Brad Brown, one of the men holding the Indians, answered, "We found these three savages out near White Oak. We figured that they might be a part of Silent Wolf's bunch."

Randy ordered some of the soldiers to take the Indians to jail. "Brad, and everyone else here, I want you to know that Silent Wolf and his followers were killed over a week ago at Townsend. Even if they weren't, it doesn't give you the authority to take the law into your own hands. I'm the officer in charge here until Major Wright gets back. These men will be held in jail until Major Wright returns and makes the decision about them. Now go on home, it's cold out here."

Margaret breathed a sigh of relief . . . until Randy fixed his eyes on her and ordered, "Margaret Black, I want to see you, right away, in my office."

She closed her eyes and took a deep breath. She and Cody followed Randy to the jail and went inside. Randy put his hands on his hips and scolded, "What in the world went wrong? Carolyn told me about Lighted Path. My God, I hate that. He was my friend. He was the one who told me about Chief Coosa and your Uncle Bill. I went along with the plan and suggested that Lighted Path go as a result of what he told me. I never dreamed any of this would have happened, or it never would have happened." He lowered his head and softly asked, "Are you okay?"

Margaret nodded and embraced Randy. "I can never thank you enough for all that you did. I'm going to have to make you that supper."

He sniffed. "You've been fixing me that supper for over a year now."

Margaret moaned. "Has it been a year already?"

Margaret began to play with the buttons on Randy's jacket. Randy pulled her hand from his coat and adamantly declared, "No! No! No! Don't you ask me one thing unless it's about George. Since I'm sure Cody has filled you in on that report, I don't want to hear anything you have to say. You constantly get me into some kind of trouble. So don't ask. Do you hear me? Don't ask!"

Margaret looked at the Indians, who were holding the bars so tightly their knuckles were white.

"No!" Randy said.

Margaret frowned. "No, what? I haven't said anything."

Randy pointed his finger at her. "You don't have to say anything; I can read your mind and the answer is no. Do you hear me? No!"

"But, Randy, they came to find me for Coosa. They didn't come to hurt anyone. If you know all that you say you know, then I'm sure you know that as well."

Randy wiped his mouth. "My God, Cody," he asked loudly, "can't you do something with her?"

Cody cleared his throat. "I more than likely couldn't if her mind is made up, but I must say, this time I agree with her."

Randy threw his hands in the air and declared, "I don't believe this. You both want me court marshaled."

Margaret tried to touch his shoulder, and he pulled away. "I don't want anything to happen to you and neither does Cody. Do you remember when George saved your life?"

Randy put his hand toward Margaret and stated, "Hold it right there, Margaret Black. It was George who saved my life, not you. Have you got that? It wasn't you."

"I know it was George, but who took care of you and nursed you back to health? I even spoon-fed you until you were able to feed yourself."

Randy widened his eyes and raised his brows. "I wish you had let me die. It would have been better than being shot by a firing squad."

Margaret lowered her head and began to talk about Lighted Path and Chief Coosa and how excited they were at the reunion. She went on and on until Randy said, "Hush! Just hush. What is it you want from me?"

Margaret smiled, took hold of his arms and kissed his cheek. "I love you, Randy. If it were up to me, I would make you a four-star general."

"Yeah, yeah. Just tell me what you want, as if I didn't already know."

"I can't let them die. Coosa trusted them to find me. I can't let anything happen to them. I wish I could tell them what happened."

"How do you suggest we make it look like they escaped?" Randy asked. "Is it going to have anything to do with me being hurt?"

Margaret's face muscles tightened as she said, "Well, not bad."

Randy squinted, tilted his head and asked, "What do you mean not bad? I want to know, what is bad to you?"

Margaret shrugged her shoulders. "Do you think being knocked out is too bad?"

Randy frowned and looked at Cody. "Just who will be knocking me out?"

Margaret gave him a tight-lipped grin and said, "Me, but I promise I'll be as easy as possible."

Randy tightened his lips. "Wow, what a comfort. When will all of this take place?"

"As soon as humanly possible," Margaret whispered. She told Randy about Holly and how she wanted someone to escort them back home and maybe the Indians could hide under the mountain of quilts in the wagon.

Randy sighed. "No, I don't want to bring Holly and her children into this. Does anyone else know about this?"

Margaret shook her head.

Cody spoke up and said, "If you get knocked out, then I guess that leaves me to take the Indians outside the settlement."

Margaret was excited.

Randy frowned. "You don't have to be so excited. So how about tonight? Cody, can you meet me at Abby's at nine o'clock?"

Cody nodded.

"Good. I go there every night to get something to eat before I go to bed. I'll bring the wagon and park it beside the jail. When all is clear, I'll put them in the wagon and head for Abby's. I'll make sure the coast is also clear there and put them in your wagon. I'll come back, and Margaret can render me unconscious. They can find me on the floor with the jail door open and the rest will be history."

Margaret tapped her lip and said, "So, Cody, what will you do? Take them to the woods and leave it up to them from there?"

"That sounds good to me. How about you, Randy?"

He nodded. "Yeah. It sounds good except being hit in the head. I don't look forward to that."

"I won't tell you when I'm going to do it, will that help?" Margaret asked.

"Tonight a nine o'clock," Randy moaned.

Margaret, Cody and Randy faced the three men in the cell. They stared at Margaret. One of them pointed at her and uttered, "Phoenix."

"I wish they could understand," Margaret said. She sighed and asked the three Indians, "Can you understand my words?" They just stared at her. Margaret thought she would try something that they might possibly understand. She said, "Chief Coosa."

They looked at each other and then at Margaret and uttered, "Coosa. Chief Coosa." One of them pointed at Margaret and said, "Phoenix. Phoenix."

Cody headed for the door. "They'll understand when we get them out of here. Everyone can recognize freedom."

Chapter Sixty-Four

News from the Front

When Cody and Margaret arrived back at Margaret's house, Holly and the children were awake. Carolyn had given Franklin a new reader and was working with him on some of his words. Diana was sitting snuggled up to her mom. Julie had put a quilt on the floor, and she and Dan were playing.

Margaret talked to Holly about going home and bringing her things back and living at the settlement. When Franklin heard them talking, he asked, "What about dad? What if he comes home and no one's there? How will he know where we are, a note?"

"We could try to get him word," Holly said.

"I like it here," Diana was quick to say.

"I don't know," Holly uttered. "We'll have to wait and see when we get closer home."

That night Cody hitched the wagon up and headed toward the fort. Margaret mounted her horse and followed closely behind. Randy pulled up at Abby's and looked around. He hurriedly moved the Indians from the back of his wagon to the back of Cody's.

Cody left the fort and headed back toward Margaret's. As soon as Randy returned to the jail, Margaret was waiting for him behind the door. She didn't want him to have time to think about it, so she hit him in the back of his head with the butt of her gun. Randy groaned and fell to the floor. Margaret took the keys to the jail and put them in the lock of the cell and opened it, pulled Randy to the front of the cell door, kissed his head and quickly left the room. She hurried back to her house and waited for Cody to return from dropping the Indians off.

It seemed like forever, but it had only been less than an hour since Cody had left the fort. Margaret enjoyed talking to Franklin as he shared his dreams of finishing school, going to college and one day running for public office. There was something special about Franklin. She wasn't sure what it was, but it was there in a big way. Suddenly, Margaret jumped up and said, "Listen, it sounds like someone coming." She hurried to the window and looked out. "It's Cody." She grabbed her coat, lit a lantern and went out to meet him. He unhitched the horses and took them inside the barn. Margaret rushed through the door and breathlessly asked, "How did things go?"

Cody continued to take the harness off the horses. "Things went really well. They couldn't understand what I was saying; however, they must have understood my intent. When I motioned for them to stay under the tarp, they lay down and didn't move until I was into the forest. Randy had filled a canteen and gathered as much food as possible for their trip home. I wish they could have had a horse." Cody hung the harness and turned to Margaret's embrace.

"Thank you so much for understanding and helping. You didn't have to and that's what makes it so special."

"You know you're welcome. Now let's get inside to a warm fire and a cup of strong coffee."

Inside, Margaret voiced her concern about hitting Randy. "I wonder if anyone's found him or if he's conscious yet. I didn't give him any warning before hitting him. I thought that would be best, for his sake."

"I'm sure he's conscious by now. It's been a good while. Surely you didn't hit him that hard, did you?"

"I'm not sure. I've never tried to knock someone out and not mean it."

Holly asked, "Margaret, did Randy say anything about an escort home?"

"Yes, he said he would arrange it for day after tomorrow."

Julie had put Dan in the bed. "I need to go home. Cody are you coming with me?"

Cody put his hat on. "Yes. That will give more room here for everyone. Besides, my things are at your house." He looked at Carolyn, held her shoulders and said, "But I'll be back in the morning."

Carolyn smiled. "By the way, Franklin, I have a class tomorrow and I would love for you to come with me."

"Thank you, Miss Morris, I would love that. Do you think it's okay, Mama?"

Holly rubbed his back. "I think that would be wonderful."

Julie and Cody left and Holly, Diana and the boys went to bed. Carolyn and Margaret sat in front of the fireplace and talked. Margaret began to chuckle.

"What's funny?" Carolyn asked.

"Can you even start to believe all that we've been through? It's like a dream. I expect to wake up any moment and realize it never happened." She turned somber. "On the other hand, I know it's real. I can still see the face of that young bugle boy. So eager to march and then in the next little bit he would be lying face down in a pool of his own blood never to blow his bugle again. Carolyn, I can still see that soldier's blue eyes when he fell on top of me. They pierced my being."

Carolyn moaned. "I remember those, but the thing I remember most, is our trip to Pine Mountain Cemetery in the mud and darkness, and Eagle Claw. That was his name wasn't it?"

"Yeah. I'm not likely to forget that name. You're right, Carolyn. That was where it all began and here I am sprinting all the way to the battlefield with my thoughts." Margaret poked Carolyn's arm. "You are so organized. Even your thoughts are organized. You can tell that mine are a bit shuffled."

"Margaret, I still can't explain how we got to the bottom of the mountain that night. I could have sworn that someone or something scooped us up and carried us to the bottom. I felt the same way when Corporal Smith brought me home."

Margaret chuckled. "I remember George's face when you told him that we had been to the cemetery. I could have knocked you off your horse for that. Then George began ranting about staying in the protected areas. I wish I could hear his voice right now, and he was where you are holding me."

"I know how you feel."

"Explain that, if you will," Margaret said.

"Not with George, but with . . . with Cody."

"Hum, really?"

"Yes. He treated me like a baby when I got back. When the doctor left, he put his arms around me and held me so gently for a long time although I wished it could have been longer."

"Did he kiss you?" Margaret teased.

"Oh my yes. I felt dizzy at the touch of his lips. I thought I would melt."

"What happened to the swooning desire for Captain Taylor?"

"I suppose it went down in history."

Margaret nudged her arm. "Do you think somewhere down the road, there might be wedding bells?"

"I don't know. I'm taking it one day at a time and see what happens."

Carolyn propped herself up on her elbow and asked, "Do you think Holly will come back to Cherokee?"

Margaret replied, "I can only hope. You know, Carolyn, Franklin is such a knowledgeable young man. I can see him going far in his future."

"I know. When I talked with him, he amazed me with his ideas and dreams."

"Diana is such a beautiful little girl, and Dan, what a cutie."

"Margaret, did she say why her husband left them?"

"No. She didn't say a lot about that and I didn't ask. I feel so sorry for her having to hide it from the children, especially Franklin."

Carolyn giggled. "I wonder how Suzie is doing in Washington?"

"She's more than likely charmed the socks off President Lincoln and the entire White House staff."

"How do you think Willie is doing? He sure seemed to love Suzie."

Margaret sat up and leaned against the headboard. "If you could have heard him in the barn talking to her, you wouldn't have to guess about his love for her. He was very unyielding about wanting her and their daughter."

Carolyn scooted under the covers and said, "We had better get some sleep."

"It's hard to sleep," Margaret said. "I can't help but think how it would have been if things had been different on the mountain. If Chief Coosa, Lighted Path and Uncle Bill had lived. I want those family paintings of Uncle Bill's to remember them by. Hum, I wonder what George will think about a Seminole Chief being my father?"

Carolyn sniggered. "I can only wonder."

"I've got to find Desan. Carolyn, I want you to pray and agree with me right now that things will work out and I will see her soon."

Margaret and Carolyn joined hands and prayed that it would be so.

Chapter Sixty-Five

Holly and Kids Go Home

The next day Carolyn took Franklin and Diana with her to school. Margaret and Holly went to Fort Howard. Margaret couldn't wait to check on Randy. She took Holly to the Trading Post. While Holly was shopping for supplies, Margaret went to the jail. When she entered the jail, there were a couple of soldiers with Randy. "Hi Randy. I thought I would drop by and see if you had heard anything from George. Why all the sad faces. Is something wrong?"

Randy rubbed his head. "Yeah. I must have gotten too close to the cell. All I remember is something hitting my head and then waking up to Private Barnes' pretty face."

"Did the Indians escape?" Margaret asked.

"Yes. Unfortunately, they did." Randy stood. "Boys, I've got to get some fresh air and a cup of coffee. I'll be back in a few minutes; watch after things for me. Margaret, would you like to join me for a cup of coffee?"

"Yes, that would be nice."

When they were outside, Randy scolded, "Why the devil didn't you give me some kind of warning before you took my head half off?"

"Did I hit you that hard?"

"Yes, Mrs. Black, you did. I've got a lump the size of a rock on the back of my head. It was good that you hit the back of my head and not the top. They thought the Indians jerked my head back into the bars. I don't know how I would have explained a blow to the top of my head."

"I'm so sorry I hurt you that bad. I thought taking you by surprise would be better than looking at you, knowing I was going to hit you."

"At least it's over."

"By the way, Randy, I can't have coffee with you. I have to pick up Holly and the baby. She's buying supplies before they leave in the morning. Who will be going back with Holly and the kids?"

"Corporal Burns. He's the only one we can spare."

Margaret gave Randy a quick kiss and headed back to the Trading Post. Margaret watched as Holly took some coins from her pocket to pay for her order. After counting it, she quickly put the candy back. Margaret spoke up. "Andy, put the candy back in the box and add a couple of handfuls of those gum drops."

"You don't have to do that, Margaret."

"I know, but what kid doesn't have a sweet tooth? Me included."

Andy loaded the supplies and the women got on board the wagon. Margaret took the reins and started to pop the line when she heard someone call her name.

She turned to see Randy rushing toward the wagon. Before she could get down, Randy was at her side.

"What's is it? Is it George?"

Randy put his hand on his chest and exhaled. "I'm in pretty good shape, but that little run took every dab of breath in my lungs. It could be related to the trauma I suffered last night."

"Randy, you're such a baby. One would think a dashing, middle-aged soldier like you, could endure a little brier scratch. All that aside, did you hear something from the troops?"

"Yes, I did. That's why I wanted to catch you. A messenger arrived while you were at the jail. He said that Major Wright was at Fort Donaldson. That's west near the Kentucky border, and they will be leaving there the middle of next week. Coming home. And yes, George is fine; however, they lost over a hundred men."

"Oh my God!"

"Yeah, but that's the price of any war. Somewhere in all of this, the good man upstairs must have a plan that's going to blow our minds, allowing all this tragedy."

"Amen," Holly said.

"Holly, forgive my manners. This is Sergeant Randy Mathis. He's the one I spoke to about an escort for you and the kids. Randy, this is Holly. . . what is your last name, Holly?"

Holly smiled. "It's Meadows and this is my son Dan."

Randy nodded. "It's a real pleasure to meet you. That's a fine looking boy you have there."

"Thank you."

Margaret gently leaned forward and patted the top of Randy's head. "You better be going. You take care of that awful wound."

"Hum, that's easy for you to say. I'll see you later, and again it was nice to meet you, Holly. You too, Dan."

Chapter Sixty-Six
Remembering Chief Coosa

That night Margaret wanted to make a special supper for her newfound friends. She invited Julie and, of course, Cody. Everyone laughed and took advantage of the lighthearted break.

Julie brought chocolate cake. Franklin and Diana were not the only ones enjoying the chocolate icing. Dan sucked the icing from his mother's finger. Margaret watched Carolyn and Cody playing with the baby, and Julie was brushing and braiding Diana's long, blond hair. She observed as Holly joined the crowd and acted so carefree. Cody brought his banjo and played every song he knew. They all lifted their voices in joyful songs, enjoying the time that would soon pass, giving way to morning and the departure of some newly treasured friends.

Julie, Cody and Carolyn all insisted on staying the night. They wanted to make sure they were there to say goodbye to Holly and the children before their early morning departure. After Franklin consumed the last piece of chocolate cake and wood was placed on the fire, everyone said goodnight.

Someone pounding on the door awakened Cody. He groaned as he pulled himself up from the floor. Margaret came through the bedroom door and asked, "Who is it, Cody?"

"It's got to be someone from the fort." Cody ran his fingers through his hair. "Who's there?" he shouted out.

"It's me," Randy called out. After Cody opened the door, Randy laughed and said, "Well, it looks as though we've had a sleepover."

Cody yawned and invited Randy inside. By then everyone was up and gathered in the living area. Holly gave the baby to Julie and muttered, "I'm so sorry Sergeant. I intended to be ready by the time you arrived. It will only take a few minutes."

"Take your time, Mrs. Meadows."

Carolyn hurried and put coffee on while Margaret fried some tenderloin, bread and eggs. Margaret looked at Cody and asked, "Would you mind getting some milk from the spring box?"

"Sure. Just let me get my coat." As he put his coat on, he asked, "Randy, what kind of weather are we going to have today?"

"I don't think it's going to be good today."

Cody started toward the door and Randy called out, "Wait up, Cody, and I'll walk with you." His words caught Margaret's ear, and she quickly cut her eyes at Randy. "Is something going on that I don't know about?" she asked.

"And what makes you think that?" Randy asked.

Margaret tilted her head and said, "I can detect when men are wanting to hide something."

"Well, you can put your pretty head to rest. I just want to walk outside with Cody. That's all."

Margaret squinted. "Is there a reason I don't believe you?"

Randy chuckled and rubbed his head. "I wouldn't lie to someone who I allowed to put a sizeable lump on my head, now would I?"

After breakfast, Cody and Randy hitched the mule to the wagon and brought it to the front of the house. Holly made sure the quilts were in the wagon the way she wanted them, and then she and the kids started their hugs with Carolyn, Julie, Cody and then Margaret. Julie took Dan and Diana to the wagon. "I'll be right out," Holly said. She took Margaret's hands, smiled and said, "I don't know how to thank you for last night. I'll treasure it forever."

"So will I. Holly, please consider coming back to stay. It would not be good only for the children, but for you as well. Will you do that?"

"I will certainly think about it. Please pray I'll be able to tell Franklin about his father. That will be the major hang up about moving back. But, whether we move back or not, we will come to visit." Holly and Margaret embraced. Holly again whispered, "Thank you for everything."

Margaret walked out with her and watched as Franklin got on board and took the reins. One pop of the lines and the mule started down the road. Everyone waved as they drove out of sight. Margaret breathed a prayer that their trip would be a safe one.

Chapter Sixty-Seven
Finding Desan

$\mathcal{T}$he morning sun beamed down, melting the snow. Julie hugged Margaret and said, "I wish they would stay here."

"I know, sis. I hope when she finds the money that I slipped in her things, she will see the only reasonable thing to do will be to come back to the people who care for her and the kids."

After everyone was inside the house and Randy had gone back to the fort, Julie asked, "Margaret, when were you going to find Desan?"

"That just happens to be at the top of my thought list," Cody remarked.

Margaret looked at Carolyn for a response. She nodded and revealed, "Yes, I was thinking the same thing. I do think you should do it before George gets home. That way, everything can be out of the way and you can enjoy his homecoming. And I can be back for my classes."

Margaret frowned and announced, "You're not going! Your arm needs to heal."

"She's right," Cody said. "Margaret, I'm going with you."

"Well it's for sure she's not going alone, even if I have to go with her," Julie stated.

"You're right, sis. I'm not going alone; Cody will be going with me."

Cody scratched his brow. "The way I figure it, we can be at the top of White Oak in only a few hours. Randy tried to tell me how to recognize the area where she lives, but I don't know. He recommended that we get off our horses before we get too close, and that we start calling out her name to let her know we mean her no harm."

"He's right," Margaret said. "I had already thought of doing that. What do you say about going tomorrow?"

Cody nodded. "The sooner the better."

Julie clapped her hands together. "What are you going to ask her?"

"I'm too tired to talk about it now. I'm going back to bed and sleep until I can't sleep anymore."

Margaret went to bed, and Carolyn and Julie went home, but Cody stayed. He wanted to make sure Margaret wasn't disturbed.

Margaret slept almost six hours. When she started into the living room, she stopped and watched as Cody stood before the fireplace with the eagle cape that Coosa had given her. He had draped it around his shoulders. She could only wonder what must be going through his mind. After a few moments, she cleared her throat to let him know she was awake. She waited a couple of minutes and went into the living room. As she thought, Cody had rolled the cape back into the rawhide. He smiled as she came and held her hands near the fire.

"My goodness. You were quite the sleepyhead," Cody said.

"I most certainly was. Thanks for staying."

Margaret could tell that something was on Cody's mind. She asked, "What thoughts are causing that somber look? I can tell it isn't Carolyn or there would be a smile involved. So what is it?"

Cody sighed and sat in the rocking chair. He began to rock. "While you were asleep, I tried to imagine how Chief Coosa looked and what he was like. Will you tell me?"

Margaret sat in the rocker. "I'll try to tell you without crying. Coosa wasn't like most Indians. By that, I mean his features, like his skin tone, were light, and he was tall and strong. When I first saw him, he had on the headdress that I have. His face was filled with character and almost no wrinkles. Actually, he looked as young as George. He wore soft buckskin from head to toe. I'll never forget the dance he did with such vigor. When he finished the dance, he threw a spear in the ground beside me. It was then he spoke his blessing over me and gave me the eagle cape." Margaret leaned forward and said, "Would you like to look at it?"

Cody blushed. "Well actually, I checked it out while you were asleep. I hope you don't mind."

"Of course not." Margaret took the cape from the roll and placed it around Cody's shoulders and stepped back. "Let me take a look."

Cody gently ran his fingertips down the front of the cape.

"You sure look handsome," Margaret said. "I bet Carolyn would melt like butter on a hot summer's day, if she could see you now."

Cody chuckled. "It does look striking, doesn't it?"

Margaret pointed at him and said, "Wait just one minute." She hurried and took the headdress from the roll and brought it to Cody. "Try this on."

Cody put it on, went into the bedroom and stood before a full-length mirror.

Margaret stood beside him and shook her head. "My heavens, you're handsome. Wow! What do you think about that?"

"I . . . I'm almost speechless. I feel an awe. What does that mean?"

Margaret shrugged. "Maybe you're feeling a little of the spirit from the grand chief who wore it before you."

After they put the cape and headdress away, Margaret and Cody talked about visiting Desan and what the meaning behind the need for the visit—the pull of the spirit—would be.

"Are you nervous about trying to see Desan?" Cody asked.

"I'm a little apprehensive . . . well, a lot apprehensive, but no more than I was about trying to see Uncle Bill. With him I was scared of being rejected by family; with Desan it's just all the spooky things I've heard. However, I trust that God will be with me and that I'll find out all I need to know with just this one visit."

As they ate supper that night, the conversation turned to Suzie Chambers, Holly and the children and then to Carolyn. Margaret raised her brows and grinned at Cody. "I think you're getting a pretty good crush on her. Am I right?"

A quick nod and Cody confessed that he was falling in love with her.

"Have you told her yet?" Margaret asked.

Cody blushed. "Well, no. What if she doesn't feel the same way?"

"Oh, she feels the same way. Trust me."

"Has she told you that?"

"Only a thousand times."

Cody's eyes widened as he put his fork down. "Are you serious? Carolyn said that to you? What else did she say?"

"That's all you'll get from me. The rest you'll have to get from Carolyn's lips."

Cody raised both hands in the air and said, "How am I supposed to sleep after hearing that?"

"The same way I can. Wishing that George was holding me tonight."

Margaret did the dishes and Cody cleaned the table. Before going to bed, they stood in front of the fireplace, held hands and prayed for a safe journey and visit with Desan, for George, Carolyn, Holly and her children.

Chapter Sixty-Eight
Desan's Story

Up before dawn, Cody saddled the horses while Margaret made egg biscuits and coffee for breakfast and the trip. Again, the sun was shining and more of the snow was melting, even though the ground was frozen. When Margaret stepped outside, she took a deep breath of the cold air and blew it out. The much needed sleep had cleared her mind, and once again she was able to keep everything in its right perspective. There was no way she could afford to break down until her mission was over and she was back home. Cody made sure the fire was out and the door was secured. They mounted horses and headed out toward White Oak to find Desan.

Fortunately, they saw no one on the trail. By noon they were nearing the top of the mountain. They dismounted from their horses and led them for a distance. Then Margaret shouted, "Desan! Desan. I'm Margaret Black. My brother, Cody, is with me. We mean you no harm. I just want to talk to you about my grandmother, Phoebe Thawbush."

Cody looked around through the trees. "We have to be getting pretty close," he said. "We're at the top of the mountain."

Margaret wiped the corner of her mouth. "I know. I feel sure she hears me, whether she answers or not is another thing. I'm so thankful the sun is shining. It's totally eerie up here. Can you imagine a heavy rain and a dense fog?"

Cody continued to survey the terrain. "I don't see any sign of a cave. Do you?"

Margaret bit her lower lip and sighed. "No, I don't, but I wouldn't expect to just see an open hole somewhere. She's lived up here forever. She's bound to have a covering on the entrance."

"Yeah, that makes sense. Try calling her again."

Margaret cupped her hands around her mouth and shouted, "Desan! Desan! I'm Margaret Black. I'm Phoebe Thawbush's granddaughter. I have my brother, Cody, with me. We're not here to hurt you. I only want to talk to you about my Grandmother Phoebe. Desan!"

Cody took his hat off and wiped his forehead with his sleeve. "Shoot. What if we don't find her? There's rock bluffs everywhere. I think this is the area Randy told us about, but I need more of a clue if this is the right place or not. I guess what I'm trying to say is, I don't know where we are. We could hunt forever and not find her."

"Well then, that's what we'll do. I intend to see her before I leave this place." Margaret yelled at the top of her lungs, "Desan! Desan! I'm Margaret Black, the granddaughter of Phoebe Thawbush. My brother, Cody, is with me. We're not here to hurt you. I just want to ask you a few questions about my grandmother."

As they turned to go in another direction, a low voice growled, "I heard you the first time, Margaret Black."

Cody and Margaret both screamed at the top of their lungs, causing the horses to stomp uncontrollably. Trying to calm them so they wouldn't get away, yet trying to see who had spoken, was almost too great a task. Once the horses calmed, they frantically scanned the area.

"Here I am. If I were a snake, I would have filled you with my poison." Sitting at their feet, behind some bushes that looked as though they were growing from the rock, sat a white-haired woman. Her hair was in braids and a leather headband with a red design was tied around her forehead. Her dark skin was leathered with age. She was short and appeared about twenty pounds overweight. She slowly pushed herself up with her walking cane. A brightly colored, woven blanket was wrapped around her shoulders. Her shoes were made of black fur and her long full skirt rested on top of them.

Margaret held her chest as she tried to catch her breath. "My word, you scared the life out of us."

Desan frowned at them and said, "If I was that jumpy, I wouldn't have come out of the house today."

Margaret cut her eyes to Cody, but didn't turn her head. Neither Cody nor Margaret knew what to say as Desan's dark eyes stared at them. She pointed her cane at them and demanded, "If you ain't got nothing to say to me, then get off my mountain."

Margaret licked her dry lips. "I . . . I wanted to ask . . ." She put her hand on her cheek and took a deep breath. "You speak English. I wasn't sure when we came if you could even understand English."

"Why wouldn't I understand English?"

"I . . . I just thought that you might only speak Cherokee."

"You're part Cherokee, and you speak English. Why is it that you think I couldn't?"

"Yes. Yes, I do speak English, and there is no reason for thinking that you couldn't."

Desan snapped, "So, are you going to tell me what it is you want from me or not?"

"Please forgive my hesitation in responding to your request, but I wasn't expecting anyone to be sitting at our feet. When you spoke and came from the bushes, we panicked. If I'm repeating myself, please forgive me. I've forgotten every word I've said to this point, and all that I was going to ask you has escaped my mind as well."

Desan tapped the side of Cody's leg with her cane. "Are you mute? Is that why you don't speak?"

"No . . . no, I'm not mute at all. It's just that every word Margaret has said sums up my feeling too."

Desan moaned. "What was all that shouting you was doing about Phoebe Thawbush?"

"Phoebe was our grandmother. I was told that you might be able to shed some light on her childhood. Is that true?"

Desan growled, "And just what do you think I could tell you about her childhood?"

"I have no idea. I just know in my spirit that I was to come talk with you, and here I am. I found out from my Uncle Bill that Phoebe was taken when she was a baby and raised by the Seminoles."

Desan put her hand up. "Enough. Let's go inside. I'm cold." Desan led the way through the bushes to the warmth of a very large cave with a fire in the center of the rock floor. The walls of the cave were lined with buckskin. Several drawings were hanging on the skin. She had pelts scattered about the floor. A cot and a couple of beautiful hand-carved oak chairs and a small chest completed the furnishings. Margaret frowned as she fixed her eyes on one of the chairs. Cody also noticed the chair. Margaret pointed to it and asked, "Where did you get that chair, if you don't mind my asking?"

Desan snapped, "What's it any of your business? It's my chair, not yours."

"I know it's your chair," Margaret muttered. "Grandma Phoebe had one just like that one. Grandpa Thawbush made it for her as a wedding present."

"Winter Snow made these chairs as well, many years ago."

Cody and Margaret's eyes brightened at the thought of seeing something made by their grandfather.

Cody rubbed his fingers gently across the top of the back and said, "His work is quite exquisite. The wood is put together with an edge so smooth it's unbelievable."

Desan pointed her cane at the chairs. "You sit in them," she directed Cody.

"Oh, no," Cody said. "You and Margaret sit in them. I'll sit on one of the pelts."

Cody sat down and crossed his legs. Margaret reached to take hold of Desan's arm to help the older woman sit down. When she touched her arm, Desan slapped her hand. "You get your hands off me. I can sit down without your help. What do you think I do when you're not here to help me?"

"I'm sorry," Margaret said. "I didn't mean any disrespect."

Desan frowned at Margaret. "Okay, we're down. So what is it you want to know?"

Margaret told Desan about the Pine Mountain Cemetery trip that started the whole thing. She shared about the paintings of Phoebe, her mother and Chief Coosa that Bill had shown her.

Desan listened without any response.

Margaret told about Lighted Path guiding her to Chief Coosa—the unbelievable moment that she saw him, the blessing spoken over her and the eagle cape that Coosa had given her. "Chief Coosa, Lighted Path and Uncle Bill were shot down by some Union soldiers who thought they had taken us hostage." Margaret took the chest from her saddlebag and opened it. When Desan saw the chest, she put her hand to her lips and gasped.

Margaret held the chest toward Desan. "Do you recognize this?"

Desan gently touched the chest and closed her eyes for a second.

"You do recognize it, don't you?"

Desan pulled her hand away, drew a tight fist and said, "What's it to you? How did you get it?"

"From my Uncle Bill. I showed you the chest because I felt sure you would know about it and its contents." Margaret leaned toward Desan. "Please help me understand if you possibly can. Anything you can share will be treasured in my heart."

Desan turned her head to the side and tightened her lips. She faced Margaret but said nothing. She glanced at Cody and then cut her eyes to her lap, still saying nothing. Margaret was beginning to think that maybe her visit had been unsuccessful until Desan held her hand to Margaret and said, "Can I see the box?"

Margaret swallowed hard as she gave it to Desan, who held it close and rocked back and forth. "I'm not crazy you know."

"Of course not," Margaret hastened to say.

"People have thought I'm a witch for so many years now. I'm not a witch. A witch would operate against the Great Eagle. I would never do that as long as I'm in my right mind." Desan sat the chest on her lap. "It's been a lot of years since I last saw this. I was with Phoebe the day it was given to her. We were raised together, you know. We were both taken from Cherokee at the same time. I'm sure your Uncle Bill told you about the mix of people that lived among the Seminole. It was there I first saw a Chinese person. She was short and talked really funny. As children, Phoebe and I tried to copy her, but it was no use.

"The chief who found Phoebe was Mighty Elk who was Winter Snow Thawbush's father. Phoebe was different from anyone in the tribe. I'm not just talking about the fact that she was Cherokee, for I am Cherokee. I mean her *spirit* was different. I stayed in the same wigwam with Phoebe, and I even knew her thoughts most of the time just by looking at her. Phoebe thought the gods the Seminole worshipped were false gods. The Medicine Man served as our spirit leader. Phoebe never believed anything she was taught about the wind god or the tree god. For as long as I can remember, Phoebe believed in one God. When she and I would lie outside at night, she would tell me about the immeasurable God of heaven and the many names that He operated under. One, I will never forget, is Immanuel. She would say 'I know that He's the true God because He is with me.'

"I would ask her how she knew His name was Immanuel. She would say, 'The black book tells me so and I feel Him in my heart. He speaks to me and I respond.'

"Mighty Elk would let us go on hunts with the braves and compete in everything that proved one was ready to take his position as a brave. Phoebe always beat the braves in every competition. Mighty Elk asked her to explain to him how she could win over the braves in everything. He wanted to hear her say, just once, that it was because of his training, yet Phoebe never gave him that credit. She said, as she held to his neck, 'Your training, my father, has taught me to run, but my strength comes from the Mighty Eagle of heaven.'

"Phoebe saw many things she thought were wrong in our tribe. The main thing that caused her blood to boil was the fact that they called on false gods. When

Mighty Elk found Phoebe by the river, there was a little black book in her things."

Margaret exclaimed, "A black book!"

"Yes, he brought the book back with Phoebe. Mandy, the woman who breastfed Phoebe, was white. Mandy was grown when she married one of the warriors, so she knew how to read and write. Therefore, she taught Phoebe to do the same. The only book that Mandy had to teach Phoebe from was the little black Bible. Phoebe believed every word of the book. She learned to pray and expect answers. One thing Phoebe learned was that Jesus was a healer. She wanted to be able to do for people as Jesus did for people in the little black book. She believed that through His name, she too could pray for people and they would be healed. Needless to say, I was the first one whom she prayed for, even though I wasn't sick. She played the part of possessing the healing gift long before it ever worked.

"One day, someone told us that one of the small children was burning hot with a fever. Phoebe felt it was time to practice on someone other than me. She went to the tent and started inside. The child's mother stopped her. 'Phoebe, go home and tell Mighty Elk to send the Medicine Man to pray for my child.' Phoebe frowned and said through gritted teeth, 'Why would you want him to come? His gods can't heal anything. There is only one God, and I came to pray for your child in His name.' The woman was so mad that her veins were popping out. She told someone who was there, to go get the Medicine Man and Mighty Elk—the Medicine Man to pray for her child and Mighty Elk to whip Phoebe for not doing as she was told. The woman went out to get fresh water for her child, and Phoebe took advantage of her absence. She hurried and laid her hands on the little girl and the fever left instantly. The mother came in just in time to see Phoebe remove her hands from her child. She grabbed Phoebe's arm and pulled her away from the bed. Before the woman could whip Phoebe, the child raised up and said, 'Mama, I feel better.'

"The Medicine Man and Mighty Eagle arrived just in time to see the woman rejoicing because her child had been healed instantly. She apologized to Mighty Elk and Phoebe. Phoebe looked at the Medicine Man and boldly stated, 'There is only one God. It is He who healed the child, not me, and most certainly not you.'

"As Phoebe grew older and wiser, she turned many people to the Mighty Eagle of heaven and earth. She would lay her hands on many, and they were healed instantly—"

"My heavens!" Margaret interrupted. "I've never heard any of this."

"The Seminole are a proud people," Desan continued, "and they didn't expect that kind of miracles from anyone but the Medicine Man. They most certainly didn't expect it from a young girl. So the Medicine Man started rumors that there must be a devil operating Phoebe's spirit. She told them that any child of the one God could do miracles if they would only believe. She ended up convincing two thirds of the tribe to believe. The Seminole living there numbered about seven hundred people at that time.

"Don't misunderstand. There were some that hated Phoebe because of the power she possessed. The Medicine Man brought her before the tribal counsel and wanted to put her to death, but the Almighty had his hand on her. Phoebe stood firm and shouted, 'Try and kill me, but you will not prevail.' She said God had assured her that He would protect her. They took Phoebe's challenge and tried to hang her three times, but the ropes snapped like a dry weed. They tried but couldn't kill her." Desan paused and shook her head.

"What is it?" Margaret asked.

"After all these years, this is still hard for me to believe. The Medicine Man tied Phoebe's hands behind her and led her to the center of the village. I'll never forget that day. Every person in the village turned out to see what would happen next. After the ropes had snapped at the hangings, everyone wondered what would happen when they tried to shoot arrows into her body. Mighty Elk turned to the Living God of heaven that day. Until then, he had harbored many doubts. After all, he had never been taught anything but the traditions of his people. The Great Spirit had been working on his heart, and that day he forgot traditions.

"All he could think about was Phoebe. He wanted her to live. By the way, did I mention she was only thirteen at the time? When I reached the center of the village, there was a tall stake driven in the ground. I trembled as they brought Phoebe with hands bound and tied her to the stake. Five warriors lined up with their bows in hand. All around, the people whom Phoebe had converted were praying for her. Their prayers turned into chants. In unison, we chanted, 'Mighty Eagle of heaven, come and save your faithful servant.' The chant rose as the warriors pulled their bowstrings to release their arrows. When they did, it thundered so loud the earth shook and streaks of lightening filled the sky. Up to that point, the sky was clear and had been clear for several days. The people continued to chant even louder. A large white cloud suddenly appeared. While the thunder rumbled and the lightning flashed the cloud exploded and the most tremendous eagle that anyone could have ever imagined came forth from the explosion. Its wingspan was as big as a towering evergreen. It swept down to where Phoebe was tied. What happened next is even harder to believe."

Margaret leaned forward in anticipation. "What happened?"

"When the giant Eagle started down, the ropes that bound Phoebe's hands fell off. The Eagle took her in his claws and swooped her up and set her on the only knoll on the north side of the village. She raised both her arms and cried a cry that I can still hear after all these years. She danced on the mountain for at least an hour, giving praise to the Mighty God of heaven who had delivered her from Satan's hands."

Margaret's eyes widened.

"The Medicine Man and his helpers were put out of the village," Desan continued. Phoebe, at thirteen years old, became the new spiritual leader of our tribe. They had a feast day to honor the Faithful God of heaven. Phoebe led the feast in prayer. She read to the people from the little black book in Exodus 19:4. She raised her voice and said, 'I bear you on eagles' wings and brought you unto myself.'"

"What did she mean?" Margaret asked.

"She said, 'God used the example of the Eagle to show how he had sent the Mighty Hunter, which is the Eagle, to bring a special people to Himself as a rare treasure, pointing out He wasn't talking about only the Hebrews, but whosoever would turn to Him and serve Him. Those eagles He would gather to His mountain and there He would train them. Afterward He would send them down the mountain to hunt and find the wounded and the lost. Then they were to bring them to the mountain. There the Great Eagle would heal them and train them.

"The celebration went on all day and into the night. Before the feast ended, Mighty Elk called all the people to attention. He too had something to say. He told about a Great Eagle that had been destroyed by evil men's fire and how the Eagle that was destroyed possessed the true words that would lead people to everlasting life. 'Many years had passed,' he said, 'and his people were in darkness . . . until one day, where the Eagle had been burned hundreds of years before, a small stream of smoke appeared and went up to heaven. The Great Eagle heard the cry that had come to Him from the smoke. It had taken all those years for the fire to be kindled and any sign of life to reappear.' He said the holy smoke that rose from the ashes prayed to be set free to share the words of truth again. The Great Eagle was pleased with the perseverance of His child and would honor the prayer. The breath of God blew on the ashes and commanded the Mighty Phoenix to arise and fill the land with His truth.

"Phoebe was dressed in bleached buckskin from head to toe. I was never sure how they got that skin so white. Mighty Elk clapped his hands, and a warrior brought this chest to him." Desan took the necklace from the chest and put it around Margaret's neck. "Mighty Elk wanted to give Phoebe the signet of his people. He fastened it around her neck and took an eagle's feather and placed it in her braid that lay against the right side of her face."

"What about the ashes?" Margaret asked.

Desan took the pouch from the chest and smiled. "The ashes weren't added to the chest until after . . ."

"After what?" Cody asked.

Desan opened the pouch and took out a pinch of ashes. "Until after he had Phoebe sit in the ash heap that he had prepared. When she sat down, Mighty Elk did a dance for ever so long. When he stopped, he took a spear from a warrior and threw it into the ground beside the ash heap where Phoebe sat. He took her hands and helped her to her feet, looked around at the people and shouted at the top of his voice, 'Oh, Great God of heaven and earth, blow the spark that this mighty woman possesses in her heart and bring new life to her and her people. Cause the spark to ignite and illuminate her path that she may light the way for others. From the ashes of death, cause her to arise like the Mighty Phoenix and display your power for all to see. Cause her to spread her enormous wings and soar to the peaks of the highest mountain. Allow the wind from her wings to refresh the souls of all mankind. May she ever be filled with your truth and peace, and may she ever find Joy on the Mountain.'

"After that, he clapped his hands and three squaws came from his tent, holding something wrapped in a piece of flawless buckskin. He unrolled the skin and held up the most beautiful eagle cape that my eyes had ever witnessed. Everyone gasped at the sight of it. He took the cape and placed it around Phoebe's shoulders. Her eyes widened and her countenance glowed as she stroked the front of the cape. The people cheered to the Great Eagle of heaven. The drums pounded in celebration. The Mighty Eagle had brought truth to a treasured people.

"Phoebe hugged Mighty Elk and embraced Mandy, the one who had taught her to read and therefore gain understanding from the little black book that was left near her blanket by the preacher and his wife who had been murdered. Phoebe then made her way to me and took my hands and whispered, 'Desan, I love you. You are my treasured friend.' At that point, everyone was celebrating as the drums continued to pound. Phoebe moved to the side of the fire. It was then she began to dance. At first her feet moved slowly and then proceeded to a rapid pace. She danced with all her might before the Mighty God of heaven and earth. Needless to say, the village was never the same again after that night."

"We didn't have any idea," Margaret said.

"People came from other villages," Desan continued, "to hear the strange words that Phoebe spoke from the little black book—words that changed people's lives. She married Winter Snow Thawbush by the end of that year. They had four children—Bill, Tyler, Lorie and Mariah. You said you were Margaret, but you look exactly like Phoebe and Mariah."

"Desan," Margaret said, "may I ask you something?"

Desan looked around and laughed. "Well, I'm not going anywhere so you may as well."

"What does all this mean? It's as though everything is going full circle, and I don't know where I could possibly fit. Grandma Phoebe I can see and even my mother, but not me. I haven't heard from heaven like Grandma did. I believe in the word, and I pray every day, knowing that God holds me in his hand, but I am not worthy to receive the chest and the contents and the eagle cape."

Desan patted Margaret's shoulder. "My dear, you don't have to be thirteen for your destiny to fall upon you. You don't have to be exactly like someone else, in your thinking or your methods, but know this, when it's time for you to enter your destiny, nothing can stop that. God has everyone's time set in motion and his callings are without repentance. In other words, God's gifts are irrevocable. They're still there whether you operate in your calling or not. For Him to go to such lengths to see that everything has been passed to you, including the cape, is a sure sign that you are another Phoenix that is coming out of the ashes. How old are you?"

"I'm fifty."

"My goodness. Do you know what the number fifty means in the black book?"

"It mean's Jubilee."

"That's right. So there is reason to celebrate. It's the anniversary of the rising of the Phoenix. What your lot will be, I don't know. Yet to some degree, I think I do know." Desan pushed up with her cane and went to an old trunk that sat at the foot of the cot. She opened it and took something out that was wrapped in a dingy cloth that once had been white. She closed the lid, walked slowly back to her chair and sat down.

"I'm an old woman, but I'm so thankful that God has allowed me this opportunity to be a part of the day He told me would come. I felt sure I must have heard wrong after all these many years." Tears filled Desan's eyes as she held the cloth up with both hands. "I was told that before I died, I would pass this to the next Great Eagle. Today that prophecy is fulfilled and the Eagle sits before me."

Cody and Margaret glanced at each other and then fixed their eyes on Desan.

"Phoebe gave me this when she and Winter Snow were married. Someone from the white settlement brought her another one. She said it was to stay in my care until the Holy Spirit told me differently. Well, today He's told me differently." Desan opened the cloth to reveal a little black book. Margaret and Cody gasped.

Desan held the book out to Margaret. "This belongs to you, Margaret Phoebe Black."

Margaret trembled as she took the book from Desan's aged hand. She wanted to say something, yet her words wouldn't form.

Desan frowned. "What was it you said Eagle Claw told you to do before you came back to the mountain?'

"He . . . he told me not to come back until I had found the mystery and penned it with my hand."

"Then go from here and pen all the events that have taken place."

Margaret nodded and hugged Desan. "I must admit I was a little scared of what I would find when we met you. Thank God those concerns all proved to be untrue."

"Is there anything we can do for you before we go?" Cody asked.

"No thank you, young man."

"Do you mind if we come and visit you again, or better yet, would you come visit us? We could come and get you and you could stay with me as long as you like."

Desan sighed. "I haven't been off this mountain in so long."

"Why is that?" Cody asked.

Desan looked to the side and didn't answer.

"By the way," Margaret said, "I met a woman who spoke very highly of you."

Desan smiled and whispered, "Holly?"

"Yes. She told me you prayed for Franklin and his cut was healed."

"He's a special boy. I knew it from the moment I touched him. How is it that you know them?"

Margaret told her how she had met them and about Holly and the kids bringing her back to Cherokee. When Margaret and Cody said goodbye and mounted their horses to leave, Desan called out. "You'll be seeing Franklin again soon."

Margaret turned. "What did you say?"

Desan shook her head and said, "You have a safe trip, friends."

Margaret frowned at Cody. "That wasn't what she said, was it?"

Cody shrugged. "I couldn't tell. Anyway we need to ride hard to get back to your place before midnight." Margaret turned for one last wave before they went out of sight.

Chapter Sixty-Nine
The Treasure

*T*here was a slight breeze, but still it was warmer than it had been for the last month. The light of the moon and the snow helped them make sure they stayed on the road. It was eleven thirty when they arrived back at Margaret's. They hadn't stopped to eat, so Margaret fixed something while Cody made a fire in the fireplace and went to put the horses in the barn.

They were too tired to talk, so they ate and went straight to bed. Morning came with the sound of someone knocking on the door. Margaret groaned as she tried to pull her tired body from the bed. She put her hands on her hips and rolled her shoulders. She hurt all over. The hard ride home had taken a toll on her muscles. Julie and Carolyn had come, eager to find out if they had found Desan. Julie grabbed Margaret and said, "Thank God you're home and you're okay."

Carolyn added, "We prayed almost all night for you and Cody."

Margaret squinted. "Come inside so I can close the door. I love the sun, but my eyes don't care much for it right now."

Julie stirred the coals and added wood to the fire while Carolyn made the coffee. "I'm starving," Margaret said.

Julie took something from her bag. "I thought you would be, so I brought breakfast from home for you and Cody."

Margaret took the bag, kissed Julie's cheek and moaned, "Thank you, Sissy."

Julie and Margaret sat at the dinner table. Julie widened her eyes and said, "I want to hear what went on with Desan . . . without any interruption. Therefore, I didn't want a long wait while you fixed something to eat."

Carolyn sat beside Julie, facing Margaret. "I also want to know what I missed."

Margaret took a bite of egg biscuit and quickly stood. She hurried toward the bedroom and said, "I have to show you something."

Julie and Carolyn watched with anticipation to see what Margaret would bring. Margaret paused in the doorway, then moved to the end of the table. She held up a dingy cloth and smiled.

"Okay, what's the big deal with a dirty looking rag?" Julie asked.

Margaret sat down and shook her head. "It's not the rag, it's what's inside the rag."

"Well, show us for heaven sakes," Carolyn said.

Margaret unfolded the cloth and placed her hands, palms down, beside the little black book and said, "Do you know what this is?"

Julie touched the black book, "Yeah, it's a Bible, isn't it?"

Carolyn squinted and remarked, "That's what it says on the binding."

"Where did you get it?" Julie asked.

Carolyn put her hands over her mouth. "Is it Desan's?"

Margaret grinned. "Better than that, it's Grandma Phoebe's."

"Oh my," Carolyn whispered.

Julie touched her fingertips to it. "This is Grandma Phoebe's? Did Desan tell you that?"

Margaret nodded. "And much more."

Carolyn poured them coffee and Margaret told all that Desan had shared with her and Cody about Phoebe and the amazing things that had taken place when she was a young girl. As she was finishing the story, someone knocked at the door.

Julie peeked out the window.

"Who is it?" Margaret asked.

Julie rushed to Carolyn and whispered, "Carolyn, answer the door. It's Willow."

Margaret's mouth dropped open as she grabbed Julie's arm. "Hide in the bedroom. She can't know you're here, or I'll never hear the end of it."

The knocking on the door grew louder. Julie hurried to the bedroom and closed the door.

"Carolyn, get the door and be calm." Margaret said as she quickly sat down at the table.

After a deep breath, Carolyn opened the door. "Willow, what a surprise. Margaret, it's Willow."

Willow peered around Carolyn into the house. Margaret hastened to greet her with a hug. "Willow, what a surprise! Come in. We were just having breakfast. Would you like to join us?"

Willow continued to scan the house as she replied, "No, thank you. I hadn't seen you around for some time. I wanted to check and make sure that everything's all right."

Margaret shrugged. "Of course, shouldn't it be?"

Willow continued to nonchalantly look around. "Is Cody here?" she asked.

Margaret took a sip of coffee and said, "Yes, he is. He's still asleep. Did you need him for something?"

Avoiding the question, Willow said, "There are two horses outside. I'm sure Carolyn didn't ride both of them over this morning." Willow smugly fixed her eyes on Carolyn. "Did you Carolyn? If you did, that would be an act that I would like to see."

Carolyn shifted her eyes to Margaret who swiftly answered. "No, she didn't, Willow! Let's cut right to it. What is it you want? You didn't get up this early and decide to ride over and check on my business did you? If that be the case, what is it that you want to know?"

Willow tightened her lips and demanded, "I want to know what's been going on the past couple of weeks. You haven't been to the fort but two or three times.

Carolyn's been sticking like glue to Julie instead of you, and God only knows where Cody's been. So tell me why Julie's hiding in the bedroom."

Margaret furrowed her brows as she glanced to the bedroom door then quickly back to Willow. Willow suddenly shouted, "Julie! Julie! You may as well come out of your hiding place. I know you're here. My maid saw you and your sidekick ride in this direction this morning."

The bedroom door opened and Cody came out. "What in the world are you shouting at Willow? Better yet, what are you doing here? Have you decided to come down from your ivory palace to your cousin's humble abode?"

She snapped, "Shut up, Cody. I have a right to do as I please without your permission."

Margaret stood. "Enough Willow," she stated firmly. "This is my house and who comes here, or when, is none of your business. I don't do that to you, and I expect the same."

Willow stood, hit the table and shouted, "I don't slip around and do things behind your back. For the past month you and Carolyn have been disappearing days at a time, and Carolyn came home wounded without you. And then you come home with some woman that has three kids. If that isn't enough, you and Cody left yesterday and didn't come back until midnight. If you're doing something illegal, I want you to stop and think about it. If you're not doing anything that's underhanded, tell me why Julie is hiding like a criminal from her own cousin?"

The bedroom door came open and Julie furrowed her brow as she rounded the table and stopped in front of Willow.

Cody threw his hands up. "What is going on here? Julie, when did you get here and what, pray tell are you doing hiding in the bedroom?"

"I told you she was here," Willow snapped.

Cody, totally confused, shouted, "What the devil is going on? Willow, how is it you know every move we've made for the last month and yet don't know what's going on?"

Willow held her head high. "At first I didn't think anything was going on; however, when Carolyn and Margaret took off for a few days, I felt sure that it had something to do with Grandma Phoebe. If it does have something to do with her, why wouldn't you care to share it with me? Is it not enough that I didn't receive a blessing from Grandma Phoebe, but you're adding to the insult by doing things behind my back?"

Julie started to reply, but Margaret interrupted. "So, that's what this is about? You can't get over the fact that you didn't get a blessing. You still blame Grandma for dying before she got to you. How childish is that? Are you never going to grow up and get this behind you? Think about it, Willow. Maybe there's a reason she didn't speak a blessing over you."

"Talk about childish. Julie ran and hid like a child. How do you think that looks to me? If you want to know the truth, it hurts my feelings. I want to be a part of the blessings and a part of you. It hurts not to know why you don't want to include me. I couldn't take it any longer. Being rejected hurts. I know you've always been somewhat jealous because I have a grander home and quite a bit more money, but all that aside, I love you and you're the only family I have here at this God-forsaken place. I just don't want to be excluded, that's all."

Margaret put her hand to her forehead and sat down. "Listen, Willow and everybody, please sit down and let's try and explain what has been going on to Willow." Everyone sat and Margaret began by saying, "Willow, once and for all, I want all this about your blessing dropped and never to be brought up again in a serious manner, understood?"

"I'll try," she groaned.

"Try isn't enough. You either promise or I'll not tell you anything. Now do you promise?"

Willow paused, then muttered, "Okay."

Margaret leaned toward her. "What did you say? I didn't hear you."

Willow bit her lower lip. "I said okay!"

"That's better," Margaret said. "Now I'll start at the first and tell you all that's taken place and what we've been doing. None of this has been done to reject you, but because I didn't feel that it had anything to do with you, I kept it between Carolyn, Julie and Cody. Had I known that you would've taken so much interest in my plans, I would have told you. To be honest, the reason I didn't tell you is because I didn't want to hear about you not getting your blessing. But that's all behind us; therefore, I'll share the events now."

Margaret told Willow everything and showed her the things that Uncle Bill, Coosa and Desan had given her. Willow was in awe. "Why didn't we ever know any of this?"

"I don't know any more than I've already told you."

Willow furrowed her brows. "Daddy never told me any of this. I can understand if someone is ashamed of something, but it seems as though somewhere down the road, after all these years, he would have mentioned it. Now he has to hear that his brother is dead. That makes me feel sick."

Margaret patted Willow's hand. "Do you want me to tell your dad or at least go with you to tell him?"

"No, I'll tell Daddy."

"Willow, be sure and tell your dad that Bill loved him very much, no matter what happened."

"Willow," Cody said, "I want to go with you to tell Uncle Tyler. If you don't mind."

Willow paused, "Of course you may go," she said. She stood and spread her arms. "For heaven sake, let's do a family hug."

They gathered in a circle, then stopped. "Something's not right," Margaret said.

"You're right," Julie added.

Willow took her arms from Julie and Margaret. "This doesn't feel right."

Cody smiled, took Carolyn's hand and pulled her to the circle. "Now it's perfect," he whispered, and they all agreed.

Chapter Seventy
Surprise Visit

A week had passed since Margaret and Cody had gone to visit Desan. Things were returning to normal as much as possible. Carolyn was back teaching full time. Cody spent almost every evening with Carolyn. That left Margaret with all the time she needed to pen all the events that had taken place, as Eagle Claw had told her to do. Her heart yearned every day for George's return. Julie and Willow grew very close and were spending more time together.

One evening, Randy came to bring Margaret a personal message. George should be home in three days. Joy filled her being, although it meant working twice as hard to finish the task Eagle Claw had given her. She wanted to devote her time to George. However, completing her writings was also top priority. Her mind was like a merry-go-round—up, down and around. She thought about the amazing, yet short-lived, events that brought her to her Uncle Bill; her real father, Chief Coosa; and Desan. She worried the old woman would die on that secluded mountain and no one would know. Margaret pulled the curtain back and looked at the winding road that led to her house. She wished she would see Holly and the children coming with her wagon loaded, ready to start a new life in Cherokee. And what of Suzie Chambers? Such an elegant woman and yet such a torn woman. She knew down deep that Suzie still loved Willie and would like to have a home with him and their daughter. Writing it all down kept it fresh in her mind. She wrote, "I stand in awe of the Great Eagle that has penned steps of my life. Who could have ever imagined such grandness in the midst of such tragedy?"

The third day had come. Margaret finished her writing for the day and prepared hopefully for George's homecoming. She wanted to ride to the fort to see if Randy had heard anything but was afraid George might come while she was away. Julie, Willow, Cody and Carolyn came that evening to visit and wait with her for George's anticipated arrival. Margaret had gone to the window it seemed a hundred times as midnight approached. Cody put his arm around her shoulders and comforted, "Honey, maybe you had better go to bed. I'll stay with you tonight."

"That's okay. I'll be fine."

"How about me staying?" Carolyn offered. "I don't have a class until ten o'clock, and besides, I want to read your manuscript."

Margaret chuckled. "I'm not sure there's enough of it to be called a manuscript, but I would love for you to read it."

"Then I'll stay. Anything I might need before morning you have."

When everyone had gone, Carolyn took Margaret's writing and went to the bedroom. "Carolyn, aren't you going to sleep in here with me?"

"When I finish reading, I'll join you."

Margaret put wood on the fire and went to bed. She had so hoped George would have made it home and he would be joining her. Around four o'clock, Margaret was awakened by what sounded like a wagon. She quickly shook Carolyn and put her robe on. "Carolyn, wake up. George is home."

Carolyn hurriedly lit a lamp while Margaret straightened her hair. Carolyn rushed to light another couple of lamps in the living room. She paused, listened closely and called out, "Margaret."

Margaret hurried through the door. "How do I look?" she asked with excitement in her voice.

Carolyn put her finger to her lips. "Shhh. Margaret, George wouldn't be driving a wagon would he?"

Margaret frowned. "You're right, he wouldn't. Carolyn get your gun."

Margaret hurried and made sure her pistol was loaded and went to the window to peek out. "Carolyn, turn the lights down."

Carolyn quickly turned the lamps down and joined Margaret at the window. "It's too dark to see who it is," Carolyn said softly.

"I know, but I just can't see George coming from the fort in a wagon. Why would he do that? He has his own horse."

When the wagon stopped, someone called out, "Margaret Phoebe Black!"

Margaret gasped when she realized the voice belonged to Desan. She quickly looked at Carolyn, grabbed a lamp and opened the door. She hurried to the porch and held the lamp up. "Desan, what is it?"

"I've driven hard to get here. Look in the back of the wagon."

Margaret froze for a moment. "Franklin," she said breathlessly.

Desan climbed down and uttered, "We need to get him inside."

Carolyn and Margaret carried him carefully, laid him on a cot near Margaret's bed and covered him up. "Stay with him, Carolyn, while I help Desan inside." This time Desan allowed Margaret to hold her arm and help her up the steps. Margaret led Desan to one of the chairs beside the fireplace and then asked, "What's wrong with Franklin and where are Holly, Dan and Diana?"

Desan lowered her head, then stared into Margaret's eyes and moaned, "They're dead."

Margaret's body instantly grew numb as she leaned back in her chair. "How are they dead? They were here not that long ago."

"I heard the boy wailing in the night. He wasn't anywhere near the mountain, so I knew the all-powerful Eagle had summoned me to find him. They were moving to Cherokee for a new life. That's what Franklin told me."

Margaret wiped her tears and asked, "What happened? Did he say?"

"He said it was so dark and the road was slick. They had a lantern tied to the wagon, but still their sight was so limited they could barely see each other. Holly didn't want to stop for the night, even though she couldn't see if she was still in the road or not. He said, with no warning, the wagon hit a boulder and threw him out, but the back wheels of the wagon went over a cliff and pulled the mule off behind it. I found Holly and the children at the bottom, lying on a heap of rocks, dead."

Frantic, Carolyn moaned, "Dead! Are you sure they're dead?"

"I'm sure. I couldn't get to them to bury them. I brought Franklin back to the mountain. He had a bad bump on his head, but other than that, he's fine. The next morning when he woke up, it was as though he had gone into shock. He hasn't spoken since."

"Did he say anything else about events before this happened to him?" Margaret asked.

"I'm not sure what he was trying to say at first; then he mumbled that someone had come to his house and told them his daddy was dead. From what I could make out, that was when Holly decided to move. Holly wanted to take turns driving so they wouldn't have to stop and they could get here faster." Desan paused, then said, "There is one other thing."

Margaret leaned forward and asked, "What's that?"

"Before he blacked out, he whispered that he didn't have any family left and he wanted me to bring him to you. He knew that you could help him. Since then, he came to but only stares into space and won't speak."

Margaret walked slowly to the bedroom and knelt beside Franklin.

Through tears, Carolyn introduced herself to Desan. "I'm sorry, Desan. This is so shocking. I don't know what to feel or think."

"That's all right, child. I understand your feelings."

Margaret came back into the room. "Carolyn, will you fix a bed for Desan?" she asked.

"Of course I will." Carolyn went into the bedroom.

Desan shook her head. "I'll not be staying, but thank you for the offer."

"Yes, you are staying!" Margaret shouted. "I'm not going to worry myself sick about you driving in the dark. You can at least wait until morning, and Cody will see that you get back safely. I won't take no for an answer, so don't say anything except yes."

"Okay, I'll stay till morning. Franklin needs to see a doctor."

Margaret pulled her robe off and stated, "I'll go get the doctor."

Desan took her arm and said, "Not till daylight!"

"Okay, I'll have Dr. Whitt come first thing in the morning."

"Hum." Desan muttered. "I think Franklin has entered his own little safe place to get away from the hurt. He'll be back after a spell. What will you do with him?"

"I . . . I don't know. My husband will be home any time. I'm sure he will help me decide."

Desan shook her head. "How is it that you would have to think about what to do with him. You don't have children. Why don't you and your husband raise him? You could use a boy around here."

"Yeah, we could. I just might think and pray about the matter."

Carolyn called from the bedroom, "Desan your bed is ready."

"I'm ready for it too." Desan stood and groaned, "I must be getting old. My bones are as stiff as a pine tree."

"Do you want something to eat or drink before you lie down?" Margaret asked.

"No, thank you."

Desan went to bed, Margaret and Carolyn sat on either side of the bed beside Franklin. Margaret stroked his blond hair and sobbed. Carolyn put her hand on top of Margaret's. "Let's pray for him," she said.

Margaret was silent. Carolyn could tell there was something Margaret was wrestling with. "Margaret, I know what you're feeling right now. I feel the same way. Honest, I do."

Margaret shook her head and groaned, "I only got to see my father and uncle Bill for such a short while . . . and now this . . . I don't understand why God would allow these tragedies. I can see no reasoning in it all. I feel angry because I know he could have prevented them. I remember I wouldn't hush about her moving back to Cherokee. I wouldn't hush. If I would have left well enough alone, she wouldn't have been out driving in the night to get back to the people who showed her love."

"Margaret, it's not your fault."

"Then why am I sitting here feeling like a criminal? In the last two months, I've killed a soldier. I've seen soldiers die. I've seen my uncle and my father and a dear friend shot down, and now, I've seen a young mother and two of her children die and for what? Tell me, Carolyn, what is it all about?"

"I know," Carolyn said as she dabbed the tears rolling down her cheeks.

"Now, here in a cot by my bed lies a young boy with no one to care for him. And he asked Desan to bring him to me. I don't know what to do. I get all these wonderful things passed to me. You think nothing could overshadow those things, but that's not true, Carolyn. The jubilant feelings have all but diminished. I feel like it's all a big trick, and I'm asking myself if it's real or if I have been deceived. It's good that George isn't here. I couldn't go through explaining everything to him right now. I couldn't."

Margaret put her head on Franklin's stomach and wept aloud. Carolyn made her bed on the floor, and Margaret lay on her own bed near Franklin. Through the night Carolyn could hear Margaret moaning and asking the Mighty Eagle for wisdom.

Three hours later Margaret gasped and sprang from the bed. She hurried to the living room and then onto the porch. Carolyn raced to see what Margaret was doing. She stopped in the doorway and saw Margaret leaning forward, gripping the banister with both hands and trembling like a frightened child. Carolyn gently put her hand on Margaret's shoulder. "What is it Margaret! Are you okay?"

Margaret tilted her head back and rested it on Carolyn's shoulder and laughed.

"Margaret, what's so funny?"

Margaret held her face in her hands. "I thought I heard cannons firing and tears from heaven falling so hard that they were causing the house to tremble, but it's only thunder. I thought there was so much pain in heaven that every angel was crying. But it's rain. The angels aren't crying but rejoicing."

A voice from behind them said, "There is rejoicing in heaven." Desan patted her shoulder. "Many victories have been won in only a short time. Margaret, a mighty war was waged on your behalf in the heavens last night. The rainstorm that's going on this morning is the aftereffect of the battle. The main thing is, the Eagles of God always prevail." Desan stepped inside the house, got her coat and fur hat and came onto the porch. "You may keep the horse and wagon, and you'll find a present for you on the back of the wagon. By the way, I put the wagon in the barn earlier."

Margaret cut her eyes to Carolyn, then quickly to Desan and questioned, "What are you talking about? You can't leave here without a horse or something."

"You're surely not going to leave in the rain, are you?" Carolyn remarked.

"The answer to your question, Margaret, is that I have another ride waiting for me. To your question Carolyn, I'll say yes, I'm leaving in the rain." Desan moved to the edge of the porch. Then she stopped and turned. "By the way, Margaret, Franklin will come around by late evening, and you won't have to spend another night without George. He's been away long enough."

Margaret and Carolyn were speechless as Desan walked from the porch to the yard. Desan tilted her head back, allowing the rain to hit her face. She laughed aloud and said as she walked down the road, "What a beautiful day to go home!" Suddenly, as Desan walked away, she disappeared before their eyes. Margaret and Carolyn were overwhelmed. As they held to each other, they realized that truly Desan did have another ride waiting for her. Not an ordinary wagon, but a noble chariot sent by the Great Eagle of heaven to carry a faithful servant home.

Chapter Seventy-One
Sweet Smell of Honeysuckle

For a while, Margaret and Carolyn knelt on the porch and worshipped the God of heaven. It wasn't until later that they noticed the weather was like a warm spring day. The peaceful sound of steady raindrops falling and the occasional rumble of thunder made it a day never to be forgotten. When Carolyn and Margaret went to check the wagon, in the back sat the two chairs that Winter Snow Thawbush had skillfully made many years before. "When did Desan put the chairs in the wagon?" Margaret asked. Earlier, Franklin was all that had been in the back of the wagon. The chairs would be treasured.

As Margaret stood on the porch, the sweet smell of honeysuckle filled the air amid what had been early winter weather. Margaret smiled as she remembered how she and George smelled the honeysuckle in early October.

Margaret was putting wood on the fire before going to bed. She paused when she heard a horse snorting. She quickly stood and wiped her hands on her gown. "George?" she whispered, then shouted, "George, is that you?"

She raced to the door when she heard George call out her name. Through tears, kisses and I love yous, they held each other for a long time before letting go.

Margaret made George some coffee and a hot bowl of soup. As he ate, she tried to explain all that had taken place in his absence. He was somewhat understanding; however, a bit of the protective husband shot forth, as George realized the danger Margaret had put herself in. After a while, George knew in his heart Margaret did what she had to do. Knowing she was okay helped him accept the quest she had endeavored. The couple went to bed quietly, so as not to disturb Franklin, just glad to be in each other's arms again.

The words Desan had spoken proved to be true. Franklin returned to normal over a period of time, and George did get home that same night.

Chapter Seventy-Two
Mission Accomplished

$\mathcal{M}$any things happened over the next few years. Wedding bells did ring for Carolyn and Cody.

Julie and Lieutenant Creed Williams were transferred to Washington, DC. There she would frequent the grand parties and dinners as she had always wanted to do. Julie herself would give many parties and dinners.

Willow and Tim Fine moved to Atlanta and the grandeur of a Southern plantation that they rightfully named Willow's Place.

Randy Mathis finally enjoyed the promised dinner and married Deloris Hays, who prepared him dinner every night.

Margaret and George adopted Franklin and loved him with a passion. George was elated to have the son that he and Toot had been unable to have.

Margaret and George made the trip to Chestnut Grove and brought back to their home the paintings of Cody, Julie, Phoebe, Mariah, Chief Coosa and her. Uncle Bill's painting of Phoebe now hung over Margaret's fireplace. The paintings of Mariah and Chief Coosa hung on either side of Phoebe. George had a painting of Margaret done, and it too took its place alongside the others.

Five years had passed since Margaret and Carolyn visited Pine Mountain Cemetery. Margaret continued to add to her manuscript almost daily. One spring day, she was sitting on her porch writing when she saw a most elegant carriage coming up the road to her house. The coachman was dressed in red and black. The four white horses were arrayed with gold tassels around their harnesses. The coach was black with gold trim. Margaret laid her book aside and slowly stood as she remembered the handsome coach that still sat in her barn. Could the passenger in the fancy carriage nearing her house be the owner of the coach parked in her barn? Could it be the one and only Suzie Chambers? The coach stopped, and the coachman promptly opened the carriage door. In all her splendor, Suzie stepped out of the coach followed by the most beautiful young woman that Margaret had ever seen. To add to her surprise, someone else exited the coach. A tall brown-skinned man. When he removed his top hat, Margaret could see that it was the father of the beautiful young woman, Willie Alexander.

Suzie insisted on leaving a sizable amount of money for Franklin's education. She vowed she could see the statesmanship in the young man who was to graduate from high school in only one month. The money assured him acceptance into Yale University—yet another chapter in Margaret's book that she had now titled, Joy on the Mountain.

She often took the eagle cape out and put it around her shoulders along with the necklace and the feather, and on occasion Chief Coosa's headdress.

Chapter Seventy-Three
Pine Mountain Revisited

In the fall of the fifth year, since her last visit to Pine Mountain Cemetery, Margaret was brushing her horse while George and Franklin had gone hunting. For the first time in those five years, Margaret again felt the pull to visit the cemetery. It was noon and there would be plenty of daylight left for the trip. Her first thought was to get Carolyn to go with her. At that very moment, she saw Carolyn riding up the road. Margaret smiled as she stood in awe of God's perfect timing.

Carolyn was elated at the thought of going up the mountain again. This time the trip would be at noonday, in the sun and without any red clay mud.

Margaret knew that she had to take the chest, the eagle cape and more importantly the manuscript. When they tied their horses at the foot of the mountain, they began to laugh aloud, remembering the last visit and all the events that had taken place over the past five years. As they neared the top of the mountain, Margaret's thoughts centered on the fact that Pine

Mountain was where she was commissioned to go and solve the mystery that would unveil her destiny. She lifted the latch, opened the gate and entered the graveyard. As they neared the white cross that sat under the massive pine tree, Margaret paused, took a deep breath and said, "Why do you think I feel so weak in my knees?"

Carolyn rubbed her chin. "Possibly for the same reason that I do."

"Yeah."

From out of the blue, Carolyn ordered, "Summon Eagle Claw, Margaret."

Margaret slowly turned her head, looked at Carolyn and frowned. "What?"

"I said, summon Eagle Claw. It was he who told you not to come back until you solved the mystery and penned it with your hand. Well you've done that, so call him."

Margaret shook her head. "Are you kidding me?"

"Do I look like I'm kidding?"

Margaret thought a moment, then shouted at the top of her lungs, "Eagle Claw! Eagle Claw!"

A light mist came from the sky and settled on the other side of Phoebe's grave. The mist cleared and Eagle Claw appeared. "You summoned me, Margaret?" he asked.

Feeling dizzy, Margaret nodded yes. Eagle Claw crossed his arms. "Have you solved the mystery as you were instructed?"

"Yes," Margaret whispered.

"Did you pen the mystery?"

Margaret nodded and said softly, "Yes, I did."

"The first time we met, you were so bold in wanting to know what I was doing here at your grandmother's grave and demanded to know what God I serve. Now you're reserved. What's the reason for that?"

"The reason should be clear to you. I stand amazed, not at you, but at the Almighty Eagle I serve . . . that we serve. His presence leaves me weak."

"You have done your task well. Did you bring the writing with you?"

Margaret put the skin down that the cape was wrapped in and took a folder from it. She handed the folder to Eagle Claw. He smiled, held it toward heaven and said, "Many will enjoy and learn from your writings." He gave the book back to Margaret. "This is a time to rejoice."

Margaret looked at Carolyn who didn't seem amazed at all, but smiled in complete agreement with Eagle Claw.

"What's going on here?" Margaret asked.

Eagle Claw uttered, "It's called destiny, Margaret."

"That's right," Carolyn said. "Your destiny has come for you at fifty-five, not twenty. You had to mature and come to a place of wisdom in order to share your wisdom with many who will read your manuscript and be blessed."

"Carolyn! You are Carolyn, right?"

"Of course, who else would I be?"

Margaret stared into Eagle Claw's eyes and said nothing.

"Don't you recognize me, Margaret?"

Margaret gasped as his face became clear. "Captain Ross? Is that you?"

He smiled and said, "The Great Eagle does work in mysterious ways. Don't you agree?"

Margaret began to chuckle then to laugh aloud. Carolyn took the cape, placed it around Margaret's shoulders and then latched the necklace around Margaret's neck. Margaret made two small braids on either side of her face and put the feather in the braid on the right side.

A slight breeze began to sweep across the mountain. Margaret looked up, closed her eyes and absorbed the sweet presence of the Mighty Eagle's spirit. After a moment, the three stepped outside the graveyard and latched the gate. Margaret looked back at Phoebe's headstone, then to Eagle Claw who was now sitting on a rock near the graveyard entrance. He was holding a brightly colored drum. He tapped the drum lightly and gradually began to pick up the slowly moving rhythm.

Carolyn leaned against a pine tree, crossed her arms and smiled, anticipating what would surely take place. Margaret put her arms through the slits on the front of the cape, lifted her hands toward heaven and slowly began to move her feet and arms to the rhythm of the drum. As Eagle Claw picked up the rhythm, so did Margaret. In a few minutes, the drum pounded and Margaret danced before the Almighty of Heaven with all her might. She was so wrapped up in her worship that she failed to see the giant eagles that had gathered and were circling overhead. Margaret had finally taken her place among the outstanding Cherokee women and the mighty eagle warriors of heaven.

Epilogue

Silence fell as the lights were dimmed in the vast exhibition hall that was filled to capacity. A middle-aged woman stood before the podium, adjusted the microphone and said in a mild tone, "This is a time that I have been longing for, as you have. I know this because you've paid a good deal of money to be here today. I want to thank you for making all of this possible. Every year, we gather here in New York City to honor women who have accomplished extraordinary goals and marked each of our lives as a result. When I was asked to present this particular exhibition, my heart leapt with joy. I asked if we could have the presentation in early October for a special reason. It was in October during the nineteenth century that this woman's destiny was set into motion."

The speaker turned to face the burgundy-colored curtain that had slowly begun to rise as the faint sound of one drum softly played in the background. A small reproduction log house surrounded by massive mountains and framed with a vast forest caused gasps to echo through the hall. A life-like mannequin of a beautiful Indian woman stood at the corner of the porch. She was arrayed in a long, white buckskin dress covered with colorful beads and long fringe. Her long, ebony hair had two small braids, each hanging on either side of her face. A large eagle feather hung from the right braid. A turquoise necklace lay against her flawless skin.

The light of that setting darkened and another one came on. The velvet curtain lifted to reveal the living room of the log cabin. Two chairs handcrafted from oak, stained with age, sat on either side of a fireplace with a rounded top. Four large portraits of three Cherokee women and a Seminole Chief hung above the mantel and enhanced the beauty of the rock fireplace. To the side, a painting of three young children, one boy and two girls, graced the wall. The light dimmed, and the final curtain slowly raised to uncover a replica of a vast mountain peak. Oversized eagles were soaring around the summit. At the foot of the mountain, an Indian chief, decked out in ceremonial attire complete with his breath-taking headdress, stood erect with a spear in his hand. At the top of the mountain, a woman sat on a large stump with pen and paper in her hand. A glorious, long, eagle cape was draped about her shoulders. Beside her on the stump sat a small chest overlaid with turquoise. She was looking out over the valley that appeared endless. Standing behind her, guiding her hand as she wrote, was the Great Eagle of Heaven and Earth.

As the drum played softly, the speaker turned back to the microphone. "There is no place in the world like the Great Smoky Mountains. Nestled in the foothills of the Smoky Mountains is a small community we know as Cherokee. Not only is that the name of the settlement, but also the name of a great people—the Cherokee Indians. The person we are here to pay tribute to was not only raised in Cherokee, but had the blood of the Cherokee flowing in her veins. Her accomplishments in writing have far exceeded anything that she could have ever imagined when she started one hundred forty years ago. For those of you who don't know, my name is Mariah Phoebe Martin. The woman I am honored to pay tribute to is my Great-Great-Great-Grandmother Margaret Phoebe Black."

About the Author

Wilma Lee Harris Styles was born August 22, 1948, in Pensacola, North Carolina, at 8:30 p.m. While still a small child, her parents bought a thirty-eight-acre farm in Fairview, North Carolina. She grew up on that farm with her mom, dad and eight siblings—four brothers and four sisters. It was there she was introduced to storytelling. Her dad's brother, Lee Harris, whom the kids called "Turk," kept them entertained nightly with his scary tales. One he told most often was about Billy Goat Gruff. Although most times he would change the details of the story, he managed to keep their eyes popped. The author recalls that she held her breath waiting for the chilling punch line. Uncle Lee died June 22, 1966.

Wilma missed him and his stories more than he could have ever imagined. Turk's tall tales impacted her life and have lived on all these years. She often smiles, remembering his convincing way of making the Troll that lived under the bridge and Billy Goat Gruff so real. Her sister Margaret carried on the storytelling tradition after Uncle Lee's death, but it just wasn't the same. Wilma had no way of knowing that she too would inherit the storytelling legacy and would be sharing her stories with you. The author lives in Inman, South Carolina, with her husband, Ray.